NEWBORN NEEDS A DAD

BY

DIANNE DRAKE

MILLS & BOON®

First published in Great Britain 2010
Harlequin Mills & Boon Limited,
Eton House, 18-24 Paradise Road, Richmond, Surrey TW9 1SR

© Dianne Despain 2010

ISBN: 978 0 263 87891 2

Harlequin Mills & Boon policy is to use papers that are natural, renewable and recyclable products and made from wood grown in sustainable forests. The logging and manufacturing process conform to the legal environmental regulations of the country of origin.

Printed and bound in Spain
by Litografia Rosés, S.A., Barcelona

Dear Reader

Welcome to the most idyllic spot I can imagine—White Elk. It's a perfect little village, nestled in the valley between three looming mountain peaks called The Three Sisters by the locals. The people are friendly, the village is picturesque and, according to Indian lore, The Three Sisters protect everyone within their shadows.

Does White Elk exist? In a sense, yes. My husband's parents retired to a place much as I envision White Elk to be. It's lovely. The people there smile at strangers and welcome them in. And the mountains… I love to stand in the valley and look up at them, but, more than that, I love to go up to the various peaks and look out across the valley. I'm a city girl. I'll admit it. But when I write these books I rarely set them in the city because I love to escape, just for a little while. I hope you love your visit to the little village of White Elk as much as I did!

Wishing you health and happiness!

Dianne Drake

PS I love to hear from my readers. Please visit my website at www.DianneDrake.com. Also, feel free to e-mail me at Dianne@DianneDrake.com, and tell me about the places in this world you love.

Now that her children have left home, **Dianne Drake** is finally finding the time to do some of the things she adores—gardening, cooking, reading, shopping for antiques. Her absolute passion in life, however, is adopting abandoned and abused animals. Right now Dianne and her husband Joel have a little menagerie of three dogs and two cats, but that's always subject to change. A former symphony orchestra member, Dianne now attends the symphony as a spectator several times a month and, when time permits, takes in an occasional football, basketball or hockey game.

Extract from *NEWBORN NEEDS A DAD*:

Maybe he'd gone a little too far when he'd kissed her.

But another time, another situation? He could almost picture himself involved with Gabrielle. Maybe even more than involved. She was everything he'd never expected in a woman. Funny, direct, honest, smart. Little Bryce Evans was going to have himself one hell of a mother, and Neil was a little envious he didn't fit into the equation somewhere, because it was a nice equation. One he'd never expected he'd want.

CHAPTER ONE

WHAT a beautiful little village! Dr Gabrielle Evans breathed a sigh of relief, shutting off her car in the parking spot marked *Guests*, in front of the quaint White Elk Lodge. She'd lived in large cities too many years. Indoctrinated herself to fast pace and convenience. Nothing about the village called White Elk seemed fast, or convenient and, right now, that suited her just fine. She was tired and, physically, she needed this stop. Surprisingly, it seemed right for her emotionally, too. Even if only for a night. Maybe two, if the bed was comfortable, the food good, a fire in the fireplace inviting, because she did have just the slightest backache, she was hungry, and the mood to settle in and be cozy was dropping down over her like a soft blanket. So much so she could picture herself sitting in front of a great stone fireplace, feet up, dozing off from pure contentment.

Nesting. Which was to be expected in her condition.

Besides, hadn't she seen a little boutique on Main Street, one with the name Handmade for Baby? That was all the excuse she needed for a short holiday here. That, and her swollen ankles. Pregnant-swollen was what she called it when her patients had the same problem. Pregnant-swollen ankles, pregnant-swollen belly. *Not to worry*, she would say. *It's a temporary condition.*

Well, temporary condition or not, she felt like stopping. Something about White Elk appealed to her sense of esthetics. It was a homey little town, its narrow streets lined with pine trees and old-fashioned streetlamps, and white picket fences surrounded the cottage homes she'd seen from her car on the way in. Cottage homes…she'd always wanted to live in a cottage. All in all, everything she'd seen so far in this Alpine-styled village was the antithesis of her steel-and-chrome condo back in Chicago, where she lived in the middle of a mixed residential and industrial area, overlooking a frantic, elevated railway on one side and the bumper-to-bumper Chicago interstate system on the other. Her wake-up call in the morning was the honking of agitated motorists trying to inch their way through impossible traffic and her lullaby at night was the clacking of the old train over the el rails.

And here in White Elk…no traffic. Just a few lazy drivers on the street, none who seemed agitated, none who seemed in a hurry. That, alone, could have been an enticement to stay over, if everything else she could see around her hadn't already drawn her in. Besides, the drive back to the airport was still another ninety miles, and her reservation home to Chicago wasn't until tomorrow. Meaning she was going to stay in a hotel room for the night somewhere. So, why not here? "And it's not like I've got anything to hurry back to," she said aloud, a habit she'd developed since she'd learned she was pregnant. Talking to her unborn baby…it's what she urged her patients to do, and in this case, she took her own advice. Chattered away to him all the time. "Anyway, what's the hurry getting back? It's not like I have a job waiting for me any more. Right now, I'm here, and here seems very nice. You should see it, Bryce. People smile. Perfect strangers wave."

Yes, a night or two here was exactly what the pregnant

doctor needed, which was why she prescribed it for herself.

Gabby pulled out her cell phone and dialed the number posted under the wooden, hand-carved Welcome sign nailed to a lodgepole. It was a lazy thing to do, but all of a sudden she felt like being a little lazy. After the day she'd had, she deserved some laziness and a nice cup of hot chocolate on top of that! "Hello," she said, when the woman who called herself Laura Stewart answered the phone. "I was wondering if you have a room available for one night." She glanced across the street and discovered the little shop White Elk Confectionary, specializing in *chocolate*. Fate? "Maybe two nights," she added, because she really did want that chocolate. Sure, it was almost spring—technically spring had sprung a few days ago, but there was still snow on the ground here, in patchy spots, so in Gabby's mind she was allowed her craving for hot chocolate. "One person," she added. Well, almost two.

According to Laura, there were plenty of rooms available, so Gabby crawled out of her rental car, stretched her aching back, decided not to look down in the inevitable lost cause of locating her puffy ankles, which she couldn't see now anyway, and forced herself *not* to waddle when she walked inside, although several friends back home had recently commented on her waddling.

"That didn't take long," the friendly-looking strawberry blonde at the desk said as Gabby dropped her overnight bag on the floor and her purse on the desk.

"I was just outside. Called from the parking lot. These days, if I can find a way to be lazy, I do it." She smiled. "Actually, I look for ways to be lazy and the more pregnant I get, the lazier I want to be."

"Don't blame you. Been in your condition three times myself, and if ever there's a time to be pampered…"

If there was someone there to pamper you, Gabby thought, her eyes going immediately to Laura's ring finger. A simple gold band there said it all. She had someone to pamper her, where Gabby did not. But that was fine because, normally, she didn't need pampering. In fact, she prided herself on her independence.

"Is this your first?" Laura continued.

Instinctively, Gabby laid her hand on her belly. Yes, her first. Unexpected. Very welcomed. "Yes, it is," she said, not really sure she wanted to go any further. People reacted differently to her situation and it wasn't a matter of feeling awkward in her very pregnant, very unmarried condition so much as it was that she didn't want to make people feel awkward around her. She was a medical doctor, she knew how these kinds of things happened, and in a moment of weakness, well, it had happened to her. No excuses, no apologies. "And I saw a lovely little baby shop down the street. I thought I might go take a look after I'm rested. I haven't really started baby shopping yet."

"You haven't?" Laura seemed genuinely surprised. "I think I was out buying baby bootees about ten minutes after the test strip confirmed my pregnancy…with my first. With my second it took about an hour, and with my third about a day." She glanced down at Gabby's belly. "I'm surprised you could hold off this long."

It wasn't so much that she was holding off as it was she was scared to make plans. "Oh, I've figured that I'd probably do a big binge shop when the time comes. You know, go crazy, buy everything in the store. But I haven't had time." And she'd had patients who'd put all their hopes and dreams into a miracle baby, like hers, only to be heart-broken. Even though she had only two months to go, she wasn't ready to invest herself in so many hopes. "Who knows, maybe Handmade for Baby will be the lucky recipient of all my saved-up baby-shopping urges once I'm rested."

Laura laughed. "Janice Laughlin will love you forever. She's the owner. Anyway, speaking of getting rested, I think we should get you to your room. The ski season's over now, except for a few brave souls who hang around hoping for late snow. So, you can have your choice of rooms—one here in the lodge—something small, a large suite. Or you can have a cabin all to yourself."

"You have cabins?" That sounded like the coziness she wanted. "With a fireplace?"

"With a fireplace."

A cabin with a fireplace in a ski-resort community, baby shopping, hot chocolate… Suddenly, Gabby was looking forward to her next couple of days. It was like this was exactly the place she was meant to be. Yes, nesting. Her patients talked about it all the time—finding the place you wanted to be, settling in, dwelling on your pregnancy. Now, for the first time, she believed she understood what that meant, and if this was, indeed, nesting, it agreed with her because she wasn't feeling so bleak, so alone, like she had too many times these past months. "A cabin… Yes, I'd love a cabin with a fireplace."

"It's a little bit of a hike to get up there," Laura warned. "Not steep, but not so convenient to the parking lot as the lodge is."

"In spite of the obvious, I'm in good shape. Just a little tired right now because I've been on the road for a while, and I *really* hate traveling. Generally, though, I'm active and a nice walk back and forth will do me some good." Especially now that she didn't get all the exercise she had when she'd worked every day.

"Good. But I still don't want you lifting anything heavy,

so I'll have my daughter carry your bags up to the cabin when she gets home from school in a couple of hours…"

Gabby shook her head. "Not necessary. All I have is an overnighter, and I can carry it myself. I didn't expect to be staying so I didn't bring much with me." Actually, she wasn't sure what she *had* expected when she'd set out on this trip. A quick announcement to Gavin Thierry, letting him know he was about to become a father, then a quick retreat? Certainly she hadn't expected much from him. After all, there'd been no lasting relationship. But to find out what she had… "Thanks, anyway, for offering."

Laura spun around the register for Gabby to sign, then handed her the cabin key when the paperwork was completed. "We have a dining room here, but if you'd like…" she took a look at the name on the register "…*Gabrielle*, I can have someone bring dinner to your cabin later on."

"Call me Gabby." Her father had been the only one ever to call her Gabrielle, and hearing someone else call her by that name now hurt. "And I appreciate the offer, but I'd rather come down to the dining room, if it's all the same to you. I think getting out, keeping myself active, is a good idea." As an obstetrician, it's what she prescribed for her patients. Then scolded them when they didn't take her advice.

"Well, if you need anything, call the main switch. Oh, and so you'll know, we do have a small hospital in the village, not that I think anything will happen. But to be on the safe side in case, well…you know…there's the White Elk Hospital, and it's pretty nice. Very good in general services for adults and, believe it or not, well known for its pediatric practices. And what we lack in big-town medical services we make up for in some very nice, very competent doctors and nurses."

Glowing praise that intrigued her, and she caught

herself wondering what it would be like working in a small town like White Elk. And raising her son here. "Well, I'm not due yet, so let's hope I won't be needing any medical care while I'm here."

Wasn't this what she wanted? A fresh start, someplace other than a large, impersonal city like Chicago? That's what she'd told herself when she'd sold her share of the medical practice to her partners and, just last week, had started the process of putting her condo on the market with the expectation of finding someplace else to start her new life. She was looking for something different, something she wasn't quite able to define. That's what she kept telling herself, anyway. What it was or where it would be were still great big questions, but she trusted that she would know it when she saw it.

Could it be White Elk? The feel was right, it was definitely different from what she'd had, but it was also so small. Moving here from Chicago would be a huge culture shock and with all the other drastic changes going on in her life now, she wasn't sure she should even think about one like this. White Elk had nice shops and a bed in a cozy cabin for a night but, generally, she liked a few more amenities around her, and a few more luxuries. This was a place where you spent a nice holiday, but to settle here?

Crazy thoughts. Pregnancy thoughts—a combination of hormones, flailing emotions over the news of her baby's father's death, and a whole lot of uncertainty. That's what it had to be. Her thinking was a little skew these days as she had someone else to consider now, and her decisions didn't affect only her. Besides, she needed to work, needed to settle somewhere the red carpet was out for an obstetrician, and what were the odds of that happening here?

"To get to your cabin, go out behind the lodge, take the

first trail to the left, and I've got you in the first one you'll come to. It's got the best view of the Three Sisters."

"Three sisters?"

"Our three mountain peaks. They overlook the valley and, according to Indian legend, take care of the people who live here. Of course, we have busy ski resorts on each of the peaks now, which is what has made White Elk thrive." She smiled. "Tourists. We love them to pieces here."

"With so many tourists I'd say the Three Sisters are doing what they're supposed to." Watching and protecting…the very same things she did for this baby she'd be delivering in a while. The same things she wished she had someone to do for her, which simply wasn't in her future.

The hike to the cabin was pleasant, the air cool and brisk, but not as cold as it could have been for the last week of March. Along the trail, little purple and yellow crocuses poked their heads out of the remnants of the last snow, giving Gabby the hope that the full burst of spring was just around the corner. By the time that happened, she'd be a mother, settled in wherever she was supposed to be. "A mother," she said, simply to remind herself. Sometimes she still couldn't believe it. This little boy inside her was a dream coming true in a way she'd have never expected in a million years. Of course, now that she knew of Gavin's death, she was a little sad. They hadn't been romantically involved. Outside of what she'd seen of him as a doctor, she hadn't even known him well enough to tell her son what kind of person his father had been other than smart, kind, considerate. Bryce did deserve to know, but what could she say? *Your mother was feeling very lonely, and very vulnerable when she met a pleasant, handsome man at a medical symposium, spent a night with him and conceived you as a result.*

Unfortunately, that's all there was to the story. It had taken her weeks to find Gavin, and weeks to get up the courage to come tell him what had happened that one night they'd spent together. But by then it had been too late. Meaning there was nothing to add to the story and Bryce would never know his father. Gavin had no family in Spotswood, where'd she'd just visited. None that she could find. And no one there who could tell her about his family either. Sad for her son, sad for her.

Gabby stopped for a moment, and thought about picking a few of the flowers for her cabin, but decided to leave them as they were, a tiny bit of inspiration fighting against the elements. "You know we're going to be fine," she said to her unborn baby. "It's just a little tough right now. I wanted you to know about him and I'm sorry I didn't find him sooner. But we'll work it out, just you and me, and I promise that if there's any information available about him…" Information, but no father.

It wasn't like she was afraid of raising a baby as a single mother, because she wasn't. In fact, from the instant she'd discovered she was pregnant, she'd been shocked, excited, scared, in awe after a lifetime being told, and believing, it wouldn't ever happen to her, that she could not get pregnant. She'd been injured in a riding accident years ago. Too much scar tissue, the doctors had said soon after. Too little hope. When she'd been fifteen, that hadn't really had much of an impact on her. When she'd turned thirty, it had. But she'd lived with it, accepted it.

Then, after all those years of believing, as the patient, and even as a doctor, that nothing could happen, she'd had the recurring feeling that maybe, just maybe she might be pregnant. Missed period one month and she'd convinced herself it was stress, that her job was demanding. Missed period the second month and she'd gone to the local pharmacy for a home pregnancy kit, then had sat it on the bathroom countertop and stared at it for three days before she'd opened it. After that she'd waited another two days before she'd actually gotten around to using it. Then, when that test strip had gone from pink to blue, she'd run, not walked, but *run* to the corner pharmacy, bought another kit, done another test. Then gone back to that same pharmacy one more time, one more kit.

A kindly pharmacist who'd seen her grabbing yet another test kit off the shelf had suggested she go see an obstetrician, and offered to make a referral if she needed one. But she was an obstetrician, and a very pregnant one, she was coming to realize. Also a very overwhelmed one. "Right now, your only problem is that your mother's very tired. But I'm on my way to fix that situation immediately."

Bryce Evans. Her miracle baby. She couldn't wait for his arrival into the world. Nothing other than that really mattered. And she was so happy…

"Thanks for making a house call. We're not busy right now, but with David out of town, it's like I'm doing the work of a dozen different people and there aren't enough hours in the day to get everything done that needs to be."

Dr Neil Ranard handed the bottle of pink bubble-gum-tasting liquid over to Laura. They called it bubble-gum tasting, and he'd successfully convinced a number of his young patients that was the case, but to him it tasted like…medicine. Nasty, nasty medicine. "Just give her the dose listed on the label and she'll be fine. There's a sore throat bug going around the elementary school and Emily is one of the many. Also I'll want to check her again in a couple of days, but she'll be ready to come to the clinic by then." Yes, he still made house calls. In a small town, that was possible, and he really liked getting back to personal medicine. Two years away had taught him so many things, but the biggest lesson learnt was that everything he needed was here. He was a small-town doctor, and that's exactly what he wanted to be.

"Can you stay for dinner, Neil? I have only a handful of paying guests checked in right now, and I'm making enough food for an army. Can't get out of the habit of cooking for a lodge full of people when the season shuts down, I guess."

"Wish I could, but I really should get back. With Walt Graham retired now, and Eric Ramsey being tied up with the twins—they're both down with sore throats—we're a little short-handed in emergency. And I've still got a few appointments to take care of at the clinic before I go make hospital rounds. But thanks. I appreciate the offer." At the White Elk Hospital and Clinic, he was the pediatrician, but family practice was also his responsibility, as well as covering Emergency when it was necessary, and doing the occasional mountain rescue. It was a varied job, and in such a small setting every doctor was called on to do pretty much whatever they had to. Medical convention aside, he loved it. Where else would he be so fortunate as to be involved in so many things?

"Can't you wait five minutes, while I get something together to send back with you? It's better than what you'll get at the hospital, and you know hospital food is what you'll end up eating." She grinned. "Think about it, Neil. Institutional cooking versus home cooking."

Home cooking, a luxury he hadn't even had those months he'd been married. It sounded good, actually. *Anything* resembling a normal life sounded good. Otherwise, for him it *would* be whatever the hospital cafeteria special was. "OK, you've convinced me. Mind if I go sit in the dining room and pour myself a cup of coffee while I wait?"

Laura dismissed Neil with the wave of an unconcerned hand, and he ambled into the empty dining room, went straight to the service bar and poured his coffee, then took a seat by the window that gave him the best view of the Three Sisters. Magnificent view, and one he had so little time to admire these days. It was also the view that had drawn him back home, even when he'd vowed, almost three years ago, not to return. But he'd returned, in part because he liked skiing when he had the time. And the fresh air. Most of all, he liked the nice people. All that, and the exciting nature of his medical practice. Here, in White Elk, he had it all. Or most of it. Because the memories of his short-lived marriage were here, too. As were the memories of the day his wife had run off with his brother.

But the good outweighed the bad. That's what he kept telling himself and maybe someday he'd even convince himself of it, because some of the memories were bitter. And forever unresolved.

Neil stretched out his long legs and leaned back in the wooden chair, trying to empty his mind of everything. Movement at the opposite end of the dining room caught his attention, though…attention in the form of one very pretty, very pregnant woman who was sizing up the various tables, obviously looking for one with the best view.

He studied her for a moment. She looked almost lonely, ambling from table to table the way she was, all by herself. And here he was, occupying the one with the view he knew she had to be looking for. Immediately, Neil sprang to his feet, and even thought to motion her in his direction, like he was the maître d'. But as he plucked his coffee mug up off the table and stepped away from it, she found her seat on the opposite end of the room, in a spot overlooking the town—all the shops, and the people bustling up and down the sidewalks.

Funny, he thought, how people had different ideas of what was perfect. Personally, his idea of perfect went to something wild, something without people. Hers went to just the opposite, it seemed.

"Your dinner, Neil," Laura said, setting the brown paper bag full of plastic containers in front of him. "There should be enough to get you through the next couple of days, and if there's not, come back. There's always more where that came from."

"Appreciate the home cooking," he replied absently, unable to take his stare off the woman, who was now seated with her back to him.

Laura, noticing his intent stare, smiled. "She checked in several hours ago," she whispered. "Not from around here. She registered her home address as Chicago and I don't know a thing about her other than that." She paused, then chuckled. "Except the obvious."

"And that she looks lonely," he commented out loud, although he'd meant the remark to stay in his head.

"You know, she did look a little lonely, come to think of it. I thought she was mostly tired, though." Laura shrugged it off as she scurried over to the other table to take Gabby's dinner order, while Neil stayed there, sipping his coffee, watching a while longer than he really should have, given his schedule.

Strangers came to town all the time. In fact, the town's economy was built on people coming here to stay for a while, whether to ski, or shop, or simply have a nice holiday. He barely even noticed them unless they had a medical problem. So what was it about this woman that caught his attention...not only caught it, but held it?

Nothing, he said to himself. Absolutely nothing at all. Right now, he didn't get involved. Not with anyone. He was married to his work, and he owned a part interest in a hospital. That was enough to keep him out of trouble, keep him fairly contented, keep him reasonably happy. Life was good. Why try for anything else?

Thinking about what had happened the last time he'd tried for something different was what propelled him back to his feet, and carried him right out the door. When he got to the entrance, though, Neil stopped and turned back to look at her, and that's when he saw her face. She was…beautiful. Stunning. Honey-blond hair falling gracefully to her shoulders, her blue eyes cast downward. Almost shyly…eyes that could only have been blue. And perfect lips. He was observing her as a physician, of course. Only as a physician.

She was what that pregnant glow was all about. He wasn't sure he'd ever truly seen it before, but now that he'd seen her, he knew what it looked like.

In that brief moment when his eyes were still fixed on her, she glanced up at him, stared outright for a long moment, then looked away. That's when Neil knew he'd better leave before good judgment was overcome with something he didn't understand, and he intruded where he clearly wasn't wanted. But once outside on the walkway, he looked back up to the window where she sat, and…was she staring at him? It seemed she might have been.

Handsome face. Rugged. Nice firm jaw, nice straight nose. With his wavy black hair, she imagined dark brown eyes. Or green. No…they had to be dark brown.

It was a face that should have been familiar, but nothing in her memory could place him. His eyes haunted her, though. So familiar. But she didn't often forget a man so handsome. Yet in that span of mere seconds, when their gazes had crossed, it had been like she'd been looking into eyes she'd looked into before. The same, yet not.

Just pregnancy hormones kicking in. Still, at first glance, he'd seemed so familiar. Then, at second glance, he didn't at all. His was one of those faces that would plague her for a while, though, until she placed him, or forgot him.

"Who was that?" she asked Laura, as Laura placed the handwritten menu on the table in front of her. Potato, vegetable and salad choices were the same with every meal, and she had her choice of meat, poultry or fish.

"Neil Ranard. He owns the family practice clinic at the hospital. And, actually, he's part owner of the hospital. Specializes in pediatrics, but all the docs there do a little bit of everything."

Would she have known him from some medical event—a seminar they'd both attended, perhaps? Or maybe a medical convention?

In theory, that sounded good, except she rarely ever had time for seminars, and as for medical conventions... She'd been to exactly one, and it hadn't been the White Elk doctor she'd fixed herself on there. So that left... Honestly, she didn't know. And she didn't want to keep thinking about it. "I think I'd like the vegetables only, if you don't mind. Bryce and I don't seem to do so well with meat these days."

"Bryce?"

Gabby laughed, self-conscious. "My baby. I'm going to name him Bryce, and I guess I'm getting in the habit of using his name. Thinking of him as a person." She'd been in the habit from the moment she'd known she was pregnant. It was going to be a boy, and she would name him Bryce after her father, a decision made the instant she'd thrown away the third pregnancy kit. Bryce...that was the only way she could make sense of things.

Laura laughed. "Boys are nice. At least, that's what I've

heard. We've got three girls, and I'm not sure if I'd know what to do with a boy now, after so many years."

"To be honest, I'm not sure I'm going to know what to do with a baby, boy or girl."

"You're…alone?" Laura asked, hesitant.

"Well, I was until about seven months ago." Noncommittal response that would suffice. Smiling, she patted her belly. "But that's sure not the case now."

"I talked to my girls too…in the womb. Read books to them, sang to them, played music for them. My husband thought I was crazy, but for the whole time I was pregnant, I wasn't alone, and I needed to make that connection." She shrugged. "Anyway, I'd better get back to the kitchen."

Once Laura was gone, Gabby turned her attention back to the window, wondering if she'd see the man, Neil Ranard, again, but he was gone. Oh, well…

"I'll take both of them." Two quilts weren't too many, and both were so adorable. So were the fifteen newborn outfits she'd bought, along with the crib accessories, the bootees, the hats… There were so many baby things she'd never thought about before and, so far, she'd bought every single thing she'd looked at. This morning her ankles were normal, her back felt fine, Bryce was kicking up a storm, and she was totally in love with Handmade for Baby. It was an amazing little store, fronted on the main street right next to a candy store. She hadn't been in there yet, but she would. And she intended to browse through the little maternity boutique that Debbi Laughlin, the baby-store clerk, had recommended.

"You staying here long?" Debbi asked. She was seventeen at most, with short, spiky yellow hair, a pierced eyebrow, and an engaging, warm smile.

"Just another day, then I'll be going back to Chicago."

Debbi arched her eyebrows over the mention of Chicago and Gabby's gaze fixed on the little silver ring anchored there that bobbed up and down. "I've always wanted to go there. Maybe even save my money and move there, go to college…anywhere but here."

"You don't like it here?" Gabby asked. So far, she hadn't found anything in White Elk she didn't like.

"It's OK, if you're old, I suppose."

Old, like she was? Gabby laughed inwardly at the thought. Thirty-three wasn't old, but to someone Debbi's age, it was ancient. "Well, I think it's a nice little town."

"Little's the thing. I don't like little. It's boring."

And Gabby didn't like big any more, but she supposed she'd have thought a small town was the end of the world when she'd been younger. She and her dad had always lived in a big city—Chicago, New York, San Francisco— and that's what she knew. *All she knew*. But those pregnancy hormones were changing her in ways she hadn't expected, for now her ideal seemed just the opposite of Debbi's and in some ways the opposite of the ones she'd become comfortable with in herself until she'd gotten pregnant. "Well, then, you'd like Chicago, because there's nothing little about it."

"What do you do there?" Debbi asked, as she folded the first quilt into a box.

"I'm an obstetrician. That means—"

"I know what it means. My uncle's a doctor here."

Was she related to Neil Ranard? "Dr Ranard?"

Debbi shook her head. "Dr Ramsey. He works with Dr Ranard when the twins aren't sick. Which they are right now, which is why I'm here and my mother isn't. She's helping Uncle Eric."

"Twins?"

"My cousins. Both of them down with a sore throat and

I told my uncle I wasn't going anywhere near them, so my mother's there helping take care of them and I'm here, doing this."

And not loving it, Gabby thought. Too bad. Life was too short not to love what you were doing.

Debbi folded the second quilt into another box, then sat it in the stack with at least fifteen other boxes. "So, did you come to take over for Doc Graham?"

"Who's Doc Graham?"

Debbi blew a bubble with her gum, then popped it. "The obstetrician. He retired so he could have more time to hike, and go skiing. If it were me, I'd retire and get out of here."

"No. I'm not here to replace Doc Graham. I'm just traveling through, and decided to stop and do some shopping."

Debbi nodded, but the expression on her face showed that she thought Gabby was crazy for intentionally staying in White Elk when she didn't have to. "So, what do you want me to do with all this stuff?" she asked.

Good question. Gabby hadn't thought that far ahead, and her first response was to give Debbi the address to her Chicago condo and have every last thing shipped there. But for some reason she didn't understand, she decided instead to have it sent back to her cabin at the lodge and figure out what to do with it later. Farewells with Debbi were brief, but she felt compelled to tell the girl to look her up if she ever made it to Chicago. Debbi's response was to roll her eyes, plug the earpieces back into her ears and listen to some tune Gabby was sure she'd never heard of.

Next, she visited the candy shop, then the maternity boutique, sending more packages back to her cabin from both shops, as well as stopping at the corner toy store and showing amazing restraint by buying only one stuffed teddy bear and a little wooden train set Bryce wouldn't play with for years. Shopping done, she felt amazingly good. Refreshed. Full of energy. So she wandered down the street, in the direction of the hospital. Deliberately.

What a cute hospital! Not at all institutional-looking, like where she'd worked back in Chicago. That was a real brick-and-mortar structure, nine stories tall, spanning several blocks, if you included the various clinics and asphalted parking lots. This hospital was quaint, made of logs, resembling a mountain lodge more than it did a hospital. If not for the sign out front indicating that it was, indeed, White Elk Hospital, she would have walked right on by, looking for a more regular-looking institution.

So, she was there. Wondering what came next. "Maybe I'm crazy," she whispered to herself. "But if they do need an obstetrician…" That's what Debbi, the store clerk, had implied. But why had she deliberately come here? To apply for the job? No way. Quaint was nice for a visit, and while she wasn't big-city obsessed like Debbi, she was reasonably sure that she agreed with the girl on the fact that White Elk was too small.

But here she was anyway. It must have been the nesting thing again. Had to be. More rushing hormones telling her to settle down, make a real home for this baby, and White Elk Village was a nice candidate for all those things. Except the idea was ridiculous. Her opportunities here would be too limited. Besides, nobody needed a seven-months-pregnant obstetrician. And at seven months pregnant, the obstetrician didn't really need a full-time job. Money wasn't a problem, but time on her hands was. She did want to work. Loved working, and she already missed it.

"But I've never lived in a city smaller than Chicago," she

said to Bryce, "and I'm not sure your mother is cut out for small-town living." Even though this small town was tugging at her. "And don't go telling me I can make a go of it anywhere I want because I'm not sure I can. There are so many things to consider, like my career, and your education."

"Excuse me? Can I help you with something?"

The sexy, smooth voice startled Gabby out of her mental conundrum, caused her to gasp and grab her belly. She rounded to face him, and caught herself staring into the most gorgeous dark brown eyes she'd ever seen. Dark brown, like she'd thought they should be. Glad they were.

"I thought I heard you say something."

She shook her head. "I was just…taking a walk, trying to get a little exercise, and I think I got myself turned around." Well, that was a bit of a lie as she knew exactly where she was. "I stopped for a moment to get my bearings and you probably heard me muttering to myself. Bad habit. I do that when I'm nervous." Better to admit that than to tell him she was engaged in a debate with her unborn child, and her unborn child seemed to be winning the argument at the moment. Muttering made her look eccentric, debating with an unborn baby made her look just plain odd.

"You're staying up at Laura's lodge, aren't you? I thought I saw you there last night."

Gabby nodded. "It's up at the top of the hill, isn't it?" she said, pointing in the direction she knew perfectly well. Was that really her, feigning the helpless woman? Good thing she had pregnancy hormones to blame it on, because there wasn't anything helpless about her. Her father had raised her well in that aspect, and she took great pride in her independence.

"It's a pretty long walk, going uphill the whole way.

Maybe I could call someone to come get you? A friend, a husband…"

"It's not so bad," she said. "Besides, I'm here by myself."

He glanced at his watch, then at the hospital. "How about I get my car and drive you back? It'll only take five minutes."

This would have been such a nice meeting had she not been pregnant, but she was, so this was only about chivalry. He was a pleasant man coming to the rescue of a damsel who didn't need rescuing. End of story. "Thanks, but I'll walk."

"Then maybe you should come inside and sit down for a few minutes before you attempt going back up." He gestured to the hospital. "Ten minutes. Find a nice, comfortable chair, put your feet up…"

"My doctor thinks I should be a little more active than that. She's of the opinion that healthy, pregnant women should be active women. But like I said, thanks."

"Then I'll walk with you."

"Because I'm pregnant? Are you one of those people who believes a pregnant woman isn't capable of doing anything? Because if you are…"

He thrust his palm out to stop her. "Whoa, I was only trying to be polite. Something my mother taught me."

"Maybe she should have also taught you that pregnant women can take care of themselves just fine."

He chuckled. Deep, sexy. "Actually, she did. And she'd send me to bed without supper for acting the way I have been." He took a step backwards and thrust out his hand. "Hello, my name is Neil Ranard. Can we start over?"

Gabby took his hand and nodded. "And I'm Gabrielle Evans. People call me Gabby…even the ones who accost me, then try to lecture me on the street."

"Then I'll have to call you Gabrielle so you won't be reminded of this rather inauspicious first meeting. It's nice to meet you, Gabrielle."

Gabrielle…it sounded so nice the way he said it. Sounded almost right and, strangely, she didn't object. Didn't object to the twinkle in his eyes either. Sexy, but mischievous. And, yes, even at her rather advanced stage of pregnancy, those thoughts still did pop into her mind. A good-looking man was a good-looking man and even her whacked-out hormones wouldn't deny that. Neil Ranard was handsome and, like she'd thought yesterday, something about him seemed vaguely familiar. "Do I know you?" she asked. "Have you come to Chicago for any reason lately?" It had to be something in Chicago as until yesterday she hadn't left the city for nearly two years.

"Actually, I've never been to Chicago, outside a layover in the airport, and that was probably five years ago. Maybe six."

"You're not famous, are you? I wouldn't have seen you on television, or in a magazine?" Or on the cover of a romance novel?

"Sorry. I'm only famous in my own mind. And even then, it's highly overrated, if not totally ignored, except by my mother and her sister."

"I guess you've got one of those faces, then," she said, still wondering why she couldn't shake herself of the feeling. "Look, I appreciate you being concerned about me, but I'm fine, and there's no need to help me get back to the lodge."

"What if I said that Laura makes the best cheesecake in White Elk Valley, and you're my excuse to go have a piece?"

"Then I'd say you're a terrible liar. But I appreciate the gesture." With that, Gabby turned and started the climb back up the hill to her cabin. She'd only gone ten steps, though, when she stopped and spun back around. He was right on her heels. "Are you following me?"

"Actually, I thought I'd go to the lodge and have a piece of cheesecake. Talking about it made me hungry for it."

"Liar!" she exclaimed, fighting to control the laugh bubbling up inside her.

He arched playful eyebrows. "I'd never lie about a good piece of cheesecake."

"But you were looking at your watch just a minute ago, which tells me you're in a hurry to get back to work. So you really don't want that cheesecake right now, and you're using it as a pretty lame excuse to make sure I can get myself back up the hill. Which I can do perfectly well without anybody's help."

His face went serious. "I know it's none of my business, but how long has it been since you've seen a doctor, Gabrielle?"

"If I'm not mistaken, I'm looking at one right now."

"I mean an obstetrician."

She smiled. "If I'm not mistaken, *you're* looking at one right now."

"No kidding? You're an obstetrician?"

"No kidding. And if I'm not mistaken, you might be in need of one here for a few weeks. According to Debbi, at Handmade for Baby."

Obvious surprise blinked across his face. "You're applying for a job?"

"Not really a full-time job. But I could fill in until your new obstetrician arrives. As it turns out, I left my old position a few weeks ago, so I've got the time."

"I've got to admit, you've caught me off guard. We were just having a staff meeting, wondering what we were going to do, and here you are, on our front walk."

As they always said, timing was everything. She hadn't meant to apply for a position, although she'd thought about it. Hadn't meant to stay here in White Elk, although she'd thought about that, too. Yes, after Debbi had mentioned that their former obstetrician had just left, the idea of staying awhile had tempted her. Now here she was, making it happen. "Well, I do come with an obvious condition." She raised her hands to her belly. "Two months to go. But I'm healthy, fit to work, and if you need me for a while…"

"Do we need you? Our obstetrician's been phasing himself out without phasing someone else in to take his place. We thought he had a while to go before he finally left so we weren't too worried, then one morning he woke up and just couldn't do it any more. It was time for him to leave."

Something she understood all too well. That's exactly what had happened to her in Chicago. She'd known she was going, hadn't known when, then one day it had been time. "Well, my credentials will check out, and I can give you some personal references."

"We'll need you for six weeks at the longest. I've got someone else coming in to take over after that, on a temporary basis until we can find someone to fill the full-time position. But we had this big gap between Walt and the temp."

"Six weeks sounds good." So did temporary. And this *was* perfect timing, wasn't it? She could work for six weeks, *part-time*, have her baby after that, and put off trying to figure out, for a while longer, what came next in her life. "Unless something unforeseen and early changes my plans."

"In which case, I'll be glad to deliver your baby."

An offer she could hardly refuse. Pregnant and

employed again. If only for a little while for both conditions. She liked it. In fact, she was excited to be working again, and didn't doubt for a minute that she could handle it. So she extended her hand to the incredibly handsome Dr Neil Ranard, and instantly a little chill shot up her arm. "When do I start?" she asked, her hand lingering in his just a fraction of a second longer than it should have.

"Five minutes ago OK with you?"

Reluctantly, she pulled her hand from his and crammed it into her jacket pocket. "Five minutes ago is perfect." Then she shivered again.

Just the chilly air, she told herself. What else could it be?

CHAPTER TWO

WELL, it wasn't a busy schedule. Fallon O'Gara, the nurse practitioner—a bright-eyed woman about Gabby's age, with wild red hair streaming down her back, a wide, cheery smile that came naturally and a laugh that bubbled through the air—handed Gabby a schedule with all of two afternoon patients for her to see. "That's it? Just two?"

"Walt Graham did help in the emergency department when he wasn't busy, but I'm not so sure we should put you on that schedule, too. Neil…Dr Ranard…said he wants you on obstetrics only, and I can't change that without his authorization. So, until I hear further, yes, that's it, unless someone else schedules an appointment with you."

"But can I change the schedule if I want to? Or maybe wander down there and put myself to work?" Sitting around all afternoon, twiddling her thumbs, would make her feel useless, and since she was on a campaign to prove that pregnancy in the workplace still had a place, she decided she was going to have to change some minds here. Or, at least, one specific mind.

Fallon laughed. "He warned me that you were a little headstrong. Told me to hold my ground with you."

"Not headstrong. I just like to work." She patted her belly. "*We* like to work."

"Well, Neil wants me to do a physical on you before you start anything. I know you're only a short-time, part-timer, but he's pretty stringent about keeping his staff healthy. And since you're so far along, I think it's best." She thrust out her hand to stop Gabby before she could protest. "I know you're an obstetrician and you know better than any of us how you're feeling and what you can handle, but rules are rules, and like I said…"

"Neil is pretty stringent." Translated to mean thorough. In her estimation, that made him a good doctor.

"On the bright side, if I don't find any problems, I'll bet you can talk him into letting you take your turn in Emergency."

"So let's do this check-up." To be honest, she hadn't had one in a few weeks, and she was due for one. "But can we do it after I see my first patient? It looks like her appointment was thirty minutes ago, and unless another one of your staff has already seen her, I don't want to keep her waiting any longer."

Fallon waved her off when a mother wrestling four little ones came through the door. They were carrying balloons and painted drawings and a vase with flowers, on their way to visit daddy, who was resting comfortably in the orthopedics ward with his leg in traction. Happy, eager, smiling faces… When she'd been young, she'd always said she wanted lots of children when she grew up. Being the only child of a single father, she'd thought a large family would be nice. She still believed that, but she was contented with one child. Elated, actually.

"So, how are you feeling today, Mrs Blanchard?" Angela Blanchard, who was sitting on the edge of the exam table, covered only in a blue paper exam gown, looked…frustrated. Not unhappy, but not happy, either.

"Not as good as you, since you're working and I'm not," she snapped. "Sorry. I'm not having a good day."

"Understandable."

"Is there some way to get this thing delivered early? Induce labor, maybe?"

A quick survey of Angela's chart revealed she was due two weeks after Gabby. She was healthy and there was nothing of alarm going on except, perhaps, her attitude. "Would it make any difference if I said that you're over two thirds of the way there and the rest is downhill from here?"

A laugh broke through Angela's mood. "The one thing I could always count on with Doc Graham was that he would be at least as grumpy as I was. And now I've got a doctor who smiles. Guess that means I have to smile, too, doesn't it?"

"It helps. You ought to try it." Gabby sat the chart aside and extended her hand to Angela. "Hi, I'm Gabby Evans, and I'll be smiling at you for the next few weeks. Five or six, if I'm lucky."

"So we're due almost the same time," Angela responded, taking Gabby's hand. She was a small woman, with short-cropped brown hair and dark brown eyes. Almost a pixie…a pixie with a sizeable tummy spread, side to side.

"Just a few weeks apart, and I know what you mean, wanting to get it over with. There are times I'd really love to see the floor again." She wrapped the blood-pressure cuff around Angela's arm and pumped it up. "Or my ankles. But I guess that comes soon enough, doesn't it?" Then she listened for the dull sound of the blood pressure through her stethoscope. It was high. Not alarmingly so, but enough that Gabby took a second reading to make sure. Again, it registered barely on the high end of normal.

"Did Doc Graham ever diagnose you with hypertension?"

Angela was instantly alarmed. "No, why?"

"You're on the verge. Nothing to worry about yet, but I want to keep an eye on it. So, do you live far from here?" she asked Angela.

"No, about twenty minutes."

"Good, then I'd like you to stop in tomorrow for another blood-pressure check."

"Should I be nervous about this?"

Gabby shook her head. "Could be nothing. Could be because you're stressing. Of course, even bringing it up puts you under more stress, which could raise your blood pressure. But I want to stay on top of this, keep it under control if it's the start of something, or rule it out if it's not." The only real concern was that, according to Doc Graham's notes, Angela's blood pressure had been normal all along. "And in the meantime, reduce your salt intake, stay away from highly processed foods with a lot of sodium in them, and if you're not walking, walk."

"I walked. In fact, that's all I did until Doc Graham made me quit working. I manage the kitchen up on the older Sister…"

"Older sister?"

"The mountain peak to the south. It's the older Sister. The one to the west is the middle Sister, and the one to the north is the younger Sister. Anyway, I'm at Pine Ridge Ski Resort up on the older Sister. Head chef, temporarily sidelined to paperwork. Which is driving me crazy, making me grumpy, probably responsible for raising my blood pressure."

"So besides the obvious, let me guess. When you're at a desk, you're not exercising, and probably eating away your frustration? And getting angry thinking about what you'd rather be doing?"

Angela laughed. "Something like that. And I should know better, being a chef and a dietician, but I've been having a craving for salty things lately."

"Well, elevated blood pressure isn't necessarily a problem when it's still in the high normal range the way yours is, so don't stress over that. But like I said, I want to keep an eye on it and make sure it isn't about something other than your change in lifestyle and..." Gabby smiled, thinking about the chocolate craving she'd been having for a while "...bad habits. So, for the next few days I'd like to see you every day to get a reading. Oh, and get back to the kitchen, at least on a part-time basis. Cook a little and use common sense." She scribbled a hasty note on her prescription pad. "According to your chart you're perfectly healthy, and I think it's good to stay working as long as you can. Light duty, though. Maybe some baking. The note gives you permission to get back into the kitchen on a limited basis, and I trust you'll use good judgment in deciding whether or not you feel like it."

"Really?" She read the note twice, blinking her surprise both times. "You're going to let me go back to work?"

"In case you haven't noticed, I'm not particularly an advocate of inactivity during pregnancy. People treat pregnancy like it's an illness, but I prefer to treat it like a normal condition, one the body's prepared to deal with."

"But Doc Graham said..." She stopped, frowned, then smiled. "I can work a little?"

Gabby laughed. "There's old-school and new-school thinking here. My dad, also an obstetrician, was a brilliant doctor, but he was very old school. Like Doc Graham. He thought pregnancy was a time when a woman should rest, put her feet up, be pampered. I, on the other hand, believe in the benefits of working through a pregnancy, if a woman's physical condition allows it. And studies back that up. My dad and I used to argue over this all the time."

"And who won?"

"He did with his patients. I did with mine." And neither of them ever budged from their position. "So, in other words, be indulgent. Of course, you're the one who has to define what indulgent is, according to your condition. Now, how about I do the rest of your physical, then we'll talk about the really important things, like decorating baby's room."

"So tell me about your hospital." Gabby caught up to Neil in the hall and fell into step with him. Big steps, tall man. Broad shoulders that swayed naturally with his steps. Neil Ranard had an impressive stature, and for Gabby to notice was something out of the ordinary. Usually she didn't pay attention, because most men looked her directly in the eyes, and she had a definite preference for tall. But he was tall, taller than Gabby by a good head, which put him well over six feet. Nice, considering how her five-feet-eight height towered over so many people. And intimidated so many men. "Tell me the five most important things I need to know in order to succeed here."

"Well, the first is that coffee breaks are essential. Do you prefer your coffee with, or without, cream and sugar?"

"We're on our way to a coffee break? That's why you're in such a big hurry?"

"Believe me, at the end of ski season, you look for any excuse you can find to take a break. For five months we're ridiculously busy. There's hardly enough time to catch your breath. Never enough time to sit down and put your feet up. Sometimes you're on call for days. Meaning, no coffee breaks whatsoever. Then the season changes and there's time to take a break, so you do even if you don't necessarily want one, because you know that will change in due course and soon you'll bemoan the fact that you don't have time to take a break. The two phases of our medical life here—with, and without, coffee breaks—are a vicious cycle."

"And you like that, don't you? I see it in your eyes."

Neil laughed. "Or maybe I just like to complain."

"Ah, the foibles of being self-indulgent. I just had a talk with my patient about that."

"My foibles have more to do with leaving here and being so damned grateful to come back, under *any* circumstance, break or no break. I was away for a while, working in a clinic in Los Angeles, somehow deluding myself into thinking that I wanted steady hours, five days a week. It was a job most doctors would envy, because I was able to live like everybody else does. You know, getting up in the morning, going to work, coming home in the evening. Weekends for tennis and golfing, which I absolutely hate, but did anyway because I had the time. It was so amazingly normal it drove me crazy inside four months. Probably because it wasn't…enough. Wasn't personal the way it is here in White Elk, and by the time I'd worked to the end of my contract, I was more than ready to come back here, where nothing is normal. For me, that makes it better." He motioned Gabby around the corner to the staff lounge, where he practically lunged at the coffee pot. "How do you take yours? I mean, I'm assuming you still allow yourself a little caffeine at this stage of your pregnancy."

"Caffeine in moderation is fine, and there's always decaffeinated coffee if the caffeine causes side effects. But I don't like coffee." She turned up her nose. "Used to, but after I got pregnant I lost my taste for it. Started craving hot chocolate."

"But you do like the coffee breaks, don't you?"

"As long as I can sit down and put my feet up then, yes, I like the coffee breaks." Which is exactly what she did. She sat down in one chair, then Neil nudged another one across the room to her, so she could prop up her feet.

"Is this your first?" he asked, sitting down next to her.

"Yes. And just so we can get past this awkward moment, I'm not married, don't plan to be married, I'm not involved in any kind of relationship with the baby's father or anyone else, and I'm very much looking forward to single motherhood. And in case that sounds defensive, I really don't mean for it to be, but I've said this by rote a few dozen times and that's just the way it comes out now." So, if that wasn't an ice-breaker, nothing was. "And it's not a secret, Neil. People will ask, they'll want to talk, and that's fine. If I'm going to be here for a couple of months, I'd rather everyone knows this isn't one of those circumstances where they need to whisper and speculate. My pregnancy is the best thing that ever happened to me, and I'm ecstatic."

"I'm glad. When I was in family practice in Los Angeles, I saw too many pregnant patients who weren't ecstatic, and it made me…sad. Sad for the mother, sad for the baby." A deep frown confirmed his sentiment, but he wiped it away after a sip of coffee, and his normal sunny smile returned. "So, you asked me about the hospital, didn't you? Five important things everyone needs to know… Well, as you've seen, it's small. That's important because we like the intimacy. We have forty beds that can expand to fifty, if we have to. Sixty in a dire emergency. Also, we offer general service here, no elective major surgeries, emergency major surgery only when it's vital, and most minor procedures are welcomed. We specialize in pediatrics, not so much because that's what we set out to do but by virtue of the fact that the two co-owners have pe-diatric specialties in their backgrounds, meaning we do get a few more peds referrals than we normally would. Although it's not technically a pediatric hospital." He paused, then grinned. "Was that four or five things?"

"Technically, four. So, you were in pediatrics?"

"Still am, but for White Elk and the whole Three Sisters area, it's too limiting, so I have a secondary specialty in family practice. Like my partner, Eric Ramsey. He was a pe-diatric surgeon, but to be flexible enough to work here he had to expand his horizons. So, besides a couple of doctors who seem to be the proverbial jacks-of-all-trades, we also have a state-of-the-art trauma department, headed by Eric, a full ob-stetrics department headed by, well, you, for the moment, a neonatal nursery, a good orthopedic set-up, and we also co-ordinate mountain rescue from here. Just a couple of ticks off full service on a very small scale—and growing, I guess you'd say. And now that's more than five."

"And I'm more than impressed. So, you're a co-owner?"

He nodded. "The hospital was struggling when I came back, and Eric Ramsey and I bought it in order to keep it going. In an area such as this you can't afford to have the hospital go under, because that affects the whole local economy. A ski resort area—and we have three ski resorts in the vicinity—needs a hospital nearby. So Eric and I decided to invest, and see if, together, we could get it back on track. So far, so good, if you don't count the fact that everybody here is grossly overworked and underpaid." He chuckled. "I get credit for the good stuff and I let Eric take credit for the bad. Although I think he says it the other way around. Anyway, you'll meet him when he gets over his sore throat…caught it from his twins. He's the one who coordinates mountain rescue, by the way."

"How many more doctors do you have?"

"Two full-time orthopedists, Kent Stafford and Jane McGinnis, John Ellis, who's another family practitioner, only he's part-time, in semi-retirement now, and we have a part-time rehabilitation specialist, Jackie Pennington, who comes in from Salt Lake city two days a week. Oh, and an obstetrician on the way, but not for another few weeks. We have nurse practitioner Fallon O'Gara, whom you met earlier and who practically runs the hospital— she's probably the most essential team member we have. And we have a couple of respiratory therapists, three physical therapists, and a dozen staff nurses. We also have a few doctors who come in to help out in the clinic on a rotating basis once or twice a month—a cardiologist and a rheumatologist. Then there's Henry Gunther, a retired anesthesiologist, on call. He moved here to engineer the ski train—trains were his hobby—so he's always close by when we need him. Then we have a number of volunteers and support staff, and that's about it. White Elk Hospital. Struggling, but surviving."

"Seems adequate for the area." And impressive. White Elk Hospital appeared to be a well-run medical facility, even if Neil did admit to a few shortcomings, and it was almost too bad she wouldn't be part of it for long. It could have been what she was looking for, professionally, anyway. Someplace nice, where people cared about each other

"Most of the time it is. And the one thing I failed to mention is that we all take our turns in the emergency department and trauma, even if that's not our specialty. At present, we don't have enough funds to staff it regularly, so we all get our chance to work there. I'm hoping that before the start of next year's skiing I'll be able to hire one more physician, another trauma doc, and bring in a couple of moonlighters. But Eric and I are still talking it over, crunching numbers, crossing our fingers."

"It sounds…compact." And not at all complicated, like so many of the large hospitals were—hospitals where the doctors fit into their own little niche and rarely, if ever, wandered out of it. Some might say there were advantages to staying where you belonged, but she liked the idea of working different areas, especially if the doctors' medical qualifications suited that. Her own father, an obstetrician, had been a general field surgeon in the army and she'd had training in general surgery, too, at his urging.

"Coming from Chicago, the way you do, I suppose it would."

"Well, coming from Chicago, the way I do, I have a different appreciation for what medicine should be."

"Which is?"

"Uncomplicated."

"In an ideal world," Neil said.

"In a real world, if that's how you want it to be. Where I worked, everything was complicated. The more complicated it became, the further away the patients seemed to get. I got used to it, I suppose, but…" She frowned. Shrugged. "It was OK then, but not any more."

"What changed you?"

"I'd like to attribute it to my pregnancy hormones but, to be honest, I haven't been happy for a while. Not unhappy either. Just existing. Nothing was wrong, nothing was bad. But nothing made me happy about my work, and I think to be a good doctor…to be the best doctor you can be…you need to be happy about your work. My dad always was. He jumped out of bed in the morning and couldn't wait to get started. He thrived in the complicated system, turned it into his playground and worked it to the advantage of his patients. I suppose I thought I should, too, which is why I stayed in practice with him so long, doing just that. But…" She shrugged again. "I wasn't suited to the manipulations, I guess you could say. I became too restless to be as effective as I wanted to be and decided I finally needed to make a change. Getting pregnant was the last shove I needed. Don't know what that permanent change is yet, but I'll know it when I see it." She was positive of that.

"So you came here, to White Elk, looking for…happiness?"

Not even close, but that was a complication she felt no pressing urge to discuss with him. "Handmade baby clothes and peace of mind. And I've already found the handmade baby clothes."

"I'm done for the day," Gabby said, plopping down onto the exam table in emergency room one. In the past two hours she'd seen one scheduled patient, one walk-in and done a regular pelvic exam on one of the staff nurses. It wasn't an overwhelming schedule, which was fine with her. Working again felt good. She'd missed it, and she was glad to be back in any capacity.

Neil, who was sitting on a chrome stool across from her, looking all rigid and uncomfortable whilst reading an outdated medical journal, glanced up, took off his reading glasses and tucked them into his pocket. "Did you have a good first day? It wasn't too much for you, was it?"

"Good first day, yes. Too much, no. In fact, it was a little slow."

"Like I said earlier, you'll learn to appreciate those lulls since they don't come too often." He put his journal aside, and stood up. "Look, are you up to a quick dinner? We're not busy right now. Fallon is down the hall stitching up a kid who took a header off his bicycle, and that's all we've had this past hour. So I was thinking about going across the street to the café before I have to come back and spend the night in emergency on call. You're welcome to join me, unless you have other plans."

"Plans? My plan this time yesterday was to go back to Chicago and get my condo ready to sell. Now here I am, working in a place I'd never heard of until…" she glanced at her watch "…twenty-nine hours, forty-two minutes ago. Meaning no plans, and I've love to join you."

"So, what do you eat?"

"Lately, everything I can get my hands on. A little light on meat, but other than that no dietary restrictions, no self-imposed taboos. Just point me in the direction of food and I'll show you what I eat."

"Then you'll love Catie's Overlook, because they fix a little bit of everything." Neil hurried down to exam three to check on Fallon, who was coming along nicely with her patient. In fact, the procedure was finished and she was at the lollipop stage—the hardest part of the ordeal, trying to get her young patient to choose between red and green. Neil took a look at the stitches, wrote an antibiotic prescription, gave the boy both the red and the green, and sent him home with his mother. Then off with his white lab coat and on with his denim jacket. A quick gesture to Gabby and they were on their way.

"So what's the specialty of the house?" she asked. Heading down the hall, his strides were long, and his heels clicked briskly on tile floor. She liked that confidence in him, liked the way he held the door open for her but didn't overstep his bounds by taking hold of her arm as she half expected him to do. "And are the portions huge? Because I eat a lot these days. I tell myself it's because Bryce is going to be an athlete and he's storing up the calories early."

"Bryce?"

"My son. I'm calling him Bryce Evans, after my father." She sighed wistfully. "That was the first decision I made after I found out I was having a boy. A fitting tribute, I think."

"I take it your father's not with you any more?"

Not her father, not Bryce's father. Things should have been different. "Not any more. Just when I was ready to make the big move, he made a bigger one. Too young, too soon."

"I'm sorry, Gabrielle. I get the feeling you and your father were close."

"We were." Stepping up onto the curb, she stopped for a moment as Bryce kicked, and laid a hand on her belly. Then she smiled. "But it's an amazing circle of life, isn't it? I lose one Bryce who meant the world to me, and another one's about to enter my life who means even more."

What an amazing woman. He didn't think he'd ever met anyone like Gabrielle Evans before. Confident, self-assured. Maybe a little too defiant with her self-reliance, probably a reaction to her having a baby alone. He guessed that she probably fought against things she didn't have to, but that was OK. It made her even more interesting. So why was it that he'd met her now, when the timing was so wrong on so many different levels? "Table for two, Helen," he said to the waitress who greeted them at the door. "Oh, and this is Dr Evans. She'll be working as our obstetrician for the next few weeks."

Helen looked down at the lump under Gabby's coat with a dubious frown, then nodded. "Which Sister?" she asked. Catie's Overlook boasted the best view in town— windows overlooking each of the Three Sisters.

"Older Sister. Better view, more lights." Not that it

really mattered, since he'd seen each of the Sisters from every angle more times than he could remember, but he thought Gabrielle might like the nicer view.

"Angela Blanchard works up there," Gabby commented as Neil pulled out the chair for her.

It was quaint, old-fashioned, all wood, and surprisingly not as uncomfortable as it looked. But on the other side of the room there were cozy, romantic booths, where several couples sat all tucked into each other. He'd done that, once upon a time. In fact, he'd brought Karen here, and he'd been the one so distracted by the moment that he hadn't noticed the obvious—that she had eyes for him, but not him alone. Well, not any more. He'd sworn off relationships a while ago, and he wasn't yet in the mood to swear back on. If he ever did, there would be no cozy booths and candlelight, though. Next time, it was going to be a matter of practicality. His one and only promise to himself was head before heart. A down-to-earth partnership.

"She came into the clinic today," Gabby continued.

"Grumpy?" Neil asked, as he took his seat, purposely keeping his back toward the row of romantic booths. "She usually is lately."

"No, not grumpy. More like frustrated with her situation. And with her inactivity. So I gave her permission to return to work, be active again on a limited basis, which is what she wanted. It had a pretty good effect on her mood."

"Ah, going against Walt Graham's sage advice to stay home and keep your feet up for nine months. His wife had seven children, and we always teased that she kept getting pregnant so she could take the nine-month holiday. Because Walt wouldn't let her do a thing. He waited on her hand and foot, and hired someone to do it for him when he wasn't there."

"And…"

"He was lost after she died. Lost a lot of the joy in his life, I think. Woke up one morning a few weeks ago and said it was time to do something else, and he did. He quit his practice. Now he's out hiking in the woods, skiing, doing the things he never had time to do before. But he's a good man, and a good doctor with old-fashioned ways."

"He sounds a lot like my father. Dad always had my mother on a pedestal. It's hard for me to even imagine the kind of love he had for her, but I think that's what Walt Graham must have had for his wife, because Dad never got over her after she died. Never dated, never looked at another woman, never took off his wedding ring."

"How old were you when she died?"

"Six. It was tough for him, raising me alone, because I was rambunctious. I demanded a lot of attention from him for the first few years, and the less time he had to give me, the more I demanded. At least that's the way it was when I was young. It got better…for me. Which made it better for my dad. But sometimes I wonder how tough it's going to be for me raising a child by myself, because I remember the nights my dad would shut himself in his room. I used to think I could hear him crying…and I believed it was my fault that he was sad. I think, though, that he was over-whelmed. He would always tell me that a child needed two parents, and he was sorry I had only one."

"He sounds amazing."

"He was. I spent a lot of time at his side, being his little assistant, walking along with him carrying his medical bag, pretending to be a doctor, too. It wasn't the way most of my friends were growing up, but I never really missed out on anything, because I loved my life, loved it that my dad included me in his medical life whenever he could. It made me feel special…important." She blinked hard, fighting back fat tears welling in her eyes. "Anyway, I know Walt Graham had his ways, but I have mine, and I don't think there's a need to keep healthy pregnant women from working, as long as they want to work, and they're physically able."

"Are we talking about Angela Blanchard, or you?"

"Both. I want her to work because she wants to work. And I want to work in the emergency room like everybody else does when it's their turn. But I got the impression that you might not want me there. If that's because you don't know me, I totally understand. But if it's because I'm pregnant…"

"I do know you. At least what I can know from a background check. You come with glowing references, Gabrielle. The kind that would make me want to put you on the emergency schedule if I had room. But I'm scheduled two weeks out, and unless there's an emergency, I usually don't change the schedule. That's why you're not there right now. The only reason. Because I am a full-fledged supporter of women, pregnant or not, doing what they want to do. Maybe we got off on the wrong foot when I told you to go put your feet up and rest, and when I tried showing you back to the lodge, but that was just me, doing a poor job of being a gentleman to a pregnant woman who seemed to be lost."

"I wasn't lost. In fact, I was on my way in when you came outside. And you're not that bad at being a gentleman," she teased. "Maybe a little more old-fashioned than you think you are, but it's nice."

Not to hear Karen talk about it. His ex-wife had accused him of so many things over the course of their marital break-up, and he was pretty sure his skills at being a gentleman had probably fallen in there somewhere. "Let's just say that I'm out of practice, and for the foreseeable future

I don't expect to be getting much practice." Work was easier. It didn't betray him the way his wife had.

"This is the part where I *don't* ask questions, right? Because I've never been very good at the distinctions. Some people say something leading, like you did, then drop it, hoping to really drop it. Others say something leading, then drop it, hoping the other person will pick it up. But I'm sensing that you don't want me to do that…to pick it up and ask questions."

"Failed marriage. In and out quickly with a lot of ugliness in the middle. That's about all there is to say about it."

"Even though I've never been married, I know that's *never* all there is to say about it, Neil, but I won't ask."

She really did fascinate him. There were so many complex layers to her, it could take a lifetime to peel them all back to reveal the full essence of Gabrielle Evans. What an astonishing lifetime that could be for some lucky man. "Are you always so direct?" he asked.

She nodded. "I attribute it to my relationship with my dad. He was a busy man, didn't have time to waste, and he'd always tell me that if I wanted to know, ask. If I wanted to be heard, speak up. Worked for him, works for me."

"Your dad was right, and being direct is oddly becoming on you."

She wrinkled her nose, forcing back an almost shy smile.

"You don't take compliments very well, do you?"

"In my experience, compliments often come with conditions. So let's just say that the one offering the compliment has to grow on me before I'm comfortable with the compliments."

"Am I growing on you yet?"

"Sprouting," she said.

Yes, she was very direct, and he liked it more and more. In fact, he seriously doubted that Gabrielle could ever lie, or be even the slightest bit deceitful. So where had *she* been when he'd been convincing himself he loved Karen? Because Gabrielle Evans, in the right place at the right time, could have changed so many things in his life.

CHAPTER THREE

"I THOUGHT you'd gone home after our meal." Neil picked up the last of the gauze scraps and tossed them in the trash, then snapped off his gloves and dropped them in the trash, too.

"I did, actually. Got ready for bed. Lay down. Couldn't sleep. Decided to take a walk, and here I am."

"Let me guess. You were the top student in your medical-school class."

"Why would you say that?"

"Because you couldn't do anything less. You're the obsessed type who never eases down, and being anything but the top student would have driven you crazy."

"Is that a bad thing?"

Neil laughed. "For most people, probably. For you, it's kind of cute. So, did you try counting sheep?"

"Did that. Got to about a million, then tried reading a medical journal. That didn't work either, so I took a walk, only it stimulated me even more."

"So you want me to do what? Bore you to sleep?"

"For me, boredom means an empty mind. An empty mind means more time to think. More thinking means less sleep."

"In other words, you came here to work."

"I saw several patients in the waiting area. You could use me, couldn't you? Since you're the only one on."

"Nobody ever wins with you, do they, Gabrielle?"

"I try not letting it happen too often."

"And I'm not getting rid of you, am I?"

She shook her head.

"Room three. Mrs Blondell. Indigestion. She probably had oysters for dinner."

"That's it? All I get is indigestion?"

"Take it or leave it, Doctor." He grinned. "Sometimes I get to win, too."

On her way to exam three, Gabby thought about how much she liked Neil. He was just…easy. Easy to talk to, easy to be around. "So, what can I do for you this evening, Mrs Blondell?"

In response, the round, ruddy woman burped. Then giggled. Then burped again. "Oysters," she said. "Happens every time I eat them."

"Have you ever thought about not eating them?"

"I limit myself to once a month." Rumbling burp. "And the consequences are annoying, but worth it."

"Then how about taking some kind of a preventative before you indulge so that you can cut down on the consequences?"

"A month's worth of preventative for one night of indulgence? That's a high price to pay for an occasional weakness, don't you think?" Mrs Blondell held her breath while Gabby listened to her chest, then her belly.

When she was finished, satisfied that nothing but a good case of acid indigestion was going on, Gabby pulled the stethoscope from her ears and took her patient's pulse. "In my experience, you're going to pay one way or another. Trust me, the cure won't be so bad, and you'll be able to have oysters twice a month, if that's what you want."

"Was it oysters?" Neil asked a little while later as they passed in the hall.

"I gave her a few antacid samples to take home with her, and prescribed an antacid to take on a regular basis."

"Which she won't take. Won't even buy. In fact, you'll find your prescription torn up and tossed in the trash on the way out."

"So why does she bother coming in?"

"Lonely. She's seventy-two, widowed, and I think some of her evenings get pretty long. She eats oysters to remind her of her husband, even though they don't agree with her any more. They went out on the twenty-eighth of every month for fifty years and celebrated their marriage with a romantic dinner."

"And had oysters," Gabby said, as a gush of weepy hormonal tears overtook her. "And today's the twenty-eighth. That's so sweet." She brushed at the unexpected tears with her hand, but Neil fished a clean tissue from his pocket and handed it to her.

"What's sweet is fifty years with the same person," he said, his voice a little thin. "More like a miracle."

"Spoken like a man who's jaded about marriage." Sniffles coming to an end, she stepped over to the nearest sink and washed her hands.

"Jaded about one marriage in particular. Admiring of the ones that make it." He gave her a patient chart. "Room five, mysterious rash. Nothing sentimental as far as I can tell."

"Well, one bad marriage doesn't a bad institution make. In my opinion."

"Eternal optimist?"

"Don't you have to be when you're a doctor? Especially an obstetrician?" She took the chart from him. "Or even someone falling in love?" Without awaiting an answer,

Gabby marched straight into a full hour of incidental complaints—nothing too taxing, nothing communicable. Because Neil was considerate. He could have stuck her with the flu patient who came in dehydrated and coughing, or the man with the gashed hand who was loud and obnoxious, but he didn't. He was protecting her. Giving her what she wanted by allowing her to work yet looking out for her at the same time.

If they'd been more than colleagues, she might have considered that a little romantic. Maybe not as much as oysters, but nice all the same.

So why wasn't a man like Neil Ranard taken? He was a looker in every way that should attract a woman. Great personality. Considerate. Good doctor. Yet he seemed to have no life outside his work. It didn't seem like he wanted one. So, why was that?

It did make her wonder, especially when she stood off to the side in the emergency department, as she was doing now, watching him work, watching him interact with other people. He was with a grumpy child. A *loud*, grumpy child with a tummy ache. The little boy had been crying for fifteen minutes, then Neil pulled back the curtain, entered the emergency cubicle, and…what was that he did? Did Neil make a funny face? She couldn't tell, but suddenly the child was laughing. No words even spoken.

The way he related to his patients was simply astonishing. And the way they responded to him… Just like the little boy did. People lit up around him. Reacted in amazing ways. Come to think of it, she had reacted like everybody else did.

Well, one thing was certain. Whatever kept Neil estranged in his personal life had to be his choice. Because as she watched him work, she noticed any number of admirers who would have loved being included in his off-duty hours. The clerk at the emergency desk who couldn't keep her eyes off Neil, the volunteer who giggled when he got near her, the grumpy little boy's mother... Neil Ranard had a way about him when he was being a doctor. Just not so much in the personal sense. "So, anything else?" Gabby asked when he left the child's cubicle. She was actually beginning to feel a little tired. "Because I think now would be a good time for me to go back to the cabin and get some rest. Unless you need me."

Rather than looking at her, he looked straight at her belly. "Your baby is the one who needs you right now... needs you to be rested." Then he looked at her. Stared straight into her eyes, with no attempt to rush the encounter—apparently lost in thought before he finally spoke. "So, go. Take care of yourself. And Bryce."

It surprised her to hear him say her baby's name. Until now, no one ever had. They always said *the baby* or *it*. But, honestly, she was pleased that he'd even remembered Bryce's name, and hearing it from someone else gave her an unexpected thrill, like she wasn't the only one in the world who thought of her child as a real person. "For once, I'm not going to argue." She arched her back, then raised her hand to rub the small of it, but Neil stepped behind her and started a gentle massage to her shoulders.

"You don't mind me doing this, do you? Chivalry may be a little old-fashioned, but sometimes old-fashioned is called for."

Rather than answering, she responded with a groan that sounded more like a purr. And did it again when he found a particularly tight muscle in her neck. "Magic hands," she murmured, not intending to say it out loud.

"In that case, gratuities accepted."

His hands moved back to her shoulders and it was all Gabby could do to keep herself from going weak in the knees and collapsing right into his arms. "And what kind of gratuity would you like, Dr Ranard?"

"Haven't decided. But I'll let you know when I think of it."

"Sounds fair. But I reserve the right to make conditions."

"I figured you would. In fact, being direct the way you are, I never thought you would have it any other way."

Gabby started to laugh, but at that moment Neil discovered a very sore spot between her shoulder blades, and what started as a laugh turned into a groan. "You know you could make money with those hands," she said, her voice a little raspy. "Open a massage therapy clinic…"

"You'd be my first patient?"

His hands splayed out from shoulder to shoulder, and his fingers applied that perfect amount of pressure—pressure that verged on both pain and pleasure at the same time. The hurt that felt so good. It wouldn't take much for her to become addicted to this…on a regular basis. "First in line." Whole body treatment. His hands everywhere… Well, that was a thought a woman in her advanced condition shouldn't be having. But she couldn't help it. If the rest was as good as this…

"I heard you and Neil had dinner together last night." Laura Stewart sat down across from Gabby and plunked her coffee mug on the table, indicating she was going to stay awhile.

"Small-town talk," Gabby replied. She'd slept in late since she had no early morning appointments, had a leisurely breakfast, and was now enjoying a lazy view of the main street, watching all the people heading off to their various destinations. Some were in a hurry, some were not. Some drove cars, others walked, a few ran. And there were a handful of brave souls on bicycles, pedaling against the chilly air, which gave Gabby the shivers, even sitting so close to the lodge's large stone fireplace, with its morning fire all crackling and cozy.

What she could see from her favorite table was an amazing snapshot of everyday life, but there was so much space in White Elk. Nothing was crammed in here. Not the buildings, not the people. And the street was not permeated with the sounds of impatient motorists honking, and passers-by shouting their anger and frustrations for anyone to hear, like she'd grown accustomed to in Chicago.

Gabby felt good here. Maybe that was what she liked best about this little town. She didn't fit in, didn't know anybody. Didn't even have any kind of a life here. But she felt good, maybe even more optimistic about her future than she had for quite a while. Truth was, she didn't especially mind the small-town talk, even when it involved her.

"Then it's true? You did?"

Gabby shrugged. "I had dinner, he had dinner. And, co-incidentally, we sat at the same table. So I guess the answer is yes, but not to the things people might imply from it."

"Ah, but rumors still fly, no matter how you might want to defend yourself. And up here, at this elevation, where the air is clearer, they seem to fly a little faster."

"You mean the rumor about the pregnant stranger and the handsome town doctor?" She laughed. "It may sound like the title of a romance novel, but I'm afraid it was just dinner. He ate. I ate, and ate, and ate…"

"We worry about Neil because he doesn't take time for himself. Doesn't have a lot of fun in life. And I'm not going to spread rumors here, or tell you anything I shouldn't, but everybody I know wants him to have... more. Good things. Happiness. He deserves it."

Laura sipped her coffee while Gabby pondered what she'd just said. So Neil was a bit of a recluse? Or maybe so dedicated to his work that he got lost in it? Honestly, she could relate to that. Her father had been much the same way, and to a great extent she took after her father in that. Her dad had buried himself in work because he'd lost the love of his life much too early. And she'd buried herself because that's all she'd known. Maybe for Neil it wasn't a bad thing, being that way. According to Laura, though, it wasn't such a good thing either. "Well, when the rumor flies your way again, would you mind infusing it with a bit of truth, that it was a casual dinner between two medical colleagues? That's all. No need for speculations."

"I think there might be some disappointment with that," Laura replied.

"Haven't people noticed the obvious about me?"

"People notice what they want to notice. Carol Vincent, the night clerk at the hospital, said Neil looked happy when he came back from dinner. Apparently that was much more obvious to her than your condition."

"And?"

"We don't see that smile on him much. That's what made it so noticeable."

"So when he does smile, it starts a rumor?"

Laura laughed. "Under normal circumstances, I'd say no. But because it's Neil, and because he's so well loved... Look, I've got to get busy. I just wanted to stop by for a moment, say hello, see if there's anything you need."

Anything she needed? Now, that was a loaded question because the honest truth was, she did need, but she wasn't sure what. "I'm fine," she said, trying to figure out what should be on the top of her list of needs. "A little surprised that I'll be staying here for a while… You don't mind me staying in the cabin, do you?"

"I love having you in the cabin. Normally at this time of the year there's no one to talk to, so this is good. And I know Angela is glad you're here. With what she's been going through lately…" Laura stopped abruptly.

"What?" Gabby asked.

"If I told you, that would be small-town gossip, wouldn't it?" Laughing, Laura scooted away from the table. "Anyway, I just wanted to let you know that it's good to have you here, and I'm hoping that after six weeks you'll decide to call it home."

A lot could happen in six weeks, but for now Gabby decided that no decision was the best one. Liking the texture of the little town was one thing, but settling down here and setting up a new life…she just didn't know if that's what she really wanted to do. Of course, she didn't know if that was *not* what she wanted to do either.

After Laura scurried off to do whatever it was she had to do, Gabby bundled up for her walk to the hospital. Her morning schedule was light, but she did have patients to see. And according to her schedule, the day was going to begin with some kind of a dedication. She wasn't sure what, wasn't even sure she was going to go see what it was about. But when she arrived at the hospital, the entry corridor was bustling with people. Dozens of them, all headed in the same direction.

"What's this about?" she asked Fallon O'Gara.

"The hospital staff voted to name the newly remodeled pediatrics ward after Neil's brother. He endowed it with sufficient funds for a nice expansion, and we're having the dedication ceremony this morning." She glanced at her watch. "In five minutes, actually. Guess I'd better hurry.

I'm the one who's supposed to meet the mayor and escort her to the podium."

A dedication, the mayor… This was a big event, apparently as much for the town as it was for the hospital. To be honest, Gabby was a little curious to meet Neil's brother. In fact, until this very moment she hadn't even known he had a brother. Not that it really mattered since she knew nothing at all about Neil. But the buzz of excitement was a little contagious, as more and more people hurried down one of the halls she'd yet to explore. So, why not? She was a part of this, if only for a while. And she didn't have a patient scheduled in for half an hour.

Gabby blended into one of the waves of people sloshing its way toward a central corridor outside Pediatrics, but when she got there, she was shocked to see at least three-hundred people packed in, shoulder to shoulder. "Come up front with the staff," Fallon called to her. "We're going to have photos taken."

Neil was standing front and center when she reached the front of the room, looking very uncomfortable about the whole thing. People were mingling, smiling, laughing and he was standing alone, not talking, not smiling, definitely not mingling.

"You don't like these kinds of things?" she asked him, feeling as out of place here as he looked.

"It was a nice gesture, donating the money, but there's no need for all the fuss. Just hang the damned plaque and be done with it."

Not only did he look uncomfortable, he was downright grumpy. And it wasn't about the plaque, she guessed. She wanted to ask, or at least inquire which face in the crowd belonged to Neil's brother, but the mayor superseded her by stepping up to the microphone and thanking the crowd for coming. "As you are all aware, a generous endowment has been given to this hospital, for the purpose of establishing a state-of-the-art pediatrics ward."

The crowd applauded, and Neil looked even more agitated.

"It is with great regret that our generous benefactor is no longer with us…"

As in dead? Gabby wondered. Or maybe he didn't live in White Elk now. A quick look at Neil's face didn't reveal the answer. In fact, as the mayor droned on for another few minutes, the tight expression on Neil's face stayed fixed. She wasn't even sure he blinked.

"And with no further ado, I'd like to ask Neil to unveil the plaque."

The audience applauded again, but Neil didn't budge.

"Neil?" the mayor prodded.

In response he gave a curt nod of his head, then walked, with all the stiffness of a robot, across the tile floor to the wall with the still-draped plaque on it. And just as stiffly, he reached up and pulled the drape away, letting the burgundy fabric slip straight through his fingers to the floor.

People applauded as the bronze letters set into marble were revealed, and it took Gabby's eyes a few moments to shift from Neil's face to the plaque, where the words *The Gavin Thierry Pediatrics Ward* simply didn't sink in at first. So she blinked twice, looked again, gasped for breath, and stumbled backwards…her head spinning, her immediate world growing dim…dimmer…

The last thing she heard was the collective gasp from the crowd as she pitched backwards.

CHAPTER FOUR

"GABRIELLE?"

The voice sounded distant, but she knew it wasn't.

"Gabrielle, can you hear me?"

There was light shining in her eyes. Bright light. She could feel the intensity of it even though her eyes were shut.

"Come on, Gabrielle. Look at me."

Someone was holding her hand, too. It was Neil. Even without looking, she knew that. Knew the tingle he caused…

"Open your eyes, Gabrielle."

She wanted to, but there was something she didn't want to see. Something she couldn't quite remember.

"How's her blood pressure?"

Now, that was a voice she didn't remember. Nice, deep, rich. Not as nice as Neil's voice, though.

"A little high. Not enough to cause her to faint."

Ah, Neil's voice. The nicest voice she'd ever heard.

"Well, the fetal heartbeat is strong. Nothing going wrong there, as far as I can tell."

The other voice again. Nice enough voice, but Neil's was better. More soothing.

"It's a good thing I caught her. She could have hurt herself on the marble floor," Neil said.

Yes, Neil's voice was the nicest. It made her feel…safe.

"Blood sugar's normal. Oh, and, Neil, I'm having the lab run a full blood panel."

"Thanks, Eric."

"Has she mentioned any kind of past medical history? Or has she been exhausted?" Eric Ramsey asked, looking down at Gabrielle. "She's not particularly pale, not underweight."

"She eats a lot. Fallon did a physical on her, and nothing came to light. Gabrielle's a really staunch defender of women working through their pregnancy if they feel well enough to do it, but now I'm wondering if she has some underlying condition she doesn't know about. Or something developing…"

Eric scratched his head. "Well, whatever it is, she sure picked a dramatic moment to faint."

"I didn't faint," she finally said. "I just…just had a momentary syncope."

"Isn't that the same as fainting?" Neil asked.

His wasn't the face directly over her when she did manage to open her eyes. In fact, when her blur came into focus she was greeted by a startling, handsome set of clear green eyes. Chestnut-colored hair, cut short. Angular face. A breath-taker for sure, but not her type. "We haven't really been formally introduced, have we?" she asked, extending her hand upward to Eric.

Quite surprised by the gesture, he took it. "I don't suppose we have."

"And these aren't the best circumstances for a proper introduction, but I'm Gabby Evans."

"Eric Ramsey," he replied, looking over at Neil, who looked almost like he was ready to pass out too. "And what I want to know from you, Gabby Evans, is what happened?"

"Odd thing about fainting. Most of the time you don't really know what happened. One minute you're there, the next you're not." She started to sit up, but Neil stepped up to the exam table and placed a hand on her shoulder.

"There's always a cause, Gabrielle," Neil insisted.

There was. She knew that. But how could she tell Neil what that cause was?

"I think I spun around too quickly, got light-headed." Horrible lie. But it was the best she could do under the circumstances. "And I'm fine now. I heard you say that the fetal heartbeat is strong. That my blood sugar is normal. So, I'm ready to go." She tried sitting up again but, like the first time, Neil stopped her.

"You're going back to work, aren't you?" he asked.

"Is there any reason I shouldn't?"

"Other than you just fainted?" he snapped.

"Look, you two," Eric interjected. "I need to go see a patient of my own, plus I think I'll look in on the patient Gabby's had waiting for half an hour. Gabby, it's nice to finally meet you *officially*, and I'm glad you're feeling better. Neil, her blood work should be back shortly. If you need anything…" Eric slipped out of the exam room without another word, his absence barely even noticed by Gabby and Neil, who were staring at each other like two rancorous tomcats ready to have a go at each other.

"I'm fine," she insisted. Truth was, she wanted to get away from him. *Right now!* Wanted to think, to figure out how this could have happened. She was pregnant with Neil's brother's baby, of all the incredible coincidences. Incredible and, she had a feeling, not in a good way. "And I'll take it easy the rest of the day." Except her hands were shaking now, and she was so cold she was shivering. Shock, followed by a faint had a way of doing all that. And Neil wasn't missing a symptom, which meant he wasn't going to let her go anywhere. "Neil, I'm really fine," she managed, as another cold chill came over her. "I just got a little claustrophobic, started to panic, with all those people standing around. I'm not a great one for being in crowds. So I spun around, got light-headed, and…"

"And scared the hell out of me."

"Are you the one who caught me?"

"Caught you and carried you here."

"Then I'm sorry to have taken you away from the dedicatory ceremony. Were you supposed to make a speech?"

"I was glad for an excuse to get away from there, but not for the reason that made it happen." He picked up a blood-pressure cuff and wrapped it around Gabby's arm. Then he inflated the ball, put the stethoscope earpieces in his ears, and listened. Moments later, he pulled the earpieces out, and removed the cuff. "Normal." Then he glanced at the fetal monitor and nodded. "That's normal, too. So, do you want to tell me what this was really about?"

"I already told you, Neil. And when the rest of the lab results get back, you're not going to find anything wrong in them. I'm fine. I just had—"

"I know. A little syncope. And just so you won't go getting any crazy ideas that you'll rest for another hour, then go back to work, I've scheduled you out for the day. You're going back to the cabin and going straight to bed. Orders from your doctor, orders from your boss."

His tone made it clear he would take no argument. To be honest, though, she didn't want to argue. Didn't know what she wanted to do except get away from the hospital, away from Neil. "My patients… It's only my second day here, and I need to—"

"We're covered, Gabrielle. Eric and I can cover, so can

John Ellis, another family practitioner. And Fallon's certainly capable of seeing patients if the need arises. So we're good here."

"Possibly half a day? I could go home for the rest of the morning and rest, then this afternoon…" She wasn't sure why she was arguing when she really did want to leave. Was it to impress Neil, show him that she could work, no matter what? Was it to prove the same to herself? She was afraid that he might decide to let her go altogether. Maybe he thought she was weak, she was a burden, he didn't need her. Horrible, horrible thought, since a little speck of optimism deep inside was telling her White Elk could be *the* place.

Neil shook his head adamantly at her suggestion. "You're not staying. And one of the good things about being the owner is that you get to boss people around." He smiled. "I kind of like it."

"Except you're not the bossy type." He didn't have a bossy bone in his body.

"Maybe not under ordinary circumstances, but this isn't an ordinary circumstance."

"Will you let me come back? When the blood tests reveal that nothing is wrong with me, and after I've spent the day resting, will you let me come back tomorrow?"

For a moment he looked surprised. Then his surprise was overcome by a generous smile. "I'm not going to fire you, Gabrielle. But I'm going to caution you the way you caution your patients, by telling you to use common sense. You, better than anybody else, know what you can do, and what you cannot do. And if that doesn't work, I have one magic word that will do it."

"What?"

"Bryce." He chuckled. "Was I right? Did that do it?"

"You were right. That did it," she conceded, not even resenting him for knowing how to get to her. Honestly, it was nice having someone care for her, and while Neil was only a casual acquaintance, he still did make her feel cared for. "Can I at least borrow some medical journals to take with me?"

"Wouldn't you rather be reading articles on how to decorate a baby's nursery?"

"Maybe I would, if the baby had a nursery. But he doesn't." And maybe he wouldn't here in White Elk after all. "So, the journals, please?"

"How about I bring them up to the cabin, along with some lunch and the results of your blood work in a couple of hours? You can rest until I get there, OK? Oh, and our security guard, Ed Lester, is waiting outside to drive you home right now, so you go on, and I'll be up in a while."

"You don't have to do that, Neil. I can take care of myself."

"Maybe I want to." His voice was tender, sincere.

A voice she could get used to.

As Neil helped Gabby first into a wheelchair, which, of course, she protested, then into Ed Lester's car, Gabby wondered why Neil was so willing to do so much for her, and she was still wondering the same thing five minutes later when Ed Lester stopped the car in front of the cabin, and helped her out. "Did you know Neil's brother very well?" she asked the gray-haired security guard, who had a firm hold on her as they walked up the cabin's wooden steps.

"Who, Gavin? We all knew him. Grew up right here in White Elk, practiced here until he and Neil…" He paused. Frowned. Didn't finish his sentence.

So Gabby asked, even though the way her heart was thudding told her the answer before Ed Lester could. "His name was Gavin? Gavin Thierry?" Even though she knew, she wanted to make sure.

The man nodded solemnly. "Damn shame what happened to him. He was a good doctor. Probably as good as his brother."

Gabby fought back a hard lump in her throat as she entered the cabin, and went straight to the rocking chair next to the fireplace. A fire would have been nice, but she lacked the physical energy to lay one. Lacked the emotional energy to do anything other than sit there and rock, and hope the numbing squeak of the rockers would keep everything else out of her mind. Because, right now, she truly didn't want to think.

But eventually confused thoughts started popping and, try as she may, she couldn't push them away. What had Ed Lester meant when he'd said Gavin had practiced here until he and Neil…? He and Neil what? Of all the times for the small-town gossip to quit on her! Especially when it concerned her, indirectly.

Which brought her to another weighty thought. Should she tell Neil about her involvement with his brother? She was, after all, carrying Gavin's son, Neil's nephew. "I don't know what to do, Bryce," she said on a heavy, discouraged sigh. "I was prepared to tell your father about you, but now that he's gone, I'm not sure what to do beyond that. Especially since…" Since what? Since she really liked Neil. Since she might be developing feelings for Neil, crazy as that seemed in two short days. "Like it would even go somewhere if I weren't pregnant," she muttered.

But she did wonder about her feelings. Naturally, she attributed them to her upsurge of hormones, and to a lesser extent the fact that she was alone and Neil was so…welcoming. So steady.

Leaning her head back against the rocker and shutting her eyes, the only thing Gabby envisioned was Neil, and in her images he was proving himself to be everything she'd ever wanted in a man. And that wasn't the hormones talking. Or the misfit wanderings of a delusional mind. "But I'm not going to fall in love, Bryce. We're fine, the two of us. No outsiders necessary. Right?"

What was she supposed to do, though, when that outsider was a blood relative to her baby? That was the question causing her hands to shake.

Slumping down into the rocker even more, Gabby sighed heavily again. Right about now she surely could have used some of her father's sage advice. There was never a time she could remember that he hadn't known what to do and say, and what had always amazed her about him had been how he'd utter just a few simple words that would make things crystal clear. She did miss him, and even now, after all these months without him, tears pooled in her eyes when thoughts of him flooded back. Daddy's girl—not because he was her only parent but because she wanted to be daddy's girl. His absence didn't change that, and the ache of missing him was an ache that was softened only by knowing that, in the coming years, there would be so many wonderful stories to tell Bryce about his grandfather.

Why couldn't life have been just a little less complicated right now?

"You know I haven't done this before," she said to Bryce, brushing away the tears with the back of her hand. "So you're going to have to bear with me until I get it right." And whether or not to tell Neil about his brother's baby was something she had to get right.

Gabby sat and rocked for the next hour, wrapped up in a cozy blanket and also wrapped in her memories of the past and her hopes for the future. She deliberately avoided thinking about Neil, pushing those thoughts right out when they crept in. After a while, when she'd finally succeeded in not thinking about him every three minutes, a sharp knock on her cabin door brought all thoughts of him right back to the forefront of her mind. He was here now, bringing lunch. She'd almost forgotten his offer. Wished she'd called and told him not to come.

But she hadn't, so she had to face him. "We're going to let the moment play itself out as it happens," she told Bryce on her way to the door. As she passed the hall mirror she took a quick glance, saw that she was a little more tear-splotched than she wanted him to see, so she pulled open the cabin door, then ran immediately to the sink in the bathroom to blot water on her face.

"You OK, Gabrielle?" Neil called from the hall.

"Fine," she called back, bent over the sink, cupping her hands under the water, then splashing it on her face. "Just washing my hands." And trying to wash away so many thoughts. Another quick look in the mirror convinced her to run a brush through her hair and tint her lips with a little colored gloss. Hasty, but not so revealing now, she decided as she turned out the bathroom light and emerged into the hall, where Neil stood waiting for her, much closer than she'd expected him to be.

"That was a long hand wash," he said, his face full of concern. "Unless you're scrubbing for surgery."

"I'm pregnant. I'm allowed to take longer doing things."

"Sure you're OK?"

She managed a smile, and a lie. "I'm OK." Which she wasn't. "And hungry." Which she was, but not nearly so much as usual. "So, let's eat." Skip the chat, go straight to the food and hope conversation between them could be cut to a minimum, because she didn't feel much like talking.

"Gabrielle, you look… Have you been crying?"

Neil reached out to take hold of her arm as she whisked by him, but as she slipped past, she grabbed the sack from his hands and hurried off toward the tiny cabin kitchen, anxious to get out of his gaze, lest he looked any deeper and discovered more. He was trying to diagnose her. She was sure of it, and if he thought he saw something, he wouldn't let her work, which would mean she had no reason to stay in White Elk. Leaving here might be the easiest solution, but it wasn't the one that felt good to her. And right now she truly needed to be back in the hospital, seeing patients and not being one. "Of course I wasn't crying. I just washed my face, got a little soap in my eyes. So, what did you hear back from the lab tests?"

"Everything's normal. Perfect."

She managed a wispy smile. "Just like I told you."

"You're right about that. You did tell me. But what you didn't tell me was why you fainted, and I think you know."

She glanced away from him, looked at the vegetable salad he'd brought for fear he could read the answer in her eyes. "You brought pastries, too?" she asked, pulling a cinnamon roll from the bag, breaking off a piece and immediately sticking it in her mouth so she wouldn't have to answer him.

"OK, I won't ask again. But if you faint again, Gabrielle, I won't be able to let you come back to work. In fact, I'll admit you to the hospital for the rest of your pregnancy. I don't like the way you're evading my question, but I'll respect your right to do it."

"I won't faint again," she said, once her mouth was empty.

"I hope not." He watched her go after another bite of cinnamon roll. "So, at least answer this question for me.

Didn't anybody ever tell you that dessert comes *after* the meal?"

She licked the gooey icing off her fingers, then finally met him eye to eye. "My dad always told me to go after what I wanted and not to let anything get in my way, and right now I want the cinnamon roll." She picked up another cinnamon roll and handed it to him. "Care to join me and indulge yourself in the best part of the meal first?" Putting her already half-eaten roll on a plate, she went to the fridge to pour herself a glass of milk. One for her and, on impulse, one for Neil who, she noticed, looked awfully tempted to take a bite of his roll. Desire over tradition. Sometimes that was a nice dilemma to be caught in.

"And you don't think I might really want the salad first?"

She gave her head a vigorous shake no as she handed him his milk. "What I think is that you're in a rut. You think you're supposed to eat the salad first, and the cinnamon roll comes last because that's the traditional order of things, but that's only prior indoctrination. An old habit. If you really like the salad better than the cinnamon roll, then by all means, eat that first. But if you like the roll better, why fill up on the food that's not your preference and risk not having room left over for the food that is?"

It made sense to her, and she remembered the many meals when her father had let her start with the chocolate cake or the apple pie before she got to the meat and potatoes because of what she'd just said to Neil. Not every meal had been that way, of course. But her father always said that because life was so usual most of the time, why not be *unusual* when you had the chance? He'd always told her that it was healthy to be different, and she'd believed him. Still did.

Suddenly, her eyes brimmed once more with tears and she spun away before Neil could see them.

"I was right. You're crying," he said, setting down his glass of milk and stepping up behind her.

"You're not supposed to notice." Gabby sniffled. "I'm having a hormonal couple of hours. Nothing to worry about."

"Would another massage help?"

A massage would be heaven. Wouldn't do a thing for her hormones, and her muscles weren't particularly stiff, which was why she couldn't allow it. She wanted his hands on her too much and that was simply a stupid thing to do. Wanted comfort. Needed it badly. Even though with Neil it was only a nice gesture meant to make the pregnant doctor feel better, to her it was too intimate, too close to her problem.

"What would help would be the rest of my cinnamon roll." She picked it up, and took a seat on the stool at the kitchen counter. "And for future reference I'll pretty much eat anything sweet. And chocolate. Salad's OK, but it doesn't get any better than this." She held up the cinnamon roll, studied it for a second, then took a bite. But she still had a lump in her throat, which made it hard to swallow.

Neil seated himself next to her at the counter and pulled a cinnamon roll from the sack. "Guess this make me officially *less* boring, doesn't it?" he asked, then took his first bite.

"Some people would call it spontaneous."

"Trust me, no one would ever call me spontaneous. That was…" He frowned, exhaled a sharp sigh, then continued. "That was my brother. His life was one spontaneous moment after another. People always called him the fun one. And I was…sensible." He attempted a laugh, but it didn't mask the true sentiment.

"Gavin Thierry?" she said, her voice oddly shaky. "The one on the plaque?" Even though she knew, she still had to utter the words and hear his response.

"That's right. My half-brother, actually." Cold, distant words.

There was so much resentment bottled up in *the sensible one*. She could hear it, even though he was trying to hide it. It was there, though, and she wondered what could have been so bad between the two. "Your brother did a very nice thing for the pediatrics ward, Neil. And I'm so sorry for your loss." It was a nice thing Bryce should know when he was old enough.

Gabby's words didn't set well with Neil, though, because he dropped his cinnamon roll onto the counter, clearly not comfortable with the topic. "We hadn't been close for a while," he said, his voice flat. "For years."

Not close for years? For Gabby, this only begged more questions. Which she wouldn't ask, even though she desperately wanted to know more for her son. And for herself, since she was the one standing in the middle of the unhappy dynamic.

Lunch was pretty quiet after that. Some general chat about the hospital. Neil going back to his traditional way of eating—main food first, no spontaneity. Gabby filling up after two cinnamon rolls, no room left for salad. Throughout the whole muted ordeal, Gabby couldn't help but wonder what had happened in Neil's relationship with his brother that hadn't been resolved even with Gavin's death. She couldn't imagine that it was old childhood resentment left over after so many years. But, like Neil, she ate in silence.

After she'd had all the food she could hold, Gabby put the leftovers in the fridge, then faced Neil across the kitchen counter. "I'm going back to work with you."

Staying cooped up here, alone, only made her think, and she didn't want to. At least, not about the things she needed to.

"Fine," he said, no argument.

She'd expected an argument. "That's all you have to say about it?"

A small smile finally crept back to his face, but not as far as his eyes. They were still troubled, distant. Still reflecting on sad memories. "Because I'm not in the mood for an argument, and if I said no, you'd argue. But you know what's best, know what you feel like doing, so I trust you in this. If you feel like working, work. Eric's still not feeling well, and I'm sure he'd appreciate you taking back your afternoon patients so he won't have to be quite so busy."

A cold breeze cut through their conversation. She could feel it, and it had everything to do with the father of the baby she was carrying. So, for now, her real question was answered. *No, she wouldn't tell Neil.* It was a short-term solution, but it worked for the time being.

It didn't make her feel any better keeping it to herself, though, because Neil had a right to know. But the question was, would he want to know?

"Time will tell," she whispered to Bryce a few moments later, as Neil waited at the front door while she stood at the hall closet, slipping into her jacket. Yes, time would definitely tell.

The rest of the afternoon passed into oblivion, as did the evening, as did the week. She worked, she avoided Neil as best she could. And she bought baby clothes. Stacks and stacks of them. Plus she made a point of eating at a different restaurant every day…places where she didn't expect to find Neil. But he was always on her mind, always a guilt that weighed heavily.

And even after seven days of knowing what she knew, she still didn't know how to deal with it. "Life doesn't come with an instruction manual," she told Bryce one night as she was settling into bed. "And your mother just isn't very good at figuring out how all the pieces fit."

She wasn't expecting an answer, but she got one anyway, in the form of a phone call from Neil.

"Are we having problems?" he asked.

"No, why?"

"You seem to be avoiding me."

"Not avoiding you. I've been busy. And resting when I'm not." True. But also a great big avoidance.

"And you're feeling good?"

"No complaints." The conversation was so stilted, so cold she could almost see the frost on the phone.

"Want to have dinner Friday night? I'm on back-up call, but I don't have to be at the hospital. And I have something interesting I'd like to talk to you about."

"Neil, I just…just don't know." She settled back into her pillows and sighed heavily. "I just don't get involved in…in personal situations. And right now I'm more in the mood to just be alone." That was true.

"So we do have a problem."

"It's not a problem. It's just that…" Why not just tell him? Accept the invitation, and get it over with. That way, she'd know if she had a future here, or if she didn't. "Look, let's have dinner together, OK? I'd like that."

Their goodbye was brief, cordial. And Gabby didn't fall asleep for a good two hours after it. She'd made the commitment to herself, made the promise to Neil, and now the real worry was setting in, because she did want to raise Bryce here, did want Neil to be part of his life. A week and a few days here and she loved White Elk, felt at home, felt like she could spend the rest of her life here. But all that was up to Neil, and he didn't even know it yet. And it scared her that when she was finally making plans, they could all blow away. Yet it scared her even more that they wouldn't.

"Your mother's not thinking too clearly right now," she said to Bryce, as her eyelids began to flutter shut. "But I promise you, that's only a temporary situation."

All the same, she hoped White Elk was not.

CHAPTER FIVE

THE next few days passed in a blur of patients and shopping, so that before she knew it the evening of her date with Neil had arrived. Truth was, as hesitant as she'd been to accept his invitation, she'd been looking forward to the evening ever since. Dreading it, of course. But hopeful. "They're going to be OK without us?" she asked Neil, trying to fasten the seat belt so it wouldn't be so tight. It was like her belly had doubled in size this past week. Maybe not so much in outward appearance as in the actual way it felt to her. Naturally, Bryce had picked this evening to be more rambunctious than ever, kicking, turning somersaults, tap dancing.

Neil chuckled. "The hospital will do fine without us for a few hours." He jiggled his cell phone at her. "And there's this. They have one too, and they know how to use it."

"OK, so maybe I worry too much. But if there were an emergency…"

"Calm down. There won't be."

"You're sure of that?"

"I've been on call five nights straight. All I can say is, I've been looking forward to this, so there'd better not be."

"Like we can control that part of our lives," she said on a wistful sigh as they turned onto the road leading out of the town, and headed for the winding road that would take them to the top of the older Sister.

Neil glanced over at Gabby, not sure if she was napping or simply relaxing. She'd been quiet for several minutes now, and he missed the sound of her voice. He'd caught himself thinking of this as a date off and on, then reminded himself this evening had a purpose. He was going to ask her to stay. He and Eric had crunched numbers, and decided they could afford her part-time for a while. Full-time when she was ready. He wasn't sure this was what she wanted, but he hoped it was because so many of the women were happy with her. Of course, he'd never really heard her talk about her future plans with any certainty, so he had no idea what she intended for herself. But maybe, over a nice dinner, pleasant music and a wonderful view of everything she could have here in White Elk, it wouldn't be so easy for her to turn him down.

On a personal note, he hoped she would stay, too. But that wasn't going to come into play, because she avoided the personal almost as much as he did. "We're winding through an area now where a lot of the celebrities have built their mountain homes," he finally said, more because he simply wanted her companionship than his pressing need to tell her which movie star lived where during ski season.

"I'll bet it would be nice, if I could see it," she murmured, sounding awfully contented.

"Did I wake you?"

"Did you want to?"

"Maybe."

She laughed. "Well, you didn't. I was just…relaxing. Enjoying the night sky. In Chicago, you don't get many stars like you do out here—the kind in the sky, not movie stars. I was remembering the song my mother used to sing to me…'Twinkle, twinkle little star…'"

"'Like a diamond in the sky.'"

"Funny, but I don't think about her too often. It's always my dad that comes to mind."

"Did he sing to you?"

Gabby laughed. "Heavens, no. He had a voice like a foghorn. Kind, gentle hands when he held a baby, though. That's one of the things I miss the most, seeing my dad with a newborn in his hands." She straightened up in the car seat, drew in a deep breath. "Did your mother sing to you?"

"She didn't have time, really. She and my dad divorced when I was still a toddler, and after she married my step-father, Gavin's father, it seems like her time was consumed with all sorts of things. But never singing."

"Was she happy?"

"I think so. She was a nurse at the hospital, she raised two sons, took care of her husband... I think she had a good life with him."

"Did you?"

"Charles Thierry was good to me. Good man, excellent doctor."

"Let me guess...pediatrician?"

"The apples didn't fall far from the tree, did they? He was a very good pediatrician."

"And?"

"And he died when I was in med school, before Gavin had a chance to go to med school. My mom remarried a few years later, and she's living happily on a beach in Nicaragua."

"But you and Gavin got along back then?"

"Like typical brothers. You know, ups and downs. Until...well, let's just say that the adult years have been all *downs* and let it go at that. I don't want talk of my brother spoiling the evening. Especially when we have such a nice night ahead us."

Whatever had happened between them was bad. Hurtful. It made her nervous, made her feel guilty.

"Well, then, let's talk about pleasant things. As I recall, you said you had something you wanted to discuss with me? It's pleasant, isn't it?"

"I think it is, but first I want to ply you with food, chocolate, more food, more chocolate, to maximize that pleasant potential."

A gentle smile finally crept back to his face, causing her to relax. Right now, this was for the best. Soon, though, she would have to tell him everything,

"I like the part about more food, more chocolate. Bribes are good, but are you sure you can afford me, Neil?"

He chuckled. "I know the executive chef. I believe she'll let me make installment payments, if I have to." Yet, the real question was, could he afford her in the ways that counted? Because if she stayed, he was going to have to figure out just how he was going to do this. And it had nothing at all to do with the finances of the matter, and everything to do with the feelings.

"Have you ever thought about what you'd be if you quit being a doctor?" she asked him.

"Why? Are you thinking about quitting?"

Not quitting so much as making a big change, and finding a way to accommodate her new life in the meanwhile. "My life is changing. Who knows what I'll be doing a year from now, other than raising my son? I mean, as much as I love medicine, I suppose that could always be a possibility. Maybe I'll want to be a full-time mom, or maybe I'll settle in a place where my medical skills aren't needed."

"You're too dedicated to quit. You'd go crazy inside a month. No, make that a week. Isn't that why you're working now, just a few weeks away from your due date? Because you need to be a doctor, because it's part of you?"

"It is part of me. But what if I found a place where I really wanted to raise Bryce, but there was no need for my services there? Yet I was so happy being there, raising my son there, that I couldn't leave? Or what if you found a place to live that didn't need a family practitioner, but you wanted to stay there so badly it didn't matter? Maybe it's the kind of place where we *want* to define ourselves by something other than our work."

"In my case, is there a woman involved?" he asked, half teasing.

"You mean you'd give it up for a woman?"

Neil made a sound that sounded like a cross between a laugh and a choke. "Hell, no, I wouldn't give it up for a woman. I'd hope that a woman who's that important to me would understand why I couldn't give it up. I came close once, and it almost cost me everything. So once was enough."

"But she wasn't the right woman, was she? I mean, you two did get…" Gabby paused, deciding not to wander down that path. It was Neil's business, and if he wanted to tell her, fine. If he didn't, fine, too. "OK, so let me start this conversation over. What if the place where you wanted to spend the rest of your life couldn't support you as a doctor? No woman involved. Which would you choose? Your heart, or your profession?"

"Is that what you're struggling with, Gabrielle?"

"Not struggling. I gave up my job in Chicago because something much more important than anything I'd ever dreamed of came into my life. No regrets there, what-soever. In fact, what I thought I was so passionate about disappeared when I realized that my baby needed some-thing different than what I had. No contest. He won, and

I don't regret that because I've discovered that when you love someone more than anything in the world, the sacrifices don't matter."

"So what you're saying is that it might not be a sacrifice, if you truly love the person you're doing it for?"

"Something like that."

"Are you talking about White Elk?"

"Maybe," she hedged.

"Well, when you are *definitely*, let me know because Eric and I crunched some numbers and we believe we could support you here as a part-timer for a while, with the option of expanding your duties in the future, when you're ready. That is, if you want to stay."

"But I thought you were trying to figure out a way to expand your trauma unit?"

"That, too. But we don't want to let a good thing go."

"A good thing, as in me?" Admittedly, the offer did give her butterflies because she wanted to stay. But it caused problems, too, as she couldn't give him an answer until she saw how he reacted to finding out about Bryce. Also, a little bit of disappointment settled over her, because she'd had this fantasy where he'd asked her to stay, and it was purely for personal reasons. He needed her, he wanted her. Not that he'd crunched the numbers and he could afford her, part-time. "Can I have some time to think about it?"

"All the time you need."

"And this was the reason you're taking me to Pine Ridge? To ask me to stay?" Again, she was disappointed. It was a silly reaction, because they were only colleagues. Still, she couldn't help the way she felt, and right now it was definitely let down.

"Part of the reason."

"And the other part?"

"I like your company, and sometimes it's nice to be part of a couple. I thought maybe you'd enjoy the evening out."

Gabby breathed a sigh of relief. It was not a romantic declaration or anything close to it, which was good. But hearing those words made her feel better. "I never dated very much. Didn't have time. Didn't have interest. Never met the right man. All of the above. And sometimes I wonder what I've missed out on, by making the choices I do. I know I didn't sound very gracious when I accepted your invitation, but I'm glad you invited me, because I would enjoy an evening out." Unfortunately, it was the end of the evening she dreaded.

"Are you thinking about staying here, Gabrielle? I mean, I don't need a firm answer, but I'm curious."

She shifted back down into her seat and twisted to stare at the stars again. *Twinkle, twinkle little star.* How she wished her life was simpler. "I'm thinking about all my options…keeping them open."

"And there's really no one else involved? You're not running away from someone?"

"No one else."

"So, would I be out of line if I asked about the baby's father?"

Not out of line so much as simply too late. It was a melancholy subject. "I told you that there is no father involved. We had a brief relationship. He was a very nice man, someone who was there when I needed to be involved. My dad had just died, I was lost. And for me, getting pregnant wasn't a concern because I never thought I could have children. Was told it wouldn't happen because…I'd had an injury when I was younger. It left me with a lot of scar tissue and opinion after opinion through the years confirmed that bearing children wasn't in my future. But never say never, right?"

"But the father…he's really not going to be involved with the baby at all?"

"No," she said, flatly. "And that's all there is to it." For now. She didn't want to ruin the evening, didn't want to drop the news on him, then spend the next few hours with a man who might not want to spend them with her. No, she wasn't going to do this now. In her mind, the scenario worked out in a specific way. She'd rehearsed it, and she was sticking to the plan.

"Sorry, I didn't mean to get so personal."

"Nothing to be sorry for. People are curious, and the only way you ever find out is to ask. But the good thing is, women have babies by themselves all the time. There's no stigma attached, no societal taboos, at least in this society. Doors are opened much wider these days for single mothers."

"And you'll be a very good mother."

She bristled right up. "Even without a father for my baby? Is that what you're implying?"

"I didn't say that, Gabrielle. Didn't imply it either. It's a good decision for you, I see it in your face every time I look at you. You're happy, and it shows. And so you'll know, if you do decide you want to stay in White Elk, accept my offer, and raise your baby here, you have a host of new colleagues who will support you."

She wanted him to say more. Wanted him to tell her how much he wanted her to stay. Wanted him to make it personal. But that was wishful thinking. Neil wasn't getting involved, the way she wasn't getting involved, even though her baby hormones were trying to turn this into something much more than it was.

Nothing was settled, and if anything, the offer that should have made her happy was beginning to feel like a dense, wet fog. A very cold one, at that.

* * *

"This is wonderful!" The tables were all adorned with lit candles and white roses in crystal vases. The light was low, the reflection from the candle glow giving off a very romantic overtone. Tonight was a night for lovers was what it said. Wasted on her, of course, but appreciated all the same. "I'm not sure what I thought this restaurant would be like, but it's…elegant." Very different from the lodge look she had expected—cedar logs, stone fireplace, animal heads adorning the wall. The restaurant was refined, its menu select, its ambiance pure class. And she felt so clunky in her one and only maternity outfit—a black skirt and black sweater—and snow boots. Clunky in and of themselves. "Why didn't you tell me it was so nice?" she hissed at Neil, who was impeccable in a gray wool suit, with his black turtle-necked sweater underneath. The beauty and the…underdressed frump.

"I thought you looked fine."

The dining room was full, the singer, an older woman in a long sequined gown, kept the crowd mesmerized by her dulcet tones, and all Gabby wanted to do was sneak through to her table and hope the tablecloth was large enough to conceal most of her. "I expected a lodge dining room like the one at Laura's. I didn't know this was a world-class restaurant."

Neil laughed. "You're being too self-conscious."

"Spoken like a man," she snapped, looking down at herself. Things went well on top, started to deteriorate around her middle, were pulled pretty darned tight over her rear end, and the boots…a concession to comfort she'd found two days ago, on sale. Faux fur that looked like she was wearing a raccoon wrapped around each ankle.

"OK, so maybe the boots aren't good," he admitted,

fighting back a smile. "But they'll be under the table, so no one will notice."

"Which is where you'll find me," Gabby muttered, as Neil took her by the arm and led her all the way over to the window. Naturally, he stopped at several tables along the way to say hello, to ask how someone was feeling, to introduce her to a highly styled couple he thought she should know. So, what could have, or should have, been a quick trip across the carpeted floor turned into twenty long minutes in which she knew people were turning their heads, asking questions. Pointing.

"I didn't know," Gabby explained to Angela, who hurried over to the table the instant they were seated. "And I apologize."

"For what? I'm just glad you're here. When I saw that Neil had made the reservation I decided to stay over and make sure your meal is perfect. Even though I won't be cooking it. But I did make a fabulous chocolate trifle for dessert, since I knew you were craving chocolate."

Gabby pulled her boot out from under the table. "This is what I'm apologizing for. I might have to have a double serving of the trifle to get me over the trauma."

"She thinks she's out of place." Neil set aside the wine menu and went straight to the menu of imported waters. "I told her she's fine, but she won't believe me."

Angela laughed. "He's right. You're fine. And I'm so glad you're here."

"How are you feeling?" Gabby asked.

"You're off duty, Doctor," Neil reminded her, then ordered a sparkling water from Belgium. "Time to relax, which you're not doing very well at right now."

"I'm fine, and I've got to get back to the kitchen," Angela explained. "And I've got your meal all planned, so please sit back, relax, enjoy yourself." She turned away, had a second thought, then turned back. "Dance. We have an awesome dance floor here. And I know an obstetrician who would tell you that the exercise would do you good."

Gabby gave her a scowl. "I don't dance." Angela was trying to turn this into a romantic date, and that wasn't going to work, no matter how romantic the atmosphere, the food or the music. But the smile she saw on Neil's face made her wonder if he thought differently. "I don't," she protested. "Never have, except for a couple of school dances when I was a girl, and I was terrible."

Angela scurried off to the kitchen, leaving Gabby and Neil to the discussion. "So you really don't know if you can dance, then, do you?" he asked.

"And I'm not about to find out."

"What if I asked you? Called in the gratuity you offered for the massage. Remember that?"

"I remember reserving the right to put conditions on that gratuity, so I'd have to say no."

"And you wouldn't find that a little rude, turning down your dinner escort that way, especially when a gratuity *you promised* still hangs in the balance?"

"If my dinner escort valued his toes, he wouldn't ask." She sat back in her chair and folded her arms over her chest. "So don't ask."

"What if I said that dancing is good for the baby?" His eyes positively twinkled with mischief.

"Then I'd say it's a good thing you're not an obstetrician, because dancing has nothing to do with fetal development."

"You're referring to Bryce as a fetus, now? And just when I've gotten use to personalizing him?"

She didn't answer as the waiter placed a champagne bucket next to the table. In it was a chilled bottle of sparkling water, which he served the way he would have served a fine wine. Gabby kept her eyes fixed on him while, across the table, Neil kept his eyes fixed on her—making her totally uncomfortable. Given different circumstances, this might have turned into the night he expected. But circumstances weren't different, and nothing was going to change. Or, actually, it would once the evening was over.

"Why are you staring at me?" she asked.

"I've never been this up close and personal with a pregnant lady," he admitted, "and I'm finding it fascinating. I'll bet you don't even know how many times in any given hour you raise your hand to your belly, and smile. And it's a warm smile, one that comes from a place I'm not sure any man could ever truly understand, which is too bad, because I've always thought men were left out of the best part. It's amazing, though, isn't it? A brand-new life about to happen. We know how it happens, know *that* it happens, but it's still amazing and all the men can do is stand back and watch."

"Want to do more than watch?" she asked. "He's kicking, if you'd like to feel."

A smile spread across Neil's face as he laid aside his napkin, stood up and went to her side of the table. Without a word, Gabby took his hand and guided it to her right side where, indeed, Bryce was making himself known. Then, instinctively, she pulled up her sweater to let Neil see the little blips her baby made on her belly when he kicked. "He's one rambunctious boy," she said, surprised how intimate this felt. Normally, she hated people coming up and touching her belly like it was their right. So many people did that. Poke, prod, pat…it made her cringe thinking about all the uninvited hands she'd had on her lately. But Neil's hands, as he laid them on her bare flesh now, and felt the kick of her child in a way no one but she had before, were so gentle, so right. What surprised her was how the baby settled down almost immediately under Neil's touch, like he knew that this man was part of his life.

"You have a good way with him. I guess that's why you became a pediatrician," she said, pulling her sweater back into place as the waiter approached the table. All too soon the moment was over, and Neil was back sitting across from her, staring again, as the waiter fussed over the table, rearranging the flowers, setting aside the candle, refolding the napkins.

Gabby liked it that Neil watched her that way. In an odd sort of way, it made her feel almost…sexy. And pregnant women were sexy. That's what she told her patients every day. But sexy had no place in *their* relationship. They weren't lovers, sharing a wonderful experience together. After this evening, after she told him the little boy he'd just felt kicking was his flesh and blood, they might not even be friends. So rather than saying anything, she took a drink of her sparkling water as melancholy slipped down over her. They had no future, no past. All they had was just this moment, which suddenly felt lonely.

Dinner went nicely in spite of the glum mood that had come on her earlier. The food was wonderful, the conversation light. Neil wisely avoided talking anything of substance, for which she was grateful, and he even managed to stay off hospital matters. Throughout the whole thing, Gabby couldn't help but wonder what it might have been like had this been a real date between two people in different circumstances. Maybe in love, or on the verge of it. But this was her lot now, and while the evening had brought on a good case of the blues earlier, she wasn't really unhappy. They were temporary, while the excitement of what was happening to her was permanent. It's all good, she decided on her way back from the ladies' room. "And things will work out the way they're meant to be," she whispered to Bryce.

She cut around the edge of the dance floor, where a dozen couples were dancing to something seductive that could have been sung by Frank Sinatra. The low tones from the tiny orchestra were so smooth and sensual, she couldn't help but slow her pace, to watch for a moment, and to listen. Which was her mistake, because Neil stepped up from behind and led her straight to the dance floor.

"Gratuity time," he whispered, as he took hold of her hand and pulled her into him as far as she could go, all things considered.

"And if I simply walked away?" She wanted to, but she was suddenly discovering that so much of her didn't want to. For a little while, it would be nice to live in the illusion that they were a romantic couple caught up in the pure sensuality of the dance. Even with her boots...and her belly.

"I'm not keeping you here, Gabrielle. I would never force you to do something you don't want to do. So, it's your choice."

Her choice...her body was already swaying to the rhythm. Swaying to Neil's rhythm. It was like she couldn't stop it. The music was drawing her in, pulling her even closer to Neil...he was holding her, they were dancing. Hands appropriate, of course. Proper dance etiquette. And she wished, dear heaven, she had on better shoes, something to help her glide more gracefully. But that didn't matter, because they took up so little of the parquet floor, dancing mostly in one small spot. Tighter together. Their proper dance etiquette relaxing into something more personal, her arms slipped around his neck as his slipped around her back. They looked like every other couple out there. So close... Her head on his shoulder now, she could feel his breath on the back of her neck. The steady in and out of it, the gentle brush of his lips…no lips. No, that wasn't his lips. Couldn't be.

Suddenly, Gabby pulled back, broke away, stared into his eyes. "I need to sit down." she said, trying not to sound as breathless as she was. Which had nothing to do with the dance.

"Are you OK?" he asked, leading her off the dance floor.

"Just a little winded. I'll be fine when I sit down."

She wasn't, though. She wasn't fine at all. In fact, she was so disquieted she wasn't able to eat a bite of the chocolate trifle Angela had sent along for dessert. "Did you kiss me?" she finally blurted out.

He looked up from his spoonful of trifle. Smiled. "I might have. Why?"

"Why would you ask me why? No, skip that, and tell me why you *might* have kissed me?"

"The moment was right. So was the mood."

"Whose mood?" she sputtered.

"Mine. Yours."

"How do you figure my mood was right?"

"Your head was on my shoulder, your arms around my neck. Since I wasn't the one who placed them there, then I figured the mood had to be yours, too."

He took another bite of dessert, and over the flicker of the candles between them she saw the pure devilry in his eyes. "I was…" Voice quivering, she cleared her throat. "I told you I didn't dance. I didn't know what I was doing."

"Then I claim the same thing. I didn't know what I was doing. *If* I kissed you, that is." A purely sexual smile crossed his face. "And that hasn't been established yet, has it?"

"I think it has."

"Did you see the kiss happen?"

"Of course I didn't. But I felt it." Had felt goose bumps rising on her flesh, too. And shivers running up and down her spine. Shivers that were still there.

"Are you sure that's what you felt?"

Oh, she was sure. But she wasn't going to tell him.

Neil scooped up a spoonful of trifle and held it across the table to her. Wiggled it ever so seductively close to her lips. And she wanted it, not because she craved the chocolate but because she craved the seduction. Or, rather, the illusion of seduction, as no man in his right mind would seduce a seven-and-a-half-months-pregnant woman. But it was so nice feeling wanted—in *that* way. And because she wanted it so desperately, she pushed herself back from the table, away from temptation. "What I felt was a man coercing me into doing something I didn't want to do, and I was just being polite, so he wouldn't be embarrassed by my rejection of him on the dance floor."

Neil laughed outright at that. His eyes twinkled, they crinkled at the corners, and he gave her the full effect of a laugh that was so contagious she couldn't help but laugh, too, at the absurdity of what she'd said. In fact, she laughed herself to tears, and took the handkerchief he offered, to dab her eyes. "OK, so maybe that wasn't really what I meant," she finally managed.

"What you meant was that you enjoyed it. Admit it, Gabrielle. You had a few nice moments out there on the dance floor when you finally allowed yourself to."

"It's been a while since I've felt like…a woman. I'm a doctor, a pregnant person, I'm a clunk in furry boots, I'm a mother-in-waiting. But a woman…"

"Believe me. Even with the furry boots, there's no mistaking the woman." And maybe he'd gone a little too far. But he'd been caught up in the moment. Smelled her perfume, held her in his arms, felt her head on his shoulder… Normal reaction, he was telling himself. He didn't date, didn't have a social life, and Gabrielle was…attractive. More like beautiful. And alone. He was only trying to befriend her, that's all. So the kiss had been a mistake, he'd admit that to himself, and deny its existence to her. Even though she knew he'd kissed her.

Truth was, he wasn't even embarrassed, when he probably should have been. Another truth was that, given the opportunity, he might kiss her again. There wouldn't be another opportunity, though, so he was safe.

But another time, another situation? He could almost picture himself involved with her. Maybe even more than involved. She was everything he'd never expected in a woman. Funny, direct, honest, smart. Little Bryce Evans was going to have himself one hell of a mother, and Neil was a little envious he didn't fit into the equation somewhere, because it was a nice equation. One he'd never expected he'd want.

"Well, right now, these furry boots are going to hike back to the kitchen and see Angela for a few minutes." She stood, then breezed by his side of the table, stopping opposite him. "Oh, and, Neil," she said, a tiny smile turning up the corners of her lips, "no kissing any other pregnant women while I'm gone. OK?"

Damn, she did make him laugh. And feel good. And, for the first time in years, feel optimistic. He watched her until she disappeared down the corridor leading to the kitchen, then turned on his cell phone and called the hospital. He'd given instructions that he wanted nothing short of a natural disaster to call him away, and at present there was no natural disaster, except, perhaps, the natural disaster he was making of the evening. Trying not to think about what he'd done, Neil slumped back in his chair, stretched legs out under the table and closed his eyes. Trouble was, in his mind's eye all he could see were his lips on her neck.

"Not a good thing," he muttered, taking a drink of the sparkling water, wishing it was something much stronger.

"You two looked good out there," Angela said.

She was taking a break, sitting in the employee lounge with her feet propped up on a low table. Gabby dropped down next to her, propped her own feet up, then compared pregnant bellies. She was carrying in a little ball in front, and an old wives' tale said that meant it was a boy. But Angela was spread out all the way around. The same old wives' tale said that meant it would be a girl.

"I felt pretty good, too. Except for the fact that I wasn't dressed properly, and my dancing shoes didn't really allow me to dance."

Angela laughed. "I'm really sorry about that. But people come in here dressed every which way. You really don't stand out as badly as you think."

"It's a nice restaurant, Angela. I can see why you missed it, not being able to cook."

"Well, I'm going to be off on maternity for quite a while, at least three months, so at some point I'll have to get used to it."

"So who'll be in charge while you're gone?"

"My sister is coming in from Arizona to take over the kitchen, and to help me. She's a nurse. Well, she was a nurse. Not sure why she quit, but she did. So she has the time, and she also has a certificate from a culinary institute. Cooking was her first career choice before she fell in love with nursing. So, she'll be here shortly and who knows? Maybe she'll stay on and cook for me since she's saying she's not going back into nursing."

"Some people just burn out." Gabby arched her back when Bryce kicked, then shifted. "I just get comfortable in one position, then he changes, and I have to change."

"Did you ever *not* want to know his sex?" Angela asked.

"Not really. I wanted to establish a personal relationship with my baby right from the start, know who he is, call him by name. Which meant he had to be more than an it—you know how people always refer to an unborn baby as it. But I didn't want that. I wanted to know who I was bringing into this world, probably from the instant I knew I was pregnant."

"Brian calls our baby *it*. In fact, in the divorce papers that arrived this morning, he stated that I can have full custody of it. Not the baby. Not the child. Not the boy or girl. *It*." She sighed wistfully. "His charge is that we'd agreed to not have children, and I tricked him."

"Oh, Angela. I'm so sorry. I'd really hoped you could work it out."

"I did, too. He didn't. But I can do this, and I've got your example to follow. And just think. If you stay in White Elk, our children will be friends, playmates." Angela pushed herself to the edge of her chair. "So, do you know?"

"Know what?"

"Whether I'm having a boy or a girl?"

Her guesses were usually right, but she never told her patients what she guessed. "Want the test? It's easy."

Angela shook her head. "I like surprises."

"Surprises and miracles." Hers, and Angela's. "You're going to do just fine with this. I'm a pretty good judge of future mothers."

"It is a miracle, isn't it? I guess I never thought of it in those terms."

"It's always a miracle, but some miracles are different. So, since you don't want to know your baby's gender, tell your friends to buy yellow for you. It goes either way."

"If *you* were buying me a baby present, what color would *you* buy me?"

Gabby laughed. "White." Then she followed Angela to the door, where she was met by Neil.

"I think it's time to go," he said, "unless you want another dance." He actually held out his arms to her, but she waved him off, laughing.

"No dancing. No food. No more anything for the evening. It's time for this pregnant lady to go home and go to bed." Of course, the road back to the cabin was long, and she was dreading the ride. But now was the time. Neil had to know.

And she decided to tell him before they left the parking lot. "Could you wait just a minute before we leave?" she asked. "There's something we need to talk about."

"You're accepting my offer to stay?"

He put the car in neutral and twisted in his seat to face her. Thank heavens he left the dome light off and they were parked in one of the darker areas, because she didn't want to see his face right now. She was afraid it would break her heart. "I'm not sure you're going to want me to stay. In fact, you may not even want to drive me home."

He chuckled, but it was nervous. "What could be so bad?"

It was already beginning to hurt her. "I just want you to know that I'll stay here until your other obstetrician arrives, because I don't want to put my patients or your hospital in a lurch. But if you get someone in here to replace me right away, I'll go." More than hurting her, it was ripping her heart in two.

"Gabrielle, I don't understand. What's this about?"

"My baby, Neil. It's about my baby."

He was suddenly alert, sitting up straight, leaning in a little closer to her. Even in the dark shadows she could see the look of concern on his face. So she looked away.

"What's wrong?" he gasped, putting a comforting hand on her arm. "Gabrielle, tell me what's wrong, and I promise, we'll find the best doctor to fix it."

"That's the problem, Neil. It can't be fixed. What's done is done."

His grip on her arm tightened a little. "What, Gabrielle?"

"My baby's father." She took a deep breath, and swallowed. "Bryce's full name is Bryce *Thierry* Evans. Gavin is…was his father."

Neil didn't respond. Not in the next few seconds. Not in the next two minutes.

"Neil?" she finally whispered. "Did you hear what I said?"

"What I heard," he began in a perfectly calm voice, "is that, first, my brother slept with my wife, then stole her. Then he slept with you and got you pregnant."

"Your wife?" she choked. Just when she thought this moment couldn't get any worse… "Gavin stole your wife?" *Worse, had she slept with a married man?*

"He stole, she went. Whatever you want to call it." Still calm, and much more in control than she'd thought he would be, Neil started the car, and it moved forward. Slowly, though.

"Don't you want to know what happened?" she asked. "Why I…why Gavin and I…"

"I'm a doctor. I know *exactly* what happened." His voice was so chilled it sent shivers up her spine.

Angry tears pooled in Gabby's eyes. She was angry at herself for hurting Neil, angry at Neil for not wanting to hear what had happened between Gavin and her. "I didn't mean to hurt you, Neil. When I came here I had no idea you were Gavin's brother, then after I found out…it was difficult. I couldn't figure out a good way to tell you. Especially after I knew you two were estranged."

"Well, at least I know why you fainted that day."

"It was a shock."

"I guess it would be." Same cold voice. "But I do have one question. Why were you in White Elk? Gavin didn't live here."

"I'd gone to Spotswood, to find him. To tell him. He didn't know. After I found he'd died, I was on my way back to the airport, and I was tired. I just wanted a room for the night. White Elk seemed so—"

"So the relationship didn't last?" he interrupted. "You and Gavin weren't together?"

"It lasted a week. At the end of that week we knew we didn't have anything worth continuing. And I didn't know he was married. I would have never—"

"He wasn't. By the time he got around to you, he'd been divorced from my ex-wife a good year."

"*By the time he got around to me?* That's not fair, Neil. I know I've hurt you, and I didn't mean to. But you weren't part of this. I didn't know you when Gavin and I were…" She paused, drew in a steadying breath. "Gavin was a nice man who helped me through some difficult days. He wasn't some predator out looking for a vulnerable woman, the way you're implying."

As they rounded a curve, and started the descent off the ridge, Neil slowed down even more.

And didn't speak again for nearly a minute. Neither did Gabby. Instead, she looked out the window, stared up at the night sky, hoping to take some comfort in the twinkling stars, but they were all gone. The night was still, no stars, a moon that was clouding over. Maybe fighting would have been better. Neil yelling, letting out his anger. But he wasn't doing that. Wasn't doing anything at all, and that's what worried her. "So, do you still want me to work until my replacement comes?" She wasn't even going to bother asking if he still wanted her to stay in White Elk, because she knew the answer to that one.

"You do whatever you want, Gabrielle."

Frigid indifference. She hated that. But that's what it was, and she'd deal with it. She'd made promises here she wanted to keep. "Then I'll work for a while longer."

"Fine."

"And leave as soon as I'm replaced."

"Fine."

"I'm sorry he hurt you, Neil. I didn't see that side of him."

No response.

"And if I'd known…" What? What would she have done differently? Gavin had been an important part of her life, and she couldn't deny that. He'd given her a baby, and for that gift, he'd always have a place in her heart. "I'm sorry I hurt you. That's not what I wanted to happen."

"You have one hell of a way of ending a nice evening," he snapped. And that's all he said until they turned onto Aspen Loop, where, in the distance, they could see red and blue lights flashing through the pine trees. Emergency lights. Everywhere. "Damn," he muttered, accelerating just the slightest.

"What is it?" she asked.

"Nothing that's going to involve you," he said. "And I mean it, Gabrielle. You're staying out of it."

"And you can stop me?" she snapped.

"I can, and I will."

"Because you're angry with me?"

"You're damn right I'm angry. Mad as hell. Don't

know what to do about it yet either. But that's not the reason."

"Then what is?"

"You're carrying my nephew. That's the reason."

CHAPTER SIX

ERIC RAMSEY was already on the scene when Neil stopped the car and got out. Gabby stayed right up with Neil, matching his fast, furious steps as he made his way over the rocky road to the guardrail that seemed to be the center of activity.

"Two vehicles involved," Eric said in greeting.

Neil was already out of his suit jacket, pulling on a pair of coveralls one of the medics had handed him the instant he'd jumped out of the car.

"One was a van," Eric continued. "Teenagers out doing whatever the hell it is teenagers do. Thank God my girls are only five." He paused, shook his head, refocused. "Anyway, the other car didn't go over. Man and woman, no significant injuries."

"How long ago?" Neil asked.

"Thirty minutes."

"Any sign of life from down below?"

"Over here," Eric shouted at the light crew, a group of volunteers whose job was to light up the scene of the emergency. They carried portable utility lights of all kinds, which would run off the generator that was being pulled into the scene at the same time. "We need them as near the edge as we can get them." Then to Neil he said, "So far, nothing from below. The van is visible. It's hung up on a ledge down there and I have no idea if it's stable, or what we'll find."

"Anybody else down there yet?"

"Not yet. We've been prepping the scene up here first."

"OK, then. Let me go get into my harness and I'll be ready in a couple of minutes." He spun to walk away, then stopped, and turned to face Gabby. "I'm not even going to bother warning you to be careful, because you'll just do what you want anyway. But this could be a long, hard night. So take care of yourself." His voice wasn't quite angry, but wasn't friendly either, and the chill in it wasn't missed by Eric, who frowned.

"Everything OK?" Eric asked, both Gabby and Neil. He looked first at Neil, then at Gabby, then back to Neil when he didn't get an answer

"Fine," Neil finally ground out. "Everything is just fine."

Eric took that as a hint not to pursue the matter any further, opting, instead, to go to the equipment truck to harness up. Neil followed immediately. "Don't ask," Neil said, waving off his partner before Eric could say a word.

Eric tossed Neil his harness. "If I'd known your evening was going that badly, I'd have called."

"Evening was fine. The ride home wasn't."

As Neil harnessed up to go down the side of the mountain face with Eric and the others, he avoided watching Gabby, who was in the process of establishing herself in the back of one of the ambulances, pulling out various medical supplies that might be needed. It was too damned frustrating. He didn't need it. Didn't need anything but the life he'd had before she'd come to White Elk.

"Anything I can do?" Eric asked, as the two of them were about to go over the side of the mountain.

"Shoot me in the leg if I ever go near another woman."

Eric grimaced. "That bad?"

"That bad."

"Maybe you just need more practice with women."

"The only practice I need is in avoiding them."

"Well, for what it's worth, I understand you two looked pretty good out on the dance floor. Actually, I heard several interesting versions of the story."

"Already?" Neil snapped, as he checked his ropes. Emergency lights were finally directed down the mountainside, and dozens of people, all of whom knew their jobs, pressed into action as two doctors and three other rescuers lowered themselves over the side of the mountain, and disappeared down into the black abyss.

Neil liked this part of the job, the physical rigors of it, the adrenaline burst. Gavin had, too. In fact, rescues like this had been one of those times he and Gavin had worked well together. Back in simpler days. *Much simpler*, he said to himself, thinking about Gabby and trying *not* to connect Gavin to her. "See anything?" Neil called to Eric, who'd come down parallel to him, while the other three came down in the second wave.

"Maybe a headlight, but I'm not sure."

Whatever they found, it wasn't going to be good. Sighing, Neil turned his attention to getting to the bottom. But not before he gave one brief thought to Gabby. What the hell was he going to do now? She had no one, and she was carrying his nephew. The normal thing, under these circumstances, would probably be to walk away from her. But that wouldn't be the right thing, and right now he wasn't sure he wanted to do the right thing. Not sure at all. "I see it!" he shouted to Eric. "About twenty feet down, and to the left. Nothing moving, as far as I can tell."

And he sure as hell wished he hadn't kissed her.

* * *

Aching back, cold to the bone, the first hour into the rescue had been an exercise in patience because all they'd done was wait. Neil and Eric were at the van, word was there were survivors, but so far no one had been sent up. Several others had gone down, though, to tie off the van to make it secure. It was a slow process. Gabby was frustrated and uncomfortable, and that was about her physical circumstances. The way she felt about Neil's reaction…actually, she was trying *not* to think about that.

People all around her were pitching in. It was an amazing thing to watch, because tables were set up and coffee was being handed around to rescuers and watchers alike. Blankets were coming out of car trunks and being wrapped around the shoulders of anxious parents waiting to find out if their children were in the vehicle at the bottom of the ravine. It was an almost surreal scene, because everybody seemed to know their place there. Everybody but Gabby, who decided to go lie down in the back of an ambulance while she waited, when the estimate for the first patient to be brought up turned into another thirty minutes. So she made her whereabouts known to one of the attendants, then stretched out, trying to fight off the dull, heavy sleep that wanted to slip down over her. Emotional sleep, she decided. Something to heal her dull emotional state.

But she didn't sleep. She just existed in oblivion for a few minutes, not thinking, not planning. Not asking herself the obvious questions. Eyes closed, and focused only on her breathing, maybe her mental escape lasted five minutes when all of a sudden Gabby had the distinct impression that she was being watched. When she opened her eyes and turned her head she saw him. He was kneeling next to the stretcher on which she was resting, his face only inches from Gabby's. "Who are you?" she whispered, so not to startle the child.

He whispered back. "Benjamin Tyler Janssen, ma'am."

Polite child, and scared to death. She could see that in his eyes. "And what can I do for you, Benjamin Tyler Janssen?" She guessed him to be seven, give or take a year.

Benjamin shrugged, didn't answer. Tears were welling in his eyes but not spilling.

"Were you in the accident?" He could have been. Maybe he'd climbed up the side of the drop-off on his own.

"No," he replied, his voice quivering as the tears got closer.

"Are you hurt, Benjamin?"

"No."

That was good. "Are you here looking for someone who might have been in the accident?"

"No," he answered again, as the tears finally began to roll down his cheeks.

By now, Gabby knew Benjamin wasn't going to be forthcoming with information, and if she wanted to find out what was going on, she'd have to ask the right question. Which could go on all night. Except the child was here at an accident scene, kneeling in the back of an ambulance. The doctor in her took over. "Is someone you know sick, or hurt?"

"My grandpa. He said he didn't feel so well, then he…" He sniffled, then wiped his tears on the sleeve of his jacket.

"What, Benjamin? You have to tell me so I can help him."

"He went to sleep. And he wouldn't wake up."

A whole list of possibilities raced through Gabby's mind. Stroke, heart attack, complete cardiac arrest. "Well, I'm a doctor, Benjamin, and I want to go see your grandfather right now. Can you tell me where he is?"

He nodded. "He's still in the car. We were going back to our room and he had to stop because of all the sirens."

Meaning they had been on the road to the lodge and had pulled over for the emergency vehicles. At least, that's what she hoped he meant. "You're staying at the lodge?"

"Yes, ma'am. We can go hiking every day. Grandpa takes pictures and sells them to magazines."

So grandpa was a professional photographer, which meant he was probably in pretty good health. Gabby hoped that would be enough to sustain him for a while. "Do you see that black bag sitting on the stretcher right behind you?" she asked, as she scooted to the edge of her stretcher, preparing to stand.

Benjamin turned around. "Yes, ma'am."

"Well, right now, I need you to be my assistant and carry it." While she carried the bag of first-aid supplies she was taking from the ambulance—an IV set-up, a flashlight, a bag of saline solution, a blanket and some incidentals. Not much, because she couldn't deplete the ambulance. So, after stuffing everything into the pillowcase she'd been using during her much abbreviated rest, she followed Benjamin out the back of the ambulance, told one of the attendants where she'd be, then followed Benjamin through the crowd, which seemed to be growing larger by the minute.

At the edge of the scene, where the number of people dwindled, and the flurry of activity had died down, Gabby stopped for a moment to dial Neil's cell phone. She didn't expect him to answer, but she hoped that at some point he would listen to his messages. "It may be a heart attack or a stroke," she started to explain. "Won't know until I get there. But we're going down the main access road. Call me when you get my message." As she clicked off, she wasn't sure that he would.

"Do you live near here, Benjamin?" she asked, hoping a little conversation would help calm the boy.

"No. But we come here sometimes. My grandpa likes the pictures he takes here."

"And no one else comes with you?"

"Just me and Grandpa. My mom and dad stay home."

Mom and dad. That was a relief, because she'd been wondering if Benjamin's grandfather was raising him. "Well, as soon as we get your grandpa taken care of, we'll call your mom and dad." Benjamin was picking up his pace, and Gabby sensed they were nearing the car. Right now they were only a few hundred yards away from the crash site and she could still see the reflection from the lights set up all around it.

"Hurry up!" Benjamin yelled, breaking into a run.

She called Neil's cell phone again. "I think I'm at the car now." She flashed her light on it. "It's an SUV, red, with a luggage rack on top." And a man slumped over the steering wheel. "Gotta go," she said, clicking off. Then clicked right back on. "And I'm not doing anything stupid," she added, then clicked off again.

"Benjamin, what I need for you to do is stay here, on the road, and if someone comes by, wave at them, try to stop them. But don't run out in front of them." A mother's advice. And it felt right.

"Is he going to be OK?"

She wanted to make promises, but she knew better. As she opened the passenger's door and looked at the man in the next seat, her patient looked so bad she wondered if there were even any promises to make here at all. "What's his name?" she asked Benjamin.

"Ben," he said, his voice quivering as the tears started again. "Grandpa Ben."

"Well, then, let me see what I can do for Grandpa Ben."

After she'd climbed inside and seated herself next to the man, the first thing she did was feel for a pulse in his neck. Nothing. She repositioned fingers, tried again, still nothing. But on a third repositioning…a pulse! Very thready, very irregular, but it was there.

"Is he OK?" Benjamin called from the road.

If only she could twist around and be more flexible. Or at least be flexible enough to have a look in his eyes. But she couldn't. The space was too cramped and she had too much bulk, so she climbed back outside the vehicle and went around to the driver's door.

"Is my grandpa OK?" Benjamin yelled again. This time more agitated than frightened. He was expecting a miracle, and she didn't want to let him down. But the situation wasn't looking good for Grandpa Ben, and the fact that she was so limited wasn't helping.

"I have to do a few more things before I know what's going on," she told the boy. Part of her wanted to hug the child and prepare him for the worst, and part of her wanted to send him back up the road so he wouldn't have to be here if, or when, his grandfather died. She remembered seeing her mother die. It had been an aneurysm, had happened fast, while her dad had been working and she'd been home alone with her mom. It was a memory no child should ever have. But she needed Benjamin here with her, needed his help. "Benjamin, what I want you to do is make a phone call for me." She tossed him her cell phone, then opened the driver's door. "Call the number at the top of my list and tell the man who answers what I'm about to tell you…"

"Grandpa Ben, can you hear me?" she shouted at her patient. He was a big, muscular man. Curly brown hair, broad shoulders. Handsome and rugged, but much too large for her to move. "Ben, can you hear me?" No response. Not even a little stirring.

She checked his eyes. Pupils equal and reactive to light. Good. "Did you dial the number?"

Benjamin nodded. "Yes, ma'am."

Such a polite little boy. Manners were important. She intended to instill proper manners in Bryce. "Did anyone answer?"

"No," he said.

"That's OK. But you've got his voice mail, right?"

"Right."

"Then say P-E-R-L. Pulse thready, tachycardia. Respirations…" She counted for several seconds. "Normal, shallow. And BP…" She pumped up the cuff, took a listen, got nothing, took another listen, couldn't hear a thing. "Can't hear it."

Benjamin repeated her word for word.

"Mild cyanosis…"

Benjamin stumbled over those words.

"Skin cold and clammy." Over the next two minutes she made all the diagnoses that she could standing next to the driver's side, leaning in. And that's as far as she could go. Physically, she couldn't lift the elder Ben out, even with little Benjamin's help. And she couldn't even climb in and administer anything. So she was stalled here. Standing guard over a man who needed so much when she could give him so very little. "Tell him I'm starting an IV with saline." After that, she needed help or the man would die. Of that, she had no doubt. Even without the proper diagnostic tools, she knew a heart attack when she saw one. A severe heart attack.

"Ben," she shouted again, hoping to rouse him. Somewhere in the back of her mind, she saw a situation where Ben woke up and with a little help from her was able to climb into the next seat over. Easy solution—she'd drive him to the hospital. But that wasn't happening. And each and every time she felt for a pulse, what she felt was the heart rhythm of a man closer to death than he had been when she'd checked him the last time.

"The man said he's coming," Benjamin shouted.

"What man?"

"The one on the cell phone. He called back. Does that mean my grandpa is going to be OK? Is that man going to help fix him?"

"That man is a very good doctor, and he'll do everything he can to help your grandpa." She took another pulse. Unfortunately, Benjamin's grandpa was failing fast. Too fast. By the time she saw headlights coming toward her, she couldn't find a pulse at all. Couldn't count a respiration.

"He's coding," she called, as Neil jumped out of the ambulance he was driving. "And I can't get him out of the car seat."

"Get what you need from the ambulance," he said, running past her. "And, Gabby, it's just the two of us. We couldn't spare anybody else from up top. They're finally getting the kids up and it's taking every medic we have up there."

In the ambulance, she found cardiac drugs and a portable defibrillator, which she handed to Benjamin to carry over to Neil. There was also a bag to force air into his lungs and an intubation tray if the field resuscitation went that far. By the time she got everything to the road, Neil had Grandpa Ben out of the driver's seat, lying in the dirt, with the SUV headlights pointed directly on them. He was doing chest compressions, alternating them with mouth-to-mouth resuscitation. Gabby's first task was to hook the leads from the defibrillator to Grandpa Ben's chest, which she did, only to find him in ventricular fibrillation—a condition where the heart was more quivering than beating. Her second was to ready the cardiac drugs as Neil did the cardioversion—shocked the man's heart.

"Damn," he muttered, when it didn't convert to a normal sinus rhythm. "Do you know if he's had previous heart problems?"

"Don't know. I looked in his pockets and in the glove box in his car and didn't find anything—no drugs. So I'm assuming not. And he's physically active."

"Of course he's physically active. Do you know who this is?" Neil asked, as he prepared to give Grandpa Ben another shock.

"Someone I should know?"

"Ben Gault, one of the most noted photographers in the country."

She'd seen his photos in an exhibit in Chicago last year. Impressive. In fact, she'd bought a couple of copies and hung them in her condo. Admittedly, Ben Gault's subject matter was responsible for some of her discontent. All the hours she'd looked at the nature he'd captured through the lens had made her realize she wanted more than she'd had. It had been the start of something big in her life. Suddenly, it occurred to Gabby that she'd been looking at the Three Sisters from different angles all those months. No wonder she'd felt at home here so quickly. "*The* Ben Gault?"

"The one and only."

After the drugs were pushed in, Gabby took the portable oxygen little Benjamin had dragged over, and attached it to the bag and mask to ventilate him. But the mask wouldn't get a tight seal. Grandpa Ben's face had huge contours that wouldn't meld to the mask seal, so the only other option was to intubate. Which she couldn't do, because Grandpa Ben was on the ground, and whoever did the intubation would have to get flat on their belly. Heaven knew, she couldn't do that now. So she took over chest compressions as Neil placed the tube in their patient's lungs.

"I'm concerned that he hasn't shown any signs of rousing, even before he crashed," she whispered to Neil, as he wiggled into a good position, then pulled up Grandpa Ben's chin to start the procedure. "I have no idea how long he's been this way, which also has me concerned."

"But he didn't crash until just before I got here, did he?"

"Your timing was perfect. And I was getting scared, because there wasn't anything I could do."

Neil didn't respond as he slipped the straight-bladed laryngoscope into Grandpa Ben's mouth and had a look at his vocal cords. Neither did she talk as she continued pumping on the man's chest. Her back already ached, her arm muscles were cramping up, and even her shoulders were complaining.

"You OK?" Neil asked, once he slid the breathing tube into place.

"Are you?" she asked in return.

He glanced up briefly. "I don't want to talk about it, Gabrielle."

"I think we should. I want to tell you about Gavin."

"*You* want to tell me about my brother?" He snorted. "Well, guess what? What you know about him is nothing I want to hear." On purpose, Neil turned away from Gabby as he taped the tube into place, then he took over the chest compressions and gave Gabby the task of ventilation. No more words spoken between them.

Gabby knew better than to pursue it. This wasn't the time. Neil wasn't ready. Maybe he never would be.

An hour later, Ben Gault was alive and doing better, tucked into one of the hospital's few intensive care beds, and except for a few words concerning their patient, she and Neil had said nothing to each other. In fact, the air between them was downright cold. She'd expected that, but she'd hoped she was wrong, that Neil wouldn't have reacted the way he had. "It is what it is," she whispered to Bryce, as she went to check on little Benjamin.

"Can I see my grandpa?" he asked.

Gabby sat down on the waiting-room sofa next to him, and put her feet up. "He's sleeping right now, but maybe in a few minutes we can sneak in there together and have a look, if you promise not to wake him up."

"Is he going to be better when he wakes up?"

"We hope so, Benjamin. We're doing everything we can to help him."

"He promised to take me to Hawaii with him this summer."

"You travel a lot with your grandpa, don't you?"

"When my mom and dad let me go. Sometimes they don't, but mostly they do."

"And I'll bet you love it." She was thinking about Bryce and how he would miss out on having a grandfather like Ben Gault. Her dad would have been great, like Benjamin's grandpa was. Bryce wouldn't have a father either. No men in her son's life, which was something she couldn't help. But Bryce would miss out on so much. For a while, she'd hoped Neil might be that man in her son's life, but the likelihood of that happening was so slim she wouldn't allow herself to hold out any hope.

"It's fun. I like it when we go hiking together, and he lets me carry his camera. I have my own camera, too. Grandpa Ben bought it for me last Christmas."

"I'll bet you take good pictures, don't you?"

Benjamin nodded.

"What things do you like to take pictures of?"

"Animals. I like horses. And goats."

"You like goats?" Gabby laughed. "I don't think I've ever really seen a goat in person."

"You've got to watch them," Benjamin warned seriously. "They can be sneaky."

Like life, she thought as she settled in to wait with Benjamin. His parents were on their way to White Elk and she'd promised them she'd take care of him until then. Already she was loving it, and thinking about life with her own son. *Thank you, Gavin*, she said to herself, as she slumped down and made herself comfortable.

She was a natural with the boy. They'd been chatting for an hour and she had such a way with little Benjamin that he couldn't help but watch. She would be a good mother to his nephew. He had no worry about that.

No worry…he actually had a right to worry. Before, he'd been concerned as a friend, as someone who had been growing more than fond of Gabrielle. But now it was different. He was connected to her baby in a way he couldn't have expected. Sure, he'd had moments when he'd thought about being her baby's father, thought about being part of her little family. It had been a nice thought then. Now it was totally senseless. To be honest, he didn't know how to deal with it, even if he wanted to. He had growing feelings for a woman who was carrying his brother's baby, and there truly was no solution for that.

But she would be a good mother. "I think you two can go in to see Grandpa Ben," Neil said, finally stepping into the waiting room.

Gabby looked up at him, and nodded. But she didn't smile. Didn't speak. And as she took Benjamin's hand and walked right by him, his heart lurched.

What the hell was he going to do?

* * *

Five days into his recovery, Grandpa Ben, as Gabby was used to calling him now, transferred to a hospital in Denver for open-heart surgery. He was stable, doing quite nicely, and it was time to unclog his two blocked arteries. All the accident victims from that night were coming along at various rates of recovery, some in White Elk, some having been transferred to other facilities. No one had died, a few had required surgery, there were broken bones galore, a few internal injuries, contusions, cuts and scrapes, but what could have been a disaster had turned into a near-miracle on the mountain.

And Gabby was feeling better, too. She was rested, no aching muscles. Going along quite nicely for a woman in her advanced condition. Avoiding Neil as much as she could. Which was easy, because he was avoiding her, too.

"So, are you looking for anything in particular?" Janice Laughlin asked.

Handmade for Baby had become one of Gabby's favorite places in town, not just because of the wonderful baby items but because of Janice. They'd become friends. Had hot chocolate together every day. "What I haven't really bought so much are toys, and I was thinking a nice rattle or two."

"I have something you might like in my back room. Plus, hot chocolate."

Hot chocolate. Words meant to lure Gabby through the curtains to the back room. Following Janice, she'd no more than stepped through the teddy-bear-print curtains when several women started applauding.

"What?" Gabby gasped.

"You didn't think we'd let you have your baby without us giving you a baby shower, did you?" Laura asked. "I know you've been doing your best to buy everything in Janice's store, but we all love to do baby shopping, too."

She pointed to a table filled with pastel-colored packages, most of them wrapped in white and various shades of blue.

"Plus, we have an ulterior motive," Ellen Patrick said. She was one of Gabby's patients, three months along, third child. "We want to persuade you to stay, and we know Neil and Eric asked. It's nice having you here, Gabby. After Walt Graham's grumpy ways…well, if we have to bribe you, that's exactly what we'll do."

The ladies all laughed, and agreed.

"I never expected this," Gabby said. Still standing in the entryway, she was too stunned to move. "I mean, I've never…" Had friends. Not in the real sense. And these women felt like real friends to her. Fallon O'Gara, Rose Kelly, Jane McGinnis, Jackie Pennington from the hospital. Laura from the lodge. Janice and Debbi from the store. Angela. Helen, the waitress, and Catie from Catie's Overlook. Even Amarelle from the confectionary shop. And these were only a handful of the women gathered there. For her. They were there for her.

Tears welled in Gabby's eyes. "I don't know what to say."

"That you'll stay?" Angela said.

She wanted to. More than anything, she did want to stay. But how could she? "So, where's the hot chocolate?" she sniffled.

"You OK?" Laura whispered, a little while later, as everyone was busy helping themselves to cake.

"I didn't expect this. And I'm a little awkward. That's all it is."

"I think it's more than that. The cake is chocolate. Double chocolate, actually, with chocolate cream between the layers, and you haven't touched it."

She wanted to tell Laura what was happening in her life

now, because maybe Laura would have some wisdom. Maybe she'd say something that would make perfect sense, make things all better. But it was Neil she really needed to talk to. It was Neil's words she wanted to make perfect sense, make things all better. But now his words were only medical. A patient consult, a recommendation, a question. Which made Gabby feel so empty, so alone. She'd never expected to miss him the way she did, but she did. In passing, in a hall, when he'd acknowledge her with the same polite nod he did everybody else, that's when she missed him the most.

"Probably just some apprehensions over being a mother. I mean, it's getting close. The most experience I've had with babies is delivering them. Once I hand them over to their mothers, that's as far as I go. I'm on to the next baby. But I think I'm getting a little scared at the prospect of keeping this one. You know, wondering if I'm going to be a good mother, wondering if I'm suited to motherhood."

"You're suited, Gabby. Being scared is natural, having all the worries you're having happens to every expectant mother. But you're going to be great, and if we can convince you that White Elk is really where you need to be, you're going to have a fantastic network of support. Just look at all these ladies…they love you. They want to be there for you."

"You're going to make me cry again," Gabby said, welling right up.

"Want to know the cure for that?" Laura asked.

"What?"

"Chocolate cake. A great big piece."

Chocolate cake. If only life were that simple. But for a momentary fix it was perfect. And maybe that's what she needed for a while…momentary fixes, one after another. It was certainly better than trying to find a fix for the big picture.

CHAPTER SEVEN

"Do we need to cut your patient load?"

Gabby bristled at Neil's words. "My patient load is fine," she snapped. "I'm managing."

"And that's why you're holding your back, leaning to the side? Because you consider the back spasm you're having right now as managing?" He reached out to steady her as she leaned against the corridor wall, but she jerked away from him. "Gabrielle, I think you need to sit down." He was concerned. Couldn't help himself.

"I know what I need, Neil," she snapped, trying to rub the muscle plaguing her.

"Does this happen often?" His first inclination was to pick her up in his arms and carry her to a chair. But he knew exactly how she'd respond, and he wasn't in the mood to wrestle a pregnant lady into a chair, even if she needed to be there. "Can I do something for you?" A massage was probably out of the question, even though she looked like she needed one.

"You can let me leave. I'm through for the evening, and I'd like you to step aside so I can go back to my cabin."

"You're not walking, are you?" Because she wouldn't make it. In fact, right now, he wasn't sure she'd make it to the hospital's front door.

"Is that a professional question or a personal one? You're entitled to a professional answer, but not a personal one."

He bent in close to her, until his face was mere inches away from hers. "What I'm entitled to, Gabrielle, are the feelings I'm feeling. I haven't worked them out yet. And you'll have to admit this isn't a normal situation. But I am concerned about you, and about the baby. I was before I knew you were carrying Gavin's child, and that hasn't changed." He straightened up. "So I'm going to drive you home."

She looked up at him for a moment, and the fight in her eyes was so visible it was almost palpable. But suddenly she backed off. "I've missed you," she admitted.

"And I've missed you, too. I've really wished..."

"Wished what, Neil?"

"Wished things were different between us."

"Even if they were, that wouldn't necessarily make things right, would it?" Another muscle spasm hit and she gasped. "Look, Neil, I'm fine. I can call a cab."

"Or you can quit being so damned stubborn, and let me help you. I'm offering to drive you a few blocks, Gabrielle. That's all it is. A ride."

"But we'll fight," she said, the defiance draining from her eyes. "And I don't want to do that, Neil."

"Neither do I."

"Then we'll just ride in total silence, and I don't want to do that either. So it'll be best if I take a cab. But I appreciate the offer."

She started to move away from the wall, but another back spasm caught her. Only this time she didn't fall back to the wall for support. Neil grabbed her into his arms, then whispered, "You're coming with me."

Surprisingly, she agreed. Although he wasn't going to let

himself read anything into it. She needed help, and he was the one most convenient. That's all it was, all he'd allow himself to think of it. Doing a good deed. "It's not letting up?" he asked, as they made their way slowly to the front door. Every step of the way she leaned into him more and more.

Gabby shook her head. "It happens. Nothing to worry about, and I'll be fine in a few minutes." She slowed her pace as another spasm hit.

"Like hell you will," Neil said, whisking her off the floor and straight into his arms even though every fiber, strand and ounce of common sense in him was screaming *Put her down and get out of there*. But with a pregnant woman nestled in his arms who was at least as shocked as he was, it seemed he was committed to this.

"I appreciate a good chivalrous act every now and then, the way most women do," she said as she straightened herself in the passenger seat of his SUV a few minutes later. "But don't ever touch me again, Neil. Because I might have to hurt you if you do."

"With what?" He couldn't help the laugh that bubbled out of him and stayed with him all the way round to the driver's seat. Couldn't help that it didn't quit when he climbed inside and started the engine.

"What's so funny?" she snapped, trying to find a comfortable position.

"The look on your face. I think you did want to hurt me, didn't you?"

"Did it ever occur to you that I didn't need, or even want, your help, since I didn't ask for it?"

"OK, so you didn't ask, but could you walk?" he asked. "Right then, could you have taken a step without someone helping you?"

"Maybe not, but that's not the point."

"Point is, you and baby Bryce—*my nephew*—need to be off your feet while your muscles are working themselves out, and leaning against the hospital wall wasn't going to do it for you."

"And if you hadn't come in, I'd have been fine in a few minutes."

"But you're off your feet now, aren't you? So, are you feeling better?" She wouldn't admit that she was. He knew that, knew she was too stubborn to give in. He'd bet his life on it. But he liked the argument and, admittedly, had missed them since she hadn't been talking to him. Even though things weren't worked out between them, it was nice to have a little interaction with her again.

"What I'm feeling is… You know what? I don't know how I'm feeling. I don't even know what I'm supposed to feel. I'm happy, Neil. Happier than I've ever been in my life about having this baby. And I'm sorry I've hurt you. But there's nothing I can do about any of it. So that's why I don't know what to do, or how to feel."

For sure, Gabrielle was one big entanglement he shouldn't be having, but common sense seemed to go into hibernation every time she came near him. Because he was tangled up, probably in more ways than he knew.

"For what it's worth, I'm not angry with you."

"It's worth a lot," she said, practically in a whisper.

"Then I hope you can understand why I'm not…" He swallowed hard. "Not getting more involved. I can't do it, Gabrielle. I just can't do it." He wanted to, though. Problem was, he didn't know how. Didn't know if he would ever know how. And it was tearing him up.

"Neil, you're going the wrong way." This very short ride seemed interminably long. Of course she understood Neil's feelings. Understood why he couldn't get involved.

It hurt, because she wanted him there with her, but she knew why that wasn't meant to be. But could they work out another relationship? One where she could stay in White Elk? One where he could be an uncle to her son?

She hoped so, but she wasn't optimistic. Although she wasn't going to give up on it yet.

"No, I'm not."

"Then why is the street to the lodge where I'm staying two blocks back?"

"Because I'm taking you to my house. I have something that just might help you in your present state."

"My present pregnant state, or my present aching-back state?"

"A little bit of both. Something my mother bought for me months ago, and I haven't had time to use."

"Which would be…"

"One of those new state-of-the-art massaging chairs. It massages back, shoulders, arms, legs, neck. Gives off a nice warm heat at the same time."

A massaging chair? Oh, my, did that sound heavenly. Her back was already much better, but the idea of spending time being massaged in Neil's chair was almost too tempting. Back in Chicago, going to a day spa for a massage had been her one indulgence. Even before she'd fallen pregnant. She would have a nice, relaxing soak in a hot tub, then have Inga and her magic hands do the massage. Of course, the hot tub was out at this late stage in her pregnancy, and Inga was still back in Chicago. But if Neil's chair worked…

Still, as tempting as it sounded, it was Neil's chair, in Neil's house, which made it off limits to her. She wouldn't let herself indulge no matter how much she wanted to. That's all there was to it. "I don't need a massage. In fact, all I need is for you to turn around and take me back to my cabin. I didn't protest when you picked me up and carried me out of the hospital, didn't protest when you put me in your car. But I'm not going home with you, Neil, and I mean it."

"Too late," he said, stopping on an uphill incline in front of what was probably the largest house in White Elk. She'd seen it from a distance on her way to the hospital, and had even wondered who lived in the house on the hill. But she'd never suspected Neil.

The house looked like a Swiss chalet towering over its neighbors below and, honestly, the more she studied it, the more she wondered about it. Neil wasn't the least bit pretentious, and she hadn't expected this of him. In fact, if she'd been asked to guess, she'd have put him in a one-room studio apartment. He was a no-fuss, no-muss kind of a man. And this house…this mansion of his was all about fuss and muss. So, what was this about? "This is yours?" she asked, just to make sure.

He chuckled. "You expected what? A cave?" After opening the car door on her side, Neil allowed her to exit on her own. No scooping her up into his arms, no other grand gestures. He simply extended his hand to her to help her out.

"Maybe not a cave." Although she could much better picture him in a cave than this. "But I expected…modest."

"Modest. An expectation of someone who never met my ex-wife. She couldn't have modest. For Karen it was all or…" he gestured to the house "…even more than all. Then, after the divorce, I got stuck with it. And I'm still stuck with it because no one in White Elk wants to buy it. So I make the best of it, since I'm not here most of the time anyway."

He walked alongside her, ready to help if he needed to, but she was steady on her feet now, no more back spasms.

Which meant she really didn't need to be here. She was curious, though, and she wanted a peek inside now that she'd seen the outside. So she'd have her look around, then she'd ask him to take her home. Or call a cab. Good plan, she decided. Safe. "Well, I can certainly say it's impressive," she said as Neil punched the front-door code into the keypad.

"It's meant to be impressive. That's why my wife bought it."

"And you didn't stop her?"

"Sometimes when you're in love you overlook things. In our marriage, this house is one of the things I overlooked."

She wanted to ask what the other things were, like had he suspected his wife was having an affair with his brother? But she didn't. Right now, the mood between them was better, and she wanted to keep it that way. If they could stay cordial, the way they were now, that might work, might allow her to remain in White Elk. So, she put Neil's wife out of her head to the extent that she could as she entered Neil's wife's house.

Inside the foyer Gabby's first reaction was a gasp. Neil's chalet was palatial, decorated so elaborately and beautifully she simply stood there a while, turning in circles, taking it all in. Rococo mirrors, crystal chandeliers, Victorian furniture… So well appointed. A place to hold a magnificent Viennese ball if anyone in White Elk ever took the notion to hold one. Definitely not Neil in any way, shape or form, but impressive all the same. "Well, my compliments to your ex-wife. She did an amazing job, and I'm surprised she'd let you keep this house in the divorce settlement, since it was, essentially, her house."

"Her house, my money. And it wasn't a matter of keeping it. We tried getting rid of it, and no one wanted it. The divorce agreement stipulated that if, or when, it sells she'll get half the money, but because of the circumstances she's never pressed me on it. Don't think she will either."

Gabby blinked. Neil couldn't get away from it. What Gavin and Karen had done to him…it was everywhere. So much so, it was finally hitting her. Made her feel sad. Uncomfortable. Especially as Neil had it within him to sound so matter-of-fact about it. "But you still live here?"

"Not too often. I have an apartment near the hospital— three rooms, enough room to turn around if you hold your breath. Which is all I really need. And this place…it's only a building. No real memories because Karen and I never moved in. In fact, most of the upstairs isn't even complete."

Gabby's knees went weak, thinking about what all that meant. Karen had gone with Gavin before she and Neil had even moved into their new home. Then, by some cruel twist of fate, he lived in a flat with barely enough breathing room while this behemoth of a house stood on the tallest hill in town, mocking him.

"Back spasm again?" Neil said, as he rushed to her side and helped her down into an upholstered chair.

"Something like that," she mumbled. "Can I just go home?"

"I think you should give the chair a try first."

"It's been a long day, and I'm really tired." True, but she also wanted time to think. Alone.

"Five minutes. It if doesn't make you feel better in five minutes, I'll take you home."

This was the old Neil, the one she liked, the one she counted on. The one she wanted in ways she wasn't willing to admit to herself. It scared her being with him, and she should have insisted on leaving, but so much of her did want five minutes more because who knew when she'd ever get another five minutes with him? "Five minutes then I'm gone."

"Gabrielle, you look exhausted, and I'm worried about you. Right now, I'm the doctor. OK? And this doctor is prescribing some rest and relaxation before you do anything. *Anything*. So for once just cooperate."

She wanted to, but she and Neil both knew that would be a mistake. "There's nothing to worry about, Neil. I'm fine."

"You sure couldn't say that twenty minutes ago, could you?"

"Spasms are…spasms. In most cases they're nothing."

"Except an indication you're pushing yourself too much."

"So what are you going to do, fire me?"

"I probably should, but I still do believe that you're the best judge of whether or not you're able to work, and I'm not going to back away from that. At least, for now."

"Just show me the chair, OK? That's why you brought me here, so let's get it over with. It's supposed to rain tonight and I want to get back to my cabin before it starts."

"Well, now that you're being so cooperative…" he said facetiously.

He showed her to the den where his mother's miracle chair was sitting, showed her the controls and left her alone. The room was nearly dark, and that was just fine with her. With the mood she was in, she really didn't want any light shining on it.

Admittedly, the deep, warm massage from the chair, once it was adjusted to settings she liked, was wonderful. Maybe not as good as actual fingers…as Neil's fingers…but she found herself drifting off, in part because she was relaxing even when she didn't want to, and in part because the soothing hum was lulling her into another world. It was a peaceful world where she didn't have so many problems. "We may have to get a chair like this," she said to Bryce, as her eyelids drooped. Then she whispered, "Five minutes more," and a contented sigh escaped her lips.

"Gabrielle?"

He had such a nice voice. The nicest voice she'd ever heard.

"Gabrielle, wake up."

She didn't want to. Not yet.

"The chair recommends thirty minutes only, so I've turned it off."

But she didn't want to go. Didn't want to open her eyes.

"Gabrielle?"

She snuggled down more in the chair, and sighed contentedly. "Five more minutes," she murmured.

"Five more minutes," he said, putting a blanket over her. But this time he didn't leave the room.

This time he sat down in an easy chair in a dark corner on the far side of the room and simply watched her for the next hour, after which she finally did wake up for real.

"Neil?" she whispered in the dark.

"Over here," he said.

"How long was I asleep?

"About an hour and a half."

"And you watched me the whole time?" That did make her feel odd. Not angry. Maybe a little flattered.

"Not the whole time. Just for a little while. You talk to him in your sleep...to Bryce. I heard you murmur his name a couple of times. I'm not sure if I mentioned this before, but I like the way you talk to him."

"We're connected. He's part of me, and it would seem so odd not talking to him. To me he's always been another person. Besides, studies show that babies in the womb do hear…you know, recognize their mother's voice. It makes our connection even closer, I think."

"I think he's a lucky little boy, having you for his mother."

The natural thing here would have been to ask Neil if he wanted to be involved in Bryce's life. But she couldn't do that, for she feared his answer would bring a screeching halt to a very nice evening, and a very nice moment between them. She wasn't ready for that, wasn't in a hurry to get back to where they'd been before this evening had started. "You know, your mother has good taste in massage chairs. I think I'm going to have to buy one of these myself."

"And put it where, Gabrielle?"

His question caught her off guard. "What do you mean by that?"

"What I mean is, where will you put your chair? Here, in White Elk, or somewhere else?"

The former ache to her neck snapped right back as her muscles stiffened. "Where do you want me to put it, Neil?"

"To be honest, I don't know. I've been sitting here thinking about that. Wondering if we could continue a relationship, given the circumstances. Wondering if it would work out if you stayed."

The same things she'd been wondering for days, but hearing him say it hurt. Maybe somewhere, deep down, she'd hoped he would ask her to stay here. It didn't even have to come with a commitment to be friends or anything else. Just hearing that he wanted her here would have been nice, and now that he'd finally voiced his skepticism, she realized she wasn't prepared to hear it. Wasn't prepared to deal with it.

"I need to leave," she said stiffly, as she pushed herself out of the chair. "I hear the rain and I want to get back to my cabin before it starts to pour."

"You're welcome to use the guest room. There's no reason for you to go outside and get soaked."

"Sure there is. I don't want to stay here." She didn't want to sound angry, didn't want to sound hurt, but she could hear all of it slipping into her voice. And she could feel the untempered emotions slipping down, trying to suffocate her. It was time to get out of there, time to get away from Neil.

Time to figure out what she was going to do. No more putting it off.

"Before you leave, how about something to eat? I'll go fix you something, as I'm assuming that you haven't eaten yet."

"What is it with you?" she snapped. "One minute you're telling me you don't want me here in White Elk, and the next you're trying to feed me."

"That's not right, Gabrielle. I never said I didn't want you here in White Elk."

"But you never said you did."

"Because I was trying to be honest. I don't know what I want."

"Did it ever occur to you, Neil, that the decision has nothing to do with you? You know I could stay here, open up my own obstetrics practice independent of your hospital. And I think I have a solid enough base already to have a chance at a good practice, because a lot of people do want me to stay. They're asking. Did you know that? There are people here in White Elk who want me here." Harsh words, and she hadn't meant to say them because, ultimately, she wouldn't hurt Neil. She cared for him too much to do that. But right now she wanted some support from him, and all he was giving her was…honesty.

Honesty. Dear heaven, what was she doing, faulting Neil for being honest, when that's what she'd wanted from him all along? Maybe she was saying these things because she was hurt that what he said in honesty wasn't the honesty she'd wanted to hear from him.

"Neil, look. I…I wanted to tell you that…"

He shook his head, held up a hand to stop her. "There's nothing to say right now that's going to make it any better. I'm sorry it is what it is, Gabrielle, but I'm as entitled to my feelings as you are yours."

"I want you to be involved in my son's life, Neil. I've known that for a while. Maybe even before I knew you were his uncle."

"And that's the big chasm, isn't it? What you want, and what I don't know if I can do."

"I'll call a cab, Neil," she said, heading out of the den. She wasn't sure if she wanted him coming after her, wasn't sure that he would. But by the time she'd made it to the front door, alone, she was sure that Neil had made his choice. A choice by which she would abide. So she called a cab, then waited outside for it under the portico so she wouldn't get wet. But after mere moments, Neil joined her, put a raincoat over her shoulders, put his arm around her shoulders. Held her close. And didn't speak until the cab pulled up.

"Give me some time, Gabrielle," he said as he helped her in. "This isn't about you, or Bryce. It's about me, and I have to figure out how I'm going to work through it."

"I'll give you whatever you need, Neil," she said, then pulled the door shut. As the cab pulled away, she turned to see if he was watching her, and he was. He was standing in the driveway, in the rain, watching. And it made her heart lurch. Caused a lump to form in her throat.

Her dad had always said that the big moments in life made indelible impressions, even when you didn't know that what you were experiencing was a big moment. He said those moments, though, would stay perfectly in the mind and in the heart so they could be replayed for an eternity. This was one of those moments. She was sure of it. Because this was the moment she knew, for sure, what she'd been trying to deny.

It had been two days since she'd talked to Neil, since she'd seen him, except in passing. Two miserable days full of rain and gloom. On top of that, she was drastically cutting back her work because it was time to do that. "Does it always rain like this during the spring?" she asked Eric. He'd just finished an emergency appendectomy, and now he was sitting in the emergency room lounge, feet propped up on the admitting desk, involved in a serious relationship with a can of soft drink. Two, actually. The one he was drinking and the one he would drink when he'd finished the first one.

"This is unusual. Normally we get the spring runoff from the melting snow, but the rain is pretty uncommon."

She plopped down on one of the emergency beds, raised the head, and was perfectly happy to stay that way the rest of the day, if she could get away with it. Finally, she was pregnant-tired. Her patients talked of it, she knew it existed, but now it was her reality. She was ready to have this baby, ready to get her body back to normal. "Why two cans of drink?" she asked him.

"I don't allow soft drinks at home. Try to keep things more healthy for the twins, so when I'm here I—"

"Sneak the drinks," she said, laughing.

"What's good for the dad isn't necessarily good for the twins."

"They're amazing little girls, Eric. I've spent a little time with them when I'm visiting Janice."

"Thank you. I'm a little biased, but I think they're pretty amazing, considering the life they lead. Dad away all the time, being shifted from Laura to Debbi, and a few other ladies in town when the need arises."

"But it's about the quality of time, not the quantity. And the quality shows on the girls." The way she hoped it would show on Bryce.

"Well, it wasn't what I planned, being a single father. It's not easy, but it works out."

"I hope so," she whispered. "I really hope so."

"You OK, Gabby?" he asked.

"Tired. Grumpy. All the usual end-of-pregnancy complaints. Nothing serious, though."

"Neil's the one who's grumpy around here. Compared to him you're a sweetheart."

"Well, I appreciate the compliment, but I'm trying hard to stay on my good behavior right now."

Eric chuckled. "Have you figured out whether or not you want to stay? I know there's a lot of sentiment to keep you here."

"Thanks to your sister. I think Janice's leading the campaign. But since you have another obstetrician coming in shortly…"

"Plans change, Gabby. We only have a temp coming in, no firm commitments yet from anyone who wants to stay. So if you want the position…"

"How does Neil feel about that? I mean, does *he* want me to stay?"

Eric shrugged. "He's not objecting."

That was a surprise, actually. It was also a little bit

hopeful, but she wasn't going to read anything into Eric's interpretation of Neil not objecting, because that might not be the case at all. Maybe he wasn't objecting outright because he wasn't yet ready to tell Eric the reason he didn't want her here in White Elk. "Well, I'm thinking about it. But I haven't decided anything for sure yet."

"But you haven't decided against us, have you?"

"No," she said. "I haven't." In truth, the decision would be Neil's. But it wasn't her place to say that to Eric. A deep sigh of discontent escaped her, and she shut her eyes for a moment.

"Maybe I should have a look at you, Gabby. I know that Neil had Walt come in a few days ago to check you, but since you're getting so close to your due date..." Before she answered, he stood, and grabbed a blood-pressure off the table next to the exam table.

Automatically, she extended her arm while he wrapped the cuff around it. "The first eight months went so fast, but the last few weeks..."

He chuckled. "Just like the twins and Christmas. They're fine for fifty weeks of the year, but those last two weeks... Hell for them, worse for me. You'll find out."

Her blood pressure was normal. So was everything else. "Any contractions yet?" he asked, as he put away the blood-pressure cuff.

"A few. False labor. Nothing serious." Which was very common. Many women lived with occasional contractions for weeks, sometimes even months before they delivered.

"And you're sure you're up to seeing patients? Because we can spread out your duty between all of us."

"As it is, everybody's already taken over my routine patient load. I'm only following a few patients on a regular basis right now, and I'm fine with that."

"Neil and I can take over."

"And I'll ask you when I need that. But I want to continue working. Right now, it's only a few hours a week, but it makes me feel…useful. And to be honest, I don't know what I'd do with myself if I didn't have anything at all to do. I'm not exactly the type who can be idle."

"That's what Neil keeps telling me."

"He does?"

"Honestly, I've wanted to put you on leave, but Neil keeps saying you should be the judge of when you do that."

It was such a simple thing, having Neil stand up for her. But it warmed her heart. "I won't put the baby at risk," she said, as Eric started to hook up the fetal monitor. But he was interrupted by a phone call, one where he didn't say a word. When he clicked off, the frown on his face told Gabby that the news wasn't good.

"An emergency coming in?" she asked.

"Not exactly. At least, not right away. But the levee up at the mouth of the valley isn't holding well. They've got engineers up there right now, who are saying that the compromise could endanger the whole area because the breach, coupled with all the rain, and the snow runoff, puts them in imminent danger of flooding. I think we're about to have to evacuate, Gabby."

"The hospital?"

Eric shook his head. "Probably not. It's built high. But White Elk would be in the way of a flood if that's what happens. And the engineers are pretty sure that's what's going to happen. So, I've got to get home, make sure the twins are safe with my sister. Then I'll come right back and start mobilizing a medical team to stand by. I'll call Neil and let him know, but if I don't get through…"

"I'll tell him," she said, sitting up. "You just go."

She didn't have to tell him again. Eric turned and ran

out of the emergency department like a man possessed. He was. He was a man going to protect his children, and she knew exactly how that felt because nothing, but nothing, would stop her from protecting Bryce.

"You need to get out of here, Gabrielle," he said, his voice calm. But calm wasn't what he was feeling, not with Gabrielle still here. She needed to be safer. He had to make sure she was taken care of.

"But we're short-staffed, with Eric gone."

"And you're not approved for emergency duty any longer."

"Do you *really* think I'm going to do something to put my baby in jeopardy? I wouldn't do that, Neil. But you do need another doctor here for a little while."

Another doctor, yes. Gabrielle, no. The need to protect her from the flood was becoming so urgent it surprised him. Right now, getting Gabrielle to safety was all that mattered. "Just leave here," Neil ordered. He fished through his pocket for a set of keys, then held them out to her. "Go to my house. I won't be there because I do have to stay here, but it's the highest spot in White Elk." With his responsibilities, that was all he could do.

"I'll be fine at my cabin."

"See, that's just it. You might be fine at your cabin, but you'd be better off at my house, and you're just too damned stubborn to listen to me. So let me put it to you in a way you'll listen—my house will be safer *for Bryce* than your cabin. And depending on how bad the flooding gets, you might be holed up there several days. So you tell me, Gabrielle. How well protected, and accommodated, do you want your baby to be?"

"That's not fair," she snapped, grabbing the keys from his hand. "You know I'd be perfectly fine at the cabin."

"But you'd be even better at my house. More amenities, if nothing else. And Lester's going to drive you. I'll call him, and by the time you get to the parking lot he'll be there waiting for you."

She started to walk away, angry. But ten steps later she had a change of heart. Neil was only trying to take care of her. He'd thought of her safety before anything else, and here she was resisting him. She didn't want to. But she was so afraid of giving in, because if she kept doing that—and giving in to Neil was the easiest thing to do—eventually it would rip her heart in two. Putting up the barriers the way she did didn't get her any closer to him, but it didn't drive her any further away either. And that's all she was allowing herself to hope for right now, not to be driven any further away. So she spun around and drew in a deep breath. "Thank you," she said. Simple words. But they brought a smile to Neil's face. A beautiful smile that would sustain her.

"You take care of yourself, Gabrielle. I'll call you when I can."

"Please, do that."

Ed Lester chose that moment to run down the hall and motion for Gabby to follow him. Another lingering moment with Neil would have been nice, but that was also the moment Neil disappeared into the emergency department.

But she had his smile imprinted in her heart as she followed Ed into the rain. For now, it was everything.

CHAPTER EIGHT

TWENTY-TWO hours cooped up now, and for most of those hours she'd stared out the window, watching the rain come down steadily, paced the halls of Neil's house, fighting the boredom, then stared out the window some more. She wasn't going completely crazy yet, but she was so restless she was ready to jump out of her skin. Being alone in Neil's huge tomb of a house was making her feel safer, but it was also reminding her just how alone she was, isolated up on the hill away from the flowing waters in the road down below. It was a lovely house to look at, and to explore the first six or seven times she'd explored it, but the emptiness around her was almost palpable. No wonder Neil didn't spend much time here. His home, every immense nook and cranny of it, had all the warmth of an institution. And she was so lonely here she wanted to cry.

She wanted Neil.

But she was glad to be there in spite of her glum mood. Glad, and even encouraged that Neil had thought of her safety above everything else. And, sure, she'd much rather have been working at the hospital alongside him, but that was all behind her for a little while. It was time to take care of herself, and get ready for the inevitable. Just thinking in those terms made her boredom easier to bear because when she thought about Bryce, everything fell into its proper place. He was going to be here soon and her *only* plans now were to deliver a healthy baby and see what life had in store for the two of them. Or the three of them, if Neil wanted to be included.

"We'll make all the decisions in due course," she told Bryce. "Whether we'll be staying here for good or going back to Chicago and regrouping. But it's going to work for us, no matter what we do. Whatever it turns out to be, it will be good. I promise you."

Reports coming in on the radio said that some of the villages farther down the valley were being fully evacuated now, and while White Elk wasn't at the same high-level risk, the flood of rushing water in the street was a concern to her. It made her feel even more trapped because now, even if she wanted to, she couldn't get out. She didn't have a car there. "It would have been nice having Neil here with us," she said to Bryce. He'd have been good company, and on a purely medical note she'd have felt safer. All the same, the last time she'd talked to him he'd said the hospital was going crazy. People with nowhere to go were stopping by. Minor injuries were starting to trickle in, too. There were people everywhere, simply loitering.

"It's good that he calls," she told Bryce. "And we like his voice, don't we? It makes us feel safer." Made her feel better too because it was soothing. Now that her real contractions were coming, she craved that comfort. She hadn't mentioned her labor pains to him yet, because she wasn't particularly concerned that four or five an hour were going to lead to anything any time soon. They were a beginning, though. Her new life reminding her that it was just about ready to start. Of course, she was still a few weeks away from her due date, and had no reason to believe Bryce's arrival was at hand. Women often had sporadic labor pains in the last couple of months, so she hadn't triggered the alarm that she was about to give birth all alone in the house on the hill, because nothing indicated that was going to happen.

"You're just reminding me that I'm not alone," she told Bryce, as another pain hit her while she was on her way to the front window to stare out yet again. This time she saw someone coming up the drive, in a truck that was well able to navigate the eighteen-inch flood waters down below.

The truck came to a stop at the top of the hill and the driver got out—someone dressed in a bright yellow rain slicker. A woman, Gabby guessed from the person's small size as the figure ran to the passenger's side and opened the door.

The passenger was Angela! Was she in labor? Was her baby picking the worst possible time to make a grand entrance? As she pulled open the door with one hand, she placed her other hand on her belly. "Don't you go getting any ideas, you hear?"

The woman in yellow stood back as Angela ran into the house. "Neil told me you were here all alone," she said, shaking out of her wet raincoat. "He thought that since we were at a higher elevation than this place, we'd be able to get here better."

"Why?" Gabby asked, taking Angela's raincoat and waiting for Angela's friend to shed her slicker.

"Because he didn't want you to be alone. When he finally got through to the resort, he said he'd been trying to call here for hours. But the phone lines are cutting in and out all over the place. Anyway, Neil said that you were here all by yourself and asked if there was any way I could get to you. I told him I was on my way, and that my sister would come with me."

"And he didn't tell me?" Gabby said.

"He tried calling you. We tried calling you. The wires are crossed or something, because it sounded like some kind of party line with several people talking. Oh, and I'm Dinah Corday, by the way. Brand-new to town, and not impressed with your weather."

"I'm not impressed with it either," Gabby commented, picking up the house phone and trying to dial out. No dial tone, though. So she tried her cell phone, and it started to ring, but cut out almost immediately. "So it's just the three of us, stranded here without communication?"

"My phone's working, off and on," Dinah said.

Dinah didn't at all resemble her sister, Gabby noted as the three women fixed hot tea and settled into Neil's den, which Gabby had decided early on was the only truly comfy room in the house. It was decorated for a man and she imagined Neil having it done for himself.

Sipping tea, wishing there was some hot chocolate in the house, she studied the sisters. Where Angela was small, Dinah was tall, statuesque. Angela's brown hair was cropped short, while Dinah's auburn locks waved halfway down her back. Their eyes were the same, though, and that's where Gabby saw the resemblance. Dark brown, feisty. "Well, it's a big house and you're welcome to anything in it," she said, then laughed, "even though nothing here is mine. So, aren't they going to need you to cook up at the ski resort?"

"My whole kitchen staff is in, running all over each other," Angela replied. "I put my sous chef in charge and, to be honest, I was glad to get out of there. People from all over the area are trooping into the lodge, trying to get away from the floods, and it's a madhouse. Too many people." Relaxing, Angela put her feet up on the sofa and settled back into the pillows. Within a minute, she was sleeping like a baby.

"How's she doing?" Dinah whispered.

"All things considered, good. I know she's had a lot to deal with lately, but she's managing."

"I'm glad you let her go back to work. Even the little bit she's doing means everything to her."

"Like I keep saying, pregnancy's not an illness, and it shouldn't be treated like one."

"Well, I'm glad she found you. I think if Dr Ranard hadn't asked her to come and stay with you, she would have anyway. She really wants you to deliver her baby, and she's been worried that with the flood…"

Gabby flinched under a contraction, trying not to be obvious about it, but Dinah caught on right away.

"When are you due, Gabby?" she asked.

"Not for a while."

"So are your contractions Braxton Hicks', or did I just see the real thing?"

"Sometimes it's hard to tell the difference."

"Unless you're an obstetrician." She took hold of Gabby's wrist to take a pulse. "Your pulse is a little fast."

"Just tired. That's all."

"Tired, and in labor?" Instinctively, Dinah positioned Gabby's legs on the sofa, then propped a pillow behind her head. Next came the quilt. "And have your waters broken yet?"

Gabby shook her head. "I've still got almost three weeks. And I've been having false labor for a little while."

"And unless I'm mistaken, I'm counting your false labor at one contraction every six minutes. Could you be a little off on your due date?"

Not even by a minute. She knew the exact moment of her conception because that had been her first time with a man in…well, forever. As well as her last time. "Due date is right on."

"So you're just going to deliver a little early."

All of a sudden, a sharp pain nearly split Gabby's belly in two. *This wasn't a false alarm.* And those pains she'd been having right along were the warning. Suddenly, she was excited. And frightened. And she wanted her dad. But most of all she wanted Neil.

Desperately.

"It's time," she finally confessed. "I've been hoping I was wrong. But you get to a certain point where you can no longer deny the obvious, and the obvious for me is that I'm going to have a baby, probably before the flood waters recede."

"Well, your timing's not very good, is it?" Dinah said, pulling out her cell phone. She searched for a signal in the den, couldn't find it, so she went to the lobby, which had a higher ceiling, and dialed the number Angela had given her for Dr Ranard.

The reception was crackly, but he did answer.

"You're the doctor?" she practically shouted.

Neil had no idea who was on the other end. The number meant nothing to him, and he could barely hear the voice. "Yes," he answered.

"Gabby...labor..."

"What?"

"She's in labor."

"Gabrielle's in labor?"

The answer sounded like yes, but he couldn't tell for sure. And as he tried asking a second time, the line went dead. "Damn," he muttered, running into exam four to Eric. "She's gone into labor, as best I can tell."

"Gabby? Did she call?"

"No, I think it might have been her friend, Angela. She's up there with Gabrielle now."

"Then I think you'd better get going," Eric said. "Take

the back road. It's at a higher elevation, shouldn't be a problem if you use my truck." He tossed the keys over to Neil.

"You going to be OK here?" Neil asked, already shrugging out of his white coat.

"Just go," Eric said impatiently. "For once, something besides this damned hospital should come first."

Ten minutes later, on the road, he could barely think straight, he was so crazy with worry. Eric's truck, a large, sturdy four-wheel drive, would get him through the muddiest of back roads without too much problem. *He hoped.* On his way out, he'd stocked it with every medical supply he could grab in two minutes, then left the mayhem of the hospital to the rest of the staff. Angela's sister was a nurse, Angela had told him earlier. But he wasn't going to have her go through this without him.

Of course, Eric had already guessed Neil's feelings for Gabrielle. Nothing had ever been said about it, but Eric had accused him of wearing his heart on his sleeve these past weeks, and that was probably the case. Even when he was avoiding her, or when she was avoiding him, he couldn't avert the glances he fought too hard to tame, couldn't deflect the longing stares he tried to deny himself, and failed so miserably to do.

He'd wanted to convince himself he didn't have feelings, wanted to convince himself that he didn't want her. But he did. There were no more denials here. Not even about the fact that she was about to deliver Gavin's baby.

That thought caused Neil's grip on the steering wheel to tighten as the truck wheels spun in a wash coming down off the side of the mountains, flowing straight across the road. Damn, he hated going so slowly. But doing something stupid, like speeding up, would get him stranded up here while Gabrielle was less than a mile away, having her baby. *Without him.* So he had to be steady, had to keep his head.

Dear God, you'd think it was his baby she was delivering, the way he was feeling. The way he was acting.

Admittedly, he was jealous. The perfect scenario would have Gabrielle pregnant with his child. He'd thought about it that way, tried blocking it out as that would never happen. But he'd also thought about a future where he and Gabrielle and Bryce were a family in the ways that mattered.

Except he'd been such an idiot lately. A great big idiot, blaming Gabrielle for something that wasn't her fault. It didn't matter right now, though. Nothing did, except getting through.

Suddenly, his cell phone rang, and he looked at the number. Eric. Damn. He'd been trying Gabrielle but not getting through. He'd hope this was her... "Yeah," he said, answering his phone.

"You can get down Canyon Circle," Eric yelled to Neil over the bad connection.

"What?"

"The Canyon Circle. I heard...open...may be passable."

"Is it going to hold?" It was at risk to wash out, and the last thing he needed was to get stranded up there. But if it held, it would be a shortcut. It might give him as much as fifteen minutes.

"What?"

"Eric! Is it going to hold?"

"Not sure...possibly." The connection cut out.

Sighing, Neil turned down a road that looked more like a wide trail, cursing the mud, cursing the weather, cursing the road. It was passable, but barely. It would take him straight to Canyon Circle, though, unless it washed out down the way. Which, unfortunately, it did. But before he got that far he made another turn onto the old national park trail, and spun himself straight into a ravine of mud, bringing an abrupt end to his trip by truck. Nothing that he could do out there, by himself, was going to get the back tire out of its rut.

"Damn," he muttered, gathering up as many supplies as he could carry. "Why the hell couldn't this be easier?"

The only answer came in the clap of thunder overhead as he started his way down the trail on foot, alternately slipping, then sliding where the trail washed out, most of the time managing to stay upright. Once his foot slid out from under him and he went straight down, still hanging on to his medical bag. Another time the bag flew out of his hands as he went down, and landed in a thicket of budding branches nearby. Luckily for him, it stayed latched, so once he'd pulled himself from the mud yet again, he grabbed his bag and continued his downward trek, slowing up a little for fear that if he injured himself, or ruined his medical kit, he might not be able to give Gabrielle the help she needed.

That's all this was about—helping Gabrielle. So for the next several minutes he grumbled about his slow pace as he sloshed through the many rivulets and washouts, but he kept it slow all the same until he reached the rear of his house. Pausing briefly on his patio, he phoned Eric to let him know that the back road wasn't good enough to get through without a lot of walking, and that he'd find his truck up there on the high ground at the trail head, stuck for the duration of the bad weather. Then he braced himself for what he had to do and headed straight through the back door. "Gabrielle," he called, as his rubber boots squeaked on the floor tiles, dripping mud in a trail behind him.

"She's in the front room," Dinah said, taking the medical kit from his hands and handing him a bath towel.

"You must be the nurse."

"Dinah Corday. Used to be a nurse, now I'm about to be a professional chef."

Nice smile, Neil thought, heading through the hall. She seemed competent, whether nurse or chef.

Entering the formal living room, he stepped inside the doorway and simply stared at Gabrielle. She looked… calm. Much more than he was, actually. And she was happy. "I expected something else," he said, as Dinah rushed around him and wrapped the blood-pressure cuff around Gabby's arm.

"What?" she asked.

"Maybe a little screaming. With what I had to drive through to get here, screaming would have been good because that's what I've been doing for the past twenty minutes."

Gabby laughed. "I don't think I'm a screamer, but how about a good frown?" With that, she scrunched up her face, held the pose for a second, then started laughing again. "I'm fine, Neil. Really. And you're the one who looks like he could scream." She pointed to the little pile of mud that had dripped off him. "Or could stand a good shower."

He glanced down at the mud puddle, a brown blotch standing out against the red hues of his ex-wife's favorite antique oriental rug. How appropriate that he ruin it in service to a woman he'd finally let himself love. "You just can't keep yourself out of trouble, can you? I mean, I sent you up here to keep you away from all the medical action, and now you're the center of the medical action. What don't you understand about keeping out of trouble?"

"Blood pressure's fine," Dinah said, next taking a listen to Gabrielle's belly, an oddly intimate procedure he wished he were doing.

"I'm glad to see you, Neil. I really wanted you here…"

"Did you?" he asked, looking straight into her eyes. "Did you really, Gabrielle? After the way things have been between us these past weeks…" He glanced at Dinah, who was obviously trying to make herself inconspicuous in this clumsy moment, then glanced back at Gabby. "I wasn't sure what you wanted."

"We need to have a talk, Neil. There are some things I should tell you, and…"

Another contraction gripped her, the hardest one yet. Immediately, he took her hand in his muddy one, and held it for several seconds as she nearly squeezed the blood out of it. "You've got a lot of strength for a pregnant lady," he said, shaking back the circulation once her contraction had subsided. "But I've still got a few more fingers for you to break if you need to, so we're good."

"I'm really happy you're here," she said, relaxing back on her pillows. "Even if Walt Graham had managed to drift in on his canoe, I'd have chosen you. And right now you've got about five minutes before I have another contraction, so maybe you'd better go take a fast shower, because yours are the only fingers I want to break."

"Are you sure about that, Gabrielle?" Their eyes met briefly, and he saw the answer there, the answer he wanted from her. But she glanced away so quickly, so awkwardly, it gave him cause to doubt again. It was her feelings for him he doubted, though, not his for her.

"What I'm sure of, Neil, is that you can't be part of this without a shower first, and I do want you to be part of it. So, go. Get yourself cleaned up, and come back ready to meet my son, because he's ready to pop out to meet his uncle."

As much as she wanted him here, it broke her heart just looking at his face…his beautiful, muddy face. She so desperately wished that Bryce was his son. That had been the fondest wish of her heart for a while now, one that she was only now able to admit. But what was done was done. In all honesty, she wouldn't change it, because one thing different in the whole sequence of events could have meant she wouldn't have Bryce.

It was a bad situation, and such a pervasively painful one she wasn't sure the hurt could ever fully heal. That was the sadness she saw in his eyes every time she looked. Yet Bryce was on his way now, and all the feelings, all the answers would have to come later.

"It's Gavin's baby?" Angela whispered, as she entered the room.

Gabby nodded. "Before I ever knew Neil, Gavin and I…" Another contraction grabbed her, much faster than it should have, and this time Angela surrendered her hand. But Gabby refused it, clutching at a pillow instead. "Go tell Neil it's happening…now."

"Just one more push, Gabrielle. That's all I need. One more push and you're a mother!"

She was exhausted. This was harder than she'd ever imagined it would be, and with no pain relief…

"Bear down, Gabrielle, and push."

Neil sounded so calm, so assured. And she was anything but assured right now. All her medical training down the drain, she was any other woman in the throes of delivering a baby, and that's all that mattered. "I'm pushing," she forced out, as Dinah propped her up to a near sitting position and held her there while Angela busied herself wiping a cool rag over Gabby's face.

"Breathe," Dinah said. "Come on, Gabby. Take a deep breath, then push that baby out."

"He's waiting for you, Gabrielle," Neil prompted. "Bryce Evans is waiting for you."

Bryce Evans… The men in her life passed before her eyes…her father, her son, Neil, even Gavin…as she bore down for one final time. Then, suddenly, it was over. Bryce was here. She was exhausted, happy… "Let me see him," she said to the deathly quiet room. "My baby…"

Dinah eased her back into a flat position, then hurried to the end of the bed—Neil's big king-sized bed—and Angela immediately stepped away. Went to the other side of the room, slumped down into a chair. Which was when the cold chill hit Gabby, spreading its icy tentacles through her veins, bringing to bear a terror like she'd never known could exist.

"He isn't crying," Gabby gasped, fighting to sit back up. Thrashing wildy, she was trying to toss off the sheets covering her. "Neil, he isn't crying! What's wrong?"

Even after Gabby rolled onto her side to see, she couldn't. Neil had taken Bryce to the other side of the room, to a dresser, and Dinah was with him, purposely obstructing Gabby's view. "What's wrong with my baby?" Gabby screamed, fighting to get up, even though she was too weak.

Dinah rushed back to the bed and gently pushed Gabby back down. "Look, Gabby. Neil's working on your baby right now. He's not breathing too well…"

"Did he aspirate?" Gabby choked.

"I'm not sure," Dinah said. But from the look on her face, Gabby knew better. It was the look she saw on her staff when a baby was born with a serious problem. Or a stillbirth.

"Is he alive?" she screamed, her voice so broken it didn't sound natural. "Neil, you've got to tell me, is he alive?" Neil's back was to her. She could see him working, bent over the dresser and working. But from the bed she couldn't tell what he was doing. "I've got to get to my baby," she said, suddenly launching herself up. But Dinah stopped her again.

"Gabby, let him do what he has to do."

"There wasn't a problem," she cried. "Never was a problem, and I've had so many tests, just to be sure." She rose up, watched. "Is that CPR? Is Neil giving him CPR?"

"Look, Gabby, I've got to go try and make a phone call. Do you hear me? I've got to leave the room for a minute, but I need for you to stay where you are, and be calm. Will you do that for me?"

A million things were running through her mind, none of them good, none of them that would allow her to be calm. "I want to hold him," she whispered. "Please, I want to hold him."

"Gabby, you've got to leave Neil alone now." That was Angela. She was huddled in her chair, looking scared to death. "He knows what he's doing, and you have to trust him. So, please…"

Gabby nodded. But she didn't lie back. Couldn't take her eyes off Neil's back. Couldn't *not* watch him fighting to save her son's life.

"I'll be back in a minute," Dinah reassured, then ran from the room.

"Fight for him, Neil. You've got to fight for him."

He didn't answer, but she knew he was. Neil could do no less.

"Is he responding?" she finally asked, then watched Neil's body language for an answer. But saw none there.

"He's alive, isn't he? Neil, please say something. Anything!"

"He's alive, Gabrielle. But cyanotic. And he's struggling."

She nodded. At least now she knew. "Breathing at all?"

"Some, but not sufficiently."

"Any guesses?"

This time he didn't answer. Rather, he looked up as Dinah ran back into the room. She was soaking wet. "I finally got through to a woman named Fallon O'Gara, a nurse practitioner. Had to go halfway down to the road to get a signal, but she said to stay here, that she's sending someone named Eric in with oxygen and an IV set-up. It's too bad out there to attempt any kind of transport before we've stabilized Bryce."

"Damn," Neil muttered. "Three lousy miles to the hospital, and I can't get there."

Dinah laid a reassuring hand on his arm. "Your medic will get here," she said. "Fallon told me he does mountain rescue, so I'm betting he'll be here sooner than you think."

He nodded gravely. Didn't speak. And that wasn't missed by Gabrielle, who'd finally managed to sit up and swing her legs over the side of the bed. One way or another she was going to get to her son. He needed her. She knew it. Could feel it deep down. So she pushed herself up, wobbled, and fell back. By the time she hit the bed, Dinah was at her side, ready to push her all the way in.

"You've got to stay strong for him," she said as she pulled the blanket up over Gabby, who immediately kicked it away.

The blanket meant she was permanently in bed, down for the count. Not having it on her meant she could get up, could get to her baby when she had to. "I have to see him," she said, this time her voice not quite so adamant. It was all beginning to sink in. Bryce was in trouble. Truly, honestly in trouble. But she trusted Neil to save him. "Please, before you take him away, I have to—"

"We won't take him anywhere before you see him, Gabrielle," Neil said. His voice was so tense it sounded as if it would snap in two. "Or hold him. I promise. But you've got to promise me that you'll be still."

She hated that promise, hated what was happening, hated more than anything that she was so helpless. So it was a hard promise to make. But she did, only because it was Neil who asked her.

For the next few minutes Neil worked on Bryce, and Gabby stayed in bed, watching everything and seeing nothing. But then, after the longest time of her life, she heard…a baby's cry. It wasn't strong. In fact, it was the cry she so often heard from a very sick baby. But it was Bryce, and he was alive, and crying the most beautiful cry she'd ever heard in her life.

"Do you want to hold him?" Neil asked, finally turning around. In his arms he held a bundle wrapped in a brown-and-blue Argyle sweater.

"Yes," she cried, pushing herself up in bed to receive her son.

"Just for a minute. He's still not doing very well." Neil walked slowly toward the bed, never for a second taking his eyes off Bryce. Then he bent, and handed him over to Gabby. "Bryce, this is your mother, and she's awfully worried about you."

Tears of joy, and fear, streaked down Gabby's cheeks as she took her son into her arms. He was a good size, and so beautiful. But he was struggling. His tiny chest was fighting so hard to take in breath, and when she put her fingertip to the pulse in his neck, she could feel his heart beat far faster than it should. And his lips…his precious little lips were blue-tinged from a lack of oxygen. So was his skin. He *was* breathing, though, and his heart *was* beating. Where there was life, there was so much hope, and for the next few minutes, as she cradled Bryce to her chest and told him stories about his grandfather, she hoped. Dear God, she hoped.

* * *

Neil looked down at his hands. They were shaking. So far, it was a miracle that Gabrielle's baby—his nephew—was still alive. Considering that he had no equipment, no oxygen, no IV…it was the power of love and sheer determination. That's all it could be. "He's doing a little better," he said, thirty minutes into the ordeal. "Pulse rate has come down a little, and he's breathing better." Not good enough, but enough to offer some hope.

"I know," Gabby whispered. "He's a real fighter."

He might be a fighter, but if Eric didn't come soon, Neil wasn't sure how much longer the fight would hold out. "Just like his mother," he whispered. He was sitting in bed with Gabrielle, his arm around her shoulders to support her, his eyes never once off Bryce, lest a change occurred that Gabrielle might miss. He was a beautiful boy. And he looked like Gavin in some ways. But he also favored Gabrielle. Bryce would have her smile, he guessed. He hoped.

"Neil!"

It was Eric. Eric, a former pediatric surgeon. Eric, the one who would make the real diagnosis and figure out what to do. Neil suspected the problem was something to do with the heart. The symptoms were all there, and with the proper diagnostic tools he was fairly certain he would discover transposition of the great vessels, where the two main arteries leaving the heart were reversed.

Normally, blood from the heart's right ventricle was carried by the pulmonary artery to the lungs, and blood from the left ventricle was taken by the aorta to the body. In the case of TGV, it was just the opposite, leaving the oxygenated blood meant to circulate through the body being pumped back into the lungs.

This wasn't something Neil could treat because he wasn't a surgeon. But Eric was. And for once Neil was grateful that their practice had such a pediatric influence. "Up here. My room."

Eric flew through the door, headed straight to the bed, and stopped short when he encountered Dinah Corday there. "You!" he snapped.

"You!" she snapped back.

"You two have met?" Neil asked.

"No, we haven't," Dinah snapped as she yanked the oxygen mask from Eric's hand.

"It was a slight tap," Eric said defensively.

"And you didn't stop to see if you'd damaged my car, or injured me," Dinah argued back as she slipped the pediatric-size oxygen mask over Bryce's face and turned on the emergency tank Eric had brought.

"I was in a hurry…emergency." Eric popped the stethoscope earpieces into his ears, then held up his hand to shush everybody. A moment later he looked up at Neil. "I think you could be right."

"Right?" Gabby choked out. "About what?"

"Neil thinks it might be TGV," Eric explained, "and at this point I have no reason to disagree because the symptoms fit. Things may turn out differently once we get the baby—"

"Bryce. Bryce Thierry Evans," Gabby interrupted.

"Thierry?" Eric questioned, looking downright shocked.

"Gavin was the father," Neil explained, not sounding as awkward as he could have.

Eric nodded, but didn't comment. "OK. Once we get *Bryce* to the hospital." He looked at Dinah. "You'll drive." Then he looked at Neil, a silent agreement passing between them. In the next instant he was gone, with Dinah soon to follow.

"What was that about?" Gabby asked, sliding to the edge of the bed.

"It's critical, Gabrielle. He'll do what he can to sta-bilize Bryce, and if it's TGV he'll probably do the balloon septostomy here in White Elk." Enlarging a small opening between the atria that is normally present at birth in order to let more oxygenated blood reach the body. "But we're going to have to send him down to the hospital in Salt Lake, where they can do more tests, as well as the follow-up surgery to reconnect the arteries normally."

"And you think it's TGV, Neil?"

"I'm afraid I do, Gabrielle. And I'm so sorry."

"Then I've got to go," she whispered. "Because when Eric does the septostomy, Bryce might not..." She stopped, unable to say the word.

"He's a good surgeon. Trust me on that. Eric will do everything humanly possible to take care of Bryce."

"I do trust you, Neil. And I trust Eric. But somehow you've got to get me there. Bryce can't go through this alone."

"I'll get you there," he promised.

Gabby glanced at Angela. "Come with me," she said. "I don't want you here alone."

Angela went on ahead, gathering blankets and rain gear, as Neil helped Gabby dress and get ready for the trip. "What if Bryce doesn't make it?" she choked as he pulled a sweater over her arms."

"He will, Gabrielle. Like I said, Eric is the best. If I had a baby who needed surgery, he'd be the only one I'd let do it."

"But sometimes the best isn't good enough."

"And sometimes it is." He pulled her into his arms and kissed her lightly on her forehead. "This time you have to trust that it is."

CHAPTER NINE

HUDDLED in the truck seat, squeezed between Angela and Neil, and wrapped so tightly in a cashmere blanket that her head was the only thing visible, Gabby didn't want to think about anything. It was too painful, too frightening. All these months connected to her son, and now she couldn't feel that connection any more. She couldn't feel anything. It was all gone, and it almost seemed like it had never been there at all. It was like those months had suddenly turned into a haze where everything was fast fading from her memory.

"Are you warm enough?" Neil asked her.

"Fine," she lied. Because nothing anyone could do would take the chill away. It was the cold, harsh iciness of fear that couldn't be quelled with a blanket, or ten blankets, or even a blast of heat from the truck's heater.

"And you, Angela. How are you doing?"

"I'm fine," she said, her voice on the edge of a quiver.

"Are you comfortable, Gabrielle?" he asked.

"Fine," she lied again. In truth, she was miserable, but not in the physical sense. It was as if her body didn't matter in all this. She'd given birth a little over an hour ago but the emotional pain had far outdistanced the physical pain of it. "Should you call Eric again?"

"We talked to him just a minute ago. They haven't reached the hospital yet."

"But I need to know about Bryce. I need to hear Eric tell me that Bryce is still..." She bit down hard on her bottom lip to keep herself from crying, as Angela reached to take her hand. Gabby knew that Bryce needed her to be strong for him, and that's what she had to do, no matter how hard that was right now. There would be plenty of time for the emotions later on. "I just need to know."

Neil hit speed dial, then handed the phone to Gabby. "How is he?" she whispered, fighting against the tremble in her voice as Eric answered.

"Fighting, Gabby. He's a strong little boy, and he's fighting like hell."

"Can I talk to him, Eric? He needs to hear my voice."

Neil glanced over at Gabby, and smiled, while she waited for Eric to give her the go-ahead. She found a brave smile to return to him. "It's not silly," she said. "He knows my voice."

"I know it's not silly. In fact, I'm pretty sure he's waiting to hear from you."

A look of hope flashed across her face. "Do you think so? Do you really think so?"

"The bond hasn't broken because he's not in your arms right now, Gabrielle. So, yes, I really think so."

"Neil, I'm so glad you're here. I don't think I could go through this without you." She squeezed Angela's hand. "You, too. And don't you worry. Things are going to go better with you when your time comes. And we'll deliver your little...baby in the hospital."

"You know what it is?" Angela asked.

Gabby nodded. "Do you want to?"

"Not yet."

Gabby actually laughed. "Well, in case you're curious,

I have a pair of baby bootees for you in my bag. When you want to know, find them. See what the color is."

"You shouldn't be worrying about me right now, Gabby," she said.

"Of course I should." She squeezed Angela's hand again, then leaned her head against Neil's shoulder. Fatigue was setting in. "Just, please, don't go into labor early the way I did, because I'm really not up to a delivery today."

"But she's so stubborn she'd have had a go at it anyway," Neil said, the affection in his voice so clear that even Angela heard it. Neil was brushing his thumb across Gabby's cheek when Eric finally told her the phone was in place and that she could say a few words to Bryce.

Gabby took a deep breath, straightened in the seat, then let her breath back out, slowly bracing herself for the most important words she'd ever spoken in her life. It was time to step up and be the support her baby needed, just the way Neil had stepped up to be the support she needed. She looked at Neil for a moment to find the calm reassurance she always found in him. Then she spoke. "Bryce, I know this isn't the way we had things planned, but you've got to trust me. The very best doctors in the whole world are taking care of you now, and very soon you'll be feeling much better. Mommy's on her way, Bryce. I promise, Mommy will be there when you need me." She swiped at a stray tear running down her cheek, angry at herself for not being in better control. And for being so frightened. She was a doctor, after all. She'd delivered babies with the very same problem and seen the successes. Yet none of that did any good when it concerned her child. Her miracle baby. "I love you, Bryce. I love you so much, and I'll be there in a little while. We're going to get through this together. You've got to believe me, Bryce. We're going to get through this together. Be strong for Mommy."

Gabby clicked off the phone, then scooted back down in the seat, and cocooned herself even tighter in the blanket, more emotionally exhausted than before. "I always let my patients know the risks associated with pregnancy, and I try to prepare them in case something like this happens. But I never, *ever* prepared myself, and I refused to let myself think about it because this may be my one and only chance to have a baby. I suppose I wanted it so badly I blocked out common sense."

"It's normal, Gabrielle. Nobody wants to focus on the negatives. Pregnancy can be such a happy time, with so much to look forward to, so not thinking in terms of the things that could go wrong is the easiest thing to do. And, in my opinion, the best. I mean, suppose you'd spent every day worrying? Suppose you went over the checklist of everything that could go wrong rather than looking forward to all the things that could go right, the way you did? All that stress could have made things…"

"Worse?" she snapped. "Do you really believe things could have turned out worse?"

Angela took hold of her hand again, but didn't say a word.

"Yes," he said, his voice grave. "They could have, and deep down you know that. Bryce is alive, which gives him a chance. And with so many people fighting for him—" Before he could finish, the cell phone jingled, and she automatically clicked on. It was Eric telling her they'd arrived at the hospital, safe and sound, that they were en route to the surgery. "We're going to do some preliminary tests first, get some X-rays, type and cross-match him for a transfusion if we need one. If I have your consent."

"Of course you do. Anything at all…just do it." As Eric was signing off, Neil swerved to avoid a crater in the road, then swerved again to miss a rock that had slid down the hill. The rain had all but stopped, but the water was still on the rise. Not fast, but steady. Making the road slick with mud, and littered with so many blind obstructions that Neil's knuckles were white from gripping the steering wheel so hard.

Gabby saw this, saw the strain on his face as they slowed to ford a rivulet crossing over the road. It was deep, up to the bottom of the truck door—Angela's truck. It was a four-wheel drive, high-rider, thank God for small miracles. Otherwise they wouldn't have gotten though, and she wouldn't be able to kiss Bryce before he went into surgery.

And she had to kiss him. In fact, that was the only thing on her mind, the only thing she focused on until they reached the hospital.

Then finally, after the longest ride of her life, they were there. And it was a sight she'd never expected. Dozens of people were standing in water halfway up to their knees, filling sandbags, while dozens of other people placed the bags around the foundations of the hospital to hold back the rising waters. Yellow rain slickers everywhere, rain boots, umbrellas of every color and size… Those who weren't involved in bagging sand were taking hot coffee to the ones who were, and a temporary aid station had been set up on a makeshift wooden platform so people could get up out of the water for a while.

As Neil came to a stop, it was like all the workers gathered there came to a stop too, and turned to look at them as he helped Angela from the truck first, and gestured to an attendant with a wheelchair for her, then went back to help Gabby, literally scooping her up into his arms and carrying her inside. No protests. Once in the door, another one of the volunteers rushed forward with a wheelchair, but Neil refused it, still holding Gabby close, still running.

They were only part way through the lobby when her cell phone rang, and as she answered it she saw Eric running toward the front of the building to greet them, cell phone to his ear. Rather than talking into it, though, he simply stuffed it into his pockets and shouted, "Gabby, what blood type are you?"

She had to think for a moment. She knew, but it had escaped her.

But Eric didn't miss a beat. Before she could answer, he shouted, "Because Bryce has a rare blood type, and I want to have a unit of blood ready before we take him into surgery."

"Rare?" she asked.

"AB negative."

Meaning well less than one percent of the population had this blood type. And she did not. So that was Gavin's type.

Neil stopped abruptly. "That was the one thing Gavin and I had in common. I have type AB negative, too." He dropped Gabby into the wheelchair after all, and followed Eric back into the emergency department. Running.

"I'm not a medical person," Janice Laughlin said, stepping up behind Gabby and taking hold of the wheelchair handles, "but I guess that answers a lot of questions. Eric said he's never seen Neil as grumpy as he's been lately, and I'm guessing that's the reason."

"That's the reason," Gabby said, feeling scared, and dejected, and so many other things she couldn't even identify.

"I'm pretty sure he loves you."

"Maybe he does, but will it matter?"

"Time will tell, Gabby. Time will tell. But in the meantime, let's go down to the waiting area while my brother does the surgery. Laura's come in to sit with you, too, by the way."

Good friends, Gabby thought. Very good friends, and she didn't want to lose them. But right now everything she loved, everything she cared for was slipping away from her and she didn't know how to hang on.

As the surgery prep took place, Gabby stayed secluded in a private cubicle in the surgery department. Janice and Laura stayed with her. So did Angela, who was resting in a bed that had been brought in for her. Janice's daughter, Debbi, was valiantly minding all the children—Eric's twins as well as Laura's three—so the women could stay by Gabby's side. She loved them for that, but she wished Neil was there, being the support her friends were.

Neil never came in, though, and Gabby was sure the strain of it all was getting to him. She couldn't blame him for staying away from her, especially now that the secret was out. But she did so want his company. More than wanting him with her, though, she desperately hoped he was with Bryce. In her heart, she thought he was. Even though he'd been put through the emotional wringer by all this, she truly didn't believe that he'd walk away. The man she…loved simply wouldn't do that.

Oddly enough, it was Dinah who'd agreed to go into surgery with Eric. But not before she took Gabby to a bed in a private room and allowed her a few moments alone with her son. "You're a beautiful, strong little boy, Bryce," she whispered, fighting back the tears threatening to spill. "You're going to get through this just fine, then we'll start our life together and forget all this happened." But could she forget the parts that involved Neil? Because, she was afraid she might have to.

For the next few minutes Gabby sang lullabies, and hugged and kissed her baby. Then, all too soon, Dinah came to take him. "I'm sorry, Gabby, but it's time."

She didn't want to let him go, so she clung a little harder.

"Gabby?"

Gabby nodded. "I know," she whispered, giving her baby one last kiss. "I love you, Bryce," Gabby whispered, then handed him over to Dinah.

When Bryce was gone, and Gabby was alone, she dropped her head back into the pillow and finally let the tears flow. "I really made a mess of things," she told Laura, who came in immediately.

"I heard."

"Everybody has, haven't they?" And by now Neil had to feel so humiliated…she just couldn't bear the thought of it.

"Nobody's judging you, Gabby. We know that Neil and Gavin had problems, but you must have known Gavin in a way that no one here did, and maybe, in time, that will be a good thing for Neil. For all of us, because we'd like to have better memories of him."

"If Neil ever speaks to me again once we get through this crisis."

"He will. But he may need some space for a while, so he can figure it out."

"I just don't know…"

"Do you love him?" Laura asked. She was fussing over Gabby, which Gabby didn't want but didn't have the strength to refuse.

"If I did, would it be enough for him?"

"Sometimes love is all there is. Be patient with yourself, and with Neil."

Gabby took the drink of water Laura poured for her, then slumped back against the pillows again. "But what if he never speaks to me again?"

"If he wants a relationship with his nephew, he will."

"That's the thing, isn't it? *If* he wants…"

"He's not heartless, Gabby. Hurt, maybe. But give him some time and distance, and he'll eventually do the right thing."

Of course he would. She knew that with all her heart. Neil was a kind, decent man. But even kind, decent men met their breaking point, and she'd practically slapped him in the face with his. "I just want this to be over, so I can have Bryce sent up to Salt Lake for the other surgery. Nothing else really matters."

"Would you come back?"

"Honestly, I don't know any more."

"Do you really think you can leave here and never look back?" Laura asked. "Because you have a life here. Friends, people who care. And that's not so easy to walk away from."

"No, it's not. And I do want the two of us to settle here. It's a wonderful little town, and I love the people. It's a perfect place to raise a child, and I've been happy, even though I haven't been here long. But…"

"Then stay here, Gabby. Settle down. Face your problems with some help from your friends. Raise your son."

"How can I do that?"

"You know what? Now's not the time to make any decisions. In fact, no decisions at all until you're thinking better. OK? So, since we're not talking about that now, do you want to hear the latest town gossip about how Eric hit Angela's sister's car and just drove off? And she chased him all the way to the hospital. I heard that the sparks are flying between those two, and not in a sexual way, if you know what I mean."

Small towns. She dearly loved this one, even with its gossip. If only there was a way she and Bryce could stay here.

* * *

Neil, standing concealed in a private cubicle across the hall from Gabby, watched her. She wasn't sleeping, even though her eyes were closed. She would never sleep while Bryce was in surgery. And if she were in any condition, she would have wanted to be in that surgery, inches away from her son, watching over him.

Which was what he had to do now. He'd been there through the preliminary tests, been there when they'd prepped Bryce for surgery. But he'd been torn, because he'd wanted to be with Gabrielle, too. Bryce needed him more, though, and there was no choice. "I'm going to gown up," he said quietly from the entry to her cubicle.

"Have you been with him?" She didn't yet open her eyes.

"Yes," he said simply. "I've been with him through everything so far."

The tears sliding down her cheeks broke his heart.

"I was hoping you were with him. You're the only one…" She finally raised her head to look at Neil, swiping at her tears as she did. "You and I, we're all he has. So I trust you to watch over my baby, Neil."

"I know you do, Gabrielle. I know you do." No more words were said, because it was time. He wanted to go to her, pull her into his arms and hold her until the pain went away. But the pain wasn't going to leave her until her baby was well. And his fear for that little boy…it was an agony like none he'd ever known.

"Neil?" Eric glanced up as Neil took his place next to the operating table.

As many times as he'd been in this very same position over the years—gowned and standing by to observe—this time seemed so daunting, almost foreign to him. Like he'd never really witnessed a surgery before. But, then, he'd never witnessed one in which he'd been so person-ally involved. "Just observing my…my nephew," he said. Bryce was so tiny, so helpless, lying there, as Eric cut into his chest. All these huge medical machines to sustain him and one small baby to sustain…it seemed so overwhelm-ing. "How's he doing?"

"Good, so far. I think we got lucky…well, as lucky as we can get with a sick baby who has a heart defect. But it's a *simple* TGV, the best-case scenario with this, and I think after he has his next surgery his prognosis will be very promising for a bright and healthy future."

Neil was more relieved to hear that than he'd expected to be. A simple deviation always had a much better outcome than a complex one, and Bryce would get to live a normal life and do all the things all little boys did. "Gabrielle will be relieved to hear that," he said, trying to sound unaffected. But the truth was, he was already seeing Bryce a few years into the future, playing soccer, or baseball. Playing it with… Neil blanked the scene out of his head. It was too cozy, and he wanted to be involved in the boy's life. Wanted to be the one playing soccer or baseball with him. But he'd been making such a mess of things with Gabrielle, even after she'd done everything hu-manly possible to make things right for him, to make things better. So, in the end, would she have him? Or would she decide it wasn't worth the effort after all?

"Neil, I had no idea the baby was your nephew," Eric commented.

Fallon, who was assisting in the surgery, looked up at Neil, but said nothing. Dinah, who'd agreed to be the other assisting nurse, however, did comment. "You have the same eyes," she said.

Henry Gunther, the anesthesiologist, who'd literally been brought in by boat due to the flooding, glanced at

Neil over the top of his glasses for a moment, then glanced down at the baby, nodding. "Yep, same eyes," he agreed. "You going to marry Dr Evans? I heard that you two…"

"Is there anybody who hasn't heard?" Neil snapped.

"Probably not," Eric said as he tied off a small vessel and extended his hand to Dinah for a clamp. Dinah handed it to him. For just a fraction of a second Eric took his eyes off his surgical field and glanced across the table at her. Her eyes caught that glance, and held it almost defiantly until he returned his full attention to his patient.

"Small towns, Neil," he continued. "You know how it is. So, how's Gabrielle doing? It's been a rough day on her, physically and emotionally, and I'm sure she's feeling the effects right now."

"She's strong." He tried to sound disengaged, but as he looked at the bag of blood flowing into Bryce's vein— blood from his own vein—he knew he wasn't disengaged in any way, and could never be. In fact, he was more engaged here than he'd ever been in his entire life. To Bryce, to Gabrielle… "And I'm pretty damned stupid."

Dinah glanced up, first at Eric, then at Neil. "Angela told me you love Gabby, but you're not doing a very good job of it. But you're allowed to be a little stupid for a while, because people in love usually do something stupid along the way, don't they? I mean, who in this room hasn't been stupid in love?"

"Great. Even the out-of-towners know," Neil huffed out. "And here I was, living under the delusion that there were still a few people who hadn't yet gotten themselves caught up in the story of how Neil fell in love with the woman who had his brother's baby?"

Everyone in the operating theater chuckled. "No one ever claimed life in White Elk was dull," Fallon commented as she pulled the suture tray over, meaning the surgery was nearing its end.

Neil took a step closer to the operating table, and saw that Bryce had pinked up quite nicely. In part, that was due to him being ventilated by Henry Gunther, and in part because the blood was flowing better to Bryce's entire body now. It was something Gabrielle should have seen, had she been physically able. Something he would describe for her. "So, everybody knows how I feel about Gabrielle?" he asked, suddenly embarrassed that Gabrielle's friends had recognized his feelings for her even before he'd admitted it to himself, let alone to her.

"Everybody," everyone in the theater said in unison.

"So much for privacy," he snapped.

"Privacy?" Eric exclaimed. "You had all the privacy you needed when you lived in California. And you hated it. Remember? In fact, you were the one who convinced me that the charm of a small town like White Elk was just what I needed."

Neil ignored Eric's comment about small towns because Eric was right. "Have you made any arrangements to get Bryce out to Salt Lake City?"

"Rose Kelly is working on it. Last I heard, there's no place for miles for the helicopter to set down, so we'll have to be creative."

"But Bryce will be fine here for a while?" Now he was sounding like a worried parent because, as a doctor, he knew the answer to that question. Bryce would be fine here for quite a while. Right now, though, he couldn't reach down deep enough to find the doctor in him, when his feelings for that baby were all over the place.

Eric glanced over at Neil. "You should go be with Gabrielle now. She needs you. And you need her."

One last look at Bryce, and Neil walked out of the operating room. He dumped his surgical gown, mask and hat into the hamper outside the door, and turned to leave the area, but Gabby was standing in the doorway. More like leaning against it. Pale. Weak. Tired. And fighting with everything she had in her to be there.

"How is he?" she asked.

The worry on her face was plain. "You shouldn't be here, Gabrielle. You're not strong enough yet."

"Where else could I be?"

"Back in bed. Resting."

"But I wanted to find out. All I've been getting are the vague reports they call out from surgery. You know, 'It's going as well as can be expected.' 'Your baby is stable.'" She slumped a little harder against the door frame and Neil immediately sprang forward to support her, to wrap his arms around her and hold her up. "How is he, Neil? You were in there, you saw him. So, how is my son?"

"He's pink."

"Pink?"

"You know, pink, the way a baby should be."

"Pink," she said, leaning her head into his chest and sniffling. "My baby is pink."

"It's a simple TGV, Gabrielle. Eric said he's in good shape and his prognosis is promising."

She nodded, but didn't speak.

"And they're getting ready to close, so you should be able to see him in a little while."

"I'm glad you were with him, Neil. Somehow, I'm sure he knew that. I was in there," she whispered, then sighed in relief. "I *was* in there. Through you."

Touched, and choking back his own tears, Neil cleared his throat. "Look, you need to get back in bed. Eric will come and let you know when you can see Bryce."

"Where are you going?" she asked.

"Other patients. I have…other patients to see." That was a lie. But right now he just couldn't deal with this. There were too many emotions, too many memories. And he couldn't sort them out and, at the same time, be around Gabrielle, because Gabrielle clouded his judgment to the point where she was the only thing he could feel. The only thing he could see. Right now, he had to have objectivity and clear thinking. Because he loved her, and loved that little boy.

But would it be enough to get him past his feelings about Gavin?

Neil signaled to one of the nurses at the other end of the hall. "Please see to it that Dr Evans gets back to her room." Then he turned and walked away. Never looked back. Wouldn't look back, because if he did, he couldn't walk away. And right now, walking away was the only thing he could do.

"Are you sure you're up to this?" Eric asked Gabby.

"It's only a helicopter ride. I'll be fine." The surgery had ended twenty-four hours ago, and she'd spent almost every hour since then either holding Bryce or sitting next to his crib, counting fingers and toes, singing lullabies, kissing his chubby pink cheeks, just watching him and falling more and more in love.

Outside, the flood waters were receding, but not significantly. Activity had died down at the hospital, though. People weren't flowing in with the current as they had only a day ago because they were back home now, trying to make sense of the damages and salvage whatever they could. Walt Graham had finally wandered in, complained that he'd made a wasted trip as Gabby had already delivered. One by one, every friend she'd made in White Elk had come in to see her, and with the flooding still going on outside, for some of them it hadn't been an easy trip in. But she'd had a steady parade of visitors who made her feel so loved, and so much a part of something wonderful.

If home was where the heart was, in just a few short weeks she'd found home. But there was another heart to consider—one that wasn't hers, or Bryce's. That was the heart she would not break no matter what happened. All the hours with Bryce, all those hours holding him and being thankful for everything she had…that's when she'd made her decision. If Neil wanted her, she would stay. If he didn't, she would leave and allow him to have his life here without the constant reminder of his brother. It would be a sacrifice, but not too great a sacrifice if it made Neil whole again.

Besides, even though home was where the heart was, her heart was with Bryce and wherever they were together, that would be her home.

She only hoped, and prayed, that Neil would be part of that.

Gabby hadn't seen Neil, though. Neither had she heard from him. It hurt, but she was dealing with it the best way she could.

"Well, Fallon's going along to look after both you and Bryce," Eric said. "And I'll be in touch as soon as you land. The hospital is on alert, and Dr James Galbraith will be standing by to assume Bryce's care. So, you're good to go."

"Dr Galbraith is good?"

"I'd trust my twins to him."

Knowing that made her feel better. She was anxious for this trip, anxious to have Bryce in the hospital where he would have his next surgery, anxious for his recovery so they could start a normal life together. Still, she'd wanted…no, she'd hoped…Neil would stop by, wish her luck, check on Bryce. Anything. That simply wasn't to be the case, though. So she hugged Eric, climbed into the back of the ambulance and took a seat next to Fallon, then prepared herself for the trip up to the top of the middle Sister, where her medical transport awaited.

An hour later, she climbed out of the ambulance that had picked them up in Salt Lake City, and stepped back as a flurry of medical activity swooped in over Bryce. He was whisked straight away to the NICU—neonatal intensive care unit—not because he was in critical condition but as a precaution, while Gabby was left behind to tend to the admittance chores like paperwork, consents and insurance.

"Father?" the admitting clerk asked, when she saw that section of the form had been left blank.

"No father," Gabby said. Then changed her mind. "Dr Gavin Thierry, deceased." He was Bryce's father and deserved that title, even posthumously.

"I'm sorry," the clerk said.

"So am I," Neil said, stepping up behind Gabby.

She spun to face him. "I didn't know you'd be here."

"Neither did I. Yesterday, when I left the hospital, I just drove. It took me hours to get out of the valley, taking all the high roads, and once I was finally out, I wasn't sure where I was going. So I came here. Took a room across the street at the hotel, and…waited."

"For Bryce."

"For you, Gabrielle. I wanted to see you."

"Your son's checked into the NICU now," the clerk interrupted. "You can go on up."

Gabby nodded her thanks to the woman, and started to head for the elevator. But halfway there she stopped, and turned back to Neil. "Are you coming?"

"Do you want me?"

"He's your nephew, Neil. He has your blood running through his veins. You have a right to be here." He had a right, but she desperately wanted him to have the need to be here, and right now she didn't know if that was the case, or if he'd come out of some kind of misplaced loyalty or obligation. "And I won't keep you out of his life, if you want to be in it."

He didn't speak as he stepped onto the elevator with her, or as he rode up to the fourth floor. And when the door opened, he stepped out without saying a word. But when Gabby gowned up and headed for the NICU, Neil said, "Tell him I'm here, and that I love him."

"Do you?" Gabby asked, not to be contentious but more because she wanted to know the answer.

"None of this has been easy, Gabrielle. Not for either of us. But whatever's happened, it has nothing to do with Bryce. He's an amazing little boy who's fighting his way through a tough situation, and he's going to need all the love he can get for a while."

"Only for a while? Because if that's your condition, then maybe you shouldn't be here. Because my son…Gavin's son…needs and deserves more than only your conditional love. He needs it strong, and he needs it forever. And if you can't give it to him that way, go back to your hotel, or back to White Elk. Or go anyplace you want to go so long as it's not here."

Gabby spun away and went though the NICU doors. Her hands were shaking. She wanted to cry. And scream. And kick the wall. Most of all, she wanted to go back outside and tell Neil that she loved him and she wanted him in her life…in Bryce's life. But on her terms, which were forever. When she looked back through the doors, though, he was gone. Beyond that, she couldn't think because she was rushed into the

NICU for her first ten-minute visit, top of the hour, every hour thereafter.

Bryce looked so helpless, lying there in the crib, hooked to oxygen, hooked to an IV. She needed to hold him, needed to feel the intimate bond she'd had with him before his birth, but that had been breached and she couldn't. In this impersonal room full of machines and other worried parents, there was no place to whisper the things to him she'd whispered over the months, or to sing him the lullabies. But she touched him—laid her fingers on his tiny chest and felt him breath for those ten minutes. It wasn't nearly enough, but she was grateful. Because when she looked at her son lying there, sound asleep and oblivious to all the things causing her so much pain, she saw a miracle. Seven months ago, when she'd learned she was pregnant, she'd known it was a miracle. And now that Bryce was here, and on his way to being healthy, she was filled with overwhelming gratitude to the man Neil hated. So maybe that situation couldn't be rectified. As much as she wanted it to be, she just didn't know. "What will be, will be," she whispered to Bryce, as she kissed him on the forehead just as her visit was up. "But no matter what, Mommy loves you and that will never change."

CHAPTER TEN

"I THOUGHT you might like some hot chocolate." Neil handed over a plastic cup, and sat down next to Gabrielle, who was stretched out in bed, staring at the wall. The hospital had checked her into a private room, more as a guest than a patient, partly as a medical privilege, partly because of her condition.

"I didn't know you were still here." She took the cup, clutching it like it was her life blood. She'd been so cold since she'd come here, so cold since she'd had to walk away from Bryce and leave him all alone in Intensive Care, and the warmth felt good on her fingers.

"I couldn't leave, Gabrielle. Right now, I'm as mixed-up as you are about how this will work out, but the one thing that I knew for sure was that I couldn't walk away from you and Bryce."

"I don't want you to leave, Neil." Gabby sucked in a sharp breath, held it for a moment, then let it out. "If that's what you think you have to do, I won't stop you. I'll honor your wishes, whatever they are. But just so you'll know, my wish is that you'd be part of our family. Bryce and me. You and me. *Especially* you and me."

Neil laughed. "You never mince words, Gabrielle. That was one of the first things that attracted me to you. When

I was married to Karen, I never knew where I stood. With you, I always do."

"Life's too short to play games, and I think I'm only just now coming to understand what that really means." It was a bit of her father's wisdom she'd taken to heart a long, long time ago. "My dad always said that when the opportunity arises, grab it and hold on for dear life, because you might never get that opportunity again."

"He was a wise man. I wish I could have met him."

"I wish you could have, too. You would have liked him. And I think he would have liked you."

"Maybe I'll get to know him through his grandson."

"Is that what you really want, Neil? Because while he's Bryce Evans's grandson, he's also Gavin Thierry's son, and that's never going to change."

"Tell me about my brother, Gabrielle. You know things about him I need to know."

Yes, he did need to know. Finally. She took a deep breath to brace herself. "We met at a medical seminar in Chicago, about nine months ago, as it turns out. It was also just a few weeks after I'd buried my father, and I was so…alone. My dad was, quite literally, the only person I had in the world. No other relatives, except a few distant cousins. We were very close, probably closer than most fathers and daughters because he was the one who raised me. So, pretty much, it was just the two of us. Anyway, I wasn't back to work yet, was pretty sure I didn't want to return to that particular practice when I was ready to work again, and I needed something to keep me occupied until I figured out what I wanted…I was pretty lost. So I went to a pediatrics seminar and figured that since I deliver babies, it might do me some good to learn some advances in pediatrics."

"And that's where you met Gavin."

Gabby nodded. "He was a lecturer. Brilliant, so passionate in his love of pediatrics. I think I fell a little in love
with him when I heard him speak, because I'd never heard
anyone with such excitement about his work. He lectured
on operating a small-town pediatric practice, talked about
how important pediatric specialties were to the more rural
or isolated areas, and outlined ways to get better service
to those areas. Maybe the most important thing he did was
tell those of us who came to his lecture to consider small-
town practice when we were weighing our options, and not
to write it off too quickly. He was brilliant, Neil. People
approached him afterwards and told him that he'd given
them something to think about."

"Really?"

Gabby nodded. "He was respected. Well researched,
well-spoken. All that, and he was nice to me when I desperately needed someone to be nice. He…he distracted me
from the things I didn't want to think about yet. One thing
led to another. So at a time when I was lower than I'd ever
been in my life, Gavin and I connected. I might have been
a little in love, or maybe a better way to put that is infatu-
ated. But it wasn't permanent. Wasn't meant to be
anything more than it was, and we knew that after a little
while. But for a couple of days we were two people who
were both going through some lows, trying to pick each
other up."

"He was going through some lows?"

Gabby nodded. "He didn't say anything about it, but
you could see it in his eyes." Eyes that were so much like
Neil's. And she'd seen that same distance in his eyes, too.

She shifted in bed, settled back more into her pillows,
raised the head a little. And shut her eyes, trying to picture
Gavin. Funny thing was, all she saw was Neil. They really
didn't look so much alike, except the eyes. Bryce's eyes.

"It didn't turn into a real relationship, Neil. We were careful, even though no one would have ever believed I could have a child, but apparently Bryce was meant to be. I wanted Gavin to be part of his son's life, if he wanted to. I was going to give him that opportunity."

"As possessive as you are about Bryce, didn't that scare you?"

"It did. I mean, he could have wanted full custody, or partial custody. He might have wanted to have influence in ways I wouldn't approve of. There were a lot of risks, letting him know."

"So why, ultimately, did you decide to do it when he probably would have never found out?"

"Because it was the right thing to do. Bryce had a right to his father, and his father had a right to Bryce." Overhead, the hospital light seemed especially harsh shining in her face, and she reached up to shut it off. Then she twisted to have a better look at Neil. "Everything was going so well in my life...I was having the baby I never thought I'd have, and falling in love with the man I thought I'd never meet. It was so perfect, and I didn't want it to end. But that day in the hospital, when I saw Gavin's name on the plaque...how could anyone be prepared for a situation like that? How could anyone even know what to do? Gavin had hurt you, and here I was, having his baby and falling in love with you." She stopped. The words had run out. There was nothing more to say that he hadn't already heard. So now it was up to Neil to make the next move. And there were so many ways this could go, it frightened her to the very core because she wanted to be a family with him. The three of them. Living in White Elk. Happy.

Only she didn't know if Neil could do that. So, now was the moment of reckoning. Her destiny laid out before her, and the choice was Neil's.

"Gavin and I were…at the time he died we were almost getting along again. He'd changed. I saw it after he'd come back from his medical seminar. He was…calm. Maybe a little more contented. And that was something I'd never seen in him before. Ever. But he'd called me and we'd talked a few times. He'd told me how sorry he was for breaking up my marriage. He, um…he begged for my forgiveness and I told him I wasn't ready yet, but maybe sometime in the future. It was the best I could do."

"That's good," Gabrielle said, her hopes growing even though she was trying to hold them back.

"Not good, but better. There were too many hard feelings to clear up in a matter of days or weeks. And I think he understood that."

"Maybe that was the sadness I saw in him. The regret for what he'd done. We all make mistakes, and maybe he was at a point where he was realizing that his biggest mistake was losing his brother."

Neil shrugged. "Maybe. But we'll never know, will we?"

"What we know is that the man I met wasn't the man who stole your wife. Something changed him, Neil, and while we'll never know what that was, it would be nice to think that Gavin's desire to have a relationship with you again caused the change. Honestly, I think he found his heart and his happiness through his medicine and, perhaps, that's where the change in him started. And you know what? I think his lecture was about White Elk, even though he didn't mention it by name. It was his passion, like it's yours."

"Karen and I weren't getting along when Gavin stepped in. She was such a…mistake. More like a lapse in sound judgment. And, to be honest, I didn't miss her when she was gone."

"But did you miss Gavin?"

"Not for a while. I remember telling him something to the effect that I never wanted to see him again…something about not crossing his path until hell froze over." He cringed. "It was reactionary, but I had a right to my reactions. And not because of Karen. She wasn't even significant in the matter. My wife was poison. She would have destroyed me, destroyed my career. And after I'd found out they'd been having an affair, I laughed at Gavin for being so gullible, told him he was welcome to her." Neil shook his head. "And the hell of it was, I never knew why they did it. Karen was easy to figure out. She was a child who got bored with her toys easily. But Gavin?"

"It could have been something complicated like a deep-rooted jealousy left over from childhood—like he perceived you were the favored one, or something as simple as being hurt that his father knew you were following in his footsteps, but didn't live long enough to know that Gavin was, too. It's hard to say what caused him to do what he did, and speculating is a waste of time because we'll never know. But the way you reacted…you said what you said because you were hurt. Gavin wouldn't have held that against you. I mean, there aren't rules governing a situation like that. But you rebuilt your life. Honorably. And in the end, even though you'll never have the answers you want, you'll have to make your life enough without those answers."

"It is enough. More than I ever thought I'd have, and I'm happy. Probably happier than Gavin ever was, and I'm sorry for that. Truly, deeply sorry."

Tears of pain trickled down her cheeks, and she swiped at them with the back of her hand. "The man I met had regrets, Neil. I saw that in him and I wish now I'd asked him." Yet how could she have anticipated, then, how her future would be eternally entwined with Gavin's? Or his brother's? Or his son's?

"Gavin and I, we'd agreed to meet. After months, I'd finally said yes, stipulating that the first meeting be on neutral ground somewhere other than White Elk. We'd have lunch, talk. We'd agreed to one step at a time. Gavin wanted to go faster, I wanted to be cautious. But we were going to sit down together and see if we could find a starting point." He swallowed hard. "I didn't know he changed his will to leave everything to the hospital pediatrics ward. He was atoning for what he'd done in the past, I think."

"Yes, I think he was."

"Even with all his faults, Gavin was a brilliant doctor. I would have liked to have heard his lecture in Chicago."

"Would you like to read my notes of it?"

He nodded, but didn't speak for a moment. Then, finally, "Gavin and I had a long way to go to make up. He said he understood that, and was willing to do whatever he had to. He was sincere, Gabrielle. I know he was sincere."

"Because he was a changed man," she said.

"Yes, I think he was. And I don't suppose I would have known how much if you hadn't…"

He cleared his throat and shut his eyes for a moment. Thinking. Processing. Trying to put it all together. The agony on his face was so strong it turned into her own agony. She could feel it. Feel the heavy burden he carried. If only there was something she could do, something more than listening. But maybe that's what he needed most. Maybe letting him unburden himself was the only thing she could do to truly help. So she waited quietly until he was ready to speak again, hoping he could feel her silent support.

"Anyway," he finally said, "Gavin wanted to see me and I had finally convinced myself it was a good thing. I wasn't looking forward to it, although I wasn't dreading it either. But I had a patient who went bad that morning and I couldn't leave the hospital. So I called Gavin, told him we'd have to reschedule, and that I'd call him in a day or so to see what we could arrange. Well, Gavin was insistent. He said he was coming to White Elk to see me, that he was ready to do it, and he had things to say that couldn't wait any longer. So he came to White Elk, and that's when...when he was killed. Traffic accident right before he got to the valley."

"Neil, I'm so sorry." Gabby scooted to the edge of the bed, dropped her legs over the side, then leaned forward and took Neil's hands in hers. "So sorry you two never had the chance to talk." She couldn't even begin to imagine what it would be like to be involved in a relationship that needed resolution as badly as Neil's and Gavin's had, and never have that chance. When she'd lost her dad, everything had been said between them. No resolution was necessary, because they'd expressed their love, fought their fights and forgiven each other along the way. Even thinking that something between them could have gone unresolved made her feel sad. For Neil, for Gavin. And for Bryce, because he was very much a part of this.

But more than ever it made her realize that she and Neil had a situation to resolve between the two of them, and that they couldn't let another day, another hour pass without saying all the things that needed saying.

"I know you can't go back and change things, and I'm sure you thought, like most of us do, that you have all the time in the world to make things right. It's just not like that, though. My little boy almost died yesterday, and that's the first time I've really understood how precious and short time is. Gavin was a good man. I knew him differently than you did, saw him in a way you'll never get to. But he was a good, kind man, and I have to think he learned from his mistakes and patterned himself after you. Because you're a good, kind man, too. His older brother...the best kind of example. He knew that, and I truly believe that hurting you was what made him sad. So maybe you didn't have enough time to make it right, but you would have, Neil. Given enough time, you two would have made up. He wanted to, and you wanted to."

"Maybe we would have. But I'll never know, will I?"

The truth was, he wouldn't. And that wasn't something she could fix. She could help him through it, though. Support him through the lows. If he would have her. If he would have Bryce. "I don't want to leave White Elk, Neil. I want to stay there and raise my son there. And I want to be happy there. When I first arrived, I didn't know what I wanted, or where I wanted to be. But I found everything...*everything* there, and I don't want to leave it. But I can't stay, if my being there makes you unhappy."

"You could never make me unhappy, Gabrielle. I knew that the first time I saw you in the dining room, being so deliberate about picking out the right table so you could see what you wanted to see. I'll admit I never expected to fall in love with someone quite so..."

"Pregnant?"

He chuckled. "That, too. But the word I'm looking for is perfect. Because you are." He took hold of her hand and pulled it to his lips, then kissed it tenderly. "I don't think I've mentioned this before, but you look beautiful when you're not pregnant. Of course, you're absolutely stunning when you're pregnant. Any chance that could happen again?"

"And that would mean?" It was definitely time to get

her hopes up. In fact, they were so far up they were floating.

"About fifty or sixty years, if we're lucky."

"And you're good with Bryce being Gavin's son? Because that's something he'll have to know when it's time."

"I'm already crazy in love with him, so I'm good," he said. "As long as you let him call me Daddy."

"Daddy suits you. But I can't promise you other children, Neil. One was a miracle." Gavin's miracle to both Neil and her.

"One's perfect. So are ten."

"Ten?" she sputtered, slipping from the bed, going straight onto his lap and into his waiting arms. "You would want ten?"

"Or twelve. Or, like I said, one."

As their lips met, Gabby thought about that day she'd first come to White Elk, amazed by what a perfect town it was. The place, from Ben Gault's photos, that had stolen her heart. Her home, meant to be even before she'd recognized it. Yes, it was perfect. But not for the reasons she'd thought when she'd made the decision to spend a night there. White Elk was where her son had been born, where she'd met the man she'd love forever, where she'd found the dream of her heart. Those were the things that made it perfect. And made it home. "I love you, Dr Ranard," she said, resting her head on his shoulder, happier than she'd ever thought was possible.

"And I love you, Dr Evans. Want to snuggle up?" He pointed to the bed.

"Right here? I mean, I just had a baby, and…"

He laughed. "Snuggle, Dr Evans. *Only* snuggle."

"In that case, I'd love to snuggle with you, Dr Ranard. Every day, for the rest of my life."

EPILOGUE

Six months later

"He's gained another pound." Neil picked up his son and held him high above his head, laughing. The adoption was final. Bryce Thierry Evans Ranard was his in every way and it was hard for either him or Gabby to imagine a time when this bouncing bundle of energy hadn't been the center of their lives.

"Eric said he's perfect. Everything checks out fine. Heart's good, lungs sound. Normal in every way. Oh, and I ran into Angela. She was there at the clinic with her baby…"

"Sarah," Gabby reminded him.

"With Sarah. Anyway, seeing Angela reminded me that we haven't had our honeymoon yet. So I was thinking that if we could find a babysitter…"

Gabby arched skeptical eyebrows. "I'm sensing a definite plot here, Bryce. Your father is up to something."

"I'm up to a short honeymoon," Neil said. After Bryce's second surgery, the three of them had settled in like a happy family, and the honeymoon had been forgotten. Tonight was the four-month anniversary of their marriage, though, and it was time for the two of them to get away. "And I've had a whole battalion of women volunteer to watch Bryce for a couple of days while we go up to Pine Ridge… couldn't get the honeymoon suite, though. It was already reserved by someone else. But we'll have a nice room anyway. Room service when we want it, lots of time alone…" Neil lowered Bryce, and looked him straight in the eye. "You may have to help me convince her," he said, grinning.

She took Bryce away from Neil. "You tell your father that your mother would love to have a honeymoon with him."

"Two whole nights," Neil reminded her.

"Two wonderful nights," she said, handing Bryce back to Neil, then picking up the bag she'd been hiding. "Shield his eyes," she said.

"Why?"

"Because he's too young to see this."

"Don't look, son," he said, laughing, as Gabrielle pulled a black, filmy nightdress out and waved it.

"Oh, and I'm the one who reserved the honeymoon suite, by the way. Already had several people ready to take care of Bryce, too." By all estimates, she had about another two months before her belly would start bulging again, and she wanted to take full advantage of that. Or, at least, two nights of it.

"Any chance we can stay away for a week?" he asked.

"With the way our medical practices are growing?" She waved the nightdress again, deliberately brushing it against his cheek. "Let's be glad we can have two nights, then promise to do it again in another month. Maybe try out a honeymoon suite at a lodge on one of the other Sisters."

"The practices are expanding, Bryce, because your mommy's a good doctor and women from everywhere are coming to see her."

"That's because your daddy turned his house on the hill into a women's clinic and birthing center." Her very own hospital, named The Three Sisters Women's Hospital. The Three Sisters who did, indeed, look after the people in their valley.

She and Neil had bought a modest little cottage on the edge of town, a perfect spot from which they could see all Three Sisters. Somehow she felt connected to them, like they'd watched over Bryce and protected him the way the legend had it. Like they'd brought her here in the first place so they could do just that.

Bryce's response was to gurgle out a baby bubble. Then laugh.

"But Mommy doesn't want to talk medicine right now," she said, tickling Neil's other cheek with the nighty. He was the perfect father. Devoted. Caring. Best of all, he didn't mind diaper duty. "But we will have to come home for a little while because Ben Gault is coming to town tomorrow afternoon. He's going to do a family photo of us." A family photo—her very own family. For her entire life, her family photo had been of two. But now, with three, then in a few more months with four…she still had to pinch herself sometimes to make sure it wasn't a dream.

"Ben Gault is going to interrupt my honeymoon? Couldn't we wait until he's here again in a couple of months?"

"We could, but I'll be showing."

"Showing what?" he asked.

She smiled warmly, and patted her belly.

"No!" he gasped.

"Yes," she whispered. "We might be on our way to the ten or twelve you wanted."

He snatched the black nightdress away from Gabrielle and let it float to the floor. When it cascaded into a puddle at his feet, he smiled. "Well, then, I don't think you'll be needing this."

She bent and picked it up, then dropped it back into the bag, gave Bryce a kiss on the forehead and Neil a deep, lingering kiss on the lips. Afterwards, breathlessly…"I think you're right."

HIS MOTHERLESS LITTLE TWINS

BY

DIANNE DRAKE

MILLS & BOON®

All the characters in this book have no existence outside the imagination of the author, and have no relation whatsoever to anyone bearing the same name or names. They are not even distantly inspired by any individual known or unknown to the author, and all the incidents are pure invention.

First published in Great Britain 2010
Harlequin Mills & Boon Limited,
Eton House, 18-24 Paradise Road, Richmond, Surrey TW9 1SR

© Dianne Despain 2010

ISBN: 978 0 263 87891 2

Harlequin Mills & Boon policy is to use papers that are natural, renewable and recyclable products and made from wood grown in sustainable forests. The logging and manufacturing process conform to the legal environmental regulations of the country of origin.

Printed and bound in Spain
by Litografia Rosés, S.A., Barcelona

Extract from *HIS MOTHERLESS LITTLE TWINS*:

Eric slipped his arm around Dinah's waist and she melted against him. "I remember the first time I saw the twins…I couldn't believe how perfect they were. "

"It puts everything into proper perspective, doesn't it? Makes you truly believe all's right with the world."

"All *is* right with the world…their world. And that's the way it should be."

"My life is too up and down to drag a baby into it right now." But in the future? Being around him almost made her believe she could have it all. *Almost.*

CHAPTER ONE

"I'LL be there in thirty or forty minutes, and don't even think about going out on your own. It's too dangerous." Dinah Corday had been studying the *Welcome to White Elk* sign for the past ten minutes, creeping inch by inch down the main road into the little village, along with the rest of the jammed-up traffic. Right this very moment, her heavily pregnant sister, Angela, was on the verge of braving the spring storm to go and stay with a pregnant friend, and Dinah wanted to get to her before she did that. But the rising waters weren't being accommodating. Nothing was. "Just don't do it, OK? I know you want to be with her, and I'm doing the best I can to get to you, but it's crazy out here. So just be patient." Easy to say, not so easy to do under the circumstances.

Glancing up at the three mountain peaks, Dinah sighed impatiently. The mountains looming over the valley, affectionately called the older, middle, and younger Sisters, were said to have magical powers. According to Ute Indian legend, they protected those in their shadow, and while she'd never given much credence to mystical things, she hoped that this one was true. Because Angela would *absolutely* go out in this flood to help a friend as surely as Dinah was stuck in the slow lane, getting more frustrated with each passing second.

Ahead, she saw people on the street running about in a congested knot like ants scattering after the demise of their anthill. Traffic was lined up bumper to bumper. Detour signs were being erected on the streets. Streetlights weren't working. And the wind was blowing so hard the water pooling in the gutters was flowing in small waves. "Promise me you're not going anywhere until I get there to take you. You're too far along…" A smile found its way to Dinah's lips. She was going to be an aunt in a little while. That was nice. Their family needed something good to happen to them for a change. It was overdue. "Just, please, stay there and take care of yourself. I'm on my way."

Angela assured her she wouldn't budge, but that didn't relieve Dinah's anxiety. Of course, that anxiety was pelting her from so many different directions these days, she feared turning around lest something else came hurtling at her. Today, though, her mind was on Angela. Nothing else mattered.

Except the traffic. That mattered, and she wanted to honk her horn, pound on her horn actually, but what good would it do? She wasn't the only one stuck in this mess and, most likely, everyone else had somewhere important they needed to be, too. So as the radio weather forecaster was predicting more rain, she crept forward like the rest of the people were doing, one car length at a time, while the waters outside were getting deeper.

After listening to another ten mind-numbing minutes of dire weather warnings, Dinah finally turned off the news station and dialed into a soft jazz station then leaned her head against the headrest, hoping to relax. She needed to be calm, not agitated, when she got to Angela. "Calm…" she muttered, while she studied the raindrops sliding their own little paths over her windshield. Some hit and trailed down in a straight line, never veering off an imaginary course, while others meandered, winding in and out, joining with other raindrops to make fatter, more interesting trails. Yet some hit, bounced, and seemed to disappear before they had their chance to slide downward to a new, unknown destiny. That was her, she thought. Hitting, bouncing, disappearing from view before her trail carried her to where she wanted to be. Hers had always been a destiny of chance, or one out of her control, like the raindrops that splashed themselves into oblivion even with so many interesting choices ahead.

Raindrops and unknown destinies…

Well, so much for clearing her mind and relaxing, she thought, trying hard to let the mellow wail of the tenor sax coming from the radio lull her into a daze. Dulcet tones, honey notes, all slipping down into her soul. This was a good day to be lulled. But as she willed the easy mood on herself, trying to force calm to her soul for Angela's sake, a thud on her bumper from the vehicle behind cut off all hope of calmness, sending her car pitching straight into the bumper of the car ahead. Not a hard impact but definitely a jarring one.

Twisting, Dinah looked into her rearview mirror to catch a glimpse of the perpetrator, but all she saw was an up-close image of a truck's shiny silver bumper…and the truck was already backing away from her. Right off, she opened the car door, ready to hop out regardless of the rain and see to the damage, but the man behind her beat her to it by stopping then jumping from his truck and running forward. He was a big, imposing man in a bright yellow slicker, the dress of choice for most of the people she'd seen here so far. Except he didn't come forward to her door like she'd expected he would. Rather, he got as far as the front of his truck, surveyed his bumper then hers, and that was as far as he went.

"Any damage?" she shouted, wishing she had one of those yellow rain slickers.

If he answered, she didn't hear him. But the rain was noisy, so were the road noises. So, after she'd fumbled an umbrella from the back of her car and opened it overhead, she tried calling to him again. "You're not hurt, are you?"

He didn't answer this time, either, so she tried once more. Admittedly, getting a little perturbed. "Did it cause any damage?"

His only response was a wave on his way back to his truck…waving with one hand, clutching a cell phone to his ear in the other. "I can't stay," he yelled, and she did hear that. "Jason, the man in the car ahead of you, said he'll take care of it, and…" The rest of his words were gobbled in a clap of thunder, and by the time it had rumbled on through, he'd jumped back into his truck and pulled around, stopping briefly at the car in front of her.

"You arrogant…" she yelled, slamming shut her car door and marching straight forward to catch him before he sped away altogether. She didn't need this today. Just didn't need this. And now, with this added delay, she was even more worried that Angela would try to get out in this storm on her own.

"You OK, Jason?" the man from the truck called to the man in the car she'd hit, who was beginning to climb out of his front seat. He, too, was dressed in a yellow slicker.

"What about me?" Dinah yelled, catching up to his truck and running to the window on the driver's side. "Don't you want to know how I am?"

The man who'd hit her did turn around in his seat, giving her a long, hard stare. "You're not hurt, are you?"

"No, but—"

"I'm sorry," he said. "But I can't deal with this right now. Like I told you before, Jason will take care of the details because I've got an emergency, and I've got to get back." He paused then smiled. "I'm really sorry about this."

He seemed sincere enough, his smile was…nice. But she didn't trust nice smiles, and sincerity was easy to fake. If anybody knew those two things, she did! Yet as she was about to shut out that nice smile altogether and demand he step out of the truck regardless of what his other obligations were, a gust of wind caught her umbrella, turned it inside out, then ripped it from her hands. Unfortunately, it tumbled end over end across the road, leaving Dinah standing in water up to her ankles, with her long, auburn hair soaked and shaggy, and nothing to protect her. She was barely even noticing the rain, though, because at this point she was too angry. "You can't just leave the scene," she yelled at the man. He was going to leave, though. That's what men did. They left. And she couldn't stop him. Couldn't stop any of them. Father, husband, fiancé, brother-in-law, strangers…all alike.

Before the stranger pulled away, though, he handed an umbrella out the window to her. "I'm sorry, but I can't deal with this right now. So, please, step back. I don't want to splash you…" He took a good look at her water-logged state and grimaced visibly. "Don't want to get you any wetter than you are."

Well, she could step in front of his truck and stop him, or grab hold of the handle on his door. But there was something in his eyes…a look she knew. Not a malicious one, not even a little mean-spirited. For an instant, something so deep there grabbed hold of her senses, willed her to step back. So she did, immediately regretting that, once again, she'd let herself be taken advantage of by a good-looker. In her life, trust amounted to betrayal. She almost counted on it, and that was a huge regret, too.

The proof of her regret was in the blow of black smoke from his tailpipe as he sped away from her, while she remained standing in the downpour, watching him, gripping his umbrella in a stranglehold, getting wetter and wetter.

"I'm glad Gabby has been such a good friend to you, especially since I haven't been of much use these past months," Dinah said to her sister.

Angela laid her hand on Dinah's. "Not your fault. We all have our problems to solve. And I've been doing fine here on my own. Good friends, good care. Nothing to worry about."

Except a cheating ski-bum of a husband who'd run away from Angela the moment he'd heard the word *pregnant*. "I'm your sister and I'm entitled to worry anyway. But like I said, I'm glad you've had Gabby here to help you get through." Dr. Gabrielle Evans. Angela's friend, and her doctor, who was on the verge of giving birth right this very moment, fully in labor. "So, how are you doing, Gabby?"

Gabby nodded, panted, grasped the edge of the bed while Angela wiped her forehead with a cool, damp cloth and Dinah positioned herself to see how dilated Gabby was. Dinah had been a pediatric nurse, but she'd had good experience in obstetrics. While there was supposed to be a doctor on the way to deliver this baby, and since taking Gabby to the hospital in this weather in her condition would be a crazy thing to do, Gabby was ready to deliver this baby right here, right now, doctor or not. And it was beginning to look like Dinah might have to come out of her self-imposed retirement to bring the baby that Gabby was already calling Bryce into the world.

"Can I do anything else?" Angela asked.

"Just sit down and relax. I don't want you getting worked up and going into labor yourself," Dinah said, truly concerned about the effect the strain of all this excitement could have on her sister. Two women on the verge of motherhood. She envied them. Once, a long time ago, she'd thought that's what she'd wanted most in the world. But the marriage hadn't worked out, and she'd gone in another direction with her life. Then, years later, along had come Charles, the man she'd hoped would be…well, it didn't matter what she'd hoped. She'd been wrong about him, too.

Still, with all these babies coming into the world…

"Relax, Gabby," she said, as another contraction gripped the woman. "I think this is going to be over with pretty soon. Bryce is in position and he's about to make his grand entrance."

"I hope so," Gabby forced out as the contraction came to an end. "Because I'm tired of this part of it."

Dinah laughed. "But you'll be a much better obstetrician for having gone through it yourself. At least, that sounds good in theory, doesn't it? And now, when you tell your patients you understand, you really will." She laid a hand on Gabrielle's belly, felt the amazing stirring of a new life just under her fingertips. Suddenly, she was glad she was there, being part of it.

"Angela tells me you've quit nursing," Gabby gasped. She was finally relaxing back into her pillows. But not for long, if her progression towards the birth remained this consistent.

"For now. I came here to cook for Angela while she's off on maternity leave, then I'll decide what I want to do after that." Dinah's sister was the executive chef at the lodge on one of the Three Sisters and, like Angela, Dinah had also gone to culinary school. But she'd quit part way through to go into nursing. Culinary school, like her first marriage, had been a hasty decision, and not the right one. But nursing…she loved it. Missed it already.

Right now, though, with so many unresolved issues, she had to step away. The reasons were complicated, and she didn't trust herself to make the right decision while she was still feeling the sting.

"I'm glad you can deliver a baby, because I didn't want to do this by myself," Gabby said, as another contraction hit. "And I was afraid I might have to."

The contractions were coming fast. In the hour they'd been there they'd sped up considerably, telling Dinah that Gabby was in an unusually fast labor. It was time to get her in position and hope the doctor arrived in time, that the floodwaters outside wouldn't hold him back. Or do what she had to do if he couldn't get through.

Funny, how she'd quit nursing, not sure she could ever go back to it. Yet here she was, doing what she'd promised herself she wouldn't do again until her life was in better control, if that were even possible now, and wondering if she'd made yet another bad choice by leaving the thing she most loved doing.

Which was the reason she'd had to leave. Because these days she was just…confused.

And sad.

Dr. Neil Ranard arrived in time to deliver Gabby's baby, and the first thing Dinah saw was just how much he loved Gabby. Angela had already told her that the baby wasn't Neil's, but deep down Dinah believed that Neil would raise that baby, because the look she saw in Gabby's eyes the instant Neil ran into the room said everything. It was nice. But what was even nicer was seeing that it was out there…true love did exist. Maybe not for her. But it was nice for others who were luckier than she was. Or smarter.

"Just one more push, Gabrielle," Neil urged. "That's all I need. One more push and you're a mother!"

Dinah propped Gabby up into position, enjoying what she was doing, even if it was a little outside her nursing expertise. It was good to be useful again, good to help. For a while, the ache of missing it was eased a little.

"Bear down, Gabrielle, and push," Neil said.

"I am," Gabby gasped.

"Breathe," Dinah said. "Come on, Gabby. Take a deep breath, then push that baby out."

"He's waiting for you, Gabrielle," Neil prompted. "Bryce Evans is waiting for you."

Gabby bore down for a final time as Dinah helped her through her final contraction. Then, suddenly, it was over. Bryce was here. But…dear God, he was blue. Dinah saw it immediately, felt her stomach roil, and exchanged a quick look with Dr. Ranard. A look that said everything.

"Let me see him," Gabby said to the deathly quiet room. "My baby…"

Dinah eased Gabby back into a flat position on the bed, propped a pillow under her head then ran to the end of the bed to see what she could do for Dr. Ranard. Or for the limp little newborn in his hands.

"He isn't crying," Gabby gasped, fighting to sit back up. Thrashing wildly, she was trying to toss off the sheets covering her. "Neil, he isn't crying! What's wrong?"

"Take care of Gabrielle," Neil whispered to Dinah. "Don't let her see…"

Even before he'd finished speaking, Dinah positioned herself between Neil and the bed, so Gabby couldn't see Neil's resuscitation attempts and the next minutes went by in a blur as she tried to calm the grief-stricken mother and help the doctor with the baby.

"Did he aspirate?" Dinah whispered to Neil, although

she didn't believe so. As a pediatric trauma nurse, her first guess was something cardiac, or related to the lungs, judging from the baby's listlessness and bluish pallor.

Not again! Dear God, not again! *How could she face another newborn dying?* Bryce had a chance to survive, Molly never had. She had to stay focused on that! *This* was the baby who needed her now. This was Bryce Evans, not Molly Collins.

"Is he alive?" Gabby screamed. "Neil, you've got to tell me, is he alive? I've got to get to my baby." She launched herself up, but Dinah stopped her, applying a firm hand into her shoulder.

More minutes ticked by, and Bryce still struggled. Outside, the floods were getting worse. The hospital had promised to send a medic with supplies, but each second seemed like an hour—a frantic, futile hour in which they were losing a battle. All the while, Dinah was forced to physically restrain Gabby from flying across the room to Neil. Neil didn't need that. Neither did the baby, who was not improving. She hated doing that. Hated it more than anyone could imagine, because she knew how it felt. Knew how Gabby felt, needing desperately to get there and being pulled away against her will.

Then suddenly Bryce quit breathing and Dinah was thrown back to that day when baby Molly had died in her arms. Regret, instant and brutal, assaulted her, causing a feeling of panic to rise up and strangle the breath from her. For a moment she was back there in that hospital room, struggling and crying like Gabby was, begging them not to take Molly away from her.

"Is that CPR?" Gabby cried, snapping Dinah back into the moment. "Is Neil giving him CPR?"

More minutes blurred in the battle as Bryce began showing signs of reviving. Bryce had Neil to fight for him, and Neil loved him. That was so obvious. There'd been no one to care for Molly. No one had loved her. Except *her*. And in the end, that hadn't been enough.

Now the melancholia threatened to pull her under.

"You!"

The voice from the doorway startled Dinah from her thoughts of Molly, and she jumped. "You!" she snapped right back at him. Of all the people who could have come, it would be *him*, Mr Hit-and-Run himself. And he was standing there, holding out a pediatric oxygen mask.

Dinah yanked the mask from the man's hands, and rushed to put it on Bryce. Then the medic opened the oxygen tank valve once the mask was in place.

"It was a slight tap," he said. "No damage."

"And you didn't stop to see if you'd damaged my car, or injured me," Dinah snarled under her breath to keep her problem with this man quiet, as she pulled a pediatric IV needle from the bag of supplies he'd brought and prepared to insert it into the baby's thread-sized vein. It's what she did, no one had to tell her. No one had to help her. It's simply what she was trained to do, and did instinctively.

As she set about her work, she noticed that Bryce was already pinking up. Not enough to think he was out of danger, but enough to be encouraged.

"You take care of Gabby," the medic whispered to Neil. "She needs you right now, and I'll take care of the baby."

Neil handed off the responsibility without hesitation, and the two men exchanged quiet words for a moment. "Thanks, Eric," Neil finally said, then ran to Gabrielle.

"You're a doctor?" Dinah asked.

"Eric Ramsey, pediatric surgeon, with a secondary in trauma." He pulled a bag of fluid from his supplies and hooked it to the line once Dinah had inserted the IV catheter. Then he adjusted the drip of fluid into the baby's veins, and immediately listened to Bryce's chest.

The next few minutes they worked side by side in total silence, both doing what they knew needed to be done to stabilize their tiny patient.

"He's a fighter," Eric finally pronounced, turning around to Gabby. "We've got him as stabilized as we can, so now I need to get him to the hospital. But I want you to hold him first."

She took her baby, and the way she clung to him nearly broke Dinah's heart. No one had loved little Molly like that…someone should have. She couldn't bear watching, the memories were too painful and she had to turn away.

"I was in a hurry…emergency." Eric stepped up behind her. "Otherwise I wouldn't have driven off like that."

"What?" Dinah asked.

"The accident. I had an emergency. I'm sorry, but—"

"But we all do what we have to do, don't we?" she whispered. "It doesn't matter what we do to the people around us, as long as it's good for us. I get it. You don't need to apologize."

"Yes, I do." Eric took a step back, shook his head. "Look, Neil thinks Bryce's problem might be TGV." Transposition of the great vessels, where the two main arteries leaving the heart were reversed. Normally, blood from the heart's right ventricle was carried by the pulmonary artery to the lungs, and blood from the left ventricle was taken by the aorta to the body. In the case of TGV, it was just the opposite, leaving the oxygenated blood meant to circulate through the body being pumped back into the lungs. "And at this point, I have no reason to disagree because the symptoms fit. Things may turn out differently once we get the baby—"

"You think it's TGV, too?" Dinah's mind raced through

the procedures. There would be a first surgery, called a septostomy, to do an immediate, life-saving correction. In that, a hole was literally opened up to allow better flow of the blood. It was a temporary measure to be followed by another surgery to make the permanent repair. She'd treated babies who'd had the surgery, seen good outcomes, seen bad outcomes.

"You'll drive."

"Where?" she asked.

"To the hospital. You'll drive, I'll take care of the baby."

The tension in the cab of the truck was so thick Dinah could have sliced through it with a scalpel. They'd been en route five minutes now, taking a back road that skirted the valley. It was muddy and slick, but it wasn't washed out. And it was on higher ground, which was what made it a safer bet than taking the road down below the house, where the water was at least as high as the bottom of the truck door. Flash-flood warnings were out now, and all the lower roads were being closed. So she and Eric were driving along what amounted to little more than a fire trail, and Dinah was so nervous that her grip on the steering-wheel hurt. All the while, neither she nor Eric had spoken a word to each other since his initial instruction to her on getting to the hospital.

Yet in his defense, Eric was busy tending to Bryce, holding him in his lap and continually checking his pulse, his respiratory status, being so tender, so caring with him while she was fighting to stay straight and to avoid the bumps and ruts, most of which she couldn't even see.

It crossed her mind that he was the doctor Molly should have had. He would have cared more than Charles had, even when hope had died. Charles, the man she'd almost married. How could she have been so wrong about him? Even thinking about it made her cringe.

Once or twice, Bryce let out a little cry then settled down again. And once or twice her heart lurched. Under the best of circumstances, this was a difficult situation. These *weren't* the best of circumstances, and she fretted about the outcome every inch of the way to the hospital.

"Are you competent?" she finally asked, not at all sorry to be so blunt. Truth was, she wanted to hear his voice, feel some reassurance that he could handle this situation and make everything right for the baby.

"Competent at what?"

"Your medical skills. Are you a good doctor?"

"I've been told that's the case." He twisted slightly in his seat to look at her. "But, then, everyone is entitled to his, *or her*, opinion, I suppose."

"I suppose," Dinah muttered. Something about this man put her in a very bad mood. Something about every man had put her in a bad mood lately, but this one in particular made her shiver. Shiver with anger was what it was, which she didn't like one little bit. Didn't like any reaction in her caused by any man. And didn't trust herself enough to know the distinctions.

"Are *you* competent?" he asked in return, the slightest trace of a smile crinkling his lips.

She was going to ignore that smile. Totally ignore it and pretend she hadn't even seen it. "Competent at what?"

"Being a nurse."

"I'm not a nurse." Keeping her voice noncommittal wasn't easy, but she did it, and did it so well she nearly believed her own words. Still, those words hurt, and the wound still bled. "I'm a cook. Here to take over for my sister when she's on maternity leave."

"A cook with good skills in labor and delivery, as well

as CPR. And you did a mighty fine job of getting that IV needle into a newborn, which is not easy, especially when the newborn is so sick. So, did they teach you those things in culinary school?"

He was smiling fully now. The man actually had the audacity to sit there and smile at her. But she was still going to ignore it. Had to be impervious... Couldn't get distracted. "Did they teach you your bad manners in medical school?"

"If I apologized for the accident again, would that make things better between us?"

"Why do things have to be better between us?" she asked, then hastily added, "But you do owe me a sincere apology and not one that's meant only to get you away from me as quickly as possible."

"Look, I told you I was in a hurry. I'm sorry I hit you, sorry I ran off and left you there, but in case you haven't noticed, the town is going crazy. We're flooding, the areas below us are submerging, the hospital is full of people with nowhere to go, some of them have injuries. I had to get to the emergency department, and stopping for something that amounted to nothing was a waste of my time."

"And I thought White Elk was going to be civil," she snapped. Gripping the steering-wheel more from anger than nervousness, she kept her eyes fixed straight ahead. "But I was wrong."

"No, you weren't wrong. Had it been any other time, under any other circumstances, I would have stopped and given you that sincere apology. But you were...not a priority. Getting to the hospital was."

OK, she understood that. And maybe he was right. No, he *was* right. And she was overreacting. Which she'd been accused of doing a lot of lately. "It's been a bad day," she conceded. A bad day, a worse week and an even worse month. And everything was still spiraling downward. "I should be the one apologizing to you."

"No apologies necessary. And you're right, it's been a bad day for everyone." He glanced down at his tiny patient. "But mostly for him."

Suddenly, all the anger and frustration drained right out of her. Sick children had a way of putting everything else into proper perspective, had a way of bringing everything else around them to a grinding halt. "How's he doing?"

"Struggling. But fighting. He's one tough little boy. So, are you a friend of Gabby's?"

"No, I only met her today, right before I helped deliver Bryce. But I'm Angela Blanchard's sister. And I'm really here to take over for her in the kitchen."

"Funny. I would have sworn you were a nurse. A damn good one, if I had to make a bet on it."

"I was a pediatric nurse and, yes, I like to think I was a damn good one, but that's in the past," she said. "I burned out." That wasn't the truth, but it was an easy explanation and people didn't question it.

"Sorry to hear that. Especially since you seem so…passionate about it. That's medicine's loss."

He sounded genuinely sorry, which surprised her. When she'd tendered her resignation, no one had even tried talking her out of her decision to quit. Then, when she'd closed all those doors on her life and walked away, no one had been sorry to see her go. No one had even blinked. But by then she'd become an awkward moment for the man who was supposed to love her. He was an upwardly mobile doctor, she was a downwardly spiraling nurse he found quite easy to leave. *You're too emotional, Dinah. You overreacted. Got yourself too involved in something you had no business getting involved in. Maybe you should have stayed in cooking school.*

But she believed Eric Ramsey sounded sorry she'd left nursing.

Except she didn't trust herself to believe anything. Not anymore.

CHAPTER TWO

"You didn't, by any chance, ever assist in a septostomy did you?" Eric asked, handing the baby over to the two nurses who'd run to greet them when they'd pulled up to White Elk Hospital's front door.

"I've seen them done. And taken care of the patient afterwards. Why?"

"We're short-staffed right now, and I could use you in the operating room if you've got the experience."

"I do have the experience," she said hesitantly. Her preference would have been helping the volunteer crews who were busy sandbagging the hospital, trying to keep the flood waters back from it. That was something she could do, something that wouldn't remind her of how much she ached for a career that hurt her so deeply.

"Then I need your experience. Normally, I'd have another doctor in there, but he's driving Gabby and your sister to the hospital right now, and everybody else is tied up. I can grab our nurse practitioner, Fallon, and she's competent in surgery, but her skills are more needed in co-ordinating everything else that's going on. So if you know your way around the operating room…"

He actually wanted her in surgery? She was flattered, but she'd walked away from being a nurse. Not because she didn't care, but because she cared too much. By rights, she should have turned him down and under most other circumstances she would have. But there was a baby who needed her…*another baby*…

"*Please* assist me. I have a very sick little boy who needs surgery, but if all my qualified staff are busy elsewhere, his surgery may have to be put off until we have the right combination of people free. You know what that could mean."

Yes, she did know. When he put it that way, what was she supposed to do? How could she walk away from Bryce the way everybody had walked away from little Molly? "OK, I was more than a staff nurse. I was the head pediatric trauma nurse in my hospital. Just in case you want to know, or check my qualifications."

"You wear your qualifications for everybody to see," he said. "And I'm a pretty good judge of that."

Better judge than she was. Once upon a time she wouldn't have hesitated. Now she wasn't sure. "Where do I scrub in?" she asked on a disheartened sigh.

Eric pointed her in the direction of the surgery. "What's your name, by the way?"

"None of your business," she snapped. If he knew her name, it got personal, and she wasn't doing personal again. Personal hurt. It devastated. And she was tired of the pain.

Eric laughed. "When you scrub, I'd suggest you use cold water. Might cool you down a little."

Well, he generally didn't like his women so feisty. Lord knew, nothing about Patricia had been feisty. She'd been the model of cool, calm composure in everything. Always smiling, always happy, Patricia had been perfect. Maybe too perfect for the likes of him. But this woman…she was spunky, boisterous, argumentative, and in just an hour or so of knowing her, she'd raised her voice to him more than his wife had in all the years they'd been together.

Yet there was something about her that wouldn't let him look away. Drawn like a moth to the flame…that's the thought that kept running through his head. But didn't the moth usually get burned to a crisp?

This woman was all fire. Get too close and you were sure to get burned. But she was on his mind anyway, and it had nothing to do with his expectations of a pediatric trauma nurse, and everything to do with feelings he'd vowed he'd never let happen. He'd had a perfect marriage once. Anything else would fall short.

Besides, he had two little daughters to consider. In his life, they mattered more than anything else and the thought of putting them through a life-changing adjustment scared him. They were good the way they were…all three of them. Very good.

His thoughts were interrupted by the arrival of Neil Ranard, desperate for news about Gabby's son.

"You look bothered," Neil Ranard said, as Eric scrubbed. "Is it about Bryce?"

Eric shook his head, but didn't answer right away, because what bothered him was the disloyalty he was suddenly feeling, thinking about the beautiful nurse the way he was. He had no business looking at another woman, and the wedding band on his left ring finger was a shining testament to that. "No, he's stable right now. Doing pretty well last time I checked. The good news is that once we've done this first procedure he should be stable enough to be transferred to get the help we simply can't provide here."

"Gabby and I have every faith in your abilities, Eric. Neither of us would want anyone else helping Bryce right now."

"I'll do my very best not to let you down."

"I know you will. So if you're not too worried about Bryce right now, what is bugging you? Hold on, this wouldn't be about working with Dinah Corday, would it?"

This time he didn't bother shaking his head, as the guilt was beginning to consume him. Because, yes, it was about Dinah – so that was her name! She intrigued him. And she was sexy as hell. Something he had no right noticing.

"Well, she's a looker," Neil conceded. "And even though we've only worked together once, she's one of the best nurses I've ever dealt with. So, which of those two qualities is distracting you? Because it's got to be one of them, since you don't know anything else about her."

"I'm not distracted," Eric snapped. "I'm concentrating, and you're breaking my concentration."

Neil laughed. "I think your concentration was broken before I came in here, and it's got nothing to do with anything medical."

"It's not what you think," Eric denied. "I don't have time, and you know that. Between my job, and my rescue duties, and especially with the twins…" He shook his head as he backed away from the sink, arms up, water dripping down to his elbows. "I don't have time, no matter how much she…or any other woman…breaks my concentration. So I'm not going to let it happen, simple as that."

"Look, Eric. I know you were totally devoted to Patricia, but she's been gone for five years, and I don't think she would have wanted you putting yourself through this. She would have wanted you to be happy again. To find a new life for yourself…something in addition to your work. And that would include finding someone else to share that life. But you haven't even taken a woman out for a simple dinner, have you?"

"Once or twice." Truth was, after Patricia had died, he'd lost interest. Hadn't found it again, either, because in his heart he was still a married man.

"Look, I know it's not easy. Believe me, if anyone knows how hard it is to pick up the pieces and move on, it's me. After my marriage broke up…" He paused, shrugged, then smiled. "But I'm working it out with Gabrielle now, and I think we're going to get married. Which shows how easily the past becomes just that—the past—when the right future opens up to you. So keep yourself open to the possibilities, because you deserve to find some happiness. If not with Dinah Corday, then with someone else."

"What if I don't want to open myself up to them? I mean, what if I like keeping myself shut off?" Eric spun away from Neil and pushed through the surgical door, stepping directly into the gown the surgical tech was holding up for him. He was back in the moment now, back in the zone. That's what always happened the instant he stepped into surgery and right now, even though the most gorgeous pair of brown eyes he'd ever seen in his life were staring over a surgical mask at him, he was focused on starting the procedure to save Bryce Evans's life.

But as he stepped up to the table, for one fleeting moment the only thing he saw in front of him were those eyes. Beautiful eyes. Distracting. Then he blocked them out, and cleared his throat. "Let's go over the surgical check list before we start."

Well, if this hadn't been quite the day! She'd helped deliver one baby, helped resuscitate that baby, and had then assisted in his surgery. All that, plus dodging a flood. By all rights, she should have been tired, exhausted, ready to find a quiet corner somewhere, put her feet up and take a nap. That's probably what she'd do in a little while, when she finally wound down. But right now she felt alive. Invigorated. It had been three long, difficult weeks since Molly's death. Three weeks to doubt herself, three weeks being berated for caring by the man who had claimed to love her. Three weeks of agony and self-doubt.

Yet in the span of only a few hours now, it was like she'd been sustained again. Sustained, validated. Made to feel normal. Of course, it would all be over with once she stepped outside the confines of this hospital. So she wanted to bask a while longer in a place where she felt like she belonged, to linger in the good feelings. Besides, she felt safe here. She'd never, ever in her life set foot into such a tiny, crazy hospital as this one, where trauma doctors had second careers as surgeons and third careers as heads of search and rescue, and where doctors still made house calls and invited total strangers into the surgery. As mixed up as it all seemed, she liked it so much she could almost picture herself belonging here, and that was a nice feeling she wanted to last for a while longer because, to be honest, she doubted she'd ever get it back.

Creeping into the intensive care nursery, where the lights were dimmed for the sleeping hours, and the green, glowing trace of baby Bryce's heartbeat on the cardiac monitor next to his bed illuminated the area like an eerie beacon, Dinah stopped halfway to the crib to admire the miracle baby lying there, breathing easily and sleeping peacefully. All was right in his world and he had no idea how people had scrambled to save his life today, how they'd put their own lives at risk to save him. Neither had he any idea how many people had already crept in to see how he was doing, or hovered outside the door, worrying about him. He had no idea that things weren't perfect, and that's the way it should always be in a child's world. Molly should have had a chance at that, if even for a moment.

Dinah loved children, loved taking care of them, loved the innocence of the smiles and giggles. She'd fallen in love with Molly. Abandoned at birth because of overwhelming disabilities, her birth mother had simply walked away. Never looked back. And had left a precious child to die alone in an impersonal hospital nursery where the duty nurses took good care, but didn't truly care. No child should ever be alone that way, and she'd made sure Molly had never been alone.

It had reawakened something in her. A longing. And watching Bryce now reminded her of the all things he would have ahead of him, things Molly wouldn't have. She wouldn't have gone home from the hospital, wouldn't have slept in a crib, wouldn't have had toys to play with. All those weeks sitting with Molly in the hospital, holding her, singing to her, she'd wanted to pretend things could be normal for the child, but she'd known…as a nurse, she'd known. All those weeks with Charles calling her crazy for getting involved. Hopeless was what he'd called Molly. But Dinah had never seen hopeless. All she'd seen had been a sick child who'd had no one but her.

How could she have been so wrong about Charles? He was a pediatrician. He was supposed to love children, no matter what their condition. Through Molly, what she'd come to know had been a man who could barely tolerate them.

How could she have been so blind?

Now, watching Bryce, and feeling so connected to him, the longing to be part of something so good was stirring again. It would be nice to sit and cradle him in her arms the way she had Molly, to whisper motherly things in his tiny ear. It was a feeling that scared her, though, because she knew the pain of loss when it ended. It was unbearable. So deep and profound nothing could touch it or make it better.

Not ever.

With her marriage to Damien, shortly after she'd graduated from nursing school, she'd wanted all the right things—the nice little house with a white picket fence. Wanted to bake pies for her husband and cool them on the windowsill in the afternoon so their sweet aromas would waft down to him as he came home from work. Wanted children playing in the yard. Wanted to snuggle with him in the evening after the children were in bed, and talk about the things that were interesting to no one but themselves—how their days had been, who they'd met on the street, what they were going to do tomorrow, and next week and next year. But that was a dream life that hadn't come true as Damien had been bored with their daydreams by the end of their first year together and already working on a way to find his life with someone else. And here she was now, at thirty-four, fresh from the last daydream fiasco with Charles, older but, apparently, not much wiser.

Well, experience was the best teacher. Maybe she had a tendency to let her heart rule her head, but this time her head was fastened on better. Avoid relationships and the problems didn't happen.

"He looks so peaceful, you wouldn't know what he's just gone through, would you?" Eric asked.

"Eric!" she gasped, startled that he'd been able to sneak up on her like that. She'd been too lost in the daydream she didn't want to have, too caught up in something she couldn't allow herself, and this lapse in judgment had everything to do with him. Not that he would be interested in her that way. Yet he was practically hanging over her shoulder now. Standing much too close. So close, in fact, that the scent of soap on his skin threatened to tip her right back into her daydream.

As a preventative to the thoughts trying to creep in, Dinah moved round to the other side of the baby's crib, laid her hands on the raised rails and relaxed a little. She was safe here, keeping so many physical obstacles between her and Eric, even if Eric didn't know what she was doing, or how she was feeling, being so close to him. "Babies are resilient. Much more than we are, I think."

"Is that why you chose pediatrics?" he asked.

"Actually, my most recent choice was a kitchen in a ski lodge." It was a blatant dodge, but she didn't want to talk about it, didn't want to look up at him for fear he could find the answers he was seeking in her eyes. And they were there, she was sure of it.

"Before that."

"In my life, *before that* doesn't matter," she said, her voice now a whisper. "I've had a few of those and now I am what I am in the moment. Don't expect anything else." He was going to respond to that. In fact, she was so sure of it she practically held her breath waiting for it, but when he didn't, Dinah finally did look up. "No response?" she asked. "No pithy little comeback?"

"Something I learned a long time ago is that when people drop those kinds of explosive statements, it's best to back away. If they want to explain it, they will. If they don't, you're at a safe distance." He grinned. "Right now, I like the safety in this distance."

"I appreciate that," she said. And truly she did. There was no point starting a new life and blurting out all the unhappy parts of the old one every time the opportunity arose. While she wasn't really here to make new friends, or find a new start, she did want to make the most of the next few weeks, especially with the people she might see occasionally. And Eric Ramsey…she had a hunch she'd be seeing him again. Nothing social, nothing even very friendly. But there was something about saving a life together that pulled people closer, at least for a little while. Besides, Eric might be here when she came to check on little Bryce. So why beat him over the head with all her baggage for what would amount to a few casual moments here and there? "People don't know when to observe boundaries. They step over the line, assume they have rights where they really have none, and the next thing you know…" They're cheating on you, or walking out of your life. "Thank you, Eric."

"Thank you, Dinah." He spoke the words, but even in the dim light his eyes said more. So much more it startled her.

"I…um…I'm glad we were able to work together." His intense stare on her was unsettling. It was making her nervous. Causing her hands to shake. Yet she couldn't look away. Wanted to, but could not. "And I'm even more glad that things are going to work out for Bryce and Gabby." The conversation was turning just plain awkward now. There was nothing more to say except goodbye. Yet she didn't want to. Not yet. "Anyway… I, um…I guess this is goodbye. I need to get back to Angela, and um…" Was it hot in here? Because she was suddenly burning up. "I'm sure we'll see each other again while I'm in White Elk. So…" She needed a fan, her cheeks were blazing so furiously. "So, I'll see you around."

"See you around, Dinah Corday." He winked.

Eric's voice so sexy she went weak in the knees. Maybe she was tired. Everything was catching up to her and a few hours' sleep would take care of whatever this was coming over her. Yes, that had to be it. She was tired. Her body was giving out on her. "Around," she repeated, not making the slightest move to leave.

Suddenly, Eric was around on her side of the crib, and before she realized what was going on...or maybe she did realize what was going on and didn't want to do anything about it, she was in his arms. Locked into a kiss. Deep, urgent. Lips pressed so hard she could scarcely find breath. Her arms snaked up around his neck like they'd done it a thousand times before, and her body willed itself into a tight press to his, until she could almost feel corded muscles, almost find her way deep inside him. But as suddenly as the kiss had started, it stopped. His awareness...her awareness... What they were doing shoved them apart with such a force that it was like a physical punch, one that knocked her back.

Of all the crazy, stupid things to do! How could she have?

And how could her knees still be wobbly from the force of one simple kiss?

Except it hadn't been simple. Nothing about that kiss had been simple, and she was reeling to find an explanation. What had caused it? Had it been about two people caught up in the moment, two people who'd waged the battle together and won? A kiss of celebration?

Yes, that made sense. A kiss of celebration. That sounded feasible, or feasible enough. Plus, she was tired. Exhausted.

Except it was a kiss that shook her to the very core. One that made her knees wobble so hard she had to grab hold of the crib rails. "I...I didn't mean for that to happen," she stammered. "I've been accused of overreacting in emotional situations, and I think you've just seen that." Although she'd never, ever, kissed anyone so impulsively before. "Sorry." Lame excuse, but it was the best she could do. "So, it's been a long day. Like I said, I want to go spend some time with Angela, see if we can get up to the lodge so I can finally get settled in."

If ever there was a perfect time to make her exit, this was it. Eric hadn't said word, not one single word in reaction. So all she had to do was grab up what was left of her strength, forget her dignity, since that was long gone, hold her head high and walk out the door. Except her feet wouldn't move when she tried. Both were planted firmly to the tiled floor and going nowhere soon. Or maybe she simply didn't want to walk around him and risk falling into his arms again.

Eric didn't move either. And his face, even in the dim lights, was painted with sheer panic and perplexity. A sure sign of what he was thinking, which embarrassed her even more. It wasn't like she'd kissed every doctor with whom she'd shared a victory, because she hadn't. Yet one minute she was telling him to keep his boundaries, and the next minute those boundaries had tumbled down—that emotional overreaction Charles had berated her for. Maybe Charles had been right when he'd told her she was more suited, emotionally, to the kitchen. "Look, Eric, I shouldn't have—"

He thrust out his hand to stop her. Still scowling. Still perplexed. "What you did today with Bryce was nothing short of amazing, Dinah. I don't want to take anything away from that."

In the uncomfortable moment between them, she shrugged for the lack of a better response.

"And for the record, I'm sorry about the way I behaved after we had that little collision on the road."

"It doesn't matter," she managed, barely sounding any more steady than she felt.

"But it does. I'd had one hell of a morning, between the floods and the hospital. My twin girls have been sick, and I had to leave to make sure they were safe, then I had to get back to the hospital right away. But they were frightened.

Wanted me to stay home with them. Cried, begged. And nothing pulls at your heart harder than two little girls begging for you to stay. So I stayed longer than I should have, was distracted when I finally did leave, and you…" He chuckled nervously, "Well, you know the rest of the story."

The rest of the story? Did he mean the part where she'd just kissed a married man? Somehow, with the casual way he acted around her, she wouldn't have guessed that about him. Who was she kidding, though? Her life was a testament to not guessing the right thing. And the right thing with Eric was that he wasn't only married, but married with children. A man with huge entanglements.

Well, something in her life was finally simple. One kiss, *and he'd been a willing part of it*, was where it ended. Actually, she was glad about that because her judgment wasn't going to be tested on this. They'd met their final boundary. Nothing came after it. Period. No doubts, no questions, nothing to wonder about. "How old are they?" she asked, at last finding enough strength to push her toward the door. "Your twins? How old are they?"

"Five, going on twenty-one. Spoiled rotten, and I'm not ashamed to admit it."

"Their names?" she asked, backing her way around Eric, keeping herself well clear of him as he stood at the end of the crib.

"Pippa. She's older by nine minutes, and she's the outgoing one. My little extrovert who can't stay out of trouble. And Paige, my very serious introvert who tends to be more clingy than anything."

By the time she got to the door leading to the hall, she half expected Eric to flip a photo wallet out of his pocket, like a kiss followed by a trip through the family archives was all in a day's work for him. But he didn't. Rather, he turned around, popped his stethoscope into his ears and had a good look at Bryce. Checked his breath sounds, his heart, his reflexes, probably glad for that whole awkward episode to be over with.

That's when Dinah escaped.

"Don't let me keep you from your wife any longer," she bit out as she fled the ICU. She made it to the hall, got halfway down it and sagged against the wall. What was she doing? How could she have failed to notice the ring on his finger? And how, even now, knowing what she did about Eric Ramsey, was his kiss was still lingering on her lips? It burned all the way through her, and as she raised her fingers to her lips, she knew it would linger a while longer. Against her will. Or maybe because of her will.

For a moment, she'd thought Eric was different. But he was like the rest of them, wasn't he? Her father who'd walked out on this family, her husband who'd cheated on her, her fiancé who'd seen a weakness in her and exploited it. Well, she'd been gullible again. It was her history. Her habit. They spoke, she believed, she got hurt.

The masses of humanity in the hall were cloying, as she regained enough strength to fight her way through them to get to her sister. So many people with no place to go, people reaching out, people in pain. But Dinah was in her own unbelievable pain, and she didn't see them all through the tears stinging her eyes. She was hurt, angry, but mostly humiliated. Her fault entirely. She had to get away. Had to find Angela and get out of there. But she was almost half the way to the waiting area when Eric caught up to her.

"Dinah!" he yelled over the crowd.

She heard him, but didn't stop.

"Dinah!" he yelled again, catching up to her and falling

into step. "Did you think I'd leave my wife at home with the girls while I was out hitting on you? Is that why you ran out? Because you thought I was…" He glanced down at the ring on his finger. "That I'd kiss you the way I did if I was…"

She tried to twist away from him and go the other direction, but Eric stepped in front of her then stepped in front of her again when she turned yet another way. "Look, Eric. I'll give you credit where it's due. You're a good doctor. But other than that, you do what you have to do, as long as it doesn't involve me. OK? I don't like men like you. No, let me restate that. I *hate* men like you, and I pity the women who keep falling for them because the result is always the same no matter how much they believe they're the one who will finally change him, finally tame the beast in him. Men like you don't tame. Once you've had a taste of what it's like to step outside the bounds of normal decency, you don't step back in. So, leave me alone. We've done what we had to do, and there's no reason to continue…anything."

Deep breath, Dinah, she kept telling herself. *Calm down*. This wasn't Damien Corday, her husband, who'd had the decency to wait six months into their marriage before cheating on her. It wasn't her father, a man who'd left his family because it hadn't been the family he'd wanted. Wasn't even Charles Lansing who'd turned on her in such a profound, hurtful way. This was Eric Ramsey, who was trying to cheat on Mrs. Eric Ramsey. Yes, pity the poor wife. But this time it was truly none of her business.

"Do I get to defend myself?"

"Against what?" Dinah snapped. She wouldn't look up at him, wouldn't take a long, slow journey into those gorgeous brown eyes because if she did she might do something stupid, like believe him. And the last thing she ever intended to do again was believe anything any man had to say. Sure, it was reactionary, but she had good cause to react the way she did.

"Against your accusations. You get to fling them at me, so I should have the opportunity to deflect them. To defend myself."

"I don't care what you have to say, Eric, because I've heard…*everything*. All the excuses, all the explanations. All the lies. There's nothing new under the sun, you know."

He opened his mouth to speak, to compound his lie, to make an even bigger fool of her, but at that very same moment a tiny figure in a pink rain slicker came running through the hall, directly to Eric, followed by an identical little figure in another pink rain slicker.

"Daddy!" Eric spun to see them, then braced himself against the inevitable as both little girls launched themselves into his arms at the very same time.

Galoshes halfway to their knees, rain slickers all the way down to the galoshes, rain hats covering up most of their faces, it was hard to see the little girls, but Dinah's heart did pound a little harder as Eric went down on one knee and scooped them both up into his embrace. They were giggling and laughing and splashing him with water dripping from their slickers, almost knocking him flat on his back in their exuberance.

"OK, girls," their mother said, coming up from behind. "I told you not to overwhelm your father. Remember he's been doing a very difficult surgery, and he's tired."

"But we brought him cookies," one of the girls cried.

"We've been baking," the woman Dinah took to be Eric's wife said. "And baking, and baking. They were bored, and they missed you."

"Well, you know how I love your cookies!" Eric exclaimed, extricating himself from the girls and standing up. Once he was fully upright, both girls immediately latched on to him again, one girl holding on to each of his legs.

"Are you coming home now, Daddy?" one of the girls asked.

"Sorry, but I can't leave here yet. We're too busy. Too many people still coming in and you know Daddy has to stay here and take care of them."

"Then can we stay here and help?" the girls cried in unison. "Please, Daddy, can we stay?"

He looked at the woman, who shrugged. "I'm going to sit with Gabby, and Debbie's coming in shortly to look after the girls. So it's fine with me if they stay for a while," she said. "Maybe you can take a break with them later on?"

"How can I say no to taking a break with my two best girls?" Eric said. He took hold of the brims of both their rain hats and shoved them up. "But first I want you to say hello to Dinah Corday. She's the nurse who helped me in surgery today. The surgery I did on Dr. Evans's baby."

Totally unaware of her presence there, in this cozy family scene, until they spun to face her, they both ran immediately to Dinah and grabbed her like she was their long-lost friend. "Hello," she said tentatively.

"Hello," they said in unison. "Do you want to eat some of Daddy's cookies?" one of the girls continued.

"That's Pippa," Eric said. "Without the rain gear, you'll be able to tell her from Paige because Pippa has brown eyes like me, and Paige has hazel eyes like her mother. Other than that, they're identical."

"And I'm taller," the one Dinah believed was Paige said. "By half an inch."

"Only when you're standing on your tiptoes," Pippa argued.

"Do not," Paige protested.

"Do, too," Pippa countered.

"And so goes the Ramsey family," Eric said, laughing. "Oh, and, Dinah. I'd like you to meet my *sister*, Janice Laughlin. The girls and I live with her, and she watches them when I'm working."

Eric lived with his sister? Suddenly the heat of embarrassment began its creep from her neck, up her throat, to her cheeks. "Hello," she said, almost choking over the single word.

"But Daddy's going to get us a great big house of our own soon, where we can have a dog and…" Paige started.

"A cat," Pippa finished.

Dinah chanced a glance at Eric, whose expression was an odd one, caught between pain and amusement. He wanted to laugh, or cry. She couldn't tell which. And she wasn't sure she wanted to know. "Look, it's nice to meet all of you…Janice, Paige, Pippa. But I've really got to go and find my sister."

"Can we go see the baby?" Pippa cried. "Please?"

"Pretty please?" Paige joined in.

"Not right now," Eric said, trying to take a firm hand. "He's not feeling very well. But maybe in a few days."

But Eric wasn't very good at that firm hand, and it showed. Even to a casual observer such as herself, Dinah saw that he was just plain gooey when it came to his little girls. They had him wrapped around their little fingers, and he enjoyed every bit of it. He would be a very indulgent father, Dinah decided. And a very good one. Something also told her that Eric wasn't a man cheating on his wife. He was a man getting over something painful, for which she felt very bad. So bad, in fact, that she turned away without saying another word, and practically ran into the room where Angela was sitting, waiting for Gabby to return from seeing her baby. "Tell me about Eric," she whispered to Angela.

"What do you want to know?"

"Is he married?"

CHAPTER THREE

"Why, I do believe you're flustered, Dinah." A smile crept to Angela's face as Dinah paced back and forth in the tiny hospital waiting room. "He is handsome, though, isn't he? Nice man. Smart. Good doctor, too."

"But is he married?"

"Oh, my… I guess you wouldn't know, would you?"

"Know what?"

"That he's a widower. I don't know the circumstances, except that it happened a long time ago, before he moved to White Elk."

Horror heaped on humiliation. She'd kissed him then accused him of something terrible. "He wears a wedding ring."

Her sister raised an inquisitive eyebrow. "I guess it's hard for him to let go. Is there something you want to tell me, Dinah?"

She shook her head, too upset to speak. From the moment he'd run into her on the road until now, nothing had been right between them except, perhaps, the way they'd worked together. Admittedly, that had been brilliant. A perfect medical union. Rare, especially for two strangers.

The kiss had been perfect, too. More perfect than she'd

known a kiss could be. But she couldn't tell her sister because that kiss had been a huge mistake. Had meant nothing. After all, she'd been kissed before, and no kiss in her life had ever meant a thing. So, why should this one?

"Well, for what it's worth," Angela said, breaking into Dinah's thoughts, "I've hardly ever seen him come up to Pine Ridge, so once you're settled in there, and working, you probably won't run into him again. *If that's what you want.* At least, until I have my baby and you have to come to the hospital and visit me. And maybe you can work that out so you won't be here when he is." She laughed, and a wide grin spread over her face. "Unless you want to be where he is."

"I'm not interested," Dinah insisted.

"I didn't say you were."

"But that's what you were thinking."

"What I was thinking was that you're a little too…" She faked a frown, pretended to think. "What's the word I'm looking for? Is it…preoccupied? You're a little too preoccupied by the man. Or obsessed."

"Am not!" Dinah argued as yet another good, firm, and very telling blush spread over her cheeks on account of Eric.

"Whatever you say."

"I say I'm not preoccupied. And I'm not obsessed, either."

"Whatever you say."

"I said I'm not!" Dinah protested again, yet the heat kept rising in her, along with the timbre of her voice. OK, so she'd never been a very good liar. As a child, that little trait had been the bane of her existence, like when she'd tried to explain away the missing candy from the bowl on her grandmother's coffee table, or when she'd been late to school. "And I don't want to talk about it anymore." Even though, avoidance was a good plan. If she avoided Eric, there would be no more hostilities, no more humiliation. No more kisses. The problem was, she wanted to see him. Bad problem. Bad, *bad* problem. Because she didn't know why. Which caused the heat in her cheeks to positively flame.

What the hell had that been about? Eric kicked the trash can next to his desk, knocking it over, spilling out the paper contents. It had been about a kiss, that's what. And now he felt as guilty as hell. Sure, he was a red-blooded man. He hadn't been without certain desires all this time. But desiring and acting on those desires were two different things, and he wasn't ready to act on them. Had never come close to acting on them, and suddenly, that was the only thing on his mind.

Five years was a long time—a lifetime of feeling married yet not having his wife here. But that's what his life had turned into. And he didn't regret it, because he truly wasn't ready to change things. The girls needed their mother's memory kept alive, and he was the only one who could do that. They were so young, and all they knew were the things he told them, so how could it be time to move past that point?

Swallowing hard, Eric looked at Patricia's picture on his desk. God, he missed her. His friends, even Janice kept telling him it was time to get on with his life, but he didn't feel like it was time. He was waiting for…well, he wasn't sure. Maybe a sign? Or, a push?

But not a kiss. That had been a mistake. Still, it had been a nice kiss, one that had reaffirmed the fact that he still had passions, albeit buried pretty deeply. Big mistake, though, because the feelings that had come immediately after… Then practically being accused of cheating on his wife when, in fact, that's exactly what he felt like, pounded him hard. He hadn't kissed a woman other than Patricia for ten years. Hadn't ever wanted to. So what was it about Dinah that had caused that to happen? And make no mistake, he'd been the one to step up to her and pull her into his arms. His initiative, his kiss.

He felt like hell for it. Pure hell.

What's more, he didn't trust himself not to do it again.

Bending down, he righted the trash can, then stood back up and studied it for a moment. Then kicked it again.

"You're stirring that sauce like a woman possessed."

Dinah spun away from the stove and almost bumped into Eric. She'd thought about him a thousand times these past few days, thought about the kiss, too, and would have called him, ostensibly to check on Bryce, even though she'd been kept up to date with the baby's progress via her sister. Which left her no reason to call Eric and stir things up between them again, except she did want to apologize for what she'd said. She'd even considered driving down to White Elk to set things straight with him. But how could she face him when she'd practically accused him of being a liar and a cheat?

Avoidance was easier, she decided. She and Eric didn't have any kind of relationship going, they owed each other nothing, had no expectations. So, for her, this was the best thing to do. She was good at it, had had a lifetime of practice. "You're not supposed to be in the kitchen. Didn't you see the sign on the door?"

"I did." He stepped a little closer, looking into the saucier on the stovetop. "Hollandaise sauce?"

"Bordelaise. And you can't be in here, looking at my Bordelaise."

"Actually, I can. I'm one of the on-call county health

inspectors. It gets me into pretty much any place I want to go. Including your kitchen."

His brown eyes twinkled so brightly she had to avert her eyes, stare at loaves of bread she'd pulled out of the oven just a while ago. "So this is an inspection?" Whirling back to the stove, she returned her wobbly attention to the thickening sauce, trying to ignore the fact that he was standing so close to her. "Aren't you supposed to notify us when you're going to do that?"

"No. That defeats the purpose of trying to find infractions. If you know I'm coming, you hide things."

She picked up a long-handled spoon and began to stir, only to find that her sauce was already sticking to the bottom of the saucier. Curdled beyond repair and sticking to the pan. He had been there less than two minutes and she'd managed to ruin the Bordelaise, so what was it about Eric Ramsey that did that to her? The high humiliation factor? Because she certainly seemed to humiliate herself every time she was near him. "So, inspect. Help yourself. Check the pantry, the cold storage. And don't forget the freezer. Or the grease traps." She set aside the ruined sauce, and decided not to start over until he was gone. Bordelaise could be delicate and she didn't want to mess up another one.

"You can't use that, can you?" he asked pointing to the saucier. "Any way to resurrect it?"

"Is insulting my culinary skills part of your duty as inspector?" she snapped. Why didn't he leave? Why did he make her hands shake?

She looked down at her trembling hands, and jammed them into to her pants pockets before he noticed.

"Your cooking skills looked pretty good. Not as good as your nursing skills, though."

"Former nursing skills," she insisted, feeling the bite of nostalgia already.

"Well, whatever you're calling yourself these days, I wanted to tell you that Bryce was sent up to Salt Lake City, he's had his second surgery, and he's doing fine. Came through beautifully."

"You could have phoned."

"I could have, but then I wouldn't have been able to give you these."

He jiggled a bag. She heard the paper crinkle, but she wasn't sensing what could be in the bag, and it was quite clear that he wasn't about to tell her. In other words, it was her move. If she wanted to find out, she'd have to turn around and look...look at what was in the bag. Look at him. Look into his eyes. "What?" she asked, without giving in.

"These." He jiggled the bag again, teasing her.

OK, so now her interest was piqued. She turned. Studied the brown bag for a moment. Thrust out her hand to take it. Inside were six cookies, chocolate chip. Misshapen, a little overdone. And quite obviously a gift from his daughters. "You've taken up baking?" she asked, trying to sound disinterested as she pulled out a cookie and headed straight to the fridge for milk.

"The only thing I bake is a frozen dinner, in the microwave, and technically I don't think that's even considered baking, is it?"

Dinah poured two mugs of milk and handed one to Eric. "Chocolate-chip cookies always have to have milk."

"Do you dunk?" he asked.

"Of course I dunk! Is there any other way to eat a chocolate-chip cookie?"

Eric pulled a cookie from the bag and was the first one to dunk. Dinah followed suit, took a bite, and swallowed. Politely. Trying not to make the face Eric was making. "They lack a little in refinement," he said. "But they're getting better."

At five, she and Angela had been baking cookies like pros. With help from their mother, of course. But Pippa and Paige didn't have a mother, and suddenly, she felt sad for them, sad for the things Eric's little girls were missing. Dinah knew how it felt having a parent missing from her life, but her parent had left by choice. He hadn't wanted daughters, or a woman capable of giving him only daughters. Pippa and Paige's situation was so different, so tragic. "Maybe I could give them a lesson or two. If you don't mind?" The offer was genuine, although she didn't know where it had come from. Dinah instantly regretted it because helping the girls would keep her in closer contact with Eric. That was something she didn't want, and could ill afford.

"You'd do that? Teach the girls to cook? Janice has been supervising them in the kitchen, but her skills are, well, not much better than theirs. But if you could spend a little time with the girls…" He dunked his cookie, and studied it for a moment. "They love cooking, and doing so many of the little-girl things I can't do with them. So, if you really want to do this, I'd appreciate it, because I've got a lot of years ahead of me, eating these things." He popped the last of his cookie into his mouth and washed it down with the milk. Big gulps of milk.

They agreed that the following afternoon would be good for the first cookie lesson then Dinah returned to her dinner preparation. But Eric didn't leave right away. He simply stood back, watching her, which made her nervous. Finally, after she fumbled her way through adding too much vinegar to a vinaigrette then having to compensate for her mistake, she confronted him. "Look, Eric. You can't stay here. If you're going to inspect the kitchen, or any part of the restaurant, do it. If not, please leave. I'm not a very organized cook yet, as you can tell, and you're distracting me. And I've got to get dinner service up and going within the next hour."

"I had dinner here last night. You're pretty good."

"You did?" That surprised her. But she never looked into the dining room, so she wouldn't have known.

"I was curious to see how you were doing. Janice and my niece, Debbi, took the girls out for pizza and a movie. I had an evening off. So I decided to come and see for myself."

"And?"

"It was good. Better than that thing I was going to throw into the microwave."

Dinah laughed. "That's high praise, coming from an obvious gastronome such as yourself."

"OK, so I'd just as soon eat a cheese sandwich as the Filet Oscar I had last night. Over the years, I've gotten used to less-than-polished meals. But as meals go, I'd say yours was pretty polished. In fact, I might eat here again some time. Might even ask you to come and be a nurse in my trauma department again some time. Our nurse practitioner, Fallon O'Gara, is going away on a short holiday, and I thought…"

"You thought wrong!" she snapped, spinning away from him and heading straight into the walk-in pantry. Once inside, she felt like closing the door behind her and turning off the light. Maybe that would make him go away. Or maybe all the bad thoughts would disappear in the dark, vanish into some little black crevice and never return.

"Dinah!" he called through the door.

"I'm busy!" she yelled back. It hurt, and she knew it showed. She didn't want him to see, didn't want him to know that one little kiss had turned her already-confused situation into more confusion than she was able to deal with. "Please, just let me do my work."

He opened the door, but didn't enter. Didn't turn on the light either. "Why did you leave nursing, Dinah? What happened? Because I took the liberty of checking your credentials, and—"

"You what?" she sputtered, flying out of the pantry and slamming the pouches of gravy starter she'd grabbed from a shelf down on the counter. "How…how could you do that?"

"I was curious. You're too insistent that you don't want to be a nurse, yet you're so passionate about it. Since I had every intention of offering you a temporary job, I checked."

"Well, good for you. Now you know." And she wanted to crawl off somewhere and be alone.

"I was told that you were competent. Competent, that's all. Which doesn't make any sense, because I saw you work. Saw how good you are."

"It's none of your business!" she snapped.

"It became my business when you stepped into my operating room to assist me."

"Which wasn't exactly my choice, if you recall. You were the one who wanted me there."

"And I don't regret that because I saw what you can do. Saw your passion. Which is why I don't understand what I was told."

"Well, believe it. It's true. I was competent. That's all there is to say, except I'm not looking for a nursing job. So you can leave now." She marched over to the hanging rack above the center prep island, grabbed a large copper pot down off its hook and slammed it down on the stove top. When it didn't slam hard enough to satisfy her, Dinah picked up the pan and slammed it again, harder this time. "What gives you the right?" she cried, spinning to face him. "I came here to cook, and to be left alone. Not to have someone like you dig into my past."

"Your past doesn't reconcile with what I saw."

"And it doesn't have to. I quit nursing. Walked away from it, and that's the end of the story. If you still want me to give your girls cooking lessons, I'll do that. But after that you have to leave me alone. That's the deal, Eric. Take it or leave it. I'll help your girls, but that's as far as we go." She brushed past Eric and went to the cold storage, where she grabbed six large onions, bundled them into her apron, and marched straight back to the prep area. "And you don't get to ask questions. That's also part of this deal."

"Then I have to accept it, don't I?"

"Do you?" Rather than waiting for an answer, Dinah set about the chore of prepping onions. Peeling off skins, cutting off both ends, she lit into them, fast and furious, alternately swiping at the onion tears with the back of the sleeve of her chef's jacket and chopping like a woman possessed.

"Look, Dinah, it was only a kiss. OK? People do it all the time and it doesn't usually mean anything."

She chopped even faster, the sound of her knife striking the cutting board and never breaking rhythm.

"I apologize for it, and that's all I can say. I'm sorry we did it, sorry I upset you."

The speed of her chopping picked up even more. In fact, she was whooshing through her little pile of onions so fast it surprised her.

"But I'd like us to get past that, and be friends. For my girls' sakes. Can we do that?" Her knife slipped. She whacked her finger, and blood immediately spilled out onto her cutting surface.

Dinah dropped her knife and jumped back, not reacting from pain because she didn't yet feel the pain. But the sight of blood on the butcher block… "I was a damned good nurse," she whispered, taking the kitchen towel Eric held out to her. "Better than competent."

"I know that. So, let me take a look at your finger," he said, taking hold of her hand.

But she pulled back from him. "It's a nick. I'm fine. Just…just leave me alone." Hurrying over to the sink, she ran cold water over her wound, and once the blood was washed away, she assessed the severity.

"You're right," he said, taking his place at her side. "It's only a nick. You'll be fine." He pulled a bandage from the kitchen first-aid kit and wrapped it around her cut, his fingers so gentle on her she shivered. "You OK?" he asked, when the gooseflesh rose on her arms.

"I'm busy, and this is taking up too much time." She slid her hand from his grasp and fought hard not to shiver again as her flesh slid across his. Even so, the goosebumps remained.

"So, what happened, Dinah?"

"The knife slipped."

"You know what I mean."

She did. He wanted to know things she didn't talk about. Deep, hurtful things. But she could make it simple, make it impersonal, then he'd go away. "I was engaged to a man who thought I was better suited to the kitchen than the hospital." She held up her finger. "And as you can see, I'm not that well suited to the kitchen. But I promise to keep the knives away from your girls if you still want me to teach them."

"Why do I get the feeling that you're making light of something that's not light at all?"

"It's complicated. And not very interesting. And if you agree to the cooking lessons then you drop this. You don't talk about it, don't ask questions, don't express an opinion. It's over, I've moved on, and that includes to the kitchen, not the hospital. That's the deal, the only deal."

"One opinion, then consider it dropped. I want you to

know that *I know* you're a talented nurse. One of the best I've ever seen. If it's the kitchen you want, that's fine, but that man who was supposed to love you enough to marry you was wrong. Now, no more opinions. I want you to teach my daughters how to bake."

It was a deal that left a bitter taste, apparently for both of them because the memories of that betrayal hurt Dinah, and because Eric wanted to know more. Much more. But couldn't ask. This was how it had to be, though. Dinah was reconciled to that because her history repeated itself and, for once, she was fighting hard not to let that happen again. Eric tempted her, and she caught herself wanting to be tempted. But she couldn't let herself be. It was as simple as that. Or as difficult.

Yet one glance into Eric Ramsey's eyes and she wondered if she could do what had to be done. Because he stirred things inside her she'd never known could be stirred.

"I thought you'd be at the hospital." At least, Dinah had hoped he'd be there, which didn't turn out to be the case because he was standing in the doorway, looking drop-dead gorgeous in his jeans and black T-shirt. A distraction like that was something she didn't need and, for a moment, she considered cancelling the cookie lesson, or postponing it until he was gone. But while she struggled against taking a second lip-licking look at Eric, a whirlwind from behind literally pitched him forward, almost into her arms—a giggling, squealing whirlwind of little girls, which jolted her back into the moment, and into the recognition that this was not about her, or Eric. She'd made a promise to Pippa and Paige, and she couldn't break it.

"Sorry about that," he said, shoving off her and trying to stand upright against the twin force jumping up and down behind his back. "They've been excited about this all morning. I couldn't calm them down."

Pippa and Paige each wore a tiny version of a chef's apron. If it weren't for the fact that the aprons were embroidered with their names, she wouldn't have been able to tell the girls apart, they looked so much alike. Pippa had the brown eyes, she remembered, while Paige had the hazel—if they stood still long enough to get a good look. Which wasn't the case right now. Pretty girls. Exuberant. They looked like Eric, with dark hair and beautiful, perfect smiles.

"We have lots of chocolate chips, if Paige didn't eat them all," Pippa said.

"Did not," Paige defended.

"Saw you," Pippa argued.

"Saw *you*," Page retorted.

"Which is why you should always buy twice as many chocolate chips as the recipe calls for," Dinah interrupted, stepping around Eric and entering the house. Nice house. Homey. But it didn't suit Eric. Of course, it wasn't Eric's house. He lived with his sister. "That way, you'll have enough for your cookies, and enough for your tummies."

The girls each latched on to one of Dinah's hands, and pulled her toward the kitchen in a collective effort. "We got everything ready last night," Pippa said. "And checked it again this morning to make sure nobody took anything." She gave her sister a dubious look, one which was returned.

"Good luck," Eric said from the doorway. He was standing there, filling up the frame, arms folded casually across his chest. Smiling.

"I think we'll manage quite nicely," she replied, wishing he'd go away. She didn't want him there, didn't want to keep looking to see what he was watching, afraid that he was watching her, afraid that he wasn't. "Am I going to teach you how to bake cookies, too?" Hopefully he'd take the hint and leave.

"On call all night, on duty all morning. Meaning nap time for me."

He did look tired. But it was a long-time weariness she saw more than anything else, and her heart went out to him. His life couldn't be easy. Between his work and his girls she doubted Eric had any time left over for himself. "We'll save some cookies for you," she promised, then turned away. Her thoughts were too cozy, she had no business sympathizing with the man. Had no business having any kind of thoughts about him.

As she began to hunt for the proper bowls, Eric motioned Paige and Pippa over to him. "Girls, Daddy's going to sleep for a little while. Be good for Dinah. Do what she tells you to do, and come get me when the last batch comes out of the oven because I like my cookies warm." With that, he kissed each one on the top of her head, then plodded down the hall. Seconds later, the distinct thud of a shutting door told Dinah she could relax. Suddenly, though, it was just her and two eager, ricocheting little girls. Sick children she knew how to deal with. But these girls…

It probably wasn't the nicest thing for him to do, leaving her in the kitchen with the girls. They were high energy on a normal day and this wasn't a normal day for them. But he couldn't be there. Couldn't watch the cozy scene going on. Back in the days when Patricia had been pregnant with the twins, she'd had so many plans, so many hopes and dreams for her family. And sometimes the cruel bite of how unfair life was simply got to him. Today was one of those days. It should have been Patricia teaching her girls to cook, Patricia and the girls in *their* kitchen, not in his sister's. Seeing Dinah in there, doing something that should have been Patricia's to do, tore at his heart, and it had nothing to do with Dinah. She was just being nice.

But, damn it, the girls were all over her, so happy to be involved in such a simple thing. When Dinah had volunteered to do this, it had sounded like a good idea. But now the reality of it made him question why he'd wanted to bring Dinah closer to their lives. The girls had a hard enough time hanging on to a mother they'd never known, and this wasn't going to make his task of keeping Patricia in their lives any easier. But something was nagging at him to move on with his life. It had been for a while, and Dinah only accentuated it.

Just look at him! An adult with children, living in his sister's home, making do. Postponing life. Refusing to move forward.

Back in California, before he'd agreed to come to White Elk, he'd had his mother to help him. She'd swooped in to take care of the girls, and promised to stay as long as he needed her. Which had turned out to be until the time he'd moved to White Elk and allowed his sister to do the same thing. He'd taken an apartment here, hired a nanny for his daughters, planning on putting life on a permanent delay. Janice had come here, with his niece shortly after, solely to help him, once it had become clear he was struggling to manage without family. Once she'd got here, she'd found a real life right away. She'd bought a house, established a business, made friends everywhere. On the other hand, he'd moved in with her, at her request, to make her care of the twins more convenient, while he'd secluded himself at the hospital. His life on an even bigger delay.

That's exactly what it was, and most of the time he

didn't think about that because it worked well enough. The girls were happy, they didn't feel the pressures. Right now, though, with Dinah assuming a mother's duty… "Damn," he muttered, dropping onto his bed. A single bed. For one. Grown men didn't sleep in single beds, and this was just another reminder of how he'd allowed things to get out of hand. It was his duty to make sure his daughters came first in his life, but what came after them? What was out there for him?

"It's not easy, Patricia," he whispered, looking at the wedding ring on his finger. For a few moments he simply stared at the glint of the gold and the plain contours of it, trying to empty his mind of everything. Yet for once his mind wouldn't empty. It was chock full of memories… good ones like the day he'd met Patricia, the evening he'd proposed marriage, the afternoon they'd married. Flashes of the day she'd learnt she was pregnant were there, the excitement of discovering it was going to be twins… hopes, dreams, futures to plan. But the bad memories were there, too…her obstetrician telling him she'd bled out during the delivery, that she was in a critical condition. Sitting at her bedside, never leaving for three days, never letting go of her hand. Never having the chance to tell her that her daughters were beautiful and healthy…

Eric swiped at the tear straying down his cheek. The kitchen. The damned kitchen is what caused this…what *forced* this. It was time.

He stroked the gold band on his finger, twisted it around, stroked it again. It *was* time. He resisted it, tried to argue himself out of it. Didn't want it. Dear God, he didn't want it. But it had to be time. He needed a life, too. Needed to be normal again. For himself. Especially for Pippa and Paige.

On a deep, sad sigh Eric slipped the wedding band

off his finger, kissed it and held it to his heart for a while. He wasn't sure how long. But eventually he stood, walked over to the dresser and opened the top drawer. There, nestled into the corner, was a small velvet box with another plain gold band. A smaller one. The one he'd placed on Patricia's finger nearly seven years ago, promising her he'd buy her something more beautiful someday. She'd laughed at him, called him silly, told him the plain gold band was all she wanted, that to her it was the most beautiful ring in the world.

It was another few moments before he placed his gold band with hers then, reluctantly, shut the box lid and tucked the box away.

Someday, when the girls were a little older, he would have both rings melted down and made into heart pendants for them. That's why he'd kept Patricia's ring. He'd wanted Pippa and Paige to have it, to have something that had been so loved by her. Now it only seemed right that they would have both rings…rings that belonged together, for ever.

Yes, that was a good idea. And it did give him some comfort as he stared at the empty, stark white band of skin on his finger. Then, for the next few minutes, he leaned against the bedroom door and listened to the laughter coming from the kitchen. It was good, he thought. Bad in so many ways, painful beyond anything he could have expected, but good, too. But, damn, it hurt.

Good, bad, or otherwise, first thing tomorrow he was going to start looking for a house for one dad and two daughters. Yes, it was time for that, too.

Funny, though, how he'd only now come to terms with that after he'd met Dinah. It had nothing to do with her, of course, but the timing was…odd. Unexpected. "One thing at a time," he whispered, plodding into the bathroom to splash cold water on his face. Taking off a wedding ring didn't mean he was going to go out and get involved right away. It was only a first step. Truth was, the second step scared him to death. Especially if it was in the direction of someone who came with so much baggage. And Dinah did have her fair share of it. Yes, one thing at a time, and that didn't include the beautiful nurse-chef-amazing woman who was in the kitchen, teaching his girls how to bake chocolate-chip cookies.

Or did it?

CHAPTER FOUR

"No, THE chocolate chips go in after the flour." Pippa had chocolate smeared all over her face. Paige, on the other hand, had wiped it on her apron. And Dinah was loving every minute of this. In fact, she couldn't remember when she'd had so much fun. It was like everything was right in their world, and their world was all there was. She was drawn into it, and happy to be there.

"But won't the flour turn them all white?" Pippa asked. "Maybe if we put them in first, then cover them up…"

"With more chocolate chips," Paige chimed in. "If we put more chocolate chips on top of the first ones, then the first ones won't get all white from the flour."

"Then how do you keep the ones on top from getting white?" Pippa asked, somewhat miffed.

"It comes off," Dinah said, trying to hold back her laugh. These little girls were deadly serious about this. They wanted to make perfect cookies, and she wondered if they strove for such perfection in everything they did. It was so cute, and she owed Eric a great big thank-you for letting her do this. "Once we get everything all mixed together, and get the cookies in the oven, everything will come right off the chocolate chips."

Both girls frowned at her, like they didn't believe her.

"But Aunt Janice makes us go to another room so she can have room to wipe the chocolate chips clean," Paige said in all earnestness.

Probably because by this time in the process Janice was tired of answering all the questions and wanted to get on with it. By last count, each girl had asked Dinah about a hundred, only she'd thought it was fun trying to find answers for questions she would have never, in her life, anticipated. *Where does salt come from? Who was the first person to ever cook food and how did they know they were cooking if cooking hadn't been invented yet? Wouldn't it be better to have a whole bunch of aprons in different colors to match all the foods so they wouldn't look dirty when food gets spilled on them?*

Maybe for Janice the questions got tiring, but for Dinah they were amazing. She liked the challenge. Liked the way the girls thought. But she was concerned that they were trying to be much older than they were and, in effect, losing a little of their childhood. Maybe because their care was, by necessity, left up to so many people? Or maybe because their father wasn't at a place in his life where he knew how to have fun anymore, and the girls mimicked what they saw. "Well, I'm sure Aunt Janice is used to doing it her way, but this way has always worked for me."

The girls looked at each other, considering something unspoken between them—that twin connection—then both came up smiling. "Can I mix?" Pippa asked.

"Me, too?" Page also asked.

"I have two bowls, so I'd say I'm going to need two good mixers." Ten minutes later, with all the ingredients split evenly between the bowls, and mixed as well as any cookie dough had ever been mixed, it was time to get the dough to the cookie pan.

"Let me warn you that this is where they eat more than they bake."

Dinah spun around, almost knocking into Eric, who had crept back to the kitchen and was leaning against the fridge, watching. Barefoot, hair mussed, shirt untucked…wickedly sexy. "Do you always sneak up on people that way?" Her voice was amazingly calm considering how nothing else about her was.

"Only people worth sneaking up on," he said, stepping aside as Dinah brushed herself against him, trying to wedge herself between the fridge and the utility drawer.

"Why aren't you sleeping, Daddy?" Paige asked.

"I discovered I wasn't sleepy. And I thought I would come out here and wait for my cookies."

"Then wait in the dining room," Dinah said, brushing up against him one more time on her way back from the utility drawer. It caused a chill to shoot up her spine, first time, this time. A chill she was fighting to ignore. Why was it that whatever governed one person's attraction to another was working overtime with her right now? She'd never been this wildly attracted to Charles. Hadn't gotten chills *ever* during her brief marriage to Damien. But Eric… It's because she couldn't, that's why! Couldn't have him, couldn't get involved. Couldn't even think about it. Couldn't! And that little streak of opposition in her that knew she *couldn't* was rebelling. Hence the attraction, and the shivers. It was simply a personal little insurrection.

Good explanation, she decided as she handed large spoons to each of the girls. She turned back to insist that Eric step away, but surprisingly he already had. He hadn't gone all the way to the dining room, but he was in the doorway, and the look on his face… It was distant. He was staring out the back window, but if she'd had a paycheck coming in, she'd bet every penny of it he wasn't seeing anything outside.

"How much?" one of the girls said insistently.

"What?" she asked.

"How much cookie dough?"

Pippa had a chunk on her spoon that approximated the amount for six cookies, which snapped Dinah back into the baking lesson. "Not quite that much," she instructed, showing the girls the proper amount. Then she showed them the appropriate spacing of the dough on the pan, and stepped away while they worked to get the unbaked cookies lined up in perfect little rows. Once, when they were halfway through, she looked back at Eric, who was still there. Physically. But his eyes were still so distant.

Propped there against the doorframe, he looked…sad. She studied him for a moment, trying not to be obvious. But something caught her eye. Something missing. So, when had he removed his wedding ring? "No, Paige. You can't squeeze them that close together. They have to have room to expand, so spread them out a little more. Just look at the first row I did, and copy that."

The girls chattered away as they finished putting the dough on the pan, while Dinah supervised. Then, as Dinah, not the girls, placed the cookies in the oven, Eric withdrew from the kitchen altogether. She thought about going after him, asking him if there was anything she could do to help, but her two little assistant cooks weren't about to budge from the kitchen while the timer was counting down the minutes, and she wasn't going to leave them alone in there. So she sat down at the kitchen table and fielded another battery of questions from the girls.

"Who was the one who decided how long a minute was?" Pippa asked.

"And how did he know it was a minute and not an hour, if no one had ever had a minute before?" Paige chimed in.

"The girls are great," Dinah said. She sat a plate of warm cookies on the table on the patio outside. Eric was leaning against the deck rail outside in the backyard, this time looking into the kitchen through the window. "You've done an amazing job with them. And if you don't mind, they want me to take them shopping for…well, let's just say, five-year-old unmentionables."

"Unmentionables?" He arched his eyebrows, even though the eyes underneath them were still distracted.

"Well, panties. Apparently Aunt Janice buys boring panties and your daughters want…"

Eric blinked himself back into the conversation. "They want new panties? You don't have to," he said.

"But I don't mind. And I sort of promised them manicures and hair appointments."

"Manicures? They're five!"

Dinah laughed. "But a girl is never too young to have her hair and fingernails done." Her eyes wanted to trail down to his ring finger, but she resisted. "And Pippa and Paige informed me they've never had a manicure. So…"

"They're growing up." He sighed heavily.

"A little bit."

"And I don't have a clue."

"Well, that's probably true. But it's curable, because I have an idea your daughters will always let you know exactly what they need, and when. Like I said, they're amazing little girls. Full of life."

"Like their mother." He cleared his throat and continued. "The girls and I…we're going to move," he said, out of the blue. "I love my sister, but she's put up with us for too long, without ever complaining. She disrupted her life back in California and moved here with us because she didn't want us coming here alone. But she's the one who got her life together, not me. And I think it's time the girls and I had a place of our own so she can live more of that life."

He was moving out? Did that mean he was starting to move on? Eventually, it always happened. Her mother had, after a while. She herself had, after her divorce from Damien, and in a sense this was part of her moving on from Charles. But Eric's situation was something she couldn't even begin to understand. "You're sure you're ready for this?" she asked, for a lack of something better to say. "I mean, I know that you have to get to a certain point where it feels right, feels like it's time. When Damien and I were married—"

"You were married?" he interrupted.

"Not for long. I was barely in my twenties. Not so smart about relationships. He was…not who I thought he was. The marriage lasted for less than a year, but I stayed near him for a year longer than that because I couldn't force myself to make the move. You know, move on. I suppose I always hoped something would change, that the situation wasn't really what it was. So I left him, reconciled, left, reconciled…"

"And?"

"I wised up when I finally realized that you don't change a cheating husband, no matter what he promises you. No matter how much you want things to be different, some things will never change."

"I'm sorry," he said, rubbing the empty spot on his ring finger. "That had to be rough."

"It was." Because she'd grown up picturing herself living happily-ever-after. Because she'd grown up wanting it. Sadly, she didn't believe in that anymore. "Moving on wasn't easy."

"I know," he said. "Not easy, but necessary. But I've put it off too long, so now…"

"Can we bake some more?" Paige called from the door. "We got them ready on the pan."

"Duty calls," Dinah said, backing away from Eric. "And it's pretty demanding."

"I appreciate this, Dinah. I know we've got a little friction going between us, and I'm sorry about that." He chuckled. "Seems like I'm always apologizing for something, doesn't it? But I do appreciate what you're doing for my girls. And if they need some new *unmentionables* and a manicure, and you don't mind…"

"I don't mind, Eric. In fact, I'm looking forward to it." She glanced down at his empty finger this time, and this time he saw her do it. But he didn't say anything.

"Eric, I'm so sorry," she whispered, laying her hand on his as Pippa ran up, grabbed her by the other hand and started tugging.

"So am I. But it was time."

The broken whisper of his voice broke her heart as her hand slid away from his.

"Pedicures, too?" Eric said, smiling.

"A girl can't really have the full manicure experience without having the pedicure, too." It had been a wonderful morning, and she almost hated turning the girls over to their cousin, Debbi. But the arrangement had been made, and now she had the rest of the day ahead of her with nothing to do as it was her day off. Angela was simply too pregnant to do anything but sit with her feet up and manage the kitchen from that position, so Dinah had a lot of empty hours ahead of her. "I promised them we'd do it again some time. And have high tea in the lodge conservatory. Father permitting, of course."

"You're kidding, aren't you?"

Smile bright, eyes wide, she shrugged. "Actually, no. We all thought it was a brilliant idea."

Eric laughed out loud. "You know they're taking advantage of you, don't you? They're very good at it. Better than I thought, apparently."

"You're probably right. But I'm a willing participant." Besides, she truly enjoyed their company, probably more than she'd thought she would. It was nice, being in the company of children who weren't sick. Although the more she was with the girls, the more she ached to get back to nursing. "I was wondering…would you need someone part-time in the hospital? Maybe the emergency department? I know you mentioned something the other day about nursing, but I thought maybe I could do something as a volunteer." Perhaps being back in a non-medical capacity would help ease the ache. "I could be a clerk, maybe check supplies…"

"Or be a nurse, like I suggested."

She shook her head adamantly. "I told you…"

"No, you didn't. But I agreed not to ask, so I won't. However, I still need a part-time *nurse*, and it's a serious offer."

Nursing scared her, though. In little bits and pieces she was OK. But how could she tell him that she no longer trusted herself for anything more than the bits and pieces? That all those words about being a good nurse were only words? That when she'd most needed to be professional in her duty, she'd let herself down? "Just forget it, OK? It was stupid of me to ask. I don't need to be back in a hospital. In fact, I don't want to be back in a hospital."

"Yes, you do. Or you wouldn't have asked. Wouldn't have come here to the hospital, to my emergency room, to tell me that you'd left the girls with my niece when that was the plan all along, and I knew you'd do that. Or you could have called and told me. But you didn't. Instead, you came here, which makes me think you want to come back. And don't tell me that we can't always have what we want, because I'm offering you the opportunity to have exactly what you want…a few hours a week in the emergency department. As a nurse, not as a clerk or someone who stocks the shelves." He stepped closer, leaned in to her. "I trust you here. I think you've lost your confidence for some reason I don't understand, and I'm not going to ask why, but I do trust you, Dinah."

"Well, maybe you shouldn't give away that trust so easily."

"And maybe *you* should trust my judgment, because I know a good nurse when I see one, and I'm looking at one right now."

She wanted to accept his offer. She *really* wanted to and, more than that, she was tempted. But he couldn't know how, in the waning moments of Molly's life, she'd lost part of herself. It was hard to explain, but it was like she was afraid to care now. The pain of it was unbearable, and to be around children was to care.

Tears welled up in her eyes, but she turned her head, blinked them back before Eric could see. "And maybe you should trust mine." Even the whisper of her voice was shattered by grief.

"Think about it. The offer will be here when you're ready."

"It's a tempting offer, and I appreciate it, but, no. I…don't think I should."

"When you're ready, Dinah. Like you told me the other day, it has to be when you're ready."

Eric stepped closer to her, so close she could feel the tickling of his warm breath on the back of her neck. So close she could smell the scent of soap on him. So close that if she turned around she'd be in his arms. Which was why she backed away, intent on leaving. She *did* want to be in his arms, feeling his comfort. Wanted it badly. Which was pure trouble.

"Can I help you with this?" he practically whispered. "I know I told you I'd let it go, but…"

"Promised. You *promised*."

"And I'm not breaking my promise, Dinah. I *will* let it go, if that's what you want. But I want to help you, if I can. I don't know what's bothering you, but if you could trust me…"

If she could trust? Well, that was easier said than done, wasn't it? Dinah spun around, found herself so close to Eric it caught her off guard, and she swayed right into him. But pushed herself back immediately. "No, Eric. I can't trust. That's the problem. I can't, and I don't want to."

"Because of what your fiancé did to you?"

Dinah laughed bitterly. "Because I lost heart. Everything I thought I was, everything I thought I could be…I was wrong. Good skills don't necessarily make a good nurse, because a good nurse needs heart. When you lose it…"

"Or when it's broken?" he said gently.

"Or when you decide you don't have it." Emphatic words. Hard to say but she had to, if she were ever to believe them. Now maybe he would leave her alone. Pull back his offer and walk away. It was for the best, she told herself. Definitely for the best.

But Eric didn't so much as flinch. "Do you want to tell me what happened?"

"No." It still hurt too much. To fall so in love with a child with anencephaly made no sense to most people. A child born without a substantial part of her brain. A child with no prognosis for long-term survival. But that's exactly what she'd done.

"Then I'm sure you'll tell me when you can. And like I said, I did check your background, and there were no complaints. No reprimands. No mention of anything bad. So, unless I discover something different, or unless you tell me something that would make me change my mind about you—and I doubt that's going to happen—I'd like you working for a few hours on the night shift, if you decide to do this."

"Why?" she sputtered, disbelieving. How could he still want her? Or trust her?

"Because I believe in you. I'm not sure why you don't, but I have enough belief for the both of us. You're a good nurse, you belong in nursing and you'll see that once you're back. Maybe even find some of that heart you've lost. So, I'm offering a part-time, fill-in position, most likely only a part of a shift on the nights you'll work. But as a nurse, Dinah. Not a volunteer."

"Well, you're either a very brilliant man, Eric Ramsey, or a very stupid one." Dinah allowed a slight smile to touch her lips. "I haven't figured out which it is."

"Been called both. Maybe if you come work for me we can solve that puzzle together." He strolled to the door then stepped into the hall. But before he walked away, he turned back to Dinah. "And just so you know, the girls want to try their hand at oatmeal raisin cookies. And Pippa thinks she'll be up to a chocolate cake pretty soon."

"Thank you," she said, feeling the slightest bit of excitement. She wouldn't let herself get too excited, though, because that required some level of trust…trust in Eric. And as much as she wanted to, she couldn't. Wouldn't. Still, her stomach was starting to churn.

Five minutes later, on her way to the personnel office,

what she'd just done finally began to sink in. She'd said yes to something she'd vowed not to do again. It was temporary position, and things would go right back to where they were in a matter of weeks, after Angela had delivered her baby and her help in White Elk was no longer needed. That's what she kept reminding herself on her way to fill out her employment papers. But that little warning voice was creeping in, too. *Not again, Dinah. Don't do this again.*

Wise words, but was she wise enough to listen to them? Because, with all her heart, she wanted to trust Eric.

Dinah's first official shift as a practicing nurse was quiet. In fact, if she hadn't been so keyed up to work as a nurse again, she could have had herself a very good nap because, except for one over-indulgent eater from the lodge and mild case of sniffles, she'd had the evening pretty much to herself. But that didn't matter. Nothing did, considering how she was back where she wanted to be, back where she belonged. So, for her six assigned hours, she patrolled the halls, tidied the supply cabinets, straightened the bed sheets, fluffed the pillows and simply existed in a place that made her happy. Dinah Corday, happy again. She desperately wished it could be permanent.

Eric called twice within the first hour, volunteering to come in if needed. But Dr. Jane McGinnis, on call for her shift, was sufficient for what seemed to be a very slow evening. In fact, she hid herself in a closed room and hung a "Do Not Disturb" sign on the door. Orthopedist by day, medical mystery novelist by night, Jane was in the middle of what she called revising a sagging middle, getting close to her deadline. Her orders were simply to leave her alone except for an emergency or unless she had the solution for getting the bound and gagged heroine out of the trunk of a car, safe and sound, while it was speeding at ninety miles per hour down the highway.

Since Dinah didn't have the solution to that one, she left Jane to her writing.

Then there was a grandmotherly-looking night clerk, Emoline Putters, on hand in the emergency department, spending her night transcribing doctors' notes, guzzling hot, black coffee and grumbling rather loudly, and often obscenely, over illegible handwriting. And Ed Lester, a man who mopped the halls and dusted the light fixtures, made his presence known a few times, pushing a broom up one corridor and down the next, but he did nothing more than nod and offer a half-salute to Dinah when she greeted him.

So, basically, Dinah was pretty much left alone.

At first she dreaded a long, empty night pacing up and down the hollow halls and listening to the squeak of her rubber soles on the tiled floor, and Emoline's muttering off in the distance, then at the halfway point of her shift she was amazed how quickly her first hours had flown by.

The hours, no matter how fast or slow, didn't matter, though. This was all about being back where she belonged. Smelling the smells, hearing the sounds. Home.

"Want me to go out and scare up some business?" Eric asked, as Dinah scurried by treatment room number three on her way to do nothing in particular.

She glanced in, saw him stretched out on the exam table, feet up, head propped up on several pillows, hands clasped behind his head. "Are you checking up on me?"

"Maybe."

She wasn't sure if she should be flattered or angry. "If that's standard for all your new employees, fine. Check. But if it's something about me…"

"Don't be so defensive. Jane called. She's at a plot

point she doesn't want interrupted unless we absolutely have to. She asked if I could back her up."

"A plot point."

"She's going to donate part of the proceeds from her book to expanding the orthopedic wing. We're in ski country here. We want that expansion, so we do what we have to."

"So we're not supposed to call the doctor on call."

"Not when she's at a crucial plot point." He swung his legs down off the exam table and sat straight up. "If we can at all avoid it."

"You run a very lenient hospital here, Doctor."

"We try to. I came from a very typical medical background, it worked. But when I got here, this just seemed like the place to…to be something different, do something different. We try to make our medicine more relaxed, more personal."

"More involved?"

He nodded. Neil and I both felt that medicine's moving too far away from being personal, which is why we decided to go in the opposite direction when we bought the hospital. We were both starting over at the time…he'd just gone through a messy divorce, I was recently widowed. Fresh starts all the way round."

"Easier said than done." She wanted a fresh start, but she hadn't yet figured how to rid herself of the stale past.

"Or easier done than said, if you want it badly enough. I wanted it and, thank God, I found White Elk."

"Then you're happy here?"

"We're all three happy here." Finally, he stood. "You could be, too, if—"

"Got one coming in," Emoline Putters' voice boomed over the intercom.

Eric chuckled. "What she lacks in finesse she makes

up for in efficiency." As he headed out toward the hall, with Dinah practically right behind him, they greeted a frantic mother leading the way while her husband carried a child through the emergency door.

"He's not responding to us," the mother cried, while Eric took the boy in his arms and rushed into the first treatment room. "Barely able to talk."

"When did this start?" Dinah asked.

"About an hour ago. We heard him moaning…"

"Has he been sick?"

The father stepped in and slid his arm around his wife's waist. "My name is Frank Jackson, this is my wife, Elaine. Our son, Henry, is ten. He hasn't been sick, at least not that we've seen. And he hasn't said anything to us about not feeling well. But about an hour ago we heard him moaning, thought it was an upset stomach, but he wouldn't respond to us when we tried talking to him… just moaned."

Dinah squeezed Mrs Jackson's arm. "We'll let you know as soon as *we* know something." She turned and hurried into the treatment room and joined Eric at the side of the exam table.

"Blood pressure's normal, pulse rate fine, pupils equal, respirations perfect," Eric said.

"He wasn't sick prior to this episode." Instinctively, she picked up his wrist to take a pulse, felt the boy flinch. "Any temperature?"

Eric shook his head as he placed his stethoscope into his ears and bent to listen to Henry's lungs. "Sound clear," he finally said. "Heart sounds good, too."

"But he's not responding," Dinah said, staring across the table at Eric. "I wonder how his reflexes are. Could be serious, if he has The Drop."

"The Drop," Eric responded, nodding. Fighting back

a smile. "Yes, very serious. Perhaps you should do that test, Nurse."

"Very well, Doctor." She picked up Henry's arm, held it steady for a moment then dropped it onto the table. There was a hesitation in movement, just for a split second, before his arm fell.

"Looks like a partial case of The Drop to me," Eric said.

Dinah glanced down at the boy, barely containing her own smile. "Thank heavens for that. Because the needle you have to use for a full case of The Drop is so big…" She held up her hands in front of Henry's face, indicating something at least the size of Eric's forearm.

Henry's face scrunched, but he still didn't respond.

"But I don't have a half-sized needle for a partial case of The Drop," Eric said.

"Then I think we can use a full-sized needle and stick it only halfway into him. Wouldn't that work?"

"Good idea, Nurse. Why don't you roll Henry over on his side and I'll get the injection ready."

"Are you going to give the shot in his bottom, Doctor?" Dinah asked.

Eric's grin was from ear to ear. "I know it will hurt worse there, but I think it's for the best. And since he's not awake, he won't feel it."

"Very well, Doctor." With that, Dinah started to roll Henry over on his side, but his eyes popped open.

"No!" he screamed. "I don't want a shot!"

"But you could get sick again," Dinah said, "and one shot should keep you from getting The Drop for at least a year."

Henry bolted upright on the exam table. "I'm not sick. I wasn't sick. I was just…"

"But you have all the symptoms," Eric said.

"I don't have symptoms," Henry protested. "I just

didn't want to go to school tomorrow. We're having a math test, and I didn't…" Big tears rolled down his cheeks. "I didn't study for it. Am I in trouble?"

"Faking an illness and scaring your parents the way you did could be very serious," Dinah said.

"And what if someone who was really sick needed our help but we couldn't take care of them because we were taking care of you?" Eric stepped up to the table and helped Henry to the floor. "And it costs a lot of money to come to the emergency room. Are you going to be able to pay for this?"

"M-money?" he asked.

Dinah and Eric both nodded solemnly.

"I have an allowance…my lunch money."

Dinah slipped out into the hall to talk with the Jacksons while Eric continued the discussion with Henry, and by the time the Jackson family left the hospital, the arrangement was made that Henry would pay back what he owed for his little prank by volunteering every Saturday morning for the next several weeks. His duty would be as the toy monitor in the hospital waiting room's play area for children.

"You spotted that one pretty fast," Eric said, stretching back out on an exam table.

"Experience. He was peeking at us when he thought we weren't looking." She laughed. "The harder they scrunch their faces, the more they're faking."

"You've used The Drop before?"

"In some variation. Threaten them with the big needle, and they'll confess every time."

"For a math test," Eric said, settling back.

"And to think you have two daughters who'll be conspiring together in deeds probably much more devious than anything poor little Henry's ever thought of."

Groaning, Eric shut his eyes. "Maybe I can fake them out and pretend I have The Drop." He raised his arm and dropped it to the table.

"Remember, that one gets the big needle."

"Might be the preferable outcome. I mean, I'm not prepared, and I know they're probably making a list of all the ways they're going to pull things over on me when they're older."

"Why wait until they're older?" Dinah asked, heading to the door. "I have an idea they've already started."

"Not funny," he called after her. "Not funny at all."

She poked her head back in, smiling. "Wasn't meant to be."

Eric's response was to groan again. And pull a pillow over his head.

Her night at the hospital had been good. Working with Eric again even better. On impulse, while Dinah was halfway into chopping the romaine for that night's Caesar, she called him. "You busy tonight?" she asked, not sure why she was doing this. But doing it all the same.

"I, um…no, I don't suppose I am," he fumbled, sounding quite taken off guard. "Not unless there's an outbreak of The Drop."

"Want to come to dinner at the lodge?"

No response, and she was on the verge of embarrassment, and regret, for being so impulsive. Was this a mistake? Maybe she should have left well enough alone. But something was compelling her… "Bring the girls?" she added quickly, to save face. "I'd love to see them, love to have them take a tour of my kitchen." For a moment she considered adding his sister and niece to the guest list, but he agreed before she got that far with the invitation.

"Sure. We can come. I assume you're cooking?"

"Yes, but when I'm on a break…" What? What could she do with Eric and the twins on one of her fifteen-minute breaks? Or even on her thirty-minute meal break? Suddenly, what had seemed like a good idea didn't seem so good after all.

"You know they're going to want to wear their chef aprons," he said. "You've made quite an impression on them, and I don't think they've had those aprons off since they had their baking lesson."

"Well, maybe it's time to introduce them to the chef's hat." The conversation had turned into something about the girls, and Dinah had the impression Eric was awkward about this. No more than she was, probably. What a crazy thing to do, inviting him out this way, and when the conversation was over she was almost relieved. All awkwardness aside, though, they'd set a time, and she'd marked a reservation in the book for the best table in the house, which happened to be one of the closest to the kitchen. Then she continued chopping, taking care not let her mind wander too far lest she chop one of her fingers again.

"So, are you going to tell me what it's all about?" Angela asked her, thirty minutes later, when she was plopping down at the chef's table in the kitchen, trying, without much success, to make herself comfortable. "Because I recognize the mood. It's the pensive one."

"It's the pensive one because I did something dumb again."

"Does it have anything to do with Eric Ramsey?"

"I'm not interested in him the way you seem to think I am."

"And I didn't say you were. But you're mighty quick to bring it up, so I was just thinking that if you were interested in him the way *you think* I think you are…"

"Look, why don't you waddle your pregnant self back

to your office and let me get the dinner service prep finished. OK?"

Angela laughed. "You were never good at hiding things, Dinah. That's why Mom always knew what we were up to. You gave us away every time, without saying a word, because it's right there, in your eyes. The whole story."

"Not the whole story," she argued.

"This time I think it's the whole story. You're interested, don't want to be, fighting not to be, and losing the fight. Am I right?"

"You know what I'm in the mood for?" Dinah purposely changed the flow of the conversation while clearing away the last of the romaine pieces and getting herself ready to cut up several loaves of crusty bread, soak them in garlic butter and bake them into croutons. She didn't want to talk about it, or think about it either. Didn't want it anywhere near her right now.

"I know what you're doing, changing the subject. But it won't work, Dinah. Not talking about it won't make it go away."

Dinah shot a scowl at her sister. "Not changing the subject. It got worn out and I was moving on to something nicer."

"What's nicer than talking about you falling for Eric Ramsey?"

Dinah reached out and patted her sister's belly. "This. I'm ready to become an aunt. So, how are you feeling? Any contractions? Any *anything?*"

"Actually, Gabby Evans came up to see me this morning. Bryce is still in the hospital in Salt Lake City, and he's doing remarkably well. She thinks he'll be home in another few days. But she came home to take care of a few things, and stopped by and had a look at me. She thinks I could go into labor any time. The baby's in position, and ready to come out and meet the world. In fact, if I haven't gone into labor in the next three or four days, she's going to induce me, or have someone else do it if she can't get here."

"Three or four days?" Suddenly, everything felt good. The world became better. "She'll get here, Angela. If there's any possible way, you know she'll get here."

"Well, if she doesn't, she doesn't. Bryce comes first for her, and I totally understand that."

Was she seeing a little apprehension coming over her sister? Considering what Angela had watched Gabby go through, Dinah wouldn't be surprised if her sister was scared to death and doing a very good job of hiding it. And considering that Angela was another victim of a cheating husband… "You're going to have a normal delivery," she said, sitting down next to her sister and pulling her into her arms. "Normal delivery, beautiful, healthy baby. We'll get through this together. Just the two of us. I promise."

"We'll get through it better if you tell me about your date tonight."

Dinah stiffened up, wondering if she still had time to call Eric's sister and niece and invite them, too. The more people there, the less the illusion of a *date*. "It's not a date. He's bringing his twins."

"Want to bet?" Angela struggled to a standing position, arched her back and headed back to her office, stopping before she was out of the kitchen. "It's OK to get involved, Dinah. I know I'm teasing you about it, and I'm probably the last person who should be giving anyone relationship advice seeing how my ex-husband is off on the slopes with a young ski bunny. But you know what? I want to be involved again. Brad hurt me, but he hasn't spoiled me because I know it's out there…true love, true happiness, all the things that make being involved with someone else good. It's there, and it *does* happen. And if it walked in the door right now, even in my condition, I'd give myself over to it in a heartbeat. So, don't reject it out of hand because you've had some bad experiences in the past. Maybe Eric isn't the one who'll be walking in your door someday. Maybe he is. But you'll never know if you don't leave that door open a crack."

Dinah wanted to take those words to heart. She truly did. But it seemed that her door swung one way. Out. She wasn't sure she wanted it to swing back in because, inevitably, any time it did, it swung right back out. And hurt her in such deep ways.

Maybe Eric would walk through her door, but she wasn't sure if she could survive him walking back out. It didn't matter, though, because she'd already convinced herself that a shut door was the best door. Even if Eric was standing on the other side of it, knocking.

CHAPTER FIVE

PREPARING a fresh salmon for the evening's sushi, Dinah was alternately slicing, discarding unusable pieces and reflecting on everything Angela had said. Her sister, so pregnant she could hardly move, with an ex-husband now flaunting his new relationship wherever he could, was still optimistic about love. That was the optimism Dinah wanted, the positive outlook that had eluded her for so long. Honestly, she envied her sister that. Wished she could be like her. Supposing Eric *did* want to get involved, not that she thought he would, but if, in some odd, twisted scheme of things that's what happened? What would be the worst outcome for her? A few weeks of something very nice with a man she found pleasant? She could do that for a few weeks. Go in with no expectations, come out unscathed.

See, that was her fundamental problem. She always had expectations. Even when she knew she shouldn't, she did. But what if she didn't? What if she could simply enter into something nice for a little while then walk away?

Yanking a piece of clear plastic from the roll, Dinah wrapped her fish in it then set about the task of removing scales from the second salmon. Thankless chore, smelly. Predictable outcome. People wouldn't care about the prep, they'd care about the end results. And that's where she always went wrong in her life—the end results. She cared too much, tried to make more happen than could, or would.

But could she enter into something without expecting anything at the end?

Grabbing up the de-boner, she looked at it for a moment then set it back with the rest of her knives. Even if she could get to the end without an expectation, there was always the possibility that Eric would want more. Then what?

"It's not going to happen," she muttered, totally disinterested in the whole salmon prep now. "Just not going to happen."

Her sous chef, a nice little man named Oswaldo—half a head shorter than she, long hair pulled back by a red bandana, pencil-thin mustache—gave her a quizzical look but didn't comment. Rather, he went about his sauce prep while she turned her attention to an asparagus risotto. Her concentration was lacking so badly, though, she couldn't even decide whether to use only the tender asparagus tips or peel and chop the whole stalk. In fact, all she could think of was Eric, his missing wedding ring…her lapse in sanity.

"You've already salted that," Oswaldo reminded her, trying to be discreet as he pushed the open salt container away from her.

"What?" she asked, trying to snap herself back into her work.

"Your risotto. Salted."

Dinah looked at the salt she'd pinched between her fingers and had been ready to dump into the risotto. This was her job now. Food prep. Slicing and dicing. *Salting*. And if she wasn't careful, she'd make a mess of that, too.

"Look, I'm going to go take a short break. Can you cover for about fifteen minutes?"

Oswaldo nodded, and she didn't miss that little glint in his eyes. He'd be happy to take over forever. Or, at least until Angela was back. And he was about to get his shot at it if she didn't shape up.

Tossing off her apron, Dinah thought about going back to her room, locking the door and climbing into bed. But fifteen minutes wasn't enough for that, so she opted for a quick walk to the rear of the lodge, and fifteen minutes in an employee-only area set up with outdoor chairs and tables. At the moment she was the only employee there, which suited her fine. Being alone, with nothing but a mountain slope and pine trees behind her, was a relief. No pressures there. Not to think. Not to react. Not to remember. Not to question herself.

"What am I doing?" she asked a chipmunk scurrying its way across the opening, heading straight for a pile of downed branches. "It's crazy. I know better. Maybe I should crawl under that pile of branches with you." Nice idea, except hiding never solved anything. Trouble was, she didn't know what did.

"So think of the moment," she said, switching her attention to a lone figure hiking his or her way up from a ravine in the distance. It was odd, seeing someone out here alone at this time of the day. Usually, they were in pairs, or more. In fact, she didn't recall seeing a single hiker out here anywhere, *ever*, so she watched the progress of the one in the distance, and got herself so caught up in his slow gait that she didn't even notice his pronounced limp until he was crossing over the back patch of lawn. Where, when he saw her, he collapsed in a heap.

Immediately, Dinah leapt up and ran to the man…a young man, not more than twenty, she guessed. Dropping to her knees beside him, she gave him a little shake on the shoulder. "Hey," she said, patting his cheeks, noticing the slight flutter of his eyelids. "Stay with me, do you hear?" Was it exhaustion? Dehydration? Immediately her fingers went to his pulse. "Stay awake."

He nodded in the affirmative, trying to speak, but a gash on his head, above his right eye, had been bleeding, substantially, and she wondered if he'd lost enough blood to make him woozy. Or was the head wound more serious than the superficial cut she could see?

"My brother…dad…" he whispered, his voice so low and raspy she was barely able to make out his words.

"We'll call them as soon as we get you taken care of." Her fingers pulled back his shirt so she could have a look at the way he moved air in and out of his lungs. His pulse was too fast, his breathing too shallow. He could have been too pale underneath the layers of dirt and blood but she couldn't tell. So she did a quick assessment, felt his arms, his legs, probed his abdomen to see if it was distended or rigid. It was not. "Where do you hurt?" she finally asked him.

"Please, my dad and my brother, they…" His eyes fluttered shut, and he fought to open them again, but it was a losing battle as he lapsed into unconsciousness.

Immediately, Dinah clicked on her cell phone and speed-dialed the first name at the top. By the time the first ring sounded, she was already going through the young man's pockets, looking for identification. First his jacket pockets, then his cargo pants…pants with numerous pockets, visible and hidden, everywhere.

"You having second thoughts about our date tonight?" Eric asked rather than saying hello.

"I have an unconscious young man, age approximately twenty, on the back lawn of the lodge. He walked here then collapsed when I got to him. Head wound, can't tell how serious, but he's done some extensive bleeding. Tachycardia, shallow respirations. Eyes responding, but very sluggish." She found his wallet in a zipper pocket midway down to his knee and pulled it out. "His belly's not rigid, there are no obvious breaks, at least nothing compound, and he stayed conscious only a few seconds before he went out on me so I don't have any idea what happened to him." One glance at his driver's license, and she added, "He's not a local. According to his identification, he's from Canada...Ontario."

"I'm on my way," Eric said. "Get him as stable as possible, and I'll make the rest of the arrangements from here."

"It's bad, Eric. I think it's really bad." She clicked off with Eric and called the main desk at the lodge. "Hello, Redmond," she said to the concierge who answered. "This is Dinah, from the kitchen. I have a critically injured young man out on the back lawn—"

"I'll call for help," he interrupted.

"No, listen to me. I've already called. What I need from you are blankets and a couple of pillows. Immediately." The boy was already shocky, but warming him up and elevating his legs could lessen the trauma, help keep him stable until Eric got there. "And I need someone to go and find his family. His last name is Dawson. This is Troy, and he asked for his brother and father."

When she clicked off, she didn't have to wait for more than a minute before one of the lodge workers came running with an armload of blankets, followed by another one carrying pillows. Redmond followed up with a first-aid kit and several bottles of water, and he was flanked by two more workers who had come only in case more help was needed.

"We've got someone going up to his cabin now. According to the registration, they're staying in one of the family cabins. And they're a family of five—husband, wife, three children."

Dinah had a sinking feeling that maybe Troy's brother and father had been with him, that they might have been injured, too. But she didn't want to voice that opinion and cause a panic. Best to leave the search to Eric, should a search become necessary.

"Dr. Ramsey called us. His ETA is two minutes," Redmond informed her.

"How?" she said, then looked up as Redmond pointed to the helicopter coming into view.

By the time it had landed on the east lawn, which had been cleared of guests by another one of the lodge workers, Dinah had Troy's feet propped up, and had him well tucked into his blankets. His pulse was still too fast, too thready, and he wasn't responding at all to her attempts to rouse him by calling his name or by pinching him. It was a serious head injury, possible fracture, with bleeding and swelling. She was convinced of it.

"Any change?" Eric shouted. He was running hard in her direction, carrying a medical bag.

"No response."

He dropped to his knees, and handed his medical bag over to her. Immediately she went for the blood-pressure cuff. Thirty seconds later, she looked over at him. "It's ninety over sixty." Too low.

"Pupils are responsive, but very slow," Eric said.

Bad sign. But not the worst-case scenario by a long shot.

"So was he coherent when you found him?"

"He was walking…more like staggering up the trail." She pointed to the south end of the lawn. "I watched him for a while because he seemed to be moving so slowly. But I didn't know he was injured. Then as he made the clearing, even though I couldn't tell, I had the feeling that something wasn't right. So I ran down there, and he…he collapsed. Wanted me to tell his brother and dad. At least that's what I thought he wanted. But, Eric, I might be wrong. I have this hunch that his dad and brother are out there somewhere, and he was the one who was coming for help."

"Damn," Eric muttered. He looked up at Redmond. "Does anyone here know for sure? Has anyone seen his family?"

"We're tracking them down now. Nobody's at the cabin, but one of our guests saw the mother and daughter go off together earlier. Didn't see the father and sons, though. So I've got my people knocking on doors right now."

"Then they could be out there?" Dinah asked, looking out to the vast expanse of woods around her, and the never-ending mountains beyond that.

"I'm going to send him down to the hospital right now, go down there with him, then I'm coming back, getting Neil up here with me, and we're going to start a search and rescue, unless I hear something different in the meantime." He motioned over two of the hotel workers, instructed them to retrieve the stretcher from the helicopter then he made a phone call to the hospital. Two minutes later Troy Dawson, who'd yet to regain consciousness, was on his way to the helicopter, while Eric lagged behind for a moment. "I think I may have to take a rain check on that dinner later on," he said, grabbing his medical bag and spinning away.

"I want to do this," Dinah said, practically running to keep up with him. She was tall, but her strides didn't come close to matching Eric's, especially when he was in a hurry.

"What?" he shouted, the noise of the helicopter getting louder the closer they got.

"Help with the rescue," she shouted back. "I want to be part of it." Because she felt obligated. Because Troy had been trying to tell her something and she hadn't been able to keep him conscious long enough to find out what. Hadn't been able to hold on to Molly long enough...

"Can you find the trail he came up on?" he yelled, then motioned her away as he climbed into the helicopter. "That could get us off to a faster start if we know where to start looking."

She was still nodding when the helicopter lifted off, watching it disappear over the older Sister in a matter of seconds. She had to find the trail... First thing she did was run to the kitchen to tell Oswaldo he would be in charge of the cooking. Next, she phoned Angela to let her know what was going on, and make sure she wasn't in labor. Then she changed into hiking boots, put on a comfortable pair of jeans and layered on a couple of shirts with a green sweater, tied her hair up in a bandana and scrounged for anything that might be of help in a mountain rescue, even though she'd never been on one before. She had her medical bag...bandages, scissors, stethoscope. More bulk than she wanted to carry, but...

Out the door in a blink, she ran to the gift shop and grabbed up a souvenir backpack.

"You can't take that!" the teenage clerk exclaimed while Dinah was dumping her med supplies inside, totally ignoring the girl's protests. After her own supplies, she added a lightweight blanket she found on one of the gift-shop shelves, as well as a flashlight, a small travel pillow, and several plastic bottles of water. On impulse, she scooped up a handful of candy bars and several pairs of fluorescent pink shoelaces popular with children. She had no idea what she'd need them for, but she felt better with a full pack.

"I said, you can't take that!" The clerk was now yelling. "I'm calling Security." Which she did. But the kindly old security officer, a man called Wallace Gilpin, who'd been perched on a chair almost outside the door, reading a magazine, scooped some packages of premade crackers with peanut butter from the gift shop shelf and handed them to Dinah.

"Protein," he said. "Not much, but it could help." Next, he dug a gold cigarette lighter from his pocket and handed it to her. "You might be needing this, too. But, please, take care of it. It belonged to my father." With the lighter, he handed her his magazine. "And this, just in case you need a fire starter."

"The brother and father were with him," Redmond called from across the lobby. "And no one has seen them come back. We've sent someone down to the village to find Troy's mother and sister. I've got a cell phone number for them, but I thought having someone tell them in person was better than a phone call."

"Well, I'm going on ahead to find the trail." In the whole scheme of a search-and-rescue operation, it would probably be a small contribution, but saving time had to be good. Especially with only a few hours of light left.

"Use this," Redmond said, handing her a walkie-talkie. "Dr. Ramsey has his own communication, but it doesn't hurt to have a back-up. And you won't get cell reception once you're too far away from the lodge. But these carry for quite a way."

"Are you sure you know what you're doing?" Angela

asked. She'd wandered down to the lobby, where Wallace was already scooting a chair in her direction.

"No, I'm not sure. But the one thing I do know is that I can't sit around and do nothing. Eric needs me to find the trail, and if there's a chance that Troy has a brother or father out there, and they need help…" She ran to her sister, gave her a quick kiss on the cheek. "Let Redmond know if you need me…one twinge, Angela, and I'll be back. Promise?"

Angela lifted her hand to wave, but Dinah was gone before she saw it. Running across the lawn, she discovered at least a dozen different trails, all starting at approximately the same place, all leading to vastly different areas. Suddenly she wasn't so sure where she'd seen Troy. At least four of the trail heads seemed likely, which meant she was going to have to go further. See if she could find traces of anything…blood, something he might have dropped.

Half way across the lawn, her cell phone jingled. "We've got Troy in the emergency room, and I'll be back in a few minutes. Any luck finding the right trail?"

"When I find the trail, will you let me go out with you?" she asked.

"We'll talk about it."

"I want to go, Eric. I feel…responsible. If I could have kept Troy talking, I might have discovered where his brother and father are. Or, if I'd noticed him sooner, gotten to him quicker…" So many things bothered her, but the thing that bothered her most of all was thinking about someone else being lost out there. "I want to go, and I don't want to talk about it."

"On my rescues, you follow my orders, Dinah."

"I'm a nurse, Eric. I always follow orders."

"But you're not experienced in mountain rescue."

"Then send me back if I get in the way or impede the rescue. But give me a chance. I need to…need to do this. The idea that a young boy is out there somewhere…" She shut her eyes, trying to not picture all the possibilities of trouble that boy, and his father, could be in. But in the dark of her eyelids, she saw bad things. "I have to do this, Eric." But she wouldn't, if he didn't want her. Because she was a good nurse. Because she knew how to take orders.

"Find the trail, Dinah. Just find the right trail."

The first two trail heads turned up nothing. She went some way on each, looking for clues that Troy might have come that way, and found nothing. It was on the third trail she discovered fresh drops of blood…probably from the gash on Troy's head. "Hello," she shouted, on the off chance that the Dawson family was within hearing distance. Of course, no one answered, not that she'd really expected them to. But on impulse, before she headed down that trail, she tied a pink shoelace to a tree branch so Eric would know where she was starting. Then she plunged into the woods, looking for more signs that Troy had come this way.

There were signs everywhere. Scuff marks in the dirt indicated he'd been dragging himself exactly where she was tracking. And she found more blood droplets, and other larger marks in the dirt…handprints? Perhaps where he'd stumbled and fallen?

But there were only signs of one person coming through here. She'd hoped for more, hoped that a few feet into the woods she'd find Troy's brother, or dad. Maybe with a broken leg. Something incapacitating, but not too serious. Of course, that didn't turn out to be the case, but she refused to allow early discouragement to get her down. Rather, she followed the obvious trail, one that was easy to read. Bargaining with God for an early success.

Everything reminded her of a giant jigsaw puzzle, and she was the only one there to solve it. "Solve it," she whispered, bending down to have a closer look at the broken frond of a fern. Nothing. It wasn't broken. Just not fully developed. And nothing else around her gave her a clue, which meant, to the untrained eye, the trail had run out not far after it had started. Maybe she'd gone the wrong way? Or taken a wrong turn?

Maybe she was letting the Dawson family down the way she'd let Molly down.

Suddenly a cold chill swept over her. What was she doing, thinking she could be of use out here, as a nurse, as…anything? In the distance, through the trees, she could still see the lodge, and the search activity mounting in the parking lot. It was time to go back. Raw, bitter discouragement *was* beginning to overtake her because she wanted to make a difference and she wasn't.

"It's not easy," Eric said, suddenly stepping up behind her. "It's never about strolling through the woods until you come across your victim."

"But I thought that if I found the trail…"

"You did find the trail," he said, holding up the pink shoelace marker. "This is it."

In her mind's eye, the scenario played out happily. She and Eric would turn the next bend in the trail and find Troy's dad and brother sitting there, waiting for someone to find them. They'd be alive, slightly damaged, but good. Except the story she saw etched on Eric's face told her something altogether different. "Worst-case scenario?" she asked.

"We run out of daylight without finding them. Or we find them and they're…"

This was going to be a long, hard search and the hard lump in her stomach was telling her the outcome might not be the one she wanted. "I'm right behind you," she whispered, as Eric took the lead. Instinctively, she looked up to see the sky, but the canopy of leaves overhead totally blotted out all but a few splotchy patches of light. "And I can run, Eric. I won't slow you down."

She followed him for the next twenty minutes, alternately running and stopping to assess the trail. Words between them were spared in order to conserve breath, but she did what Eric did. She observed everything, looking off to the sides of the trail, looking up, looking down. Once, when they stopped to take a drink of water, she asked the question she feared asking. "What happens if we have to go back?"

"We could lose the trail. It could be wiped out by a light rain, or a good wind. Since it's spring, that's highly likely."

"And you don't stay out after dark?"

"It depends on the situation. Normally we don't keep the volunteers out. Too many people out in the dark becomes a risk factor itself. But I have some specialists who go out at night, and Neil's getting them ready to go right now. He'll send them on an alternate trail, one that parallels us."

"All I can think about is that if we have to turn back, what if Troy's brother and father are only over the next hill? How do you make the decision to quit, and start again tomorrow, when you could be so close?"

"Judgment…experience. I don't ever like to quit, but if I'm leading the field team, I have to think about their safety first. Neil and I have a good group of volunteers who'll put their own lives at risk to save someone else, and it's up to me to make sure they don't put their lives at risk." He took one more swig of water from the plastic bottle, held it out to her, and when she refused another drink he capped it and clipped it to his belt. "It's only going to get rougher up ahead, Dinah. We need to cover more area, faster, because daylight is getting to be a huge factor now."

"Am I slowing you down so far?" she asked.

"No, but I don't want to make this miserable for you, since you've never done this type of thing before."

"What makes me miserable is knowing that…" She swallowed hard, trying to fight back the emotion. Eric didn't need her to be emotional out here, didn't need her thinking with her heart when a search and rescue such as this followed logical, ordered procedures. "I can do this, Eric." She trusted that completely.

Actually, she trusted Eric with all her heart. Too bad her heart hadn't found him when she could have given it to him. Because now, there was nothing left to give away except tatters. But, then, Eric had a few tatters of his own. So maybe knowing she couldn't have him was part of the attraction she felt for him. If nothing else, it was safe.

Safe. Yes, she wanted to be safe. But how safe? "And I'm ready to run."

He reached out and squeezed her hand. "When this is over, remind me to tell you how amazing you are."

"I've got part of the team going up to the ridge, looking for a vantage point," Neil relayed to Eric. "We might get lucky and find them by looking down, if we have enough daylight left. Oh, and Redmond's just heard from the boy's mother. She said her husband and the boys were going out to camp, but she didn't know where, except they'd mentioned renting a rubber raft. Troy is eighteen, by the way, and his brother, Shawn, is twelve. William, the father, is forty, and in good health."

"Where is she right now?" Eric asked.

"She's gone to the hospital to be with Troy. He hasn't come round yet, and it's not looking good. Scan shows a skull fracture, and they're getting ready to fly him down to Salt Lake City for surgery. He's got a subdural hematoma, too. Mrs Dawson will be going with him."

"Damn," Eric muttered. It would have been so easy to let the concierge know where they were going. But people came out here and did…foolish things. Foolish, like taking two sons and going off God only knew where for an adventure. Skilled outdoorsmen left word, drew their course on maps and left them behind as a reference. They checked in with the national park authorities. Told their wives. But amateurs went and assumed things would work out. Sometimes they prepared properly as far as the gear they took, sometimes they didn't. More often than not, they didn't do the proper research, didn't tell anybody anything. More often than not, they were the ones he was sent to rescue. When there were fatalities, they were the ones who usually died.

No, he didn't have a good feeling about this at all. Then he thought about Dinah again, and had to smile. For an amateur in outdoor rescue, she'd done it all right, sort of. Her inexperience taken into account, she'd left her markers for him, kept in touch, gathered up odd, but good supplies, according to the security guard. Good instincts. Untrained, but with a natural knack. Someone to train properly in rescue later on. If she stayed…

"Is Dinah keeping up with you? Because I could get someone from the hospital to run the base camp and come in to pair up with you. Or…" Neil chuckled. "Maybe you'd rather be pairing up with her?"

Eric studied her for a moment, standing off by herself, looking in every direction, studying, taking it all in. "What I'd rather be doing is having a nice quiet dinner—"

"With Dinah?" Neil interrupted.

"With Dinah," Eric admitted. "But right now we're

taking a water break, eating protein bars, and getting ready to run another mile or two."

"Toward the river," Neil said. "If they were carrying a rubber raft…"

"Then they wouldn't have gone too far."

"Maybe the rapids?"

Eric cringed at the thought. Inexperience on the rapids equaled tragedy. "Let's hope they were smarter than that."

"Well, I've got twenty people out, and another group ready to go. Let me know what you need." With that, Neil clicked off and suddenly it was just the two of them, alone. No civilization around to buffer them.

"Ready to go again?" Eric called. Damn, he admired her. He was working her hard, pushing her far more than he should push anyone without the kind of experience he needed from a volunteer out here, yet he knew she wouldn't let him down. There was nothing in Dinah he didn't trust and he only wished she trusted herself half as much as he did.

"Ready," she called, slinging her pack back over her shoulder. "How are we doing on daylight?"

He glanced up at the sky. It would be dark too soon…a sobering thought. He hated the night because that's when victims died most often. Maybe because with sunlight there was hope. Maybe because with the night came the feeling of cold, lonely desperation. "Not good. But the river's not too far off and we should make that in good time, and hope they didn't go much farther than the first entry point we'll come to." He glanced down at the ground, at a speck of blood splattered against a brown leaf. "Damn," he muttered. They were running out of time. Everything inside him was screaming that, loud and clear.

"Well, I'm up for a nice, hard run. Ready whenever you are."

Dinah Corday was intense, dedicated…like no other woman he'd ever encountered, and he wasn't sure how to handle her…or handle himself around her. But the one sure thing amidst all his confused feelings was that he felt more alive around her than he'd felt in years. After Patricia, he'd spent so much time feeling lost, feeling alone. Feeling like he'd lost his only chance at true happiness when she'd died.

But Dinah stirred things in him. Familiar things as well as things he'd never felt before. Things that made him want to crawl up in a ball and pray they would go away, and things he wanted to shout about from the top of the older Sister. He was happy. He felt disloyal. Mostly, though, he liked being with Dinah, however it happened.

He fingered the shoelace in his pocket as he headed off down the trail they'd been following for the past hour. Couldn't help but smile as he twisted the shoelace around his index finger.

CHAPTER SIX

ERIC clicked on his radio. "Look, Neil, I think he was coming from the river and got turned around. It's easy to do up here, since this is close to where the river cuts in. What I'm not seeing though is any sign that three people came through here together recently. So I think Troy taking this trail was an accident. I don't think we're going to find anything on it, which means I'm going off trail and heading straight over to the river."

Neil's expletive was brittle and explosive. "Look, I've got the team on the ridge now, but they're too far away, not going to get to the river before you do, and I don't think you're going to get to a point where you can meet up with them before I have to call them back in for the night."

"Well, I'm betting that the Dawsons wouldn't have gone too far upriver. Maybe as far as the rapids. It's still a good hike up there, but I think can make it before dark, and I'm not inclined to turn around."

"The rapids are another hour ahead of you, and I'm not happy having you and Dinah out there after dark, as Dinah isn't experienced."

Dinah listened to the exchange, following along behind Eric who was still going forward at a fast pace. He had an uncanny sense about this, like he anticipated what he was about to find before he found it. And he didn't talk. Not a word, except when he reported back to Neil every few minutes. Every ounce of his physical energy, as well as his mental concentration, was spent on the search, and he was so pulled into it, Dinah didn't dare speak lest she snapped his focus the way the twigs snapped under their boots. In fact, she was almost afraid to breathe in case that little distraction knocked him out of the moment.

It was an amazing thing to watch. This wasn't Eric the doctor. It was Eric the hunter. The rescuer. A man who took away her breath each and every time he paused to look at something—a disturbed leaf, an imprint in the dirt. A man who took away her breath for no other reason than he was Eric Ramsey.

"We're going to climb," he continued to Neil. "That'll cut off more than half the time, and I think we'll still have enough light left to get us all the way down to the river. Why don't you go ahead and send the second team out, have them come in from the north? Then we'll be good for a while."

"The second team?" Dinah asked, after he'd finished talking to Neil.

"My night crew. It still gets cold up here after dark, too cold if either of the Dawsons are seriously injured, so we're going to stay out for a while. Are you up to it?"

"I'm not quitting, Eric. If you go on, so do I. But what if they're not at the rapids?" One guess out of so many places scared her because right now, in the near-darkness, the woods around them seemed so much bigger than they did during the day, and trying to place Troy in one particular spot was such a daunting task. But Eric was experienced. His guesses…hunches…were based on such a solid foundation she had to trust him.

Trust. There was that frightening word again. It seemed to come up so much when she was with Eric.

"Sometimes you just have to guess. Three people and a rubber raft…inexperienced. The raft is heavy. If you want to put it in the water you're not going to spend the whole day hiking, trying to find a good starting place, but you want to go far enough to feel that you're really out in the wilderness. If they got as far as the rapids they wouldn't have gone beyond that because even the most inexperienced outdoorsmen wouldn't shoot those rapids in a rubber raft. So that would put them someplace downriver from there. Until now, the river was too far off trail, but it starts to cut back in just east of here, so I think they would have tried rafting somewhere between here and the rapids, hopefully closer to this point than the rapids."

"Well, I'm prepared to stay out here all night, if that's what we have to do. You know, I've packed food, water. A blanket and a pillow, too."

"A pillow? You brought a pillow?"

"I thought I might need it. And it could come in handy, couldn't it? I mean, my pink shoelaces did."

"Don't look down," he said to Dinah. "You'll get dizzy, so look up at me, do what I tell you, and you'll be fine."

Look down? It was hard looking anywhere with her eyes squeezed tightly shut. "Isn't there another way to get to the bottom from up here?" As rockfaces went, this one was small. She knew that. But she'd never climbed anything more than a flight of stairs, and this was just plain scary. That, plus the fact she wasn't especially fond of heights. She would have preferred letting Eric do the climbing while she took the long way down, walking. But he wouldn't hear of it. Wouldn't leave her alone. And time was running out. That was the winning argument. Shawn

Dawson and his father needed help, and if they didn't take this shortcut to the river, their rescue efforts would have to end for the day. Thinking about the young boy out there, hurt, scared…that's what propelled her to the edge of the cliff, and had her standing there, toes over the edge, trying not to look down.

"So how do you just step off the edge?" she asked, forcing herself another inch forward.

"You trust me. I've got you tied, you'll be fine. And this is a very easy beginner rock to climb."

"If you want to climb," she muttered, bracing herself for the inevitable.

"Turn around, watch me, and I'll lower you over."

"And if you drop me?"

"I've never dropped anybody before."

If only he knew how much of an issue trust was for her. Of course, this was not a question of emotional trust. The worst she'd get from this would be some cuts and bruises. They healed. Emotional bruises didn't, so this was a far easier trust to have. "OK, well…" She turned around, grabbed hold of her ropes and backed to the edge.

"You're going to be fine, so just lower yourself over the edge and walk, don't bounce, down the side. Trust me, Dinah, this is easy. You can do it."

"Easy for you to say," Dinah grumbled, then drew in a deep breath and took a big leap of faith over the edge. Literally.

The first step off was the worst. The immediate sensation was that she was falling…nothing between her and the ground but air, lots and lots of air.

"You're doing fine," he called. "Just don't swing too much, and you'll be down before you know it."

"Trust him," she muttered out loud, as her feet connected with the rockface and she was grounded again.

"Trust him…trust him…" In a way, it was like falling in love—that first feeling of falling or floating, the eventual sure footing. Of course, in her case, she always plummeted hard after the first few steps. Never did find her sure footing. "Trust him…" Those two words were becoming her mantra.

"Keep going," he said, looking down over the edge at her. "You're doing a fantastic job."

"Like you'd say anything else to someone who was dangling in midair." When she finally gathered enough courage to take a look at that *fantastic* job he claimed she was doing, she saw she'd gone only a few feet. Problem was, it was a short forty-foot drop, total. Something that should take her only a couple of minutes, according to Eric. But those forty feet were insurmountable, and she was stuck swinging in midair, couldn't get back up, couldn't force herself to continue on down.

Suddenly, panic turned her lungs into lead. Nothing was moving in and out. Her head was getting light, her fingers and toes tingly. It had to be a panic attack coming on. She'd never had one, but she recognized the symptoms. Dangling off the side of a cliff in mid-panic. She *had* to trust him, there was no other way to get out of this, to get on with the rescue. The rescue…that's where she had to focus her thoughts. Shawn needed her. His father needed her.

Eric trusted her to do this…trusted her.

About a minute into the ordeal, when her lungs finally gave out and forced her to breathe again, she realized she'd been biting down on her lips so hard they were bleeding. But something else was happening. Suspended there, as she was, a feeling of exhilaration was coming over her. Her slow progress was mounting into an unexpected victory, not only of will but of trust, and by the time she'd reached firm ground at the bottom, she was ready to have another go at it. But looking up, watching Eric scale down with the skill and grace of an aerial artist, she wondered if she'd ever have the chance to do that again. With Eric. Because it was his trust in her as much as her trust in him that had got her to the bottom.

"You OK?" he asked, as he hit the ground. Immediately, he grabbed hold of her arm and pulled her into him.

She went willingly, fell against his chest and caught her breath there. Lingered a moment longer as the adrenaline rush passed. "That wasn't so bad," she said, still a little winded.

"Then we'll do it again sometime, when I've had more time to teach you."

"I'd like that, and next time I won't be such a baby." She hoped.

"Trial by fire isn't the easiest way to learn. But you did a good job, Dinah."

Trial by fire...that's all her life had been since she'd been in White Elk. And she'd plunged into some very dangerous fires lately. "Trial by fire might not be the easiest way to learn, but it sure does make you move forward, like it or not."

After their quick embrace he went right back to work, gathering in his ropes. Once he'd wound them over his shoulder, he pointed in the direction of the river. She could hear rushing waters from where she was. In a way, it reminded her of the unexpected power she found in Eric. On the surface he was tranquil, but when she got close she sensed the currents rippling in him, the ones she didn't expect, like the currents that surprised her now, in the sounds of the river.

She hoped they would find Troy's brother and father once they reached the river's edge, but the chances of that happening weren't too good. And the real test was going to be figuring out which way to go—upriver, or down. The real test of this rescue, the real test of her life. Which way to go?

They hiked for several minutes, Eric in the lead, Dinah following, flanking him off to the left by about twenty yards. Not close, but not so far from him that she couldn't see him. She kept her eyes darting back and forth, looking for signs of life, signs that someone had been there recently. Imitating Eric in her actions. But since this was not a blazed trail, she didn't expect to find much. And once again she didn't speak, barely dared breathe for fear that, even at this distance away from him, if she broke Eric's concentration, he might miss something.

Then suddenly, something caught her attention. It was still another few feet off to her left, but she darted off course and dropped to her knees when she came upon it. A shoe. A single shoe, size eight, boys'. Fairly new. "Eric!" she called. "Over here!"

Eric barely looked at the shoe. Rather, he rushed on by her. "Shawn!" he called, then listened for a moment. "William! Can you hear me?"

To her ears there was no response, but something propelled Eric to a spot another hundred feet away. "Shawn, can you hear me?" he called. "Shawn!"

Again, she heard nothing...but she listened, dear God she listened hard. "Shawn!" she yelled, standing back up and turning in circles. "Shawn, William! We're here to help you! Can you hear us?"

She knew children, knew how they responded. When they were frightened, they hid. Shawn would be scared to death. But the question was, if his father couldn't respond, would Shawn be able to respond to them if he could hear them? If that was his shoe...

"Dinah, over here!" Eric yelled, motioning her over to an outcropping of rocks. They were practically at the river's edge now. And that's where they found the second shoe. It was on the foot of a young boy. Eric was already making the initial assessment—taking a pulse. Dinah flew into action, pulling her flashlight from her backpack and looking for pupillary reaction. Normal. His respirations were weak, though. And his skin was chilled to the touch. Even though Troy had obviously wrapped his own jacket over his brother before he'd gone for help, Shawn was suffering mild hypothermia.

"Shawn," Eric said, patting his cheeks, trying to awaken him.

"Shock?" she asked.

"And mild exposure." He picked up the totally full bottle of water Troy had obviously left with his brother. It was still full. "Dehydration's setting in."

"Broken leg." Dinah ran her hands lightly over the boy's extremities, frowned then grimaced. "Both legs, I think."

"No distension in his abdomen," Eric responded. "But he could still have internal injuries." He looked up at the rocks, expelling a frustrated sigh. "Wish we knew what happened to him."

"Shawn, can you hear us? Can you wake up and tell us what happened to you?"

In response his eyelids fluttered, but his eyes didn't fully open.

"I think Troy must have carried him this far, then left him where he thought it was safe. Probably because he couldn't carry him any further." Eric grabbed the walkie-talkie and clicked it on. "We have one victim, twelve-year-old male, unconscious, possible broken legs, possible internal injuries. I'm going to splint his legs and leave

Dinah here while I go and look for his father, unless the other crew gets in here before then. What's their estimated time?"

"Not going to make it before dark," Neil said.

"Well, have them keep to the river. And get a helicopter in here, because I'd rather evacuate the boy as soon as possible, while we still have a little light, and deal with the father when we find him." Eric and Neil discussed arrangements while Dinah snipped the fabric back from Shawn's legs to get a better look. What she saw made her cringe. Both were definitely broken, so badly that the angles of the breaks were obvious even though the skin itself wasn't broken. This poor child would require numerous surgeries and months and months of physical therapy.

But he was alive, and while she wrapped Eric's thermal rescue blanket around him and placed her little travel pillow under his head, the familiar pang hit her. This was what she needed to do—take care of children. "Shawn, you're safe now. Just stay with us, and we're going to take you to a hospital not too far from here. Your mother is already there, with Troy. She's waiting for you."

For the next few minutes, sitting and talking to Shawn the way she was, taking his vitals and cleaning various scrapes and cuts on his arms and face, she thought about where her heart truly was. No matter what she'd told Eric, no matter how much she wanted to believe she had no heart for this, she did. There was no denying it. "Can a helicopter land here?" She asked Eric, after he'd clicked off from Neil.

"There's a place, downriver, about half a mile. We'll have to get him ready to travel then get him down to the pick-up point. Neil's going to fly in and take him from there."

"Have they called his mother?" she asked Eric.

"I'm sure someone will."

"But she needs to know. Right now. Someone who loves this child needs to know he's alive!"

Eric studied her for a moment then smiled. "Right away," he said gently. "We'll let her know right away." He clicked his radio back on to Neil. "You think of the things no one else does," he said to Dinah. Then he gave her a curious look, but said nothing.

"What?" she finally asked him.

"You'd make a wonderful mother."

She looked down at Shawn, and automatically took hold of his wrist, feeling for a pulse. "I need to be stable in my own life before I can be responsible for another person. And in case you haven't noticed, my life isn't too stable these days."

"You underestimate yourself, Dinah."

"Or maybe you overestimate me."

"Actually, I think I estimate you just right. And what I've estimated so far is about perfect."

"Don't," she whispered to him raggedly. "Please, don't have expectations of me."

It took approximately thirty minutes to get Shawn stabilized and down to the rescue spot on a makeshift stretcher Eric lashed together from tree limbs. It was an amazing thing, watching him. He was so resourceful in the woods, not a moment of hesitation. Born to do this, she thought as she fashioned splints to the boy's legs. "He's warming up," she called, as Eric was cutting the last of the tree limbs. "Pulse is evening out, blood pressure's up."

"I just heard from Neil and they'll be en route as soon as we signal. Also, the second crew found William Dawson and they're taking him out right now. He's about a mile upriver, conscious, extreme hypothermia, back injury, possible internal injuries. The raft got caught in river debris, they got tossed around pretty badly on the rocks. He was trapped in the water, leg caught between a couple of rocks, couldn't get loose, so Troy tried to carry Shawn out…"

Not a great ending, but not a horrible one, either. For that, she was relieved. "Your father and brother are fine," she told Shawn, as Eric came back with the last of the tree limbs.

"We're going to take you to the hospital, and you'll be fine in no time. Just a little while longer…" She glanced up at Eric, his rugged form stunning, even though the only light on him now came from their flashlights. "We did it. I mean, we actually did it."

"You've got good instincts out here."

"I was so afraid I'd slow you down, or do something wrong, something that could have been dangerous."

He bent, took Shawn's pulse then steadied the boy's neck as they lifted him onto the makeshift stretcher. "This is what you need to do, Dinah. Rescue, nursing…either one, or both. You're wasting your time in that kitchen."

"And my ex-fiancé, Charles, said I was wasting my time as a nurse."

"Then he's an idiot on two counts. One, for letting you go. Two, for not recognizing how extraordinarily talented you are."

Together, they carried Shawn to the rendezvous point, where Neil met them and took over from there. The night had finally dropped down on them, and Dinah felt a huge sense of relief once she saw the stretcher being lifted into the helicopter, with Shawn strapped in. She didn't glance away until the chopper had made a wide turn and was headed away from the river, its lights a shining beacon of success against the black sky. That's when the true feeling of relief washed over her that all three of the Dawsons would be safe. That's also when her knees gave out and she sat down, cross-legged, on a boulder near the river.

Eric propped himself against the rock, but didn't sit. Rather, he leaned, arms folded casually across his chest. "From here, winding our way back along the river, it's going to take about three hours."

Dinah's reply was a groan.

"We could cut back through the woods and save some time, but I'm not especially interested in a tough hike at this point, which is what that would be. So…"

"So, let me rest for a few minutes," she said, every ounce of tiredness creaking its way into her voice.

"Do you like camping?" he asked.

"You mean, staying here tonight?"

"Get a good night's sleep, head back in the morning."

"I'm not much of a camper," she said. "But I wasn't much of a climber either, and that turned out pretty well, considering how I was scared to death."

"Well, there's nothing to be afraid of out here. We'll build a campfire…"

If it weren't for the fact that she was weary to the bone, that could have sounded romantic.

"I could camp."

"You could do anything you set your mind to. I'm not sure you believe that, but I believe in you out here, Dinah. Depended on you as much as I depend on any one of my rescue team."

"You shouldn't have," she whispered. "In the end, it just doesn't work out. I know we had a good outcome today, but maybe it could have been better if you'd put your trust in someone else."

Eric expelled an impatient breath. "See, that's how you

always react. You pull back. Don't want anybody to trust you. It's damn frustrating, Dinah, because I see how good you are. Everybody sees that but you, and I don't know what it would take to make you see the same thing we all see in you."

"What you see in me isn't real," she said, her voice totally flat.

"Why, Dinah? Tell me what this is about? Let me understand."

"There's nothing to understand."

"That's you pulling back, Dinah. Or pushing me away. And I want to know why. We've worked together, saved lives together… I need to know why the things you do so well are the things that make you so sad."

"Because I lost a little girl once, Eric. A patient. Her name was Molly, and nobody loved her enough to stay with her. She was abandoned, and forgotten because she wasn't lucky enough to have been bestowed with anything that could be construed as a good quality of life."

"What was wrong with her?" he asked, his voice going from agitated to gentle.

"Anencephalic. On life support for her few short weeks."

"I'm sorry," he whispered.

"So was I. And in the end it broke my heart. She trusted me. I mean, I know that most people would say she didn't even know I was there, but I think she knew, and I couldn't…" She drew in a deep, ragged breath. "After it was over, I just sat there for hours, holding on. I wouldn't let her go…couldn't. They tried to take her away from me and I couldn't…wouldn't let go. I mean, I knew she'd died. Knew all along she couldn't survive. But in the end, I just…" Tears broke free from her eyes, and she swiped at them with the cuff of her sleeve. "They had to physically remove me from the room. They took her away from me and sedated me. Afterwards, Charles recommended I take a long leave of absence, or reconsider whether or not I should even be a nurse because he thought I might not be emotionally fit to care for patients, getting involved the way I did. And he might be right. I…I don't know. But Molly's the reason I couldn't walk away from this rescue. It's not in me to leave a child who needs my help. And she's also the reason I can't get involved…because I'm afraid my emotions might cloud my judgment. In a kitchen, the worst I can do is burn my sauce. But in a hospital…"

"I'm so sorry for your loss," he said, his voice so controlled it was barely audible against the night sounds beginning to start up from the bushes and trees.

"I expect you've had your share of patient losses. And I know it's not easy. But for me, I've never gotten past the place where it's personal. Taking care of every one of my patients…my children…is so personal. I can't detach myself the way some of my colleagues did."

"Which is what makes you better than just about any nurse I've ever seen. Which is why your little Molly knew you, Dinah. She felt your heart, felt your love. Charles was wrong. Getting involved is what makes you so good."

"But getting involved broke my heart."

"Because you had no one there to support you. And I'm sorry you didn't. You deserved better, Dinah." He lowered himself to the ground and pulled her down with him. Then sitting there, at the base of the rock at the river's edge, he pulled her into his arms. "You really deserved better."

"Why do you believe in me so much?" she whispered.

"Because until you came along, I was still a married man. In my heart, I'd never seen the need to be any other way. It worked. I got along. Then you…"

"You took off your wedding band for me?"

"No, I took it off for me. And for my girls. They need me to move on with my life, because they're growing up, becoming individuals who need more than a father who stopped his life years ago. And I need me to get past this because it's time. That one I give you the credit for. You've made me get involved again, made me aware of my girls in new ways."

"I thought it must have been very difficult for you. Especially since you have the girls there every day to remind you of the things you wanted in your life, things that you'll never have."

He took hold of her hand, but not to hold it so much as to caress it. To rub his thumb over the sensitive mound beneath her thumb and massage the areas above with his forefinger. Slow, gentle swirls tracing from side to side, moving up to her knuckles, exploring each one with delicacy and such skill...surgeon's hands. Then he explored her fingers, one by one, starting at the base and with his thumb and first two fingers, moving to the tip, stroking gently, over and over. Each finger. Again and again.

By the time Eric finally took hold of her whole hand, she was as seduced as if he'd made passionate love to her, as sated as she'd ever known she could be. All that from only a touch. The jolt of it sizzling all the way down to her toes. As he took a firmer grip, her toes curled, and the muscles in her legs tightened. She wanted to be seduced. Oh, how she wanted to be seduced. But she wasn't sure that was Eric's intent. "If we do spend the night here I have candy bars," she said, her voice in a wobbly whisper. Of all the silly things anyone could possibly say at a moment like that, here she was, babbling on about candy bars. "And crackers with peanut butter. Bottles of water, a flashlight, a lighter, which I have to take good care of because it belongs to—"

"You'd flunk my course," he said, his voice in low harmony with the night sounds of the forest. Seductive, full of suggestion. Primal.

"Your course?"

"Wilderness survival." He leaned over and kissed her on the jaw. "I'm a very good instructor."

"Are you sure about this?" she asked as ribbons of moonlight flowing played wickedly with him…casting him in a half-hidden aura that was so seductive she had to force herself to breathe. Was she ready for this? Was Eric ready? Last time they'd saved a patient together they'd come together in a kiss. But this time a kiss wouldn't be enough.

"I have rules, Dinah. They've governed everything I am, everything I do, for such a long time."

"Do you want to break them?" It was a hopeful question, but she feared the answer, because even if he did want to break *his* rules, she still wasn't sure she could, or would, break her own. It was a dangerous line they were walking now, skirting the obvious, so close to toppling over. Afraid of what would happen when they did. Or if they didn't.

"I loved my wife, Dinah. It was a good marriage. No problems. Patricia was everything I'd ever wanted and she made me happy beyond belief. Sometimes, when I go home from work, I still expect to find her there. Except I've had as many years without her now as I had with her. And I wonder if I want to be stuck where I am, if it's a subconscious choice or if something else is stopping me from moving forward. I mean, right now *we* should be naked together. Wrapped up in your blanket, getting warm from each other's body heat. But here I am, talking about my wife. Make no mistake, though, I really want to get naked with you."

"Maybe it's not the right time for us. It happens. The right people meet at the wrong time. I mean, I came to White Elk set on spending this part of my life being alone and trying to figure out all the mistakes I've made in the other parts of my life so I don't make them again. Getting naked in the forest with a handsome doctor was nowhere in those plans, not even at the bottom of the list." Although had there been a real list, being naked with Eric anywhere would have been climbing its way to the top at this very moment.

"But what if it's the right time, and we're so dead set on being resistant that we don't see it?"

"Ah, yes, breaking down the barriers. Sometimes the hardest ones to destroy are the ones we can't see."

"Are you threatened by my feelings for Patricia?"

"Not threatened. I like knowing how passionate you were about her. It tells me what kind of man you are." The kind she'd never been lucky enough to find. *Until now.* Although she did worry some that if she let herself get involved with Eric, Eric might not let himself get involved with her. Not in the way she needed. It wasn't his fault, and it wasn't even necessarily something she wanted to discuss with him because, as of this very moment, they weren't involved. Flirting with the idea, yes. Doing the deed…she simply didn't know if that could ever be a reality for them.

"So what do we do?" he asked. "Right now, when any man in his right mind would be seducing this beautiful woman rather than sitting here on the river bank listing all the reasons why he's not, what should we do?"

"Start over. Take it a step at a time, with no expecta-tions." But full of realization.

Eric pulled off her bandanna and ran his fingers through her tangled hair. "Well, then, beautiful stranger, my name is Eric Ramsey, and I'm quite capable of rescuing a fair damsel lost in the woods should the need arise."

"And I'm Dinah Corday, lost in so many ways, who would welcome a rescue should the need arise." She took his hand in hers and felt the immediate sensation between them. A spark, or maybe a sparkle. Or maybe an illumination as bright as the stars above.

"How will I know when the need arises?"

"It's arising," she said, her voice as tranquil as the rustling leaves on the trees surrounding them. Sliding her hand up his arm, she liked the feel of it. Strong arm. Lean. Well-muscled, and larger than her grasp around it. Was she causing goosebumps on him somewhere the way merely the feel of his arm was causing them on her? "I'm not an old-fashioned girl, Eric. My life may have suited me better had I been, but there are only so many moments given us for the things in which we find pleasure, and we waste too many of them." No, she was not old-fashioned, but not smart in love, either. Yet this wasn't love, she was telling herself hard and fast as her fingers refused to cease their journey over his flesh. Not love. Not love. Couldn't be. She wouldn't let it be.

He chuckled, the rumble of it resonant in his chest. "There's no way I ever had that impression of you."

"And that's good?" Suddenly she wasn't sure why she was being so bold. Did she want to be seduced by him? Or to seduce him? Silly questions. Of course she did. She had almost from the moment he'd left her standing in the rain with his umbrella while he'd driven off.

"It is, if you've got that blanket you said you did."

"I had a pillow, but it went with Shawn," she added, reluctantly letting go of his arm so she could pick up her backpack. If ever there'd been a time when she didn't want to lose the feel of flesh to flesh, this was it, for she feared that in the mere seconds it would take to unzip the pack and pull out the blanket, he would change his mind.

Or she would lose her nerve.

"What I have in mind doesn't require a pillow."

After she'd pulled the blanket from the backpack, she saw exactly what Eric had in mind. Somewhere in the urgent tumble of shedding clothes and exploration so frantic that it promised to explode, the blanket was totally forgotten, and the pile of discarded clothes on the bed of pine needles was enough. They were naked and entangled, the night was chilly, and neither one of them noticed anything but each other while the natural heat of so many emerging emotions cocooned them in a fire that wasn't even touched by the raw elements surrounding them.

"Are *you* sure?" he asked, much more quickly that he'd anticipated. More quickly than he'd wanted. He'd come prepared, and debated whether or not he should. Debated whether or not he could go through with this, of if guilt would pull him away from her. But now…

"We don't have to," she whispered, sensing his apprehension.

"Yes," he choked, "we do."

"Then I'm sure…"

He responded with a guttural moan then plunged deep and hard, bringing her to an immediate climax that coaxed him to his own. To start with the final act the way they did… Dinah liked that. She also liked that afterwards they spent their leisure pleasuring each other with the less urgent things that came of lovers taking their time to get to know each other. The little pleasures, the little discoveries. It was nice….nicer than she'd ever dreamed this could be. She craved the slow exploration of his hand on her, craved the building of a trust she'd never thought she could have. Because here, with Eric, she was vulnerable and trusting. And for the first time in her life, it didn't frighten her. It's exactly what she wanted to be—with him, and for him.

CHAPTER SEVEN

ANOTHER blanket would have been nice, but they were wrapped so tightly in each other that it didn't matter. Nothing about them was cold. And everything was perfect. His body matched hers, inch for inch, in a hard press. Sensually, though. Not sexually. He felt good, squeezed tight to her, pulling her into his contours. She felt the way a woman should feel with a man so close to her they were practically sharing one heartbeat. "I've never done...*this* outside," she whispered, as the kisses he was trailing down her neck threatened to rob her of breath. The chill of the sensation radiated all the way down to her kneecaps, tiny little prickles of pleasure with every kiss.

"Neither have I," he said, breaking a perfect cadence just long enough to start a new journey from her neck down to her breasts. "But I think it's already become my favorite thing to do in the great outdoors."

"Are you going to add this to your wilderness survival course?" she gasped, as he teased her nipple with his tongue first, then his teeth. She arched to him, wanting more.

He didn't stop long enough to answer. Rather, he mumbled a very rough "Uh-uh" as his hand came up to claim the breast his mouth hadn't yet claimed.

In the distance she heard the call of a night bird…was he courting his lady love? Or was he alone, looking for a lady to love? It was a sad, mournful call, one she knew so well in her heart. One that had temporarily fled from her.

"What was that sigh?" he asked, finally pulling back a little.

"Just thinking what tonight would have been like if we'd gone back to town."

"Are you glad we didn't?"

"Very glad," she whispered, words murmured as his lips claimed hers full and hard.

The kiss was so hard and full of long-held passion that she feared her lips would bruise, or that she would bruise Eric's lips. But as what couldn't possibly intensify did just that, and as she felt the deep probing of his tongue, and returned it, she kicked off that single blanket and rolled over until they were side to side. Then she pulled back enough so she could see his face. His beautiful face.

"What are you doing?" he asked.

"Just looking."

"But it's dark, there's not really much to see."

He was wrong, though. There was everything to see, and it made no matter that there wasn't sufficient light. For she saw it in her heart. And it frightened her, because she wanted it so badly.

But this wasn't love. Wasn't love. Couldn't be love. Could it?

"There's always something to see." Sliding her leg across his hip, she wiggled closer, pressed her lips to his ear. "If you know what you're looking for."

What she was doing to him, in the explicit moves, in the subtleties. As he rolled on top of her, so ready to take her again, it was clear that this second time would be as fast as the first. There was no subtlety in what he needed or what she wanted. "Do you know what you're looking for?" he practically groaned.

"I think I do." In the perfect spot underneath him, finding the perfect rhythm with him… "I think I really do." Though knowing and truly having were so far apart.

"Eric, do you read me?"

The crackling noise from the walkie-talkie startled her awake, and at first blink Dinah was surprised to find that she was totally naked underneath the blanket. At second blink, she was surprised to find she was totally alone.

"Come in, Eric."

It was Neil's voice. She recognized it.

"Come in, Eric. Can you hear me?"

Rolling over on her belly, suddenly very self-conscious about her condition, she grabbed the walkie-talkie from atop her backpack. "Eric's not here right now," she said, struggling to sit up and keep the blanket wrapped tight.

"Tell him that the Dawsons are all stable. Everything's fine here, and we were wondering when the two of you were going to head back. We don't need to send a rescue team out to find you, do we?"

Even though Neil was chuckling at the suggestion, Dinah felt totally humiliated.

"We can have a helicopter out there to get you in the next ten minutes. Unless you care to camp out there a little longer."

"Ten minutes is fine," she said, trying not to sound as despondent as she felt. Had it been that bad for Eric? Was he having morning-after regrets? Was he still battling over his feelings about his wife, and now feeling guilty about what they'd done? She felt horrible about that. Didn't want to cause him any pain. But she was afraid that's what she'd done.

"Seriously?"

"Seriously. I'm not sure Eric will want the ride, but I do." He'd said he had rules. She'd known her own rules. And broken them. Another case of her emotions ruling her head. "And I'll be ready."

"Then ten minutes it is."

Well, it was something she couldn't fight. Something she *wouldn't* fight. And maybe it was good to find out now, before they…what? Got too serious?

Dinah sighed, tugging on her clothes. Eric had to be in the throes of complete emotional regret. "But I knew," she said, slinging her backpack over her shoulder, getting ready to hike on down the trail to the pick-up point. If she met up with Eric somewhere along the way, she'd simply pretend that last night hadn't happened. That would make it easier for him. Ignore the deed and soon the fact of it would be forgotten.

Except she wouldn't forget. She'd expected…well, it didn't matter what she'd expected, did it? It was what it was. She should have known better. Nothing was going to change.

As it turned out, Eric wasn't too far off from the campsite, which surprised her. He hadn't gone off and left her at all, which was what she'd thought he'd done. In fact, he was sitting on a rock, staring out over the river, mere yards from where they'd slept. In sight all along. Yet so far away in the things that mattered.

He had to get back to her. She'd be waking up soon, wondering where he was. Then she'd be jumping to the wrong conclusion. Well, not exactly the wrong conclusion because when he'd opened his eyes that morning, he'd wanted to feel guilty, wanted to feel disloyal. But all he'd felt was good…good in a way he hadn't felt in such a long time.

That's what had sent him off to be alone, to think. Because his feelings scared him. The fact that he *had* feelings after so many years scared him even more.

Oh, he'd been accused of hiding—behind his job, behind his daughters, behind his sister. Too many times one woman or another had approached him, shown interest, tried being friendly only to have him brush them off when their overtures proved more than he'd wanted from them. But that's what had always made it easier for him, what had always made it better. He had excuses. Places to hide. Safety in a life he really didn't belong in.

But Patricia wouldn't have wanted this. She would have wanted him to be happy, to get on with his life, find someone else, be normal again. In theory, it sounded easy. In practice, it was so damned hard because it wasn't in the plan. His life had been set the way he'd wanted it, everything laid out. Perfect. Then she'd died and left him floundering. What to do without her? What to do with the girls?

Honestly, it had been easier just sticking to the original plan—the original plan minus Patricia. Except easier was getting so frustrating lately because he wanted…needed a new life. Being with Dinah made him see what he wanted in that life and, logically, he should have been feeling guilty. But he wasn't. And it hurt, letting Patricia slip away. He wasn't guilty, though. Just reconciling. And sad.

Dinah made things better. Made them good. Changed everything. Yet she was running away from him as hard and fast as she could. She'd take a few steps closer then bolt. One night brought them closer, but didn't bring them together. The thing was, being together scared him, too. So maybe he was running away as hard as she was, and hadn't even realized it. Or why wasn't he waking up with her right now, making sweet morning love to her the way he should have been?

Sitting on a boulder jutting out over the river, with the early sun beginning to shine down on his shoulders, Eric watched the water flow by. It moved along no matter what happened, the way his life should have. But his life had been stagnant for so long, sitting in a little dammed-up pool off to the side, flowing nowhere. Until Dinah. "Dinah…" he murmured. He didn't want to hurt her. If ever there was a woman he could love again, she was the one. So unlike Patricia in just about every way, she attracted him like he'd never expected anyone could again. And it was a different feeling of attraction, something so unexpected. With Patricia it had been calm, steady, all about a sense of well-being. With Dinah it was wild, crazy, off balance. And, God help him, he wanted that in his life. But was it fair to Dinah when he wasn't sure if he could get to the place where it was truly good with him…good without all these doubts in himself? She deserved more.

Eric stood, stretched, and looked around him. In the distance he could hear the sound of an approaching helicopter, and wondered if Neil had sent someone to get them. A brisk morning hike would have been good. Very cathartic, and very long. Almost three hours from here. So maybe a short ride was best. Time to get back to reality and see what happened next. Maybe he needed some distance from Dinah…just until he was sure he wouldn't hurt her, just until he was sure about…himself.

Dinah…Thinking about her brought a smile to his face, and quickened his step as he hiked back to the spot where they'd spent the night. But halfway there, he met up with her, and even though he'd expected her to come at him with a vengeance for leaving her alone, even though she had never really been out of his sight, she simply looked up at him. "Our ride's here," she said. "I decided I didn't want to hike out this morning."

She was avoiding the obvious, but he saw it in her eyes. The questions, the doubts. She couldn't hide it. She couldn't hide anything from him, and it unnerved him, being so aware of her. "It's not easy yet, Dinah. Whatever this is going on between us…it's not going to be easy. We're both still fighting against it and I needed a few minutes to think. That's the only reason I went off by myself."

"I understand," she said.

But she didn't. She doubted him, and he saw that in her, too. It killed him that such a little thing had hurt her because he didn't want Dinah hurt by anything, most of all by him. "I didn't leave you, Dinah. I don't want you thinking that I did."

"People leave. It's not a big deal. They leave, you move on."

"But I didn't leave."

"And I *said* I understand. So let's just get in the helicopter and get back, OK? I have a shift at the hospital this morning, and I have to cook this evening."

Well, she'd shut the door. Shut it and locked it up tight and he didn't know how to open it. He wanted to be optimistic about their future together, but he wasn't sure he knew *how* to be optimistic anymore. For Dinah, though, he really did want to be.

"I'm glad you saved all of them," Janice said, then immediately turned Eric's daughters loose on him.

"I called the hospital in Salt Lake on the way in and they told me that Shawn is in surgery, his father is in Intensive Care and Troy is waking up, doing better than expected. I wish all our rescues could turn out that well."

Now that he was back, Pippa and Paige were going wild, holding on to him, trying to out-talk each other, telling him all the little details of their night without him. "They don't know what he does, do they?" Dinah asked Janice.

"They know he's a doctor, and that he helps make people feel better."

"But they don't know about the rescues?"

"He thinks they're too young to understand. He's afraid they'd be worried, especially as they don't have a mother."

Dinah dropped to her knees in the grass then sprawled out. She wasn't physically tired so much as she was emotionally worn out. Too much had happened, too much to think about, and she just wanted to stay there in the grass for a while, empty her mind and stare up at the sky.

"By the way, I have a message from Angela," Janice said, standing over her, looking down.

Dinah opened her eyes. "She's OK, isn't she?"

"Fine. Perfect."

"Not in labor?"

Janice shook her head. Then smiled. "But she said to tell you that she named her new daughter after your grandmother."

Dinah bolted straight to her feet. "She had her baby? When? Why didn't someone call me? Is she in the hospital? Is the baby OK? Who delivered the baby? Did Gabby get here, or did—?"

"Whoa," Janice said, thrusting out her hand to stop the outpouring of questions. "Everybody's fine. Angela is in the hospital, and she wouldn't let anybody tell you because she knew you'd come back to her in the middle of the night, and she thought that was too dangerous. So everyone here had to promise…"

"Neil knew?"

Janice nodded. "That's why he offered the helicopter to get you back here."

"And Eric?"

"Not Eric. He'd have tried getting you back here in the middle of the night, and we decided it was better for him to rest."

"I can't believe no one said a word to me."

"Your sister's request."

"But she's OK? You wouldn't be keeping something from me, would you?"

"Other than the fact that it's a girl, her name is Sarah, she weighs seven pounds, and she's beautiful, there's really nothing else to tell you except that Angela wants to see you as soon as you can get there."

As soon as she could get to the hospital turned into about fifteen minutes, as Dinah bypassed her room, a shower and a good meal at the lodge. She hopped in her car, drove straight to the hospital, parked in the no-parking zone at the front and ran in the door, fully aware that she looked like she'd spent a night on the mountain.

On the way to the maternity ward, she paused to look at the babies in the nursery. Three of them. All beautiful, all of them causing a lump to form in her throat. The one on the left was her niece, as it turned out. Naturally, that was the baby she'd already picked as the prettiest. Of course, she'd never met a baby that wasn't beautiful but as it so happened, little Sarah was the one who brought tears to her eyes.

As the nurse held her up for Dinah to get a better look, a lifetime of possibilities for Sarah passed before her eyes…dance lessons, school plays, girlfriends, pretty dresses, boyfriends, first date, first kiss… First longing, and it was hers. To have a baby of her own. She'd subjugated that desire for so long then with Charles she'd thought about it again. Except after he'd given her the diamond ring he'd also given her the news that he'd had a vasectomy years ago to avoid the possibility of children. He would treat them as patients but he didn't want them interfering in his real life.

She'd been disappointed. Told him so, and asked him to reconsider. Maybe they could adopt? Or he could have a vasectomy reversal. He did reconsider, but not about having children. That's when he'd started to reconsider whether or not he wanted her. And she'd started to reconsider whether or not she wanted him.

But now…*this* was what she wanted. It was like her biological clock had reserved all its ticking for this very moment, and now it was ticking like crazy. She wanted a baby of her own. Wanted that joy Angela had. Wanted that feeling of complete fulfillment. It's what made sense to her more than anything else.

"She's a real looker," Eric said, stepping up behind her. "Even though she hasn't got any hair yet, I think she's going to be a redhead like her aunt." He slipped his arm around Dinah's waist and she melted against him. Quite a pair they were, dirty, tired, bruised and scratched, and standing in the hall smiling at the babies. "I remember the first time I saw the twins…I couldn't believe how perfect they were. Perfect fingers and toes, perfect little eyes and noses…"

"It puts everything into proper perspective, doesn't it? Makes you truly believe all's right with the world."

"All is right with the world…their world. And that's the way it should be."

"And then they have to grow up," she said on a wistful sigh.

"Like I said before, you'll be a good mother, Dinah."

"My life is too up and down to drag a baby into it right

now." But in the future? Admittedly, she could almost see that happening, with Eric. Thinking with her heart again.

"Only if you want it to be up and down."

"That's not what I want, but so far it hasn't been under my control." Spinning away, Dinah headed off in the direction of her sister's room, half expecting Eric to follow, but when she didn't hear the clicking of his heels on the tile floor, she decided it was for the best. Being around him almost made her believe she could have it all. *Almost.*

"Well, I see you fixed yourself up for the occasion," Angela said. She was sitting up in bed, looking happier than Dinah had ever seen her look. Positively glowing.

"I slept on pine needles," she said, plucking one from her hair. "Climbed down a rock. Waded in an icy cold river." And made love like she'd never known it could be. But that didn't show on her, and she was going to take care that it wouldn't.

"And you look radiant. I heard the father and both the boys are going to make it."

"Why didn't you let somebody call me?" Dinah asked, pulling up a chair and sitting down next to her sister.

"Because you were needed out there, and I was fine here. Brad's mother and sister flew in. And Gabby got here in time to do the delivery, so I had a veritable force of strong women here to help me through, when you take into account that half the women in White Elk stopped by because they knew you were out on the rescue and thought I might need a birth coach."

"She's beautiful, Angela. Sarah is so beautiful, and amazing.

"Then you've seen her?"

"We came to an understanding about her first date, and her first kiss, and her wedding dress."

Angela laughed. "Sounds to me like you might have a few mommy dreams going on of your own. So, did something happen out there in the woods you want to tell me about?"

"Nothing that matters," Dinah said, trying to sound less wistful than she felt. "It was…difficult."

"The rescue, or what came after?"

"Both. Eric and I, we…we got closer, I think. But it scares me. I know I trust him, with all my heart. But I get too emotional, make bad decisions…"

"And you think Eric might be a bad decision?"

"No. But I think he might be a wrong decision, at least right now. He's still got…"

"Patricia?"

Dinah nodded. "And it feels like I'm pushing him away from her."

"Is he ready to be pushed?"

"That's the thing. He might be. But maybe he's just responding to, well…you know."

Angela grinned. "So it was a nice night in the forest after all?"

Dinah grinned back. "It was, and that's what scared me. I think I should have waited. I mean, it wasn't that long ago that he took off his wedding ring, and now…" She shrugged. "I don't want to make a mess of this, and I don't want to hurt him. But I think I'm doing both."

"Then maybe he's the one you should be talking to."

Sighing, Dinah pulled another pine needle from her hair. "Maybe I will. Anyway, let's talk about you now. Like, if Brad's mother is here, what about Brad? Have you talked to him?"

"Briefly. Nothing's changed. He didn't even want to know if I had a boy or girl. But his mother and sister have had it with Brad, and they want to be part of Sarah's life. Begged me to let them be a part of it."

"Are you going to let them?"

"How can I not? They love her. What Brad's done is his choice, but I'm not going to punish the people in his family who love Sarah because he doesn't."

"It's his loss, and he doesn't even know it." Dinah smiled at her younger sister. "You're going to be a fantastic mom, you know that?"

"I'd be even better if you'd consider settling down here in White Elk with Sarah and me. Give it some serious thought, Dinah. I know this situation with Eric is up in the air, but you don't have a real home. Mom travels all the time so it wouldn't make sense to live near her since she's never in the same place more than a month or two. Which leaves your favorite sister and your favorite niece, both of whom really want you here. I intend on raising my daughter right here, and I really, *really* want you to be part of our lives. Janice was telling me how good you've been with Eric's daughters, and I want that for my daughter… from her aunt."

Settling down… It sounded so good. Sounded good when Angela initially asked, and sounded good an hour later, as Dinah was letting the warm spray from the shower slide down her tired, aching body. It still sounded good thirty minutes after that, on her way back to the hospital to cover half a shift.

But sounding good didn't mean it was going to be simple. And what she and Eric had started…that didn't make it any easier.

Had they really started something? She wondered. Pondered. Remembered. Fantasized. She was trying not to feel so contented about it, but she was contented. There was no denying it. She was totally contented and it scared her to death because she still didn't believe that the kind of contentment she was feeling could come without pitfalls. She wanted to believe, and Eric made her come close to believing, but she was still on the edge of that ledge, looking down, not sure whether to take the leap or not. And this time she didn't have Eric there to encourage her. It was her leap to take on her own. Probably the biggest leap she would ever take in her life. If she took it at all.

CHAPTER EIGHT

"I WANT those!" Pippa squealed as the three of them passed the lodge's gift shop. This was girls' day out for Paige, Pippa and Dinah, and right now Pippa was practically jumping up and down over the prospect of buying pink shoelaces. Shoelaces like the ones Dinah had used to leave a trail for Eric.

"Did your daddy tell you about the shoelaces?" Dinah asked, wondering how much Eric had said about their rescue. Or, specifically, about her.

"He said you acted like a girl," Paige volunteered.

"And what's wrong with acting like a girl?" Dinah asked, smiling. "Did your daddy tell you what's wrong with acting like a girl?"

"He said it's very good, that he likes it. Did you and Daddy have a picnic? Is that why you were in the woods?" Paige asked.

Picnic wasn't quite the word to describe what they'd had. In fact, there wasn't a word to describe it. Wasn't a word to describe the way she was feeling because of it either. Happy. Excited. Scared. It was a jumble of mixed emotions, and she was a jumble of mixed confusions because there'd been no aftermath. No mention. No overtures. No nothing.

Two days later, it was like nothing had happened between them. They'd worked a couple of shifts together at the hospital, stayed strictly professional about it, and…nothing. Eric had gone his way, she'd gone hers. No knowing winks. No suggestive smiles. Cordial nods, for heaven's sake! "Yes, we definitely had a picnic," she explained, trying to shake off the gloomy mood trying to slip down over her, trying to remind herself that Eric's feelings toward his wife most likely had everything to do with what was happening between them now. She understood it, sympathized. Told herself it was for the best since she wasn't looking for any kind of a real commitment. Of course, for just a little while…a moment in time, she'd thought that maybe… "So, are you two ladies ready for high tea?"

Pippa looked longingly at the pink shoelaces in the gift-shop window as Dinah hurried the girls off to the conservatory and left them there for a few minutes in Redmond's capable hands while she went to the kitchen to check on the progress of the evening meal prep. As it turned out, everything was under control. Her staff was busy chopping, dicing, slicing… Unfortunately, knowing she supervised a well-run kitchen didn't give her the feeling of accomplishment she longed for. In fact, she wondered why she was still in White Elk. Angela was surrounded by women fussing over her and the baby, the kitchen was well managed by Angela's support staff and the ambitious, if not ubiquitous Oswaldo. All in all, her presence in White Elk was almost superfluous. She'd come because she'd been needed but, as it had turned out, nobody here really needed her.

Just when she'd thought she might stay, it seemed like it could be time to go. Because certainly, she couldn't face Eric day after day, if she caused him any discomfort. He had his life here, his work, his family. She had…a few hopes, maybe the makings of a dream.

"How do we look?" Pippa and Paige asked in unison as Dinah entered the conservatory a few minutes later. They were in pink floral dresses, identical, and one of the servers had given them matching hats. Grinning, giggling, blowing kisses into the air, they were capturing the attention of all the people there to partake of high tea.

"Fabulous," she said, responding with a curtsey to each girl. If she did leave White Elk, saying goodbye to these girls would be one of the hardest things she'd have to do. It was amazing how much she'd come to love them in such a short time. "Absolutely stunning and beautiful."

The girls grinned from ear to ear then Pippa stepped forward and motioned for Dinah to bend down. "We can have finger sandwiches or ladyfingers with our tea," she whispered, "but we don't want *fingers*." She held up her hand and wiggled her own fingers for Dinah to see. "Can we go somewhere else and have ice cream?"

"You know you're not supposed to ask," Paige reminded her. "Daddy said so. It's not polite."

"But how are you supposed to get what you want if you don't ask for it?" Pippa argued. "And I want ice cream, not fingers. That's why I asked."

Sound reasoning in a five-year-old's mind, Dinah thought, but the differences in their personalities were coming out in a big way, and it was interesting to see. Pippa had absolutely no trouble going after what she wanted, while Paige was more thoughtful about it, trying to abide by the rules more than her sister did. Even if those rules did stipulate they had to eat *fingers*.

Eric was going to have himself a handful in the years to come. Lucky man because his girls adored him. And lucky girls because they were adored by their father. "I'll talk to Estelle, the woman in charge of the tea, and I think she can probably find you ice cream. But so you'll know, finger sandwiches don't have real fingers in them. Usually, it's something like a cream cheese spread or cucumber. And lady fingers are simply cakes. They're called fingers because they're about the size of a finger."

The girls regarded each other for a moment, settling on an unspoken agreement. "Ice cream," they both said. Something in their expressions said they were staying on the safe side.

Tea was nice. They talked, the girls chattered on and on about the things they liked to do—swimming, playing video games, watching movies, going for walks. They wanted riding lessons, wanted ballet lessons, wanted new bicycles…all normal things. And it was so fun being involved in all that. As the hour progressed, they made plans for more shopping trips, another high tea and a talk with White Elk's resident ballet teacher…although Dinah did tell them it was all subject to their father's approval.

She liked their inquisitiveness. Hoped that if she ever had children of her own they'd be just like these two. Children of her own…a thought that had come to mind so much lately. Especially when she held her brand-new niece, Sarah. Foolish thought for someone who seemed to be heading toward the exit.

Trying to wipe out all thoughts of the things that *weren't* happening in her life, like babies and twin daughters and relationships, Dinah took each girl by the hand after tea was over and led them down the hall to the gift shop, then bought them pink shoelaces. Why not? It was fun indulging them, and for all their exuberance, and their long wish list, these little girls were not spoiled. They were a delight, two people she loved spending time with. Two girls so much alike they were practically the same, except they weren't. She could see the differences more and more all the time—differences that would be more noticeable to a woman…to their mother.

There were times, like today at high tea, watching
Pippa and Paige charm every last person in the conservatory, that she could see herself being their mother. It wasn't
a fantasy, wasn't even a fond wish, because with that wish,
by necessity, would come Eric. Yet if a woman were
afforded the opportunity to hand-pick the children she'd
want to have as daughters, she couldn't see herself picking
children other than Pippa and Paige. They were well
adjusted, well behaved, smart. A true extension of their
father.

And of their mother. That was something she couldn't
forget because that, she feared, was the final stumbling
block to any kind of relationship she and Eric might have
had. Maybe, just maybe he couldn't see her as mother to
his children. Good as their playmate or babysitter, but not
their mother.

Too emotional to be a good nurse, according to Charles.
Too emotional to be a good mother, according to Eric?

Or maybe just not the right mother… She sighed on
that discouraging note. If he was finally getting past
Patricia as his wife, but not *her* as the girls' mother…well,
that was something no one could deal with. Not her. Not
even Eric.

"You look rested," Eric commented. Offhand comment, one
he'd make to anyone, in a tone of voice he'd use on anyone.

"I'm fine," she said, shutting his office door. "Look,
Eric, we need to talk."

He set aside the patient chart he'd been reading.
"About the girls?"

"The girls are wonderful. We had a lovely time at high
tea this afternoon, and unless you don't want me involved
with them, we've made plans for a few more outings while
I'm still here."

"Still here?"

"In White Elk. I just tendered my resignation here at the hospital. Pending finding someone to replace me. I won't leave you in a bind."

"Where the hell did this come from?" he snapped.

"I'd never planned on staying. I was here to help my sister, and she's being overrun with help with the baby now, her kitchen's in good order, and there's no reason for me to stay. I've been thinking about going to Costa Rica for a while… I know someone there who operates a small resort and there's an opening in the kitchen for a sous chef."

"A sous chef?"

He was being too calm. She could see the explosion about to erupt. His mouth was drawn into a thin line, his eyes narrowing. The thing was, she couldn't interpret his anger. And maybe she didn't want to. "It's a good job, nice area. I'll have my own little cottage…"

"That's what you want? Your own little cottage?"

"It's a good opportunity." And he wasn't asking her to stay. Somewhere in her plan for this conversation, she'd envisioned the version where he'd pulled her into his arms and asked her to stay. "Good salary, wonderful climate."

"Oh, so you want a little cottage *and* a nice climate?" Words spoken harshly.

"What I want, Eric, is a life. In case you haven't noticed, the one I'm living right now is pretty much bits and pieces of other people's lives. I work a hospital shift here and there at your pleasure, cook at my sister's pleasure. The only thing I do that could be remotely construed as my own life is what I do with Paige and Pippa. So if a little cottage and a nice climate are what it takes to get me closer to having a life of my own, that's what I'm going to do." Even if it broke her heart.

"And what happens to Paige and Pippa when you leave?" he asked, his anger rippling even closer to the surface. "What happens when they come to look forward to ladies' day out, and you're gone?"

"Then you can have a daddy day with them every week. So long as you do little-girl things with them. Because they need that, Eric. I mean, you should have seen them at high tea with their hats and pretty dresses, having so much fun."

"I don't do high tea."

Unequivocal, flat response. He didn't intend on budging one inch in his position. "Or pink shoelaces?" she asked, bending down over the desk so he couldn't ignore her the way he was trying hard to do. "Because they are little girls who need little-girls things like pink shoelaces."

He cleared his throat. Pushed back in his chair, pushed his chair back. "If they want pink, I can buy them pink."

Well, his intent was clear, and she had no place in it. Any delusions of staying had been wiped away now. He'd had his opening, his chance to ask her to stay. Even a hint at wanting her to stay…for him…would have been enough. But he was hiding behind Paige and Pippa now. Which meant Eric considered her, and what they'd done, a mistake. He didn't want to deal with her. She made him nervous. Reminded him of things he didn't want to be reminded of, things he didn't want to leave behind. And there was no way to fight it. Not that she would. Eric had every right to his feelings.

And she had every right to hers. Well, at least now she knew. This was probably for the best, she decided. What had happened with Eric…she'd never done anything like that before. Never just jumped into anything so quickly, so intimately and spontaneously as she had with him. But what was the point of getting involved only up to a point? Which was what their involvement would have been—

only up to a point. So it was good she knew. The best thing. She understood Eric's regrets, his confusion. Yet, still, she'd hoped…

But it hurt. She wouldn't deny it. Knowing came with a fair sting to it.

"Look, do you still want me working my shift? Like I said, I've agreed to keep working here until you can find someone to replace me," Dinah said, struggling to keep the wilting emotion from her voice. "But if you'd rather not keep me around…"

"Why wouldn't I want you working your shift? And where the hell did you ever get the idea I didn't want you working here anymore?"

"Well, for starters, what happened that night in the woods…"

He backed away from her even more. "Has nothing to do with you being here."

"Sure, it does. I mean, look at you now. You can barely be in the same room with me. How can that make for a good working relationship, even if it's only for a few more days, until you replace me?"

He dropped his head back on his chair, drew in a deep breath, and shut his eyes. "Damn," he muttered, nearly under his breath. "I don't want you to leave."

"But you don't want me staying, either, do you?"

"I don't know what I want. But it's not about you, Dinah." He opened his eyes. "And I'm sorry that's the way it seems. I'm just…"

"Look, let me make this easy for you, OK? I'll leave then you don't have to deal with…me. I know it's not easy for you, Eric." She glanced at the picture of Patricia on his desk. Beautiful woman. Bright eyes, warm smile. The woman Eric loved. "I understand that, and I don't want to make things more difficult for you."

"Costa Rica makes them more difficult for me."

"But Costa Rica makes things easier for me. I get… involved, Eric. I can't help myself. That's just me, though. I can't detach myself, put the various aspects of my life into individual compartments the way you seem to do. It would be good if I could, because I wouldn't end up doing so many dumb things, like falling for the wrong man."

"Falling for the wrong man?"

"You know that's my history. I haven't kept any secrets about that."

"So when you say *falling*, what, exactly, do you mean?"

"You know, *falling*…spending time with, enjoying the company of, wanting more time with." Making love with more than one night. "That's all." No mention of love intended.

"Look, Dinah, I know we haven't had much time to ourselves, but—"

"No time to ourselves, Eric? *No time?*" That was his choice, and maybe it was a good choice since she'd gone and done it again—fallen for the wrong man, love possibly intended. "But that's fine. I'll stay out of your way while I'm still here, and in another week or so, you won't even have to worry about that." She glanced at Patricia's picture again and thought about Eric. Maybe someday, someone would have that same kind of enduring love for her.

"Stay out of my way? Where did you ever get the idea that I want you to stay out of my way?" He pushed himself from his desk chair, and started to round the desk, but this time Dinah was the one who backed away from him.

"That's what you've been doing, isn't it? And I understand, Eric. I totally understand."

"Good, then maybe you can explain it to me because it's driving me crazy. I mean, all I can think about is that night in the woods, and when I let those thoughts distract me, I might as well hang up the white coat because I'm no good to anyone. Which isn't what my patients need from me. If anything, my preference would be to have you in my way as much as I can."

"I distract you?" she asked, still backing away as he came toward her. Backing, but in smaller steps now as his steps toward her grew larger.

"What did you think? That I'd make love to you once, and that was it?"

"Maybe. Since that's the way it was, and you've barely even spoken to me since." Her back to the wall next to his office door, she had two choices. Stay where she was, pressed into the bookshelf on her right, or scoot to the left and slip out into the hall. "I don't make good decisions, Eric. I've told you…"

"And you don't think I'm a good decision?"

"That's not what I meant."

He clicked the lock on the door. "It's not what I expected, Dinah. None of it is and I'm trying to sort things out. Trying to let go, and hang on, and change and adjust. And that's why I've been avoiding you. The only reason." In the next instant she was locked in his embrace, their lips together. Urgent. Hungry. His fingers pressing down the sides of her spine better than the feel of any fingers on her, ever.

She arched against him, felt the hard outline of his erection on her pelvis and rocked herself into it. Craving it. Craving him, as his hands moved forward, pulled up the green cotton scrub top she was wearing and sought her breasts. Even through the thin silk of her bra, the feel of his hands cupping her, exploring her made her want more, lust for more. Give more of herself to him.

Eric groaned as her tongue sought his, sucked his, and he groaned even louder while she yanked his scrub shirt loose from his pants and ran her hands over his belly, up his chest, twining her fingers in the mat of soft chest hair, flicking his nipple, squeezing, teasing… It was only when her fingers returned to his belly and were frantically engaged in untying the drawstring to his scrub pants that she caught herself. "We should probably get a room if we want to do this," she said, her voice so rough with want she didn't recognize it.

Her words were the bucket of cold water they needed, because Eric stepped back, shuddered, ran his hand through his hair then let out a final groan. "You make me want to do things I've never done," he admitted.

"Is that good?" Her immediate fear was that he felt conflicted, or guilty. It was always the big wall between them. The thing she always feared. And she couldn't argue or compete with that. "Or bad?"

A smile crept to his face. A deliciously sexy smile on his lips that eventually spread to his eyes. "Very good." He opened his arms to her, and she practically fell into them. "I'm not sure what we're going to do, at least in the long term, and I'm positive of what we'd do in the short term if we let ourselves. Which leaves us in between, doesn't it?"

"In between isn't bad," she said. In fact, it felt very good. Everything she'd hoped for. Of course, she didn't hope in the long term, which was what made the in between what it was. Perfect, for now. "Is it?"

Eric didn't answer, though. He merely sighed, and held her. This time very tenderly.

Tender was nice. She liked tender. In fact, this was the first time anyone had ever held her this way, and she was discovering it was the way she'd like to be held forever.

Forever, and only by Eric.

Which meant… No! It couldn't mean *that*, could it?

* * *

She'd been gone thirty minutes, and he still wasn't sure he could leave his office. Just thinking about her made him weak. Got him aroused. Plunged him into the throes of a conflict like he'd never imagined could exist.

But she was short term here in White Elk. That's what she kept saying, and that's what he had to fix on. If he trusted his whole heart to her, could he trust her to stay? She was always so close to running, and he needed stability in his life. The problem was, Dinah didn't think she had stability in her. She did, of course. It was obvious to anyone who looked on. But she fought so hard against it and, truly, he couldn't bring that kind of conflict into his girls' lives. They loved Dinah, and would love her more and more as days turned into weeks, turned into months. She wouldn't hurt them intentionally, he knew that. But the big *what if* still haunted him. What if she did leave? What if he couldn't move forward enough in his life to keep her here?

Moving on... Glancing at the picture of Patricia he still kept on his desk, he smiled wistfully. She'd been important for so long. Maybe longer than had been good for him. He'd taken off the ring, but it was finally time to take off the marriage. Because he wasn't married, and to move forward meant he had to free himself. That was the first step...anything else wasn't being fair to Dinah. And anything else made him feel guilty, made him feel disloyal...*to Dinah*. So he had to move on, or maybe move away from. He wasn't sure which. "And I wish you were here to tell me," he said, picking up the picture.

He studied his wife's face. Beautiful. Angelic. Everything he'd loved. But so long ago, and for the first time in all these years he felt the distance. That's what he'd always feared the most, but somehow it wasn't as bad as he'd thought it would be. Because of Dinah. She was filling that gap. "I'm lonely, Patricia. I need…I need everything again. And I'm at a point in my life when I want it. I'm ready to start over." A lump came to his throat. "Her name is Dinah…Dinah Corday. She's so…so different from the things I thought I had to have in a woman. But she fits. I'm not sure why, and I'm not even sure she wants to, but these are my first steps, and I'm stumbling because I don't want to lose you…never wanted to lose you. Yet I can't hang on any longer. But even after I took off the wedding ring I still held on because I didn't know if I could move on.

"She's good with the girls, Patricia. She loves them, and they love her. And you'd love her for the way she loves our daughters. This isn't easy for me, though. Until now I've been in limbo because I didn't want to let go, didn't want anything different from what we wanted, but…" He kissed the picture, as he did every day, and sat it back on his desk. As he continued looking at it, though, the image of Dinah's face was beginning to cloud his vision.

After another long moment he picked up Patricia's gold-framed photo, hugged it to his chest, kissed it one final time and laid it gently, face down, in his bottom desk drawer. Then he picked up his phone and dialed.

"Janice, I need a favor. There's something I want you to pick up for me at the hospital. It's in the desk drawer. Take it home, put it away for the girls…"

Afterwards, it wasn't a good feeling settling over him. Wasn't a bad one either. More like it was a necessary feeling. One that had been a long time coming. Because of Dinah.

"Dinah…" He whispered the name as he settled back in his chair, shut his eyes and conjured up her image. So now what was he going to do about Dinah?

CHAPTER NINE

DINAH'S shift at the hospital went quite smoothly. She treated stomachaches, sprains, earache, and a mysterious rash that turned out to be a berry stain. Eric stayed in Emergency as doctor on duty, and every now and then, out of the corner of her eye, she caught him staring at her.

No staring back, though. She was a complete, total mess. Maybe in love. Maybe not. Maybe leaving White Elk. Maybe not. Maybe, maybe, maybe! That was the sum total of her life up until now, and she was only just beginning to see it for what it was. Patterns repeating themselves, over and over. Patterns she ordained because she didn't believe she could get past them. Who knew? This could have been what her subconscious was telling her she deserved, and maybe that's why she simply couldn't let herself go yet again.

Because I...I hide behind excuses. She made mistakes. She was too emotional. She didn't trust. Eric wasn't over his wife. But...they were excuses, and everybody could invent excuses for almost anything they wanted to avoid. And she wanted to avoid... Dear God, it was so simple. *I'm scared of being hurt again.* Her father, her husband, Charles, Molly... Every time she loved, she got hurt. Which was why she was ready to run...because she wanted to avoid the inevitable. To give her heart away, then to have it broken every time…

But Eric wouldn't hurt her. Not intentionally, anyway. Still, his attachment to Patricia… If she forced him to move past that, he would eventually come to resent her. But if he couldn't get past that, their relationship would never be totally theirs.

"Eric, we need to talk," she said, catching up to him in the lobby as the shift ended. She had exactly four hours to sleep then she had to get up and start meal prep at the lodge. But she could make do with three and a half hours of sleep, she felt so strongly about this. They needed to talk. Needed to work this out now, or walk away from each other before they were both hurt too badly. And the one thing she never wanted to do was hurt Eric.

"Sorry, but I'm on my way up to the resort on the middle Sister. They've had an outbreak of food poisoning, and I need to go inspect the kitchen and tend a few patients there. If you'd care to go along…"

So much for good intentions. Dinah declined with a shake of her head. "Don't have time. I've got to be on duty to cook in a little while. But make sure you check the walk-in fridge. In most professional kitchens there's always something lurking in there that should have been thrown out a month ago."

"Wish you'd go with me," he said. "I could make you my unofficial assistant health inspector. But since you can't, can we do this another time?"

She was disappointed, but she understood. His duty as a doctor called, and her duty as a chef wasn't too far behind. "Tomorrow, then?"

"Dinner tonight? I could come to the lodge…"

She shook her head. "I have a dinner meeting to serve.

A hundred businessmen coming to eat, drink and be merry. And they have a huge menu ordered."

"So they probably wouldn't notice one more if I just showed up."

She laughed. "They wouldn't, but I would. And I don't need the distraction."

"You're saying I would distract you?"

He took a step closer to her, his eyes full of that familiar devilish glint, which caused Dinah to back up a step. "I'm saying that something might, and it *could* be you." Mercy, why did everything that happened between them have to sizzle so? Because she was positively hot, and in more ways than she knew she could be. And all from such an innocent little suggestion!

"Well, then, I wouldn't want to come between a hundred hungry men and their food, would I?" Grinning, he took another step closer. "Or would I?"

"Only if you're the one who gets to explain why their risotto is dry."

"Nothing worse than dry risotto, I always say. Tomorrow, then? I have an appointment in the morning to look at a house, and a woman's opinion would be nice." Advancing yet another step, he got close enough to her to bend low and whisper, "Especially when you're the woman." Then he gave her a quick kiss on the neck, and straightened up.

Dinah glanced around to see if anybody had noticed, and when she saw that the only eyes staring at her where those of a gold and white koi swimming in the lobby aquarium, she breathed a sigh of relief. Having this…this whatever it was with Eric in private was one thing. But she didn't want it going public, didn't want people knowing or speculating. That turned it into something it wasn't. Put her in a position she didn't want to be in. Or didn't want to admit to herself that she wanted to be in.

"Did I embarrass you?" he asked, chuckling at her reaction.

"No." Big lie, and Eric realized that, because he was already stepping away from her, a wide grin smeared across his face in his retreat. She did want him to retreat, of course, but part of her didn't want it at all. "Well, maybe a little."

He laughed out loud. "Well, I'm on the verge of embarrassing you even more. So maybe I'd better get going."

"Then I'll see you tomorrow morning," she said, turning and practically running in the opposite direction. She didn't stop until she reached the side entrance door, where she discovered she'd gone to the wrong door, he'd gotten her so flustered. Flustered, confused. What on earth was she doing?

It was a lovely house. Open, spacious. A log cabin, actually, with a vaulted ceiling reaching up so high the only thing Dinah could think about was how to dust the cobwebs off the light fixtures in the ceiling.

She and Eric had said very little on their way inside, but only because the realtor, Robert Tucker, was on their heels, chattering on about every last little detail concerning the house—when it was built, why it was empty, how much land came with it. He was a veritable fountain of facts, probably because he could taste the sale. The minute they stepped through the front door, she saw the look on Eric's face, a look that said he'd come home.

And here she was, trying to figure out a way to dust his home. Even decorate it, fantasizing about a large, over-stuffed couch in front of the huge stone fireplace and picturing a king-sized bed in the master suite. Places to curl up and be comfy.

"You like it?" Eric asked.

She liked it so much she could see herself living there. Of course, she wasn't going to gush about it. It wasn't going to be her house. But if she could have chosen the perfect place for her and Eric and the girls, this would have been it. "I think it will be great for you and the girls. The bedrooms are huge. They'll love that. And there's great space out back for them to play. You could put in a swimming pool, maybe their own little playhouse."

"Buying something like this is a big step," he said on a sigh.

"Trepidation's natural. But let the girls have a say in decorating their rooms, and you'll be fine."

"With two five-year-olds in charge, you really think I'll be fine?" He pulled a sheet of paper from his pocket. "This is their list of demands, and it starts with a fenced yard for a dog…a cat, a pony, and a goat."

"A goat?"

Eric shrugged. "Beats an elephant, I suppose."

"And I suppose you'll give in to them."

"On the dog. Maybe the pony."

"But you'll draw the line at a goat? What if the goat is actually more important to them than the pony or the dog?" she teased.

He chuckled. "You're always on their side, aren't you?"

"It's hard not to be."

"Patricia would have liked that. I always figured she'd be more indulgent with the girls than I would be, and she'd be happy knowing that you're the one indulging them. And that the girls like you. Which they do, Dinah. You're at the top of their best-friends-forever list."

Surprisingly, that touched her, and tears filled her eyes. "Do they ever talk about their mother?" she asked, fighting back the sniffles that were sure to follow.

"Not really. I'm all they've ever had, and I'm not sure

I do a good job of keeping Patricia in their lives. I've always been afraid it would make them too sad."

"Or give them part of their identity," she whispered, as the tears finally broke free. "It's a delicate balance, a balance they need."

"What gave you part of your identity, Dinah? What was your delicate balance? Because I want to know you, know what makes you so afraid."

Dinah glanced out the large picture window at Robert Tucker, who was staring back in at them, his face alight with eager anticipation of a sale. She couldn't do this now. Not when he had Patricia on his mind, because he might think she was attacking Patricia, or that she was jealous. Which she was not. Truthfully, she admired the way he loved his wife. But the things she needed to say to him had to be done when Patricia wasn't the first thing he thought about. It had to be about them, with nothing else between them, so it would have to wait. "We don't need to talk about that now. Not when Mr. Tucker is about ready to jump out of his skin. From the look on his face, I think he has plans for the commission he'll make on the sale, and he's anxious to go spend that money."

"Dinah, I do want to talk about it. I want to know…"

She shook her head, thrust out her hand to stop him. Sniffled. Shook her head again. "No. You've got a house to buy. That comes first. For the girls."

"Why do you always do that?"

"What?"

"Act like what you want doesn't matter. Or run away. Because that's what you're doing…running away."

"But right now what I wanted to talk about *doesn't* matter. The house does."

Eric blew out an impatient breath. "You know, you were the one who said you wanted to talk. And I want to listen. But I can't hear you from a distance, Dinah, and that's where you keep yourself."

"Because that's where you want me kept." She hadn't meant that to slip out, but in part that's how she felt.

"Where the hell did you ever get that idea?" he exploded. "I mean, I have issues I'm working through. I'll admit it. I've been stuck in a place that I wasn't ready to leave. But never, ever have I wanted you at a distance. It's you who puts yourself there, who won't let yourself go. Won't let yourself move on. While I've been struggling to find a way to put Patricia in my past and get on with my life, you've been struggling to find a way to stay in the distance. Oh, you get close, move a little forward, but then you retreat. You say you want to talk then you won't. So what am I supposed to do, Dinah?"

"I don't know," she whispered.

"You don't know? After what we've been trying to find for ourselves, that's what it comes down to? You don't know what you want me to do? Or is it that you don't know what you want?"

She looked at Robert Tucker again, and the look on his face was worry now. He feared the loss of his sale.

But Dinah feared the loss of her heart. The first true loss of her heart.

It was so damned frustrating trying to figure her out. He wasn't sure he could, and at this point wasn't sure he wanted to. Granted, the emotional stress of Dinah's last relationship, on top of losing the child she'd come to love, had to be overwhelming. He understood that. Those were things he wanted to help her through, help her overcome. But it was the other thing that frustrated the hell out of him. Dinah was a brilliant, accomplished woman. She had amazing credits as a nurse with skills that surpassed her credits. She had amazing credits as a chef. Plus she was a natural when it came to search and rescue. She was also good with children in a way he'd rarely seen before. Yet she retreated. In fact, she'd almost raised it to an art form, she was so good at it. It was like she'd make her way to the front of the line then immediately remove herself to the rear of it, always on the verge of turning and running away from the line altogether.

He was positive he could see what she wanted. Earlier, when they'd walked through the house he'd decided to buy, the look on her face had been one that said home. She wanted to be there, with him, with the girls, yet when she'd realized that's what she wanted, she'd pulled away. Not just pulled, run as hard and fast as she could. Figuratively. Had they not been in an area of White Elk she didn't know, she'd have probably done her running in the literal sense.

Of course, his own situation didn't help matters any. But at least he was working on it. Trying hard to move forward. Not only for himself but for the girls. They needed more than he was giving them, and Dinah was showing him how much. Oh, not in an overt way—*Eric, do this. Eric, do that.* But she was so tuned in to the girls, so in touch with their needs and how, even at age five, they were growing up. He had to be more sensitive to that, and until Dinah had showed up, he hadn't been aware that he wasn't being responsive the way he needed to be.

"So, what do I do?" he asked Pippa an hour later. She was looking up at him none too patiently.

"Put the flour in the bowl, Daddy! *Just put it in the bowl.*"

They were baking cookies. Or at least trying. The three of them, decked out in aprons, were making a huge mess of Janice's kitchen. Pippa and Paige wanted to bake, but

Dinah hadn't been available. So here he was, being the worst cook in the world. But being it with his daughters, at Dinah's suggestion. "Just do it, Eric," she'd told him. "It's about the process, not the results."

And it was a nice process, really. Dinah was right. The experience itself was much better than the cookies would probably be. So why didn't he know that, and why did she?

It was frustrating. He wanted to be a perfect dad. But his shortcomings were mounting. Or maybe he was simply more aware of them now. "Then what comes after the flour?" he asked, truly wishing Dinah was there. It was a wish on his mind more and more because he could see her as the perfect mom to his daughters—the only person he'd thought of that way other than Patricia. But more than being a perfect mom, he could see Dinah as the perfect wife. The wife he wanted.

Paige handed him a measuring spoon. "You measure out the salt, then the baking soda. Be very careful it's only what the recipe says. Dinah says that in baking, you have to be exact."

Amazing, she even sounded like Dinah. "And what happens if I'm not exact?" he teased.

Both girls turned up their noses. "Yuck," they said in unison. Then Pippa continued, "You'd have to throw it out and start all over because it should be the best you can make it."

"And who told you that?" As if he couldn't guess.

"Dinah did," Paige answered. "She said no matter what you do, you have to try your best."

"You two really like her, don't you?"

They nodded eagerly. "But sometimes she's sad," Pippa said. "Why, Daddy?"

"Sometimes people get sad. Even doctors don't always

know why. But if I knew how to make Dinah feel better, I would," he said, grabbing the carton of eggs Paige was handing him. "So what do I do with the eggs, and do I put the eggshells into the cookies, too?"

"Daddy!" Both girls giggled, tugged on his apron, tried to push him away from the cabinet.

"You know what?" he said, after a ten minute tussle with the girls. "Let's leave the cookies until later. I'm in the mood to take my two best girls out to a nice dinner."

"At Dinah's restaurant?" Pippa asked.

"At Dinah's restaurant. And you can order off the adult menu. *Escargots*, if you want."

"What's that?" Pippa asked.

"Snails." Eric kept a straight face. "Cooked in garlic butter. Yummy."

"Eew," the both squealed, scampering away to get dressed.

An hour later, dressed in a grey suit he hardly ever wore, escorting two of the prettiest girls in town, one dressed in a lavender A-line dress, one dressed in yellow— the dresses bought on a shopping trip with Dinah—and both wearing colored lip balm she'd also bought them, the Ramsey family made their grand entrance into the Pine Lodge Restaurant, where they were escorted to a table with the best view in the house, as Eric had requested.

"I don't want snails on my menu," Pippa told the maître d'. "Daddy said we could have the adult menu, but it has snails and we don't like snails."

Paige was responding with a firm shake of her head, turning up her nose.

"Very well," the maître d' said, making a big production of handing each of the girls the children's menu. "This is the menu without the snails." He handed the same menu to Eric. "And it's not necessarily for children. We have a very fine chef here who will prepare anything on this menu just the way you like it." He glanced at Eric. "In adult portions, if requested."

"She's going to marry my daddy," Paige said quite loudly.

"Who?" the maître d' asked, as Eric frantically shook his head, trying to stop his daughter from making a pronouncement that shouldn't be made.

"Dinah. The chef. She's going to marry our daddy," Pippa volunteered. "They picked out a house today."

The maître d' responded with the arching of his eyebrows then backed away. "Your server will be Jeffery, and he'll be here momentarily. Please, enjoy your meal." He handed Eric an *adult* menu then left.

"Who told you I'm getting married?" Eric asked, trying to keep his voice down.

"I heard Aunt Janice tell Debbi. She said if you were smart you'd marry Dinah." That from Pippa.

Paige continued, "And you're smart, Daddy. You're the smartest man we know. So that means you're going to marry Dinah!"

"Look, girls. Dinah and I are...friends. We haven't ever..."

"Champagne, sir?" Jeffrey said, setting two flutes of bubbly down in front of Eric. "And for the girls, ginger ale. Compliments of the house, to celebrate your engagement to Miss Corday."

"See, Daddy!" Pippa exclaimed. "Everybody knows."

Eric dropped his head into his hands, and groaned. How could one little dinner with his daughters have gone so wrong, even before the first course?

"So, I hear we're engaged?" Dinah said, stepping up to the table. She was dressed to cook, hair done up under a chef's hat, wearing a white chef's jacket and black and white checkered chef's pants, spatula in hand. "I was just asked if I wanted to step out of the kitchen and have a celebratory flute of champagne with my intended and his family."

"Even she knows," Paige cried. "That means you are!"

Eric's response was to leave his head in his hands and groan again.

Dinner went quite nicely, considering the way it had started. He'd ordered a spinach and squid linguine in garlic cream sauce, from the adult menu, while the girls had chosen chicken, from the children's menu. Except for her one brief appearance at the table, Dinah had stayed in the kitchen. They'd made arrangements for a late-night dessert together after he'd taken the girls home and tucked them into bed. He looked forward to that because it had been Dinah's invitation, the first right and proper date between them, she'd called it. Truth was, they hadn't had that first date yet. Not a real date. Admittedly, he was nervous.

So, after he'd accepted Dinah's offer, he'd explained to the girls that he and Dinah were not picking out a house together, were not getting married. They'd taken the information well, but a mischievous look that had passed between the girls told him the matter was not closed. At least, as far as they were concerned, it wasn't.

Ice cream was the chosen dessert for the girls, while Eric passed on the last course, contented to drink his coffee and stare out the window at the sunset. It was a beautiful evening. Clear. The sun was casting a golden haze over the top of the older Sister, a spectacular sight. This was a good place to live, and he'd never regretted moving here with the girls. Oh, he'd resisted at first, when Neil had suggested it. Neil was from here, and they'd met when Neil had come to California to take a job. Neil's heart had never left here, though, and he'd wanted to come home almost from the day Eric had met him. Somewhere in the middle of Neil's two-year contract, he'd convinced Eric that White Elk would be a good place to raise Pippa and Paige. And, as it had turned out, it had. Now he didn't want to leave here. Didn't have the same desires he'd once had for big-city medicine and an upwardly mobile career. This was good. And finally moving on made it even better.

He *was* moving on, too. Slowly, sometimes not very surely. But he was in the process, thanks to Dinah. She was showing him there was still a lot of life waiting for him if he wanted to have it. With Dinah, he did want to have it. And if nothing else came out of their first right and proper date tonight, he was going to beg…get down on his knees if he had to and beg her patience. The picture of it in his mind was ungainly, but he would do whatever it took to keep her here, to keep her from running away.

For the first time in years, Eric was anxious to see what life held in store for him.

"More sprinkles, please," Pippa said to Jeffrey, who'd inquired as to her satisfaction with the ice cream.

"Me, too," Paige chimed in.

Eric smiled. Yes, it was a very good life. He only wished… Glancing at the kitchen door for the hundredth time that evening, he stopped the thought. No point in wishing. Dinah wasn't ready to step over the line. Wasn't even ready to come close.

He was a patient man, though. Maybe that would be enough to get him through until she had a change of heart. Or maybe that's what would eventually do him in. For now all he had was time…time to wait.

Taking another sip of coffee, he looked out over the mountaintop again, admiring the splendor of the amazing palette of colors against the darkening sky. Johnny Mason's yellow plane, a twelve-passenger commuter, was making its lazy way through the sky. The Canary, everybody called it. The Canary, which was available for rescue and transport whenever he needed it.

Johnny was good that way. So was everybody else here. Nice, solid people. People who cared.

"Can Johnny see us?" Paige asked. "We're almost as high as he is."

"No, it's too far away. And right now Johnny is concentrating on landing." The small airstrip on the middle Sister had been built recently, with two or three small commuters using it regularly, as well as several private planes. During the ski season private planes flew in celebrity skiers practically every day. This evening, though, Johnny was flying in Fallon O'Gara. She was a backbone of the hospital, maybe the most essential person there, and while no one begrudged her a short holiday, he was glad she was coming back. White Elk Hospital simply ran better with Fallon there.

"When can we ride in The Canary?" Pippa asked. "Because Johnny said he'd let us if you will."

Eric chuckled. "He did, did he?"

Both girls nodded.

"We'll talk about it when you're eight."

"Seven," they protested in unison.

"Nine," he argued back.

"Seven and a half," they countered together.

"Ten," he came back one more time.

"Eight," they finally agreed, smiling like the victory was theirs.

Eric took another sip of coffee, thinking what a lucky man he was as he watched The Canary head into its landing. Coming about, it made a sweeping circle and headed directly for the middle Sister then dipped its nose to start its descent. Then, all of a sudden… "Oh, my God!" He dropped his half-full coffee cup on the table, as half the people in the restaurant gasped and screamed. Then he bolted to his feet.

Immediately, Dinah flew from the kitchen. "What is it?" she yelled out over the cries of practically all the people dining there, who were transfixed on what seemed to be nothing outside.

"Plane crash," Eric whispered, hoping the girls hadn't heard. But, of course, they had, for they had their faces pressed to the window, the same way another thirty diners in the restaurant did. "Johnny Mason's plane went down," he choked out, already dialing on his cell phone.

Without missing a beat, Dinah threw her chef's hat onto the table and was untying her apron as she spun around. "I'll be ready to go in two minutes," she called behind her, running as hard and as fast as she could on her way to her room to get ready.

"Neil," Eric said, when his partner answered. "Johnny Mason's plane just went down. As best as I could tell, it's over the landing strip or close to it. I'm already halfway there, so I'm on my way."

Neil agreed to call a full-out rescue, but before he hung up, Eric reminded him, "Fallon's on that plane." It was a sobering thought, yet one he couldn't dwell on as he dialed his sister's number next. "Janice, there's been a plane crash—The Canary's down. I'm up at the lodge on Pine Ridge with the girls and I need you or someone to come and get them."

"Daddy!" Pippa and Paige cried together. "What's wrong? Why are the people yelling?"

"Because there was an accident up on the middle Sister," he said, as he punched in Jess Weldon's number, keeping his fingers crossed that Jess was home and ready to go. Jess had a helicopter, kept it parked in a field behind his house. He was usually ready to go at the drop of a hat. "And they're afraid people might be hurt."

"Are you going to go help the people who might be hurt?" Paige asked.

"Yes, sweetheart, Daddy's going to go help the people."

"Could you have an accident, too, like they did?" Pippa asked. "And get hurt?"

That was the question he never, ever wanted to answer. The reason he'd never told the girls what he did, other than being a doctor. It would scare them, and he didn't want that. It would also raise the inevitable question—the one Pippa had just asked. So he'd avoided the truth, but he'd never lied to the girls, and he wasn't going to start now. "I'm always very careful that I won't get hurt. It could happen, but Daddy's very safe and he doesn't want you to worry about him."

"Aunt Janice does," Paige said.

His girls were so perceptive. It amazed him, scared him and made him proud at the same time. "Look, we'll talk about this when I get back. It'll probably be some time tomorrow. OK?"

Both girls nodded a skeptical, frightened agreement, and Eric pulled them into his arms and hugged them. "We'll finish making those cookies when I get back, and I'll call you later tonight. Promise."

"I'm ready," Dinah shouted, on her way back through the dining room. She was dressed in jeans and boots, wearing a heavy sweater over a T-shirt. Her hair was pulled back into a ponytail, and she was carrying her medical kit, looking every bit the rescuer.

Eric simply stared for a moment. She was in her element, doing this. In her element being a nurse, too.

Something about her life had to change and, God willing, he had to be the one to do it. He had to be the one to make her see that she could trust him but, more, that she could trust herself.

Pippa and Paige were left in Jeffrey's capable hands until Janice could get there, and once Eric knew they were going to be fine, he ran to his truck, motioning Dinah to follow.

"Do you know where it went down?" she asked, finally catching up to him. He was already halfway out of his suit, getting ready to change into the clothes he always kept with him in the event of an emergency. While he unbuttoned his shirt, she helped him get the necktie off. While he was pulling off his pants, she was holding out a pair of jeans for him to put on.

"I'm pretty sure he was on his approach to the little landing strip up on the middle Sister. Oh, and Fallon O'Gara was supposed to be flying in. She's been on a holiday in Salt Lake City. Falling in love, I think."

"Oh, no!" Dinah gasped, grabbing Eric's boots for him.

"I talked to her earlier. She said she was going to try and catch the last flight in. Which was Johnny Mason's."

"Maybe it wasn't Johnny's plane that…" She couldn't bring herself to say "crashed". Plane crashes signified such awful things.

"His plane is yellow, bright yellow. There's no mistaking it."

"Was the plane you saw yellow?"

Eric nodded.

Dinah grimaced. "Since it didn't flame, that's good. Maybe they made the airstrip after all."

"Neil's already had a call from Ella Clark. She runs the landing strip up there. She said the plane's down." He glanced at his watch. "Ten minutes now."

"How long will it take us to get there?"

Eric glanced up as Jess Weldon's helicopter came into view. "A few minutes," he said, bending into the back of the truck, pulling out equipment—ropes, bags, tools.

"The drive would take thirty minutes, this will take less than ten." Eric waved Dinah toward the chopper and led the way, leaving Dinah to run after him, her arms loaded with the supplies he hadn't been able to carry. But when she got to the helicopter, she was surprised to find its pilot stepping out.

"It's a two-seater," Eric yelled. "And I need you more than I need Jess." He said something to Jess, tossed him the set of keys to his truck, and Jess turned and ran toward the parking lot.

"What are you doing?" Dinah practically screamed, her eyes still fixed on the departing pilot.

"Get in!" He yelled the command then climbed into the pilot's seat. Blindly, Dinah obeyed, but once she was strapped in, she shut her eyes and refused to open them.

"I hope you know what you're doing," she yelled, gripping the edges of her seat so hard her knuckles turned white. She could feel the lift, hear the rotors pick up velocity as they headed straight up. But she still couldn't look down. Couldn't even get her eyes open to look, even if she'd wanted to. "Are you really a pilot, too?" she shouted. But he didn't answer. So she ventured a peek in his direction, only to find him talking into a headset. Before she could close her eyes again, she caught sight of the ground, saw dozens of people down there looking up…at them. They were getting smaller and smaller, which meant… Dinah gulped hard. Of all the incredible things not to know about a person, this had to be the most incredible. Because he was a pilot, an honest-to-goodness pilot, and a very skilled one judging from the way he handled the aircraft.

"Why didn't you tell me?" she shouted at him when he had finished talking into the headset.

"It never came up," he shouted back.

Her hands loosened their grip a little as they turned and headed for the middle Sister. But she couldn't sit back and relax.

"See if you can spot the crash site," he shouted, then added, "With your eyes open."

"My eyes *are* open." Becoming more and more open all the time. Eric was an amazing man, the man of any sane woman's dreams. Of course, climbing into a helicopter with him might be pushing the sanity point a bit far, but this was a man who kept getting better and better. Maybe the man to make her believe that she *could* believe.

"It's just ahead, but I'm not seeing…"

"They didn't make it," Dinah shouted, practically jumping out of her seat. "I can see it. It's just to the…" She didn't have her bearings. Didn't have a clue which direction was which. "Over there." She pointed.

Eric brought the helicopter round, hovered over the spot for a moment then turned the helicopter in the opposite direction, descending just on the edge of the landing strip. "Watch your head when you get out," he shouted, as they touched down. "Give the rotors a minute…"

The words fell on deaf ears. Dinah bolted out, grabbed her medical bag and a few of Eric's tools, and took off running across the end of the landing strip, heading into what was, essentially, a cleared area at the base of an old ski slope that had shut down years ago, when the Cedar Ridge Lodge had been built on the other side of the mountain. No one was up there yet, except a single truck she saw ahead of her. It was parked off the gravel road, its driver's door open.

"Dinah," Eric called, from behind, running hard to catch up to her.

"I can see it, Eric." But not for long, as it was getting dark. And that didn't bode well for the rescue, if the victims weren't all contained in a small area.

He caught up to her, and they paused together at Ella's truck. Looked. Then, as if there was an unspoken agreement between, ran to the crash site, Dinah going to the left, Eric to the right.

"Full plane," Ella cried. She was on her hands and knees next to a passenger, feeling for a pulse. "I called it in."

Dinah dropped to her knees beside the woman, but Ella gave her a grave shake of the head. "I don't think this one will be needing your services this evening."

After she'd confirmed what the old woman already knew, Dinah stood back up, looked around. Saw someone sitting up, way off to the side of the crash. "Are you going to be OK?" Dinah asked Ella.

"I've been running one airstrip or another for fifty years. Sorry to say, this isn't my first crash. I'll be fine."

The next two people Dinah checked were injured, but stable enough. And grateful to be alive. But she came upon the pilot, at least she assumed him to be a pilot because he wore a bright yellow T-shirt with the word *Pilot* across his chest in blue. Except *Pilot* was covered in bright red blood, and poor Johnny had no pulse. In a quick assessment, Dinah counted three serious conditions, and her stomach roiled. Johnny had a puncture wound to the thigh that was leaking a fair amount of blood, a gash to his head which had rendered him unconscious, and a huge bruise to the chest, which was going to be the injury she had to fight hardest. Death was never easy, and she didn't like losing to it. It wasn't inevitable for Johnny, though.

"Dinah!" Eric shouted from somewhere on the other side of the wreckage. "Are you OK?"

"I'm fine! Doing CPR," she shouted back. She was starting chest compressions now, hoping it would be enough. "What's the estimated arrival on anybody getting here?"

"Ten minutes tops."

Ten minutes. She could do this for ten minutes. But what if someone else here needed those ten minutes, too? "Then I'll be good over here."

"Do you need anything?" he shouted.

Other than their first right and proper date? It seemed something always got in the way, that they always had more important things to do. What an amazing team they made. A team…she'd never thought of her and Eric in those terms. "I'm good. Oxygen would be nice as soon as we get it up here, though." Yes, they were an amazing team. Maybe with some kinks to work out. But amazing, all the same. "Well, Mr Pilot," she said to Johnny Mason. "You'd better make this worth my while, because it's just you and me for the next ten minutes, and I don't want you letting me down in the end. I have expectations, and you'd better not ruin them for me. You hear?"

Expectations. She looked across the crash site as Eric was about to climb through the plane wreckage. Yes, she did have expectations. "It's just you and me," she whispered. You and me, meaning Eric and herself.

CHAPTER TEN

"NEED some help with that?"

Dinah looked up, saw the silhouetted shadow of a large, looming mountain man. To her, he looked like a grizzly bear.

"You know CPR?" she asked him, wondering where he'd come from.

"In my clean-shaven days I was Dr. Walter Graham, obstetrician. Formerly a full-time doctor at the White Elk Hospital and currently part-time when I take a notion to work. In my unshaven days, I'm Walt. I was up on the overlook, getting ready to hike down the other side, when I saw the plane come down." He knelt, nudged Dinah aside and assumed his place doing CPR. "You're faster than I am, can get to more people. You go on. Johnny and I will be fine here."

"Rescue crew should be up here any time now." She grabbed her medical bag and stood. "Call me if you need something." Then she ran for the crushed fuselage, wondering if Eric was still inside. But halfway there, the faint call of someone in the distance caught her attention, so she stopped, listened. Couldn't pinpoint it.

"Hello," she called. "Can you answer me?"

There was no response.

"Can you tell me where you are?"

Again, no response. The only sound she could hear was the crunching of truck tires on the gravel road. Help was here but, damn, she really needed silence. Really needed to be able to hear. "Hello?" She tried one more time then held her breath, hoping, praying…

A faint moan, coming from somewhere to the side of the crash site. But where, exactly? "Eric, over here. I've got someone over here and I can't find them."

No time to wait for the portable lights to be set up, no time to wait for the rescuers to be organized. Dinah dashed off to the wooded area on the edge of the clearing, and started her search. "I'm coming," she called out. "Don't give up. I'm on my way."

"Dinah, where are you?" Eric called.

"Just at the tree line," she yelled back, flashing her light in the direction of his voice. "I heard someone moaning."

"Any other response?" he asked, once he'd caught up to her.

"No. And it was just the one moan. I mean, it could have been an animal, but… Is everybody accounted for at the site? All the victims?"

"Everybody but Fallon. And there's some confusion about whether or not she took the flight. It turns out that Johnny had her on the manifest for tomorrow morning. Her cell phone is off, but we're trying to contact her friends right now."

"Then she could be out here."

"And we'll find her if she is." For the next few minutes they made their way slowly through the underbrush, pushing back branches, climbing around bushes, in places practically dropping to their knees to crawl, the under-growth was so dense. They stayed apart, not talking but close enough to see one another, except Dinah couldn't look at him. Because to look was to admit her feelings. And to admit them was to change everything.

But changing because she was in love? That wasn't such a bad thing, was it?

After all, she did love Eric in a way she'd never known. Not with anybody, ever.

"One small step," she whispered. But, really, wasn't it more like one gigantic leap of faith?

"Eric, come in," Neil radioed from the crash site. "We've heard about Fallon."

He clicked on his radio. "What?"

"She was on the plane. And she's not one of the victims. We have eleven, not including the pilot. One fatality and ten survivors, three of them critical, one extremely critical, six stable. Fallon's not one of them and we've looked everywhere inside the grid we laid out. She's not here, and there's nothing to suggest she's buried in the actual plane wreckage somewhere."

Eric stood up, brushed the dirt off his knees. "Then she's here somewhere, where Dinah said she was."

"I'll get another team in to you right away," Neil said, then clicked off.

"Fallon," Dinah called from somewhere off to his left.

"I think so."

"No, it's Fallon. I've found her."

He didn't want to ask. Didn't want to know.

"She's alive, Eric. Unconscious, pretty badly injured, but alive."

In mere seconds he was at Dinah's side, assessing the pupils of Fallon's eyes. "Responsive," he said, so relieved he nearly went weak at the knees.

"Can't get a blood pressure on her," Dinah said, and immediately started probing Fallon's belly. "It's rigid. Probably internal bleeding."

Eric was checking for bone injuries and gaping wounds. "No compound fracture, but I think she's got several facial fractures, probably a shoulder fracture... can't tell about her neck and spine."

"Eric." Dinah leaned in close to him. "She's losing her airway. Her breath sounds are diminishing pretty quickly."

"Damn," he muttered, immediately putting a stethoscope to her lungs. Dinah was right. Her breathing was being compromised...shutting down. But before he could say anything, Dinah was already pouring an iodine scrub on Fallon's throat—an iodine scrub he kept in his medical bag.

"You have a blade?" she asked him, as he took Fallon's pulse.

"In the pocket on the right side." He bent closer to Fallon. "You stay with me, you hear? It's going to be a rough one, but I'm going to pull you through it...Dinah and I are going to pull you through it, Fallon. And what we have to do now is trach you..." Cut a hole in her windpipe to allow her to breathe. "You've got too much swelling in your trachea, but hang in there with me. We'll get you to the hospital in just a few minutes and get some pain meds into you."

Dinah handed the scalpel over to Eric, and squeezed his hand at the same time. Without a word, she poised herself with a flashlight, ready to provide light for the procedure, but Neil arrived with several volunteers, who all carried flashlights and spotlights. And in the blink of an eye, Eric had performed the life-saving procedure, sliced a tiny hole into Fallon's throat, through the skin, through the cartilage. With no time to spare.

"She's going to be fine," Dinah whispered, as Neil

handed her a plastic tube to insert into the tiny incision Eric had made in her throat.

Eric glanced over at her, too overcome to speak. What they did together...professionally, it was a perfect fit. But personally...yes, he would definitely get down on his knees to beg Dinah's patience with him. "I'm glad you were here," he said, his voice rough. Maybe beg more while he was down there.

"Well, I seem to be getting better at emergency rescue."

"Not for that," he said. "For me. I'm glad you were here for me."

It took fifteen more minutes to stabilize Fallon for transport, fifteen minutes getting the IV in her vein, getting oxygen started. Fifteen minutes trying not to look at the facial fractures, the cuts, the unknown conditions that could only be diagnosed in the hospital. But she was alive, and that's what Eric kept telling himself as his team stabilized her neck and strapped her to the stretcher.

Rescue was always personal, but never this personal. And he was drained, physically and emotionally.

"She's going to make it," Dinah reassured him, slipping her arm around his waist. "I know she's in rough shape right now, but she's going to pull through."

"That was a good call on her breathing," he said, leaning in, savoring her physical support as much as her touch.

"And that was pretty slick work, getting her airway opened up so quickly." She leaned her head into his side. "We're good together, aren't we?"

"Perfect." So now that he knew, without a doubt, what he wanted, all he had to do was figure out how to make it happen. What would it take to convince Dinah to bridge the distance she always drew between them? *Bridge it permanently.* "Look, will you do me a favour? I'm going to stay here and clean up the site. Pick up the trash, make sure we're not leaving any equipment behind. Do you mind going to Pippa and Paige? They were too close to this, and I don't want them to be scared. I'll call them when I get out of here and get cell phone reception, but I'd feel better knowing you're with them until I can get home. Janice is good, but even the girls recognize that she gets nervous. Right now, as they saw the plane, and I'm sure they've heard all about it, I'd like you to—"

"You don't have to ask, Eric. I'm on my way." She stood on tiptoe and kissed his cheek. "Too bad you haven't moved into your new house, because I saw a Jacuzzi there, and that would sure be a nice place for us to relax once the girls are asleep for the night."

"Damn," he groaned. "That's the best offer I've had in years, and I have no way of taking you up on it."

"Not now you don't. But maybe in a while…"

"Do you mean that, Dinah?"

"I want to mean it, Eric. I really want to mean it. But it's not easy to admit, not easy to do, and my life is still a mess…"

That distance again… Damn, what was he going to do? Rather than trying to find the impossible answer, he pulled her roughly to his chest, breaking that distance, if only for the moment, and kissed her hard and fast on her lips, then pushed her away. "We'll continue that later, but I want you going down the mountain with the team now. OK?"

She kissed her fingertips, dirty as they were, and brushed them across his lips. "OK." Then she trotted down the trail after the rest of the team.

Eric kept the flashlight trained on her until she was out of sight then he began the clean-up. Truth was, he could have come back in the morning. There was no great hurry to get this done. But right now he wanted to be alone. He had a lot of thinking to do. And he needed to do it now.

* * *

"I was just checking on Fallon, and she's in pretty bad shape," Dinah whispered to Janice. Pippa and Paige were busy in the kitchen, making sandwiches for Eric. Ten sandwiches and counting, made out of every conceivable thing from the kitchen that could be slapped between two pieces of bread. Including the cookie dough. "We lost one, several are critical, most are stable, though."

"Which is a blessing," Janice said. "Although, I'm so sorry for the one who didn't make it." She glanced at the pendulum clock on the wall. "How long before he'll be home?"

"Actually, I thought he'd be here by now." It had been only two hours, and maybe it was merely her eagerness to be in his arms that had protracted those hours into an interminable length. "But who knows? Maybe he's taking some of the equipment back to the hospital, or even checking on some of the victims who'll be treated there? He's probably in the emergency room right now, totally unaware of the time."

"He needs someone to make him aware," Janice said. "Don't get me wrong. I've been happy having him here, and I love Pippa and Paige. But they need another life…all of them. And I…well. So do I. I'm not getting any younger, and there's this really nice man who owns a little café across the street from my shop. We have lunch together a couple times a week, and we've even gone out in the evenings. Yet…"

"You haven't been able to bring him home."

Eric's sister shook her head. "My daughter, Debbi, has a life. She's decided to go to Chicago next month, after she graduates from high school, and one of Gabrielle's friends there is going to make sure she doesn't get herself into too much trouble. Which means I'll be alone for the first time in eighteen years. And I'm looking forward to it. Though

I'll be sad to see her go, sad to see Eric and the twins go, too."

"Sad, but not sad."

"Does that sound terrible, Dinah?"

"It sounds normal. And you deserve it."

"But I worry, because Eric is so caught up in the past. And I want him to move on with his life. This house he's buying is a good thing, and I have an idea it has something to do with you. So does his taking off his wedding band, and finally putting Patricia's photo away."

"Her photo?"

"The one on his desk at work. He called me the other day, had me come and take it."

Dinah had seen him stare at that photo so often, seen that distant look in his eyes when he did. These changes couldn't be easy for him, and yet he did them so quietly, and with so much strength. Not like her, making her changes kicking and screaming and being so resistant. Even tonight, when he'd asked her if she meant it…the Jacuzzi with overtones of so much more…she hadn't said she meant it. She'd said she was *trying* to mean it. Then said it wasn't easy. Wasn't easy… In truth, it was the easiest thing she'd ever done, falling in love with Eric. And the instant he walked through that door, she was going to tell him so.

"Still no word?" Dinah asked one of the rescuers who was still lingering in the hospital, helping to get all the plane crash patients settled in. It had been four hours and she was pacing the emergency department halls now, making a nuisance of herself.

"He's fine, Dinah. Sometimes Eric likes to unwind after these things. He's gone off before. Don't worry." George Fitzhenry, one of team leaders, squeezed her shoulder. "He's had a lot on his mind and sometimes you simply need to get away to think."

"I suppose you're right." George knew Eric's habits, and he wasn't concerned. So she shouldn't be concerned either. She was, though. Everything in her screamed she had to be concerned. "But he was anxious to get back to Pippa and Paige."

"And he knows they're in bed by now. I think it's too soon to be so worried. Eric will turn up when he's ready."

"But couldn't we do some kind of preliminary search?"

George shook his head. "It's too soon. People haven't even gotten home from the last effort. But if he hasn't called or come back in another hour or two, we'll look for him. Right now it's better to wait."

"Sure," she said, starting to turn away. But the voice screaming in her head wouldn't let her turn away. *Trust yourself, Dinah! Trust yourself!* That voice wouldn't let her be talked out of what she felt, what she knew. *Trust yourself, Dinah.* Eric's life depended on that! "He's in trouble, George. You're wrong about this, and we do need to be worried. Something's wrong, and I'm going back out there to look for him. I'll need someone with me so I'm going to go find Neil and tell him to call a rescue. *Now.*"

After Dinah found Neil, and demanded action, he shut the patient chart he'd been writing in, retracted the point on his pen then tossed both pen and chart on the desk. "I'll have a team ready in twenty minutes."

Twenty minutes…too long. But going out there alone was stupid. Eric would be the first one to tell her so. Now it was a matter of fighting her will, because everything inside her wanted to run for the door and not look back. The deeper sense inside her, though, the sense Eric had put there, was holding her back, forcing her to finally do this the right way. Because it was Eric's life on the line. Eric… "I'll be waiting." Waiting the longest wait of her life.

Neil ran the effort without a hitch. A dozen people were at the hospital door in a matter of minutes, still dirty from the night's earlier rescue, ready to go back out, ready to find Eric. In those few minutes while she waited, Dinah tried his cell phone over and over. Tried to get through to Ella Clark, to see if Eric's truck, driven there earlier by Jess Weldon, was still there, but Ella wasn't answering. Neil said she took off her hearing aid at night.

Various people from town called in, all reporting no sign of him. Apparently, there was a foot search going on. People were walking the streets, looking for his truck. Not that Eric was the type who would be so irresponsible as to simply wander off this way. He wouldn't, and Dinah was biting her nails with worry. "The first thing I'm going to do when we find him is hug him and tell him how much I love him," she said on the cell phone to Angela. "The second thing I'm going to do is…tell him again how much I love him."

"He's going to be fine," her sister reassured her. "He probably has a flat tire."

Or he'd fallen off the side of a mountain somewhere. "Look, I'll call you. Neil's got everybody ready to go out so I've got to run." And run was what she did. To the truck, to climb into the front seat with Neil. To the site where they'd last seen his truck at the landing strip the instant Neil had stopped his own truck. To the place in the woods where they'd found Fallon, to make sure he'd cleaned the site. Which he had. By the time Neil had caught up with her, she already knew everything there was to know at that particular site. Eric wasn't there.

"I have people tracking him down the road," Neil explained. "Driving it, taking the side roads. Walking it, to look for any indication of where he might have gone over."

"And that's it? That's all we can do?"

"Eric's not given to doing stupid things. He knows how to leave signs if he's in trouble, and he knows how to take care of himself until we can get to him."

Words meant to calm her down, but it wasn't working. "Look, I'm going to get out and walk down the main road like the others are doing. Maybe I'll see something…" She shrugged. "Maybe I won't, but at least I'll be doing something other than sitting." Something was better than nothing.

So she climbed out of Neil's truck and began her descent down the road leading away from the middle Sister, thinking about the Ute Indian legend. If ever there was a time when the Three Sisters needed to protect someone in their shadows, this was it. Looking up to the oldest Sister, which towered over this, the middle Sister, she prayed for the three of them to work their magic, and work it fast.

Rescuers in front of her, sweeping the road with their flashlights, walked slowly, looking everywhere. It was a methodical search as they hunted two by two, darting off the road into the underbrush every now and again then returning to the road, dejected. Coming up behind them, having a second look at everything the way she was, was probably a waste of time, but she was trying to think like Eric now. He had been going to clean up and go to the girls. He might have been in a hurry… Had the girls called him? Or had he called the girls, like he'd promised? Flipping open her phone, she wondered. "Hello, Janice," she said when Eric's sister answered.

"Did you find him?" Janice choked.

"No, not yet. But we've got a dozen people out on the

mountain, and at least that many in town. There's a good chance he's had trouble with his truck." No one knew that, no one had even speculated, but Janice needed to hear something reassuring, although Dinah wasn't sure if she'd said it for Janice's sake or for her own. "But what I need to know is if he called the twins. I remembered him telling me that he'd call them when he got out of here, so I was wondering…"

"Just a minute," Janice interrupted, then dropped the phone. Almost immediately, she was back on. "He did call them. Told them he was on his way home, and to get the cookie dough ready."

"And that's all?"

"That's all they said, except they wanted more chocolate chips."

Wanted more chocolate chips. The words kept coming back to her, nagging, not letting go, for the next several minutes on her trek down the road. More chocolate chips… "Neil," she said when she called him on his cell phone. "If I were on the middle Sister and wanted to go and find a bag of chocolate chips, where would I go?"

"What the hell are you talking about, Dinah?" he snapped.

"Chocolate chips. Where would be the best place to find them on my way home from the middle Sister?"

"Is there a point to this?"

"I don't know…maybe." Would he have gone for chocolate chips?

"You'd go to Bertie's Convenient Store, open all night. At the fork, halfway down the main road, you'd take the road to the west, go about a mile, and if you knew the short cut, you'd come to the giant boulder—it looks like an old lady with a crooked nose—and take the dirt road around it…more like a wide, dirt path."

"Would Eric know the short cut?" she asked.

"Would Eric have gone to Bertie's for chocolate chips?" Neil asked, gunning his engine. Before Dinah could answer his question, he'd pulled up alongside her. "Get in," he said, barely stopping.

She was in, door not quite shut when he took off, but not before he'd radioed his position to several of the rescue team. "It makes as much sense as anything else does." Dinah fastened her seat belt. "Everything he does is for the girls, and if they wanted chocolate chips, I think he'd go out in a blizzard to get them."

"Well, apparently he's more predictable for you than he is for me, because there's no way I'd have put chocolate chips together with him going missing."

"Let's hope he's predictable this time." Gripping the side of the seat as Neil took the turn at the fork, all she could do was stare out the window, hoping to see something…anything. But all she saw was a dark, nearly starless night, where glowing eyes stared out from their bushy hiding places, and bugs darted in and out of the truck's headlights. Truth was, there was nothing to see. Without light it was hopeless. But waiting until morning was unthinkable. Neil knew that, every rescue worker out on the hunt knew that. Yet they were there, doing what they had to do, breaking Eric's own rules about this kind of night search, to find Eric. "So, how much farther to this boulder?"

Neil lifted his hand from the steering wheel at the same moment he stepped on the brake and pointed to it. "Right there."

In the night shadows, it did resemble the profile of an old woman with a hooked nose. "Should we drive, or walk?"

"Eric's truck is heavier than mine so he might have gone

this way. But I can't drive it because after all the rains and flooding we've had recently, my truck will get bogged down." He stopped the truck directly under the old woman's nose. "So we'll walk for a while and see what we can find."

Words said to no one, as Dinah was already on her way out the door.

Together, they walked about half a mile down a rutted, muddy path, slipping and sliding, most of the time hanging on to each other to keep themselves upright. "The tracks look fresh," Dinah said, shining her flashlight on the road.

"Kids in town like to come down this way. They use it for a lovers' lane."

"Well, it's isolated enough." Too isolated, she thought, while trying to extricate her boot from a particularly deep rut…one that looked like it could open up and swallow the whole town of White Elk. Stopping, she bent to help her foot slip back into the boot and dropped her flashlight. It plopped, more than rolled, and its beam fixed on a little grassy patch off to the side of the road. She didn't pay attention until after she'd got her boot back on and was going to get her flashlight. That's when she saw it. A pink shoelace.

Dinah gasped. "He's here," she whispered, then immediately yelled, "Eric, can you hear me? Eric!"

"Eric!" Neil yelled, not sure why or how Dinah had decided this was the place. But he yelled again, and began frantically sweeping his light from one side of the road to the other.

"Eric," Dinah yelled again. "Where are you?" She grabbed up the shoelace, tucked it into her pocket, and studied the spot for a moment. "I think the tracks are his," she said, looking on down the road, still seeing nothing.

"I think he came this way, something happened, and he tossed a pink shoelace out the window as a sign."

"A pink shoelace?"

"Long story," Dinah said, moving on ahead in mud halfway up to her knees now. Neil was flanking her on the right, keeping his distance and keeping his eyes peeled for anything on that side of the road. But Dinah was the one who found it…found the spot about three hundred yards away when the tire marks veered off… "Here," she choked, running straight into the waist-high prairie grass, following tracks that had flattened the grass. "Eric, can you hear me?"

In response, a honk. Which brought immediate tears of relief as she followed the trail until it came to the overturned vehicle. It was on its side. Lights still on, shining into the trees. "Eric," she choked, dropping to the ground to look into the cab.

He smiled at her. Cut, bloody. Half-strangled by the seat belt. Beautiful. "I thought you'd never get here," he choked, his voice hoarse.

Well, the first thing she wanted to do—hug him—wasn't going to happen right now. He was too injured. A quick assessment revealed a broken leg, as best she could tell without moving him. Probably a dislocated shoulder, too. So no hugs from her. But in her heart she was hugging him forever. However, the second thing she'd said she'd do… "I love you," she whispered, crawling in and cutting away the seat belt while Neil radioed their location to his teams. Muddy tears were streaking down her cheeks. "I love you more than anybody I've ever loved in the whole world, and if you ever do this to me again, I'll…" She sniffled, cut through the shoulder part of the seat belt, and pulled away the remnants of the air bag which Eric had already punctured and deflated.

"You'll what?"

"I'll love you more than anybody I've ever loved in the whole world."

He was coming home today. It had been a crazy seven days, subduing the twins who would have surely injured Eric in their enthusiasm to hug him, and trying to get his house ready so he wouldn't have to go home to Janice's cottage. He was going to need a medical bed for a while, and she'd had it set up right in the front room of his new cabin. Dr. Kent Stafford, one of White Elk's full-time orthopedic surgeons, had actually recommended Eric to a rehab facility for a couple of weeks, but Eric had refused. Said he wanted to be with his girls. Said over and over he wanted to be with Dinah.

So she was busy making sure that would happen.

As it turned out, he *had* been going after chocolate chips that night. In a hurry. Taking the short cut. His truck had slipped out of control in the mud, the brakes wouldn't hold it, and it had picked up speed in its descent. On a flat surface, nothing would have happened. But rolling down the side of a foothill… The Three Sisters had been watching over him because, by rights, he should have been killed.

And the pink shoelace…he'd tossed it out the window when he'd realized he was going to take a long, bumpy ride to the end.

"In the middle of the front room?" Those were Eric's first words when the medic rolled him in the door. His broken leg, now in a cast, was elevated. A pink cast at Pippa and Paige's insistence. He was shirtless, but the brace supporting four broken ribs covered most of his chest. And his arm was in a sling. A mess, but such a handsome mess that tears welled in Dinah's eyes.

"In the middle of the room," she said, smiling so widely it almost hurt.

"I was hoping for some privacy."

She waved to George Fitzhenry, who'd brought him home and was on his way back out. "In your condition, Eric, privacy's the last thing you need. Especially if you're thinking what I think you're thinking."

Eric sighed. "So how are you going to lift me into bed?"

"I have a few friends coming by later. And you're getting a full-time nurse. Hired the best one I could find."

"That would be you."

"That would be me. And I'll be full-time nurse at White Elk Hospital as soon as my private duty is over."

"Meaning?"

"You know what it means."

"But I want to hear you say it. No, I need to hear you say it."

Yes, he did, and she wanted to say it to him. "I'm going to stay, Eric—here in White Elk, here with you and the girls. With my sister. *I want to stay here.*"

"Do you know how good that sounds?"

"It couldn't sound any better to hear it than it feels to say it. Because it's what I truly want to do. I mean, I kept telling myself that if I walked away from everything I'd found here in White Elk I'd be fine. Better to be alone, keep myself hidden, than open myself up to getting hurt again. I wanted you so much, but I was scared…scared I wasn't enough, scared I'd let you down, scared you'd be disappointed. So it was easier to push you away, even run away…"

"To Costa Rica?" he said, smiling.

"It was never about running to someplace. It was always about running away from something…in this case, you."

"But I wouldn't have hurt you, Dinah."

"Not intentionally. But what happened if we woke up one morning and you decided that I wasn't…"

"Patricia?"

She nodded. "And the thing is, it wasn't even about Patricia. I'm so glad you had her, so glad you had such a wonderful marriage with her. I just didn't feel like I could be enough for you after you've already had perfection. For me, it's always easy to hide behind excuses, which is what I've been doing, Eric. The men in my life leave, I'm too emotional to be a nurse, Charles betrayed me…excuses. And I wanted to turn you into another excuse. But you wouldn't let me. And I know I was forcing you into that position by distancing myself, as you called it. Getting close then shoving you away. Even resigning from the hospital."

"I would have come after you, Dinah. Don't you know that I've been trying to figure out all along how to keep you here, or what to do if you did run away?"

"You were?"

"Of course I was. I mean, I've made a mess of things myself, and I know that. So maybe I've kept myself at some of that distance I've accused of you keeping while I was trying to figure out a way to make this work between us. I was always afraid that Patricia would be an issue…"

"I understand your feelings for her, Eric."

"An issue for you, Dinah. I never wanted you to think I was comparing you, or putting you second. But when you love someone it's hard to let go. Which is why I wasn't going to let go of you no matter what happened. Even if I had to go all the way to Costa Rica to get you."

"You would have?"

"I would have," he said.

A shuddering sigh over took her. "I loved Molly, and that day when she died, when I kept holding on to her…I couldn't bear the pain. That's why I left nursing. As much as I loved, it just hurt so much, and there was nothing I could do. Molly was going to die and I knew that, but I think I blocked it from my mind because when it happened…I went to pieces, Eric. I went to pieces, and how can you be a good nurse if you get that emotional?"

"The best nurses and doctors do get that involved, Dinah. Loving someone that deeply is never anything to be ashamed of, and hurting when you lose them is natural. You loved a little girl who desperately needed someone in this world to love her, and the Dinah I know will do that again and again because that's what makes her extraordinary…as a person, as a nurse."

She paused for a moment, shut her eyes, fighting back the tears. "When Charles pulled me away, physically restrained me and had me sedated, I'd never felt more betrayed…more pain in my life. He told me I was being an idiot, opening myself up to being hurt, that what I was suffering was my fault. That I was weak."

"Loving someone never makes you weak, Dinah. It's what makes you strong. Builds you up. Makes you better."

"But I was so wounded, and I just didn't want to…to bleed that way anymore. My father, my husband, my fiancé, Molly… I convinced myself it was easier living life alone. That maybe Charles was right."

"He was wrong, and it's not easier. I've been alone for years and I think I'd convinced myself of the same thing, that it's easier that way. And it wasn't the pain I was running from so much as it was the fear of starting over. I'd had everything I'd ever wanted in life then lost so much of it, and for me it just became easier not to want any of it again. I had my work, my girls… By all standards, that makes me a very lucky man. Then I met you, and…"

"I made you miserable."

"Sometimes, because I had to reevaluate where I was and what I was doing, and, as you've seen, I've been pretty resistant to that. But you also made me incredibly happy, and I don't think I ever counted on having that kind of happiness again. Or maybe I'd convinced myself I didn't need it. And to be honest, I did feel guilty…not because of Patricia, or moving away from Patricia. I felt guilty because I wasn't feeling guilty, if that makes any sense. All along I think I expected some huge blanket of guilt to drop down and smother me if I ever looked at another woman…thought of another woman the way I have you. Maybe I even counted on it happening so I wouldn't have to move on with my life. Then, when that didn't happen, when I realized that I was getting happier, I wasn't sure how to handle it."

"Well, we're quite the pair, aren't we? Me running away from the things I love most because I'm afraid of getting hurt, you hiding because you're afraid of being happy. You know, I wanted you to let me down, Eric. I fought like hell to make you do it so I didn't have to face myself, and I fell more and more in love with you each and every time you wouldn't be pushed too far."

"I know."

His voice was so gentle it melted her heart. "Every time I did, I wanted you to come and get me. And every time I was so afraid you would, and even more afraid you wouldn't."

"I know that, too."

"And you still want someone as crazy as me raising your daughters?"

"Crazy's good," he said. "As long as it's crazy in love."

"And I am, Eric. I fought myself and lost miserably. Which means I've won everything."

"Damn, I wish you could be sitting in my lap," he said. "Because I want to show you how crazy in love feels."

"You can't even put your arms around me," she said, sniffling. "But I can put my arms around you…a little bit. If you trust me to do that without hurting you." Crossing over to his wheelchair, Dinah bent down and eased her arms around him, barely touching him. But it was a good touch. *A perfect touch.* "Thank you, Eric. You've given me everything, and I don't know how to repay you."

"Marry me?" he asked, quite simply. "I know this isn't the most romantic proposal, and just let me warn you that if you say yes, we're going to do it as soon as we get the license, even with me in this pink leg cast, because I don't want to spend another day of my life without you. Also be warned, the girls already have the wedding planned. They've been working on it for days, and I think their intent is to upstage us."

She started crying again. "It sounds beautiful… perfect." She backed away for fear she'd hurt him, and propped herself against the hospital bed.

"It was a long time coming, trying to forget Patricia."

"But you don't have to forget her, Eric. She was such an important part of your life…of the lives of three of the people I love most in this world. She took care of you, loved you, gave you two amazing children, and for that I love her, too. So you shouldn't forget her…none of us should."

"When I fell in love with you, that's what I came to realize. It wasn't about forgetting her. I loved Patricia with all my heart, and that won't change. But I learned my heart has room to love someone else, too…love someone else with all my heart. And that's how I love you, Dinah. That day in the rain, when you fought with me, it was like I woke up for the first time in many years.

Woke up, felt alive. Then every time after that… There were so many things in me that I'd put away. Things you reminded me were still there. And I want that with you, Dinah, all of it."

"You don't mind pink shoelaces, do you? And pink and purple walls in the girls' bedrooms? Because we've already talked about it and it's a unanimous decision. Pippa's walls will be pink on the top half, purple on the bottom, and Paige's walls will be purple on the top half, pink on the bottom. Not negotiable. The goat is negotiable, though. But not the pony or the dog." She smiled. "Although I can think of some things I'd love to negotiate on my own. Like a honeymoon, *without the girls*, once you're healed."

"Care to tell me what you have in mind for that honeymoon?"

"And get you all excited? That could hurt a man in your condition."

"My only condition is totally, incurably in love."

"Well, in that case…" She bent over and gave him a circumspect kiss on the forehead.

"Not good enough."

Another one on the tip of his nose.

"Not good enough."

One on each cheek.

"Closer, but still not good enough."

This time she kissed him on the lips. Tenderly, and rather quickly. But there would be time for more. A lifetime for more. "Oh, and so you'll know," she whispered in his ear, "I'm taking over your duties with the rescue team. I think I have a knack for it."

"You're not trained for it."

"I'll get my training."

"But you're getting married, going to be a mother, going to be a nurse…"

Dinah gave him a broad smile, folded her arms across her chest, and looked down at him. "Trust me, I know what I'm doing."

"You know, you're sexy when you talk that way. I like a woman who knows what she's doing." He arched wicked eyebrows.

"Staying with the man I love is what I'm doing," she said, taking his face in her hands and going straight for his lips this time. "For the rest of my life."

MEDICAL™ 2-in-1

Coming next month

THE MIDWIFE AND THE MILLIONAIRE
by Fiona McArthur

Midwife Sophie Sullivan hates arrogant playboys like Levi Pearson! But when a helicopter crash leaves Levi and Sophie stranded together in the Australian outback, these two opposites find one thing in common – their attraction to each other!

FROM SINGLE MUM TO LADY
by Judy Campbell

Single mum Jandy Marshall wants nothing to do with high-flying city doc Patrick Sinclair. But Patrick has a big heart and a big secret… Could he be the Prince Charming this Cinderella nurse has been waiting for?

KNIGHT ON THE CHILDREN'S WARD
by Carol Marinelli

Heiress Annika Kolovsky is pursuing a career in nursing, but nothing prepares her for working alongside sexy paediatrician Ross Wyatt! Ross goes above and beyond for his tiny patients – but will he do the same to win Annika's heart?

CHILDREN'S DOCTOR, SHY NURSE
by Molly Evans

Determined to make the most of his new job, paediatrician Dr Mark Collins finds his new colleague, timid nurse Ellie Mackenzie, an unexpected attraction! As work forces their lives to intertwine, it's clear they hold the key to healing each other's heart…

On sale 4ᵗʰ June 2010

millsandboon.co.uk Community

Join Us!

The Community is the perfect place to meet and chat to kindred spirits who love books and reading as much as you do, but it's also the place to:

- Get the inside scoop from authors about their latest books
- Learn how to write a romance book with advice from our editors
- Help us to continue publishing the best in women's fiction
- Share your thoughts on the books we publish
- Befriend other users

Forums: Interact with each other as well as authors, editors and a whole host of other users worldwide.

Blogs: Every registered community member has their own blog to tell the world what they're up to and what's on their mind.

Book Challenge: We're aiming to read 5,000 books and have joined forces with The Reading Agency in our inaugural Book Challenge.

Profile Page: Showcase yourself and keep a record of your recent community activity.

Social Networking: We've added buttons at the end of every post to share via digg, Facebook, Google, Yahoo, technorati and de.licio.us.

www.millsandboon.co.uk

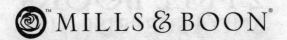

2 FREE BOOKS
AND A SURPRISE GIFT

We would like to take this opportunity to thank you for reading this Mills & Boon® book by offering you the chance to take TWO more specially selected books from the Medical™ series absolutely FREE! We're also making this offer to introduce you to the benefits of the Mills & Boon® Book Club™—

- **FREE home delivery**
- **FREE gifts and competitions**
- **FREE monthly Newsletter**
- **Exclusive Mills & Boon Book Club offers**
- **Books available before they're in the shops**

Accepting these FREE books and gift places you under no obligation to buy, you may cancel at any time, even after receiving your free books. Simply complete your details below and return the entire page to the address below. You don't even need a stamp!

YES Please send me 2 free Medical books and a surprise gift. I understand that unless you hear from me, I will receive 5 superb new stories every month including two 2-in-1 books priced at £4.99 each and a single book priced at £3.19, postage and packing free. I am under no obligation to purchase any books and may cancel my subscription at any time. The free books and gift will be mine to keep in any case.

Ms/Mrs/Miss/Mr _____ Initials _____

_____

Surname _____

Address _____

_____

_____ Postcode _____

E-mail _____

Send this whole page to: Mills & Boon Book Club, Free Book Offer, FREEPOST NAT 10298, Richmond, TW9 1BR